Stay With Me

A
SUGARLAND CREEK
NOVEL

BROOKE MONTGOMERY

Sugarland Creek series
Reading Order

Come With Me (Prequel)
Here With Me (#1)
Stay With Me (#2)
Fall With Me (#3)
Only With Me (#4)
Sin With Me (#5)

Each book can be read as a stand-alone and ends in a happily ever after. However, for the best reading experience, read in order.

Content Warnings

This book contains the following that may trigger some people, so please read with caution:

loss of a loved one / suffering with grief
mention of drugs / being drugged
anxiety attacks / anxiety disorder
animal sickness (on page)
animal death (mentioned)
drunk driving that leads to death (graphic)
death (on page)
accidental pregnancy (if you don't like pregnancy topics)

There is no cheating and there is an HEA at the end

Acknowledgments

To Echo Grayce, Charity Ferrell, Britt Johnson, and Morgan Medri

Here's to Girlhood:
Early morning chats
Late night chats
Buddy reading
Sharing daily dog pictures
Supporting each other through thick and thin
Being obsessed with Taylor Swift & Travis Kelce
Sending dozens of TikToks to each other
Laughing at ourselves and at each other

I couldn't do this without you. Thank you for being in my life!

And to the amazing women I was fortunate enough to meet and spend a week with in a mountain cabin teaching, learning, laughing, and becoming lifelong friends... I'm forever grateful for you!

I light the fire when it's cold out
    And she lights up the room
    I hope that she'll love me forever
    She hopes I'll be back soon
    I take her out to the movies
    She takes away my pain
    She is the start of everything
    And I'll be there 'til the end

From all my airs and graces
    To the little things I do
    Everything is pointless without you
    Of all the dreams I'm chasing
    There's only one I choose
    Everything is pointless without you
    I'll wait for you
    You'll wait for me too

-Pointless, **Lewis Capaldi**

Playlist

Listen to the full *Stay With Me* playlist on Spotify

Beautiful Things | Benson Boone
See You Again | Wiz Khalifa, Charlie Puth
Pretty Little Posion | Warren Zeiders
Before You | David J
I'll Be There | Jess Glynne
My Person | Spencer Crandall
Take My Name | Parmalee
Let Em Go | Nate Smith
Wild as Her | Corey Kent
Love's A Leavin' | Warren Zeiders
Treat You Better | Shawn Mendes
Sin So Sweet | Warren Zeiders
Growing Old With You | Restless Road
Dirtier Thoughts | Nation Haven
Die First | Nessa Barrett
Tennessee Twister | Wesley Green
Glad You're Settling | Jessica Baio

Welcome to

SUGARLAND CREEK

RANCH AND EQUINE RETREAT

SUGARLAND CREEK, TN

~Welcome to Sugarland Creek Ranch and Equine Retreat~

The town of Sugarland Creek is home to over two thousand residents and is surrounded by the beautiful Appalachian Mountains. We're only fifteen minutes from the downtown area, where you can shop at local boutiques, grab a latte, catch a movie, or simply enjoy the views.

We're an all-inclusive ranch. While we provide rustic lodging, each cabin is handicapped-accessible with ramps and smooth walking trails. If you need assistance with traveling between activities, we'll provide you with a staff member to pick you up in one of our handicapped-accessible vehicles at any time. Please request at the front desk or dial '0' on your room phone. We're here to help in any way we can.

To make your stay here the best experience, meet the family and learn about everything we have to offer at the retreat to ensure you have the vacation of a lifetime!

Meet the Hollis family:

Garrett & Dena Hollis

Mr. and Mrs. Hollis have been married for over thirty years and have five children. The Sugarland Creek Ranch has been home to over three Hollis generations. When the family officially took over twenty years ago, they added on the retreat to share their love of horses and the outdoors with the public.

Wilder and Waylon
Twin boys, the oldest

Landen
The middle child

Tripp
Youngest of the boys

Noah
The only girl and baby of the family

Whether you're here to relax and enjoy the views or you're ready to get your hands dirty, we have a variety of activities on the ranch for you to enjoy:

Horseback trail riding & tours
(10:00 a.m. and 4:00 p.m.)
Hiking, mountain biking, & fishing
(Maps available at The Lodge)
Family Game Nights
(Sundays and Wednesdays)
Karaoke & Square Dancing
(Friday and Saturday nights)
Kids Game Room
(Open 24/7)
Swimming
(Pool open 9:00 a.m. to 9:00 p.m. each day)
Bonfires with s'mores
(Fridays)
...and much more depending on the season!

The Lodge building is staffed 24 hours a day. It's home to our reception & guest services, The Sugarland Restaurant & Saloon, and activities sign-up.

Find all of our current information at sugarlandcreekranch.com.

We pride ourselves on serving authentic Southern food, so please let us know if you have any dietary restrictions or needs to better serve you. We offer brunch from 8:00 a.m. to 1:00 p.m. The restaurant is open for dinner from 5:00 p.m. to 9:00 p.m. If you wish to dine or find other activities off the ranch, we're less than an hour from Gatlinburg and are happy to provide you with suggestions.

Thank you so much for visiting us.
We hope you have the best time!

-The Hollis Family & Team Sugarland

See map on the next page!

C

D

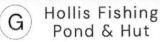
J

H

E

SUGARLAND CREEK

RANCH AND EQUINE RETREAT

SUGARLAND CREEK, TN

Prologue
Tripp

"What?" I snap into the phone, then roll over and flick on my bedside lamp. This better be good.

"*Duuuuuuude,*" Billy shouts over the loud music playing in the background. "Why aren't you here? There's so much pussy, man."

Rubbing my eyes, I clear my dry throat. "Are you seriously callin' me at three in the mornin' drunk off your ass?"

I have to be up in three hours, and I only picked up my phone because I forgot to turn it on silent mode.

"I'll come get ya!" he yells louder.

I stretch my arm to avoid my eardrum getting blown out. "Billy, no. You can't drive. And I gotta work." Ranch chores start before sunrise.

"It's the last party before graduation! Live a little and come out to Miller's! There's like three kegs and a dozen bottles of

1

liquor." The slurring of his words gets worse as I sit up and blink until my eyes adjust to the bright light. "You gotta get over that stupid crush of yours anyway."

"Not interested," I say harshly. Not about the crush part, but the drinking and partying part. But I don't say that. "Stay there, Billy. Crash on the couch or find a bed."

"I gotta find me a lady first…" He cracks up at his own words. "There are so many options, bro. I'll save ya one. You want a blonde or a brunette? I already called the redhead. She looks feisty. *Rawr.*"

Jesus Christ. I pinch the bridge of my nose and blow out a breath, trying not to lose my shit on his drunken, stupid ass.

Billy Hendersen's been my best friend since kindergarten and has always been a decent guy, but after his parents split up last year, he's been wild and reckless. After showing up late to football practice multiple times, he eventually got benched. Then he pulled three no-shows at his part-time job and got fired. Now he's hanging on by a thread to graduate.

"No, thanks. Imma go back to bed." Groaning, I fall back on the mattress.

"You *suuuuck.*" He shouts something at the party, and they all holler in return. "That's it. I'm comin' to get ya. I'm sick of your *mopey sad, woe-is-me* attitude. I'll drag your ass out of bed if I haveta."

When I hear keys rattling, I sit up in a panic. *Goddamn him.*

"No! Fine, I'll come. Just *don't* drive." I grab clothes out of my closet and toss them on the bed. "And I ain't actin' that way, so shut the hell up."

"Nah…you're just sayin' that. You ain't gonna come unless I carry you out here. Which I'll do because I'm twice your size." He cackles to himself, and then I hear the sound of an engine roaring.

"Billy! Goddamn, I'm comin'!" I nearly shout. Everyone in the house is asleep and the last thing I need is to wake up my parents as I sneak out of the house. "Get out of your truck. *Now.*"

"Betta hurry up then…" His taunting voice is unsettling, urging me to get dressed and slide on my boots in a hurry.

"I'm on my way. Seriously. Stay there." Once I grab my wallet and keys, I go downstairs and rush to my truck. I need to keep him on the phone so I know he doesn't do anything stupid.

He revs up the gas as if this is a game. "Wanna race? If I get to your house before you get here, you owe me a hundred bucks."

Fucking hell. "Dude, I'll give you two hundred to stay put."

"What fun is that?" I hear him shift into gear and my heart races at the thought of him driving not only intoxicated but in the pitch black. There are no lights on these country roads, and Miller lives on a small dairy ranch with dim lighting. I've gone to his parties several times, but everyone always crashes in the loft of the old barn. No one's allowed to leave if they've been drinking.

"Where's Miller?" I ask.

"With Sabrina."

"Go find him for me," I demand, hoping it'll stall him a little longer as I speed over.

"I ain't walkin' in on them fuckin'. Noooo, thank you."

"Billy, stay there. Please. I'm already on my way," I grit out between my teeth.

"You fucker! That's cheatin'!"

Then I hear wheels squealing as if he's driving on pavement and my heart drops to the bottom of my stomach.

"Try and beat me!" He antagonizes with a loud *yee-haw*.

I know there's nothing I can say to get him to turn around at this point, and the only thing I can do is try to get to him before he crashes.

"Billy, no speedin'. I'm already on my way. Just turn around. *Please, man.*" I'm not above begging at this point.

"Don't think so, bro. Prepare to lose your *mon-aye*!" He drawls out the last word with a laugh.

Before I can continue to reason with him, he hangs up the phone.

Goddammit.

I slam my foot down on the gas, hoping I can find him before he gets too far. It's a ten-minute drive to Miller's, but I need to somehow make it there in five.

As I keep an eye out for his truck, I call his phone, but it goes straight to voicemail.

I do it again, and the same thing happens.

All the blood rushes to my ears. I tell myself his phone just died, that he's probably been on it all night. Too anxious to wait, I call Miller and am relieved when he answers.

"What's up, Hollis?"

"Billy's behind the wheel, and I'm on the way to your house now. I want you to keep an eye out for him in case he drives back. He needs his keys taken away."

"Ugh, what the fuck? He's wasted."

"No shit, Sherlock. Hence my panic."

"I'll go outside now and look out for him." I hear ruffling in the background as if he's getting his shoes on.

"Great. I'll let ya know if I find him."

Once we hang up, I continue driving, confused as hell when I don't come across any vehicles by the time I get to Miller's. He's standing on his porch with a few others when I approach.

"Did he show up?" I take the steps two at a time.

"No. You didn't see him on your way here?"

I lift my cap and brush a hand through my hair, worried about where the hell he is. "Either he got lost or went the wrong way. I'm gonna keep lookin' for him." I backtrack down the steps.

"I'll come with you," he says, and we both hop in my truck. Considering how drunk Billy is, it's possible he didn't even go in the right direction.

We stay silent as I drive, turning in the opposite direction of my house. Miller tries calling him a few more times with no response.

"Maybe he pulled over and is sleepin' it off..." Miller suggests, but it does nothing to settle the uneasiness taking over.

Flashes of Billy and me over the years surface. Memories of us causing trouble and messing around on the ranch have my chest tightening in fear. The thought of something happening to Billy has my palms sweating against the steering wheel.

"Over there…" Miller points ahead to headlights beaming on the other side of the road, and I lower my window.

"Shit. Is he in the ditch?" I squint through the pitch black, but there's a faint scent of smoke in the air.

"Holy fuck, his truck's flipped over!" Miller's gruff voice is filled with panic.

As soon as I shift into park, we jump out and run over.

"Billy!" I shout, lowering myself to the driver's side window. It's shattered, but I can't see inside.

"Turn on your flashlight," I tell Miller.

"Is he in there?" he asks, pointing his phone toward me.

"Billy?" I poke my head in as far as I can. "He ain't here."

"What the fuck? Maybe he got thrown or climbed out?"

I pull my own phone out and turn on the flashlight so I can look at the passenger's side.

"That window is shattered, too. He coulda crawled out of either one. Fuck!"

"Is that blood?" Miller's shaky tone grabs my attention, the light pinned to the spot he's referring to. A pool of red liquid.

"Shit. He probably smacked his head or cut himself. We need to find him. I'm callin' the sheriff."

"Wait, why?"

I wave out my hand as if it isn't obvious.

"Dude, we're underage. He'll ticket everyone at my house."

"I wasn't drinkin', and you weren't drivin'. He ain't gonna be worryin' about that when there's a missin' teenager."

He sighs but doesn't argue. As soon as I get the dispatcher and tell her what's going on, Wendy informs me she'll send someone out. That could take ten minutes or two hours. Sugarland Creek's a small enough town that there's only a handful of deputies on staff.

I grab a couple of larger flashlights from my back seat, then toss one to Miller.

"Let's start walkin' around and see if he passed out somewhere. He couldn't have gone far with injuries. Hell, he could be bleedin' out. We need to find him and fast." The harder my heart pounds, the harder it is to get my words out.

"Billy! Billy! Where are you?" I shout into the distance.

I try his phone again to see if I can hear it ringing, but it sends me straight to voicemail again.

"Look on the other side of the road in case he crossed it," I tell Miller. "He couldn't have gone far."

We shout his name, flashing my light between trees and up and down the ditch.

"Maybe someone picked him up?"

"Or maybe we're going the wrong way," I bite out, angry at the thought. If he was going back to Miller's, then we're headed in the right direction, but if he's heading to mine, then he'd be in the opposite direction.

"Let's head back to my truck and wait for the sheriff. Maybe he'll —"

I stop dead in my tracks when I spot something up ahead in the middle of the road. It's too big to be a small animal, but it could be a deer. My gut tells me it's not.

"Billy!" I yell, pointing when Miller looks at me. "That him?"

Sprinting with my breath caught in my lungs, I exhale when I confirm it is.

"Christ, Billy. Wake up." I kneel beside him and Miller comes to his other side. Billy's on his stomach as if he face-planted on the cement.

"Hold your flashlight up," I demand so I can turn him over, then place two fingers on his neck. Blood covers his forehead and cheeks. "I don't feel a pulse." Then I lean down until my ear's above his mouth. "He ain't breathin'."

"Oh my God." Miller's whispered voice is filled with desperation.

"I'm gonna do CPR. Back up and keep the light on him."
Once my hands are in position, I start chest compressions.

After a solid minute and breathing into his mouth twice, Miller
interrupts my counting. "Lemme take over, man. You're gettin'
tired."

"Do it fast and hard," I tell him, then take the flashlight from
him. "C'mon, Billy. Breathe, breathe!"

Miller does mouth-to-mouth before going back to his chest.
After another thirty seconds, we switch again.

"I feel a pulse," Miller confirms. "It's weak, but I swear it's
there."

I check for myself, and he's right. It's slow and faint, but his
heart's pumping and that's all that matters.

When I put my ear to his mouth, I say, "He's breathin'."

Barely, but at least it's something.

"Billy, can you hear me? Squeeze my hand," I tell him, placing
my fingers in his palm. But he doesn't.

"Should we move him to the side of the road?" Miller asks as
we continue to try to get a response from him.

"I don't think we're supposed to in case he has a neck or head
injury. Billy? Can you move?"

No response.

I grab my phone and dial the sheriff again to give the
dispatcher an update.

"I've let him know. He's almost there," she says after putting
me on hold, and a wave of relief washes over me. "I notified the
EMTs, too. You did the right thing. Hang tight, boys."

"Stay with me, okay? Help's on the way." I take Billy's hand
in mine, waiting to see if he'll squeeze or make any movements
at all.

"Um...Tripp?" Miller's shaky voice puts me on edge.

"What?"

"He's uh...his lips are turnin' blue."

I place my fingers on his neck again and feel for his pulse. "It's
weak, but it's still there."

With my hands on Billy's shoulders, I give him a little shake. "Keep breathin', man."

Miller's face looks like he's seen a ghost. "What if he lost too much blood? Or went too long without oxygen? He could be—"

"Shut the fuck up, okay? He's *fine*. He's gonna be fine. Once the ambulance gets here, they'll give him oxygen and fluids. He'll survive this."

He has to.

He's my best friend—a fucking idiot—but my best friend nonetheless.

Finally, we hear the sirens and lights approach, followed by the EMTs.

We get out of their way when they place an oxygen mask over his face and put him on a gurney. The sheriff asks me to stay behind so he can get my statement, but I tell him he'll have to follow me to the hospital because I'm not waiting.

As I drive us into town, I call my brother Landen, then our parents. Miller walks home since he has a house filled with drunk teenagers and wants to make sure no one else drives.

After ten minutes of sitting in the waiting room, my brother and parents show up. I explain more of what happened, and then Billy's mom and dad barge in.

The nurse at the front desk wouldn't tell me anything, but they promised to call his parents so they could at least give an update.

"Marissa," my mom calls, cautiously walking up behind Billy's mom.

"Dena, oh my God!" Marissa cries into Mom's chest as she wraps an arm around her.

"It'll be okay." Mom strokes her hand up and down Marissa's back. "He's a fighter."

We wait for what feels like hours before a doctor emerges. William and Marissa walk over, desperate for good news.

Standing, I inch closer so I can overhear their conversation.

"Is he okay?" Marissa asks.

"Unfortunately, he lost a lot of blood. We don't know how

long he went without oxygen, so we did a PET scan after the CT, and the results are concerning. He's on life support to help him breathe, but I'm afraid he won't be able to survive without it."

"*What?*" Marissa shrieks and my knees threaten to give out.

"He's brain dead?" William stutters. "Is that what you're tellin' us?"

The doctor's gaze lowers for a moment before they make eye contact. "I'm so sorry."

My throat burns as I swallow down the lump that's preventing me from inhaling. Everything freezes around me once I take in his words. His diagnosis.

It's wrong. He's *wrong*.

"He'll wake up," I say defiantly. "Billy will wake up, and he'll be fine. Just watch."

"Is it possible?" Marissa asks the doctor. "Is there a chance he could wake up and be okay? Maybe his brain just needs time to heal. It's still early. Right?" Her anxious voice echoes across the room.

My parents approach me from behind as the floor threatens to flip me upside down. Dizziness and blurry eyes take over my senses, revving up my panic.

"There is always a chance. Of course, miracles do happen. But in Billy's case…"

"*Don't say it,*" I spit out. Billy isn't a statistic. He's going to open his eyes and prove the doctor wrong. I know it.

"I'm so sorry," the doctor murmurs.

"Can we see him?" William asks.

"Of course. One of the nurses will bring you back." He nods once before exiting from the same direction he entered.

After a few minutes, a woman approaches and leads us through the emergency doors. She explains that he's in the ICU and we need to prepare ourselves. Before I can ask what that means, I look through the glass door and see for myself.

He's hooked up to machines and bandages cover his head where the glass cut him. We stand around his bed in silence.

"We gave him a dose of pain meds so he can't feel anything. We'll keep him comfortable until a decision is made." The nurse's reassuring voice does nothing to dim the ache penetrating my chest.

The decision is we wait until he wakes up.

"Thank you," William says after she excuses herself.

Marissa takes Billy's hand and cries, keeping her focus on his face. My parents stand next to me as I stare at my best friend, who's never looked this quiet and calm before. He's pale, but when I touch him, his skin is warm—a contrast to how he felt just hours ago in the middle of the road.

"How am I supposed to let you go?" Marissa sobs and my mother comes over to comfort her. William stands emotionless as if he can't wrap his mind around what's happening.

Me neither, if I'm being honest.

After half an hour, the nurse returns and offers blankets to anyone who wishes to stay. There's a couch and recliner on the other side of the room, but I won't be able to sleep.

How can I when my best friend is dying?

A week later, hundreds of people show up at Billy's funeral.

His friends and family give speeches, praising him for his kind heart and willingness to help anyone in need.

They speak about him as if he's been gone forever.

But it's only been seven days since I talked to him.

Six days since the doctors confirmed with a second PET scan that he had no brain activity.

Five days since his family had to make the hardest decision of their lives.

Four days since we stood around his bed and said our final goodbyes.

Three days since I held his hand during his honor walk before they donated his organs.

Two days since my first anxiety attack brought me to my knees.

But only one day since I relived that night, wishing I'd just agreed to come so he never got behind the wheel in the first place.

And with that comes a lifetime of guilt.

Chapter One
Tripp

TWO YEARS LATER

"Get that Swedish Fish-sized boner away from me."

Jesus fucking Christ.

"C'mon, Daisy. Let's go." I grab her shoulders in an attempt to steer her away from whatever douche was stupid enough to grind on her. If I knew she couldn't handle herself, I would've taken care of the asshole myself.

Of course, in true Magnolia fashion, she jerks out of my grip.

"Don't call me that," she hisses, whipping around and narrowing her eyes.

My lips curve up in an amused grin because no matter how many times she scolds me, I'll never stop our little inside joke. Calling her any flower name except her own. She claims to hate it, but the blush on her cheeks tells me otherwise. She loves having my attention.

"*Sunflower*, it's time to go," I emphasize my favorite flower name for her. Usually *Sunny* for short.

"*Mag-no-lia*," she drawls out in slow, drunken breaths, poking me in the chest three times right above my left pec where Billy's name is inked on my skin.

"I'm gonna call you *pain in the ass* soon if you don't get movin'."
I pull her finger off me. "My truck's outside."

"Where's Noah?" she asks, glancing around for her best friend
—and my little sister—as more people bump into us. They're two
years younger than me and get on my nerves regularly.

"Landen already took her out. We're just waitin' on you, so…"
I motion for her to get moving, but then a guy stumbles over with
a red cup in his hand and tobacco chew in his lip.

"You're lookin' sluttier than usual, baby pop. Wanna go
upstairs?"

I squeeze my eyes to stop myself from punching his brains out.
But in reality, between the two of them, it's Magnolia I should be
holding back.

"*Excuse you?* Did you just call me a *slut*?" She stands straighter
on her heels, which only pushes out her already revealing chest
more.

His gaze lowers down her half-naked body, and he licks his
lips with a throaty groan. "You got a rep for a reason, baby girl.
Show me how good you suck dick so I can experience it for
myself."

Magnolia's jaw tenses as all five foot two inches of pure sass
squares up against his six feet of muscle. "The only thing I'm
gonna show you is—"

"And we're leavin'…" I bend my knees, lift her up, then haul
her over my shoulder. Her mouth's unfiltered on a good day, but
when she's been drinking, there's no telling what'll come out. The
last thing she needs is to get arrested and expelled before
graduation.

"Put me down, Tripp Hollis!" She pounds her fists against my
ass. Landen notices us approaching and quickly opens the back
door. My brother's two years older than me, and the only one out
of the four of us actually legal to drink.

She squeals when I toss her in next to Noah, then I slam the
door before she can cuss me out.

Fucking hell. I didn't sign up for this bullshit, but when my little sister called and needed a ride, I couldn't say no. So I dragged Landen out to come help since I knew Magnolia would be a handful.

"You can't just throw me 'round like a rag doll," she slurs once I hop in the passenger's seat.

Landen backs out of the driveway while Magnolia continues running her mouth. He gives me a sideways grin and steals a glance at her like a lovesick puppy.

"Are you listenin' to me?" She leans forward and flicks my ear since I ignore her. Once she gives up, she rests her arms on the back of the seat as Landen drives us down the dark country road.

I tilt my head to where she's hovering and get a whiff of her coconut shampoo. Even drunk off her ass, Magnolia Sutherland still smells like fucking heaven.

And I hate it.

"Tryin' not to," I murmur.

After five minutes of driving, Magnolia covers her mouth. "Oh shit."

"Oh shit, *what*?" Landen asks in a panic.

"Pull over!" Noah yells.

When Landen jerks my truck to the side of the road, we jump out. Noah helps Magnolia down, and the moment she bends over, she empties her stomach.

I shake my head. "Fuck. How much did y'all drink?"

Noah holds Magnolia's ponytail and rubs her back. "I only had a few, but she was takin' shots in between playin' beer pong."

"I'm totally fine." Magnolia stands a moment later, wiping her mouth and chin.

I snort at her ability to act normal two seconds after throwing up.

Her dark brown hair is a wild mess, her makeup is smeared, and her white top is covered in beer stains.

But still, she's the most gorgeous woman I've ever seen.

And equally off-limits.

I try to keep my distance, but she's been around our family for as long as I can remember, so it makes it hard. Wherever Noah is, Magnolia's close by.

"No pukin' your guts out in the truck," Landen warns. "No one wants to smell that. You good?"

"Definitely!" She puts a finger to her nose, then switches hands and does it again. "Practically sober now. If I knew how to drive a stick shift, I could drive y'all home myself! But no one will teach me." She pushes out her bottom lip in the most adorable pout.

Landen laughs, holding the door open and motioning for her to get back inside. "Even if you did, Tripp doesn't let chicks drive his truck. It's a rare beauty."

"Wow, sexist much?" she scolds.

"It's a 1974 Ford 250 Highboy Crew Cab! I've been workin' on it since my freshman year," I defend. "The only reason Landen's allowed to drive it is because he helped me restore it and knows I'll kick his ass if he treats it badly."

"That's right, baby!" He waves his fingers at her. "These aren't only good for hand necklaces."

"You're gonna make me throw up again." Magnolia makes a gagging noise as he helps her into the back seat. She stumbles slightly, and Landen snorts at how drunk she clearly is.

"Ma's gonna kill you," he taunts Noah when Magnolia drapes across the bucket seat.

She shoots him a death glare. "Not if she doesn't know."

"There's no way she ain't gonna hear the four of us walkin' upstairs, especially with your drunken asses trippin' along," I say, then buckle up again.

Magnolia sits up and leans forward until her face is perched between Landen and me. "Guess y'all will have to carry me bride-over-the-threshold style."

Landen laughs, putting the truck into gear, and then glances at her. "Could haul you over my shoulder with one hand, sweetheart." He flexes his arm, then smacks his palm over his bicep.

I roll my eyes, then suppress a groan when she squeezes his muscles. I'm the one who just carried her out of that party without breaking a sweat, and she's acting like Landen's a god when he flexes.

Get me outta here.

"But I ain't riskin' Ma catchin' me sneakin' y'all back inside. Last time I got in trouble, she nearly shipped me off to Canada," he adds before pulling back onto the road.

"Well, we can't have that now, can we? So we'll have to make a *plan...*" Magnolia emphasizes the last word. "Noah and I will sneak up to her room first and make sure no one wakes up. After a few minutes, we'll text you when it's safe to come in."

I look over at Landen, surprised he's actually considering it, and then he nods. "Fine. But after ten minutes, I'm comin' in."

Ten? I'm waiting three tops.

As we get closer to the house, Landen turns off his headlights. I don't bother moving but look back to make sure the girls are getting out.

"Ten minutes," Landen reminds them.

"Keep your panties on." Noah snickers.

They use their phone flashlights and slowly make their way up the porch steps before opening the front door. Dad sleeps like the dead after working twelve-plus hours a day, but my mom's always been a light sleeper. Having a houseful of five kids made her aware of every little noise.

"So what was Magnolia doing when you found her?" Landen asks when the silence gets too loud.

"Two seconds away from kickin' some guy's ass for touchin' her," I say flatly. "Then two seconds after that, another guy came up and called her a slut. That's when I hauled her ass out of there. I knew the moment she kicked him in the balls, a fight would break out, and it wouldn't be too much longer before the cops showed up."

Landen chuckles. "She's a fiery little thing."

"Tell me again why you like her?" My voice is mostly taunting since I have no room to talk.

"Besides how beautiful she is?" He arches a brow. "She's fun, has a good sense of humor, a playful personality, and as you know, she can handle herself. Bold and sexy. What's not to like?"

I nod in agreement but keep my mouth shut.

It's one thing to know who your brother likes, but it's another when it's the same girl you've liked for years.

When I found out he had feelings for her, I shoved mine aside the best I could and pulled away. Landen and I have always been close. I'm not sure what he'd say if I told him I like her too, but I didn't want to find out and have a girl come between us. Landen's a great big brother, a good guy, and after the heartbreak his high school girlfriends put him through, he deserves a nice woman in his life.

"It's been five minutes. Let's go." I grab the door handle before he can stop me.

Moments later, he's following me up the steps, but we both freeze when the doorknob doesn't turn.

"Those little shits," Landen murmurs, reaching for his keys to unlock it.

But the door doesn't open when he turns it.

"What the hell?" I ask, shifting the knob back and forth. "They deadbolted it."

Landen grabs his phone and clicks on Noah's name. After one ring, it goes to voicemail.

I call her next but get the same thing.

"Goddammit. We go save their asses, and they pay us back by lockin' us out of the house. If Ma wakes up, she's gonna think we were the ones out past curfew." I shake my head, my hands balling into fists. Although Landen and I are adults, we still live at home and abide by the rules as a form of respect for everyone who gets up early to work on the ranch and retreat.

Pulling Magnolia's number up, I call her next. To my surprise, she picks up.

"Hey, handsome. You lookin' for a rowdy cowgirl for the night?" Her seductive drunken tone nearly has me choking out a laugh, but I'm too pissed to give in.

"Open. The. Door."

"You sound mad, cowboy. You need a little *relief*? That'd make ya smile, wouldn't it?"

"Oh my God! Stop using your porn voice on my brother!" Noah scolds in the background.

Pinching the bridge of my nose before I lose my patience, I blow out a slow breath. "Unlock the deadbolt and let us in."

"And what're you gonna do for it?"

I look over at her car parked next to my truck.

"I'll tell ya what I *will* do if you don't…" I threaten.

"Mm…tell me more."

"That little red Beetle of yours is gonna find itself floating in the pond if you don't let us in."

"You wouldn't dare!" Her voice is harsh now as if that slapped her back to reality.

The pond's located on the retreat side of the ranch and would take us less than three minutes to get it there.

"Don't think I can hot-wire a car? Think again, *Marigold*. I'll push it in myself and watch it drown."

"You're evil," she hisses.

"Way to fold, Mags!" Noah snickers.

"He threatened Big Red! What am I supposed to do?"

"You know he's lyin'. But go ahead and let him win. Just don't stumble on your way down," Noah warns.

"You really thought this was the best way not to wake my parents?"

"I was hopin' we'd make a deal of sorts, but since you're no fun…"

Seconds later, the door whips open and Magnolia stands in front of me in nothing more than a baggy T-shirt.

My T-shirt.

I mimic her amused expression. "What kind of deal?"

Landen sidesteps me with a muttered *finally* and walks around Magnolia. Considering we work in a few hours, I don't blame him, but I stay planted in the entryway because I'm too intrigued.

"One where I tell you a secret, then you tell me one."

I move closer, shutting the door behind me and never taking my eyes off hers. Magnolia's chest rises and falls rapidly as I hover above her.

"Where'd you get that?" I jut my chin toward her body.

"Your closet." Her voice is barely above a whisper.

I reach for the hem, then roll the fabric between my thumb and finger. My other fingers graze against her soft, tan skin, and her breath hitches.

"Why're you wearin' it?"

The corner of her mouth tilts up. "It smells like you."

Licking my lips, my throat tightens as I battle with the words I want to desperately say but can't.

Take it off. Let me touch you. Give yourself to me the way I want to give myself to you.

But I don't say any of those words.

When Billy died, a part of me did too. It doesn't feel right to be out having fun when he can't. He made one bad decision, and it affected everyone who loved him for the rest of our lives. I want to hate him for being so stupid, but he was hurting and acting out the only way he knew how.

And it cost him his life.

So instead of partying and making the same mistakes, I focus on my family and work, which has been enough for me. It helps keep the anxiety attacks away — *usually.*

But Magnolia tempts me. She gives me hope, and that's a dangerous feeling.

It's bad enough that Landen wants to date her, but if there's one thing I know to be true about her, she goes back to her dipshit ex anytime he decides to get his head out of his ass. Travis is a year younger than me, and when we played football together my senior year, we actually became friends. They'd been on and off all through high school, which is why I never took her little flirty comments to heart, but it's also why I never reciprocated them. Bro code means you don't date your friend's exes and you most definitely don't date your brother's crush.

Taking a step back, I shove my hands in my pockets and lower my gaze to her bare legs. "Put it back in my room when you're done."

Without waiting for her to respond, I walk away.

Chapter Two

Magnolia

THREE YEARS LATER

"It's my birthday, bitches!" I scream and throw my arms up. Everyone cheers and holds up a shot glass. I'm finally turning twenty-one, and I'm making the most of it. I invited a few of my girlfriends over to pregame at my boyfriend's house, and then we're going to the Twisted Bull for the real celebration. There's a large dance floor and a mechanical bull, but I'm only interested in the alcohol and music.

"Here, babe. Made you a drink." Travis winks, handing me a red cup.

"Ooh, what is it?" I smell it, and hints of fruit hit my nose.

"Special birthday drink to make sure you have the time of your life tonight." He wraps an arm around my waist, pulling me into his chest and kissing my lips. "I want you to let loose and have fun."

I smile wide at my boyfriend, then gulp half of it down. We've had our ups and downs over the past few years, but he's finally maturing. We used to fight about silly, stupid shit, and now he's more considerate of my feelings and what makes me happy.

"It's delicious!" I shout over the music, then take another long drink. "Wanna dance with me?"

"I will in a bit. I'm playin' bartender before we head out."

Pulling him down for a heart-stopping kiss, I grin at how sweet he's being. "Thank you for all of this."

His palm cracks down on my ass, and I yelp. "Anything for my woman."

"Noah!" I shout when I see my best friend walk in with two of her brothers. "You guys came!"

I jump into her arms, and luckily, she catches me. The alcohol is catching up to me already.

"Of course!" She laughs and hugs me.

"You brought the snooze team with you?" I arch a brow at Landen and Tripp.

She gives me a pointed look. "They're our DDs. Be nice."

Tripp limits his alcohol and never gets drunk unless he's at home. Even though he's twenty-three, he's never been a big drinker. I suspect that has to do with his best friend in high school dying from a drinking and driving accident five years ago.

I already know Travis isn't going to like them being here. Before we got back together, Landen and I went out on a date last year. I was surprised to learn he liked me that way but figured I had nothing to lose since Tripp was blind to all my signals. When he asked if he could kiss me at the end of the night, we discovered there were no sparks between us and agreed to stay just friends.

But even so, Travis hates him simply for that reason.

"Well, perfect! Because we're partyin' hard tonight! C'mon, Travis is makin' drinks!" I grab her hand, then pull her behind me toward the kitchen.

Tripp and Landen stand behind us while Travis makes Noah a cocktail.

"You two want a beer?" Travis asks them once Noah has her drink.

"Nah, we're drivin'," Tripp explains.

23

"Oh, c'mon. One won't kill ya. Take it." Travis holds out a bottle, but neither reaches for it.

"I said *no*." Tripp's harsh tone sends a shiver down my spine. "I don't drink and drive, man."

They have a stare-off before Travis shrugs and takes it for himself. "C'mon, doll. Let's dance."

When I turn, I find Tripp's icy glare on me as I take Travis's hand. His hot-and-cold attitude confuses the fuck out of me because one minute he'd give me a sign he likes me, but then a minute later, he acts like he can't get away from me fast enough.

It's why I gave up trying and decided to give Travis another chance. I'm a goddamn catch. I shouldn't have to convince a man to be with me.

Travis and I dance in the middle of the makeshift dance floor and halfway through the second song, I feel a hole burning in the back of my head. Noah's next to us, dancing with our friends from high school, so I spin in Travis's arms to see what else is going on in the room.

Tripp's drinking out of a water bottle and Landen whispers something to him. Tripp's brows are furrowed, his eyes locked on Noah and me. I sip more of my fruity drink and get lost in the music while keeping my gaze on him.

Arching my back, I rub my ass against Travis's groin, and he tightens his hold on me. "You keep doing that, and I'm fuckin' that tonight."

I playfully elbow him, but he squeezes my arm.

"I'm serious, Maggie. Trust me, you'll like it." He spins me around to face him, and I scowl.

He knows I hate being called *Maggie* and even more when he doesn't respect my boundaries.

"I thought we had this discussion already." One where I told him *no freaking way*.

"I'll get ya nice and prepped, dollface. By the time I'm done edgin' you, you'll be beggin' me for my *thick* cock in your ass." He winks, and it makes my skin crawl.

Thick? If a number two pencil was thick, *then yeah, he's thick.* But I have a low pain tolerance, and nothing sounds worse than giving him the green light to touch me there.

It'd be one thing if he were talking about rough sex or even role-playing. We've experimented in the past, and it was hot as hell, but this is one thing I won't budge on. It makes me uncomfortable, and he seems to think me saying *no* is foreplay to him getting what he wants.

Knowing he's been drinking and not wanting to have this conversation at the moment, I brush him off. It's not worth fighting about when tonight's about celebrating and having fun.

"I'm ready to go to the Twisted Bull. Noah?" I look at her, and she nods eagerly.

"We'll ride with her brothers since you're drunk," I tell Travis.

"The hell we will. I'm drivin' you." He squeezes my arm again, but this time it's hard enough to leave a bruise.

"You've been drinkin'," I remind him, keeping my voice steady so he doesn't blow up in front of everyone. "Tripp and Landen can drive us there and then we'll Uber home."

He pinches his lips together and scowls in the direction of Noah's brothers before finally looking at me. "Fine. But I want you close to me all night."

Normally, I'd think his possessiveness was hot, but he's acting more like a dick than a loving, protective boyfriend.

"You will be, I promise." I wrap my arms around his neck so he calms down.

I finish the last of my drink before we get into Tripp's truck. We can't all fit in the front and back seats, so the rest of my friends pile in the bed and sing loudly to the music on our way there.

Noah nudges me, grabbing my attention, then tilts her chin toward the phone in my hand. When I unlock the screen, I find a text.

NOAH

Everything okay with you and Travis?

As discreetly as I can with Travis on my other side, I type out a response.

MAGNOLIA

Yeah, he just didn't want to ride with your brothers, but I told him he had been drinking and it was best he didn't drive.

NOAH

He keeps glaring at Tripp. I thought they were friends?

MAGNOLIA

Me too. I'm not sure what's going on with him tonight. But I'm determined to have fun and not let his moody ass ruin it.

NOAH

You better not! You only turn twenty-one once, and then it's all downhill!

She laughs when she watches me read her message.

"Bitch." I chuckle.

As soon as I pocket my phone, we pull into the parking lot.

"You're here to have fun tonight, okay?" Noah reminds me as we link arms and walk toward the entrance. "Just keep cruisin' and shake it off. Or whatever Taylor Swift said."

I burst out laughing at the reference. She's a closet Swiftie.

Travis puts his hand on the small of my back as we go inside and brings his mouth close to my ear.

"I'm sorry for earlier. I just hate sharin' you."

The sincerity in his voice has me smiling. Travis isn't good at processing his emotions or showing them, so I know it's not easy for him to express when something's bothering him.

"It's just for a few hours, and then I'll be all yours once we get back to your place," I reassure him, losing my grip on Noah and wrapping my arms around his waist. "You still owe me a birthday gift anyway."

He tilts my chin with a devious grin. "And I plan to fulfill it when I get you alone." His other hand lands on my ass with a smack. "Gonna pop that cherry."

I roll my eyes, not wanting to argue about it again.

"Want a drink?"

"Yes, please! Somethin' with a big pineapple in it. Oh, and get a strawberry margarita for Noah."

He chuckles, then brushes his lips to mine. "You got it, doll."

"He seems in a better mood, huh?" Noah comes to my side.

"Yeah, he'll be fine. If his mood swings don't make me kill him first." I laugh, but when I glance at her, she's giving me one of her side-eye *looks*. "What?"

She shakes her head, staying silent, but she doesn't have to say anything. I already know what she's thinking.

But I'm just going to have to prove to her she's wrong about Travis this time. We've had our problems, but I can tell he's really changed and wants us to work out.

"Where'd your brothers go?" I ask to change the subject.

"They went to play pool and darts. I'm sure they'll be back in a bit to babysit me. Oh, I love this song! Let's go dance!"

Noah grabs my hand, drags me to the dance floor, and we let loose with our friends. Travis catches up to us and hands us our drinks. He then secures a tabletop and chugs a beer while watching me.

"Lemme try your piña colada," Noah shouts over the music after I've sucked down half of it. "I haven't tried one before."

"Yeah, can I taste yours?"

We swap, and I moan at the sweet strawberry puree flavor. Instead of switching back, we keep drinking each other's. Oh well, I'll get another one later.

After dancing for five or seven songs and a pound of sweat across my forehead, we stumble our way back to Travis. Our drinks are nearly empty, but I want to do shots before getting another fruity one.

"We need to do some blow job shots! And Sex on the Beach!" I shout. "Oh, and I need a piña colada since Noah stole mine."

Travis's eyes lower to our glasses and his jaw clenches. "Noah drank yours?"

"Yeah, she wanted to try it, and then we forgot to switch back." I shrug because who cares? We share our things all the time.

"Fuck," he mutters, threading his fingers through his slicked-back blond hair. "Um, okay. Just stay here. I'll be right back."

Travis goes to the bar and then my gaze finds Tripp with some redhead hanging on his arm.

"Maybe I shoulda dyed my hair, and he woulda liked me," I mumble toward Noah.

"Huh? What're you —" Then she realizes who I'm looking at. "Oh, shush your mouth. Tripp has his own issues. It has nothin' to do with your hair color."

"You sure?" I blink a couple of times when my vision gets fuzzy. "He's lookin' at her like he's ready to devour a medium-rare sirloin steak smothered in mushrooms."

Noah snorts, hanging closely as we study her brother. "Of course you'd know his favorite meal, you psycho stalker. But if it's any consolation, I'd say he's lookin' at her like she's a bowl of cold pea soup."

I furrow my brows at the visual. "What's that mean?"

"He hates soup. And pea soup is the worst of 'em all."

We're in a fit of giggles by the time Travis returns with a tray of shots. Noah grabs one, then holds it up high. I wave our friends over and tell them to grab a shot, but I take one of each for myself.

"To the motherfuckin' birthday girl and my best friend!" Noah shouts, and everyone hollers in return. By how much she's yelling tonight, she'll have no voice tomorrow.

We down them quick and easy before slamming the glasses on the table. Then I hold up my second one. "Who wants a BJ?"

Travis shoots me a disapproving scowl, so I ignore him. If he doesn't want to have fun with me, then I'll find someone else who will.

The commotion of our little party gets Tripp's and Landen's attention, and they walk over.

"Tripp, you wanna BJ?" I ask mostly to toy with him but also to see if he'll actually do it.

"Am I supposed to know what that means?" His gaze shifts from mine to Travis, who's no doubt giving him a murderous glare.

"Kneel in front of me and do what I say," I order.

Once Tripp begrudgingly does what I ask, I stand in front of him. "Now open your mouth."

He raises a brow, but I nod confidently. Once he does it, I tilt back my head and pour the shot in but don't swallow. Holding it in my cheeks, I lean over Tripp, then spit the liquid into his mouth. Before he can swallow it down, I smash my lips to his.

His eyes widen as his throat moves.

"Yeah, go birthday girl!" one of my friends cheers, but I'm too stuck on the fact that my lips are touching Tripp's to holler back.

After all this goddamn time, and it's happening like this.

In front of my boyfriend. Oops.

Neither of us moves, our mouths glued, yet both too afraid to take a taste.

"That's enough," Travis barks, yanking me back.

I stumble on my heels and blink my eyes open to get used to the bright lights.

"That's how a BJ shot works?" Landen asks, helping Tripp to his feet.

Shrugging, I wipe my lower lip. "It's how I do it."

Lies. I made it all up to see if Tripp would take the bait and he did.

"Hot damn, now I need me a cowboy to give a BJ shot to. Any takers?" Noah skips around, looking for a victim. She hasn't dated since she and Jase broke up last year, so I'd love to see her finally

29

getting back out there again. Between working on her family's ranch and a busy horse training schedule, she hasn't made time for it.

"You might wanna get your sister home soon before the ecstasy kicks in," Travis tells her brothers in a hushed voice, but I overhear every word.

Did he say *ecstasy*? When did Noah take that?

"Excuse me?" Tripp's booming voice can be heard from a mile away.

Oh fucking shit.

"You drugged our sister?" Landen snaps.

"Wait, what'd you do to me?" Noah's voice falters as she stops dead in her tracks.

"Shit. No, I-I didn't mean to. It was for Magnolia, but she didn't keep her own fuckin' drink, so it ain't my fault," he hisses, shooting a glare at me.

"*What?*" I shriek. "You drugged me? And it's somehow *my* fault?"

"Well, if you'd stop swappin' spit with everyone, it wouldn't be a big deal." He stands in front of me as if to block me from everyone else. "It was part of your gift. I wanted you to have fun and let loose for...*later.*"

I step back from him, trying to comprehend his logic.

"You can't just drug me without my consent, then get mad I didn't end up takin' it. How could you do this?"

He closes the gap between us, lowering his mouth to speak. "You wanted to try anal, so I thought this would help ease your nerves. This way, you wouldn't even feel the pain."

"When the hell did I say I wanted that? I've been tellin' you *no* for weeks!"

"Yeah, because you thought it'd hurt, which is why I got the Molly for you."

"Oh my God. That cannot be your excuse." My head bobbles and the floor starts to open in front of me.

"Are you…how much of your drink did you have before you gave it to Noah?" he asks, holding my shoulders.

"Like a third of it, probably. Less than half." I try to remember, but I can feel the blood rushing to my ears, and it's freaking weird.

"Shit, you probably drank some of it then."

"Guys. I'm feelin' it. Holy shit. I love you so much, Magnolia. You're my best friend." Noah's smile is so wide and goofy I can't help but laugh.

"You dumbass, look what you did to her. She's high as shit." I smack his shoulder, but he doesn't even flinch.

"You will be soon, too. We should get home. I'll order an Uber." He unlocks his phone screen and clicks on the app, but I don't want to go yet. And right now, I don't want to go anywhere with Travis after this.

Tripp steps between us, taking me off guard and nearly making me fall back on my ass. Luckily, Landen's close enough to grab my arm and keep me on my feet.

"You ain't takin' her anywhere, asshole. You drugged them, and you've been drinkin'. Take your fuckin' Uber and go home *alone*." Tripp gets in Travis's face with his hands balled into fists at his side.

Oh shit, this isn't good.

"Fuck you, Tripp. She's my girlfriend, not yours. So back off." Travis shoves Tripp's chest, then leans around him to find me. "Magnolia, let's go. We'll wait for our ride outside."

I'm too dazed to be angry because all I feel is relaxed and happy. Glancing at Noah, I notice her toothy grin, and by the way she's hanging on Landen tells me she's beyond trippy.

"Landen, take 'em to my truck. Now," Tripp says without glancing away from Travis.

"Dude, no. You can't have her. She's *mine*!" Travis sounds like he's ready to kill him.

"Why're you being so goddamn loud? It's a party! Let's

dance!" I raise my arms and lift on my tiptoes. "Oh my God, I love this song! Noah, let's—"

"No!" Tripp grabs my hand and pulls me away from the dance floor. Landen follows with Noah in his grip, and I pout.

"It's my birthday! I don't wanna go!"

"Me neither!" Noah whines. "We can have a dance party at my house!"

"Yes!" I shout at the same time Tripp and Landen bark out, "No!"

"The fuck? *Magnolia*!" Travis catches up, grabs my arm out of Tripp's grip, then raises his fist. Before I can warn Tripp, Travis punches him in the nose.

"Oh my God!" I squeal, falling back into another body.

Landen shoves Travis, then kneels to check on Tripp.

Shit, I see blood.

"Let's go!" Travis yanks me toward the door, making me lose my footing and my heels.

"Slow down!" I bend to grab my shoes, but before I can, Travis hauls me into his arms.

"Those are my favorites!" I whine.

"I'll buy you new ones. We need to get outta here before…"
Before the cops show up.

"Magnolia!" Noah shouts behind us with Landen on her tail. "We didn't ride the bull!"

"Oh my God! We have to!" I yell back, then turn to Travis and kick my legs. "Lemme down!"

"You hate the bull, Maggie. It's just the Molly. It'll wear off."

I scrunch my nose. "Who's Molly?"

"You definitely have some in your system. Why would you share your drink?"

"Asks the person who put drugs *in* my drink," I mock as he searches for our ride in the parking lot. Perk of being in a small town is not having to wait long for an Uber, but a part of me doesn't want to go back to his house. I don't trust him even if I am feeling an adrenaline rush.

"Maybe I should stay with Noah and go home with her so I know she's okay," I say when he sets me down.

Travis opens the passenger door and shoves me inside. "Just shut up and buckle yourself." He slams the door in my face before I can respond.

Oh, he's more delusional than I thought if he thinks he's getting anal after this.

Chapter Three
Tripp

I*'m going to fucking kill him.*

I lost track of Magnolia after her loser boyfriend hit me in the face. That asshole can't even stick around to fight it out. He bailed out like the little bitch he is.

Since Landen's keeping an eye on Noah, I focus on finding Travis. I need to stop him before he takes advantage of Magnolia in her drugged-up state.

Sprinting outside and between parked cars, I find Travis pushing her into the back of a black SUV. He shouts something at her, and when he nearly slams the door into her bare foot, I see red.

As he rounds the back, I whip open her door and remove her buckle. "Get out. Now. *Quick.*"

Her eyes shoot to mine as Travis notices from the other side.

"The fuck?" he grumbles, reaching for her across the seat.

I push Magnolia against the seat, then lean over her body and slam my fist in Travis's face. He curses, flailing back and cupping his nose.

When I hear my truck's engine roaring behind me, I grab Magnolia's hand and launch her over my shoulder.

"Hey!" she squeals.

When Landen hops out of the driver's seat and opens the back, I set her down and motion for her to scoot over so I can sit next to her since Noah's in the passenger seat. But either way, I'm not giving Travis another opportunity to take her.

As I shut the door, this asshole grabs it and tries to pry it open. I lean back, covering Magnolia from him, and with all my strength, slam my boot into his chest. When he falters, I grab the handle and slam it closed.

"Go, go, go!" I yell at Landen.

The tires squeal against the pavement, and when we finally hit the main road, I blow out a breath. "Jesus fuck. He's like the Ghostface in *Scream* who never dies."

"Technically, there were several Ghostfaces," Noah tells me, and I thank her with an eye roll.

"You okay, Sunny?" I ask Magnolia and notice her eye twitching. "Come here."

The events of what happened tonight with the rush of serotonin hitting her bloodstream are confusing her about how she should be feeling right now.

"I'm so horny right now," she blurts out with a laugh. "Do you wanna do anal?"

I blink hard. "The fuck did you just say?"

"What? That's why Travis gave it to me, so it wouldn't hurt. Would hate for it to go to waste now."

That sick motherfucker. I'm going to kill him.

I should've kicked him in the dick instead, so he couldn't ever use it again.

"I don't care how high or horny I am, there's no way a cock is touchin' my booty hole," Noah says, then turns and adds, "I poop out of there."

My nostrils flare and inhale a long, frustrated breath. *Dear God, please erase that sentence from my sister's mouth out of my mind fucking immediately.*

"Okay, so no anal." Magnolia nods as if it was even on the

table. "We could sixty-nine, doggy, reverse cowgirl, or hell, eat whipped cream off each other. I'm game for any of those."

Fuck me. I shouldn't have let her kiss me or played into her little BJ shot game because her listing a variety of sex positions is getting me hard now that I know how her lips feel against mine. Her telling me to kneel and open my mouth should've been my clue. But I saw the way Travis was treating her tonight and wanted her to have a good time on her birthday.

"*Tulip*, no one's havin' sex tonight." *Unfortunately.*

Magnolia frowns and her nostrils flare, which is freaking adorable, but I'm not giving in no matter how much my dick wants to.

"How about you, Landen? We did go on that date. Wanna continue it in the bedroom? I'm way more flexible now."

His eyes shoot to mine in the rearview mirror, and I want to smack that grin off his smug face. I never admitted to him that I like Magnolia even after they decided to stay friends, but a part of me wonders if he suspects it.

It was pointless to say anything after that anyway since she started dating Travis once again—as she always does.

I hate that even after what he did tonight, she'll crawl back to him and take the blame for his actions. Even if I shared my feelings with her right now and told her we should be together, I'd always worry about the day she left me and went back to him.

Though I can't figure out why she does because he's a controlling asshole who treats her like shit. It's like he has a spell on her that prevents her from seeing her worth and just how awful he truly is.

Travis and I used to be cool until I found out he'd cheated on her, then gaslit her into thinking it was her fault for invading *his* privacy when she looked at his phone. And somehow, she ended up apologizing to him.

Then he lost all my respect the minute he started taking advantage of her when other guys would murder someone just for a chance to have her.

But after tonight, he'll never take her for granted again.

I just need to convince her she deserves better.

"You can't sleep with Landen!" Noah giggles, glancing at me before she looks at Magnolia. "Tripp would get jealous."

Goddamn her.

"Of *Landen*?" Magnolia cackles in disbelief.

"Of any guy you're with, *duh*!" Noah rolls her eyes. "He was ready to murder Travis tonight. He abandoned his own sister to get you."

"I knew Landen had you!" I defend. "Plus, I wouldn't let any guy take advantage of a woman who'd been drugged. Especially a friend of yours. So shush your mouth."

Magnolia smiles at me, and I hate that it calms my racing heart. "So you only saved me because I'm Noah's bestie? No other reason?"

Instead of falling into her trap, I tighten my lips to hold back from spilling everything.

"You did kiss me earlier…" she reminds me as if I could possibly forget.

"Against my will," I tease. Not that I minded *at all*. But when she does shit like that, it messes with my head.

If she wanted to kiss me so badly, why is she dating that loser?

"You're right. So we should even the score."

"What's that mean?" I ask, knowing I shouldn't.

This is definitely another trap.

"You get to kiss me now. Or hell, do *anything* you want to me. This high is makin' me needy and so, *so* horny. Plus, I deserve birthday sex."

I cover my groin so she doesn't notice the bulge forming in my jeans. She needs to stop talking and confusing my dick.

Turning away from her, I growl, "No."

"Wh—"

"Because unlike your douchebag *boyfriend*"—I meet her pleading eyes—"I don't take advantage of women under the influence or fool around with those who are in a relationship."

She winces as if I verbally slapped her, but she needs to hear it. Innocently flirting with guys is one thing, but cheating isn't something I want to be involved in. Even if they break up after this, I'd just be a rebound.

"You're not stayin' with him after this, right?" Noah asks her.

"The Statue of Liberty will walk before I ever take him back. Plus, he never wanted to do anything I wanted to do. Even go to the movies! What kind of psychopath hates the theater? So yeah, we are never, ever gettin' back together." Magnolia shakes her head as if she truly means it, but I know better than to get my hopes up she'll smarten up this time. "I'll need to grab my stuff from his place at some point. That'll be fun."

"You ain't going alone. Landen and I will come. Waylon and Wilder, too, if needed." Our older twin brothers are more unhinged than both of us together.

Magnolia's hand reaches for my thigh, but before I can stop her, she pulls back. "You really consider me a little sister type, dontcha?"

It's on the tip of my tongue to tell her the truth, but I also don't want to lie and pretend she's right.

"I consider you a friend, *Orchid.*" I lighten my tone so she doesn't scold me for using my nickname for her.

"Ugh. *Friend?* I have enough of those."

"You deserve better than him. I hope you realize that," I tell her instead of acknowledging her *friend* comment. "Relationships aren't supposed to be this hard. *Love* isn't supposed to be this toxic."

"Since when did you become the expert?" Noah chimes in with a chuckle. "You've never had a serious girlfriend."

"Because I don't want just a fling and that's all girls my age are interested in." And that's not even a lie. At twenty-three years old, I'm ready to find my person and settle down. I work hard on the ranch every day. It'd be nice to come home at the end of a long day to someone I love.

"What about that redhead at the bar? She seemed into you,"

Magnolia asks with a hint of jealousy in her tone, but I don't even know who she's referring to. My eyes were glued to her most of the night.

As Landen drives down our long driveway, I'm confused as to why most of the lights are on in the house with how late it is. Though Noah lives in the cottage behind our parents' house, I don't trust these two on their own tonight. When our cousin Mallory moved in last year after her parents died, Noah moved out so there was enough space for Mallory to have her own room.

Once Landen parks, I help Magnolia out, then carry her up the porch stairs since she's not wearing any shoes. The door whips open with Wilder and Waylon standing in the entryway, looking like smug fuckers.

"What're y'all doin'?" Landen asks as I set down Magnolia on the warm floor.

"Sheriff Wagner called Dad. Y'all in *trouble*," Wilder singsongs, leading us deeper into the house.

"For what?" I snap, watching Noah and Magnolia rush to the kitchen. Moments later, I hear them digging through the pantry for snacks.

"Landen! Tripp! Get your asses in here," Dad shouts from the living room.

"Good luck. I'm going to bed." Waylon checks out, but I don't blame him. Five a.m. comes early when it's close to midnight.

"Nah, I'm stayin' for this."

I glare at Wilder, tempted to punch him just for being a taunting asshole, but my knuckles are still sore from hitting Travis.

Landen and I walk in, dragging our feet like dogs with their tails between their legs. I've no idea what the sheriff said, but I'm playing innocent until proven guilty.

"Care to tell me why Sheriff Wagner called ten minutes ago asking about your whereabouts?" Mom asks with a hand on her hip.

Dad's intimidating scowl means if we get caught lying, he won't think twice about putting us on bitch work for a month.

"Not sure." I shrug, shoving my hands in my pockets while Landen stands silently next to me.

"Cut the bullshit. What'd y'all do? It'd be better if we know before he comes and arrests you," Dad states.

"Arrested for what?" Landen asks.

"Aggravated assault." Dad folds his arms across his broad chest. "So tell us again. What'd you do?"

"It's not their fault," Magnolia comes in with a mouthful of food. "My boyfriend, well ex, drugged my drink and when he dragged me out of the bar, Tripp punched him before the Uber could take off."

"And kicked him in the chest the second time he tried to take her," Noah adds.

With a groan, I squeeze my eyes and tilt my head back, silently cursing my sister for adding to my charges.

"It's true," Landen says. "He was just protectin' Magnolia."

"True or not, someone called 911, and Travis is tellin' a different story," Mom says.

"What's he sayin'? There's witnesses anyway to prove he punched me first." I stand taller, plant my feet firmer, and hold my stance. I'm not going to jail for that fuck face.

"That you assaulted him and abducted his girlfriend," Dad explains.

"I'm not his girlfriend anymore!" Magnolia interjects.

I shake my head at the part she's focused on. "And I clearly didn't *abduct* you…"

"Well, duh." She takes a bite of a brownie that Mom and Gramma Grace baked yesterday. "Can't we just call the sheriff and explain what actually happened? We can give our statements, and Tripp will be off the hook."

"It ain't that easy." Dad shakes his head. "It'd be better for Tripp to turn himself in and give his full testimony. Then they'll confirm his story with the witnesses, and if he agrees with your version of events, you'll be released."

"You can't be serious."

"Better to get ahead of it. Our lawyer will show up first thing in the mornin', and if the sheriff's in a good mood, you'll get points for not makin' him drag you in."

"This is fuckin' bullshit." I'm close to losing my temper and the only thing holding me back is Magnolia being close enough to inhale her perfume.

I'd punch and kick Travis a thousand times if it meant he kept his slimy hands off her.

I'd face the sheriff, give my statement of the *truth*, and then prove I was within my rights to defend myself and Magnolia.

"Fine," I spit out before Mom can scold me for my outburst. "But the girls need to stay here tonight. That asshole laced her drink with ecstasy, and Noah drank from it, too. The comedown from it could make them depressed. They probably have a couple more hours until it's out of their system."

"I'll stay up with 'em," Wilder says, finally approaching from watching the shitshow. "No way I'm going to bed now anyway."

"Aww...you *love* us," Noah teases.

Magnolia chuckles. "No, he loves the drama."

"C'mon, son. I'll drive you." Dad goes to walk past me but then pauses with his hand on my shoulder. "Proud of you for watchin' out for Magnolia."

Lowering my gaze, I nod, then follow behind him.

"Don't lose your temper with the sheriff, Tripp. Orange ain't your color," Wilder taunts.

I flip him off, and he smirks.

"And don't worry about your chores. They'll be waitin' for ya when you get back from prison." He chuckles, and I'm tempted to get one last punch in before leaving.

"Tripp, wait." Magnolia comes up behind me and wraps her arms around my waist, pressing her cheek against my back.

"Thank you for riskin' your life to save mine. You're a good friend."

Friend.

Maybe I'll ask the sheriff to shoot me instead of putting handcuffs around my wrists. At least it'd put me out of my misery.

But I'm the one who called her a friend first, so I can't even be mad at her for it.

I pat her hand once before removing her body from mine. Without facing her, I say, "Go to bed, Rose. Sleep it off and don't get your stuff from his house alone."

She pulls my arm, quickly grabbing my attention, and I meet her eyes over my shoulder.

"If you insist on callin' me flower names besides my own, Sunny's my favorite. Sunflowers are a sign of positivity, happiness, and hope."

The corner of my lips tilts up slightly that she's not giving me shit about it for once. "I'll remember that."

Then I walk away before doing something I'll regret—like kissing her for real this time.

Chapter Four

Magnolia

PRESENT DAY, TWO AND A HALF YEARS LATER

"Have a *mag-nificent* day!" I emphasize the *mag* part that matches my name, then smile wide as Mrs. Hollis grabs her latte and places a five-dollar bill in the tip jar.

"Thanks, Magnolia. You too." She winks, then gives me the same warm smile I've known all my life since she's my best friend's mom.

Every Tuesday and Friday, I park my mobile coffee business, Magnolia's Morning Mocha at the Sugarland Creek Ranch and Equine Retreat to sell frou-frou drinks to the workers and guests. On the other days, I serve downtown, depending on what other events are happening. I stick to the touristy areas, then on Saturdays, I move to the farmer's market and work the morning rush of shoppers looking for fresh veggies and flowers. They love to get their caffeine boost before leaving, and I love being my own boss instead of working at my old coffee shop where Mrs. Blanche underpaid and undervalued my ideas.

Now, I get to write cute board signs like *Pay with cash and it's free #GirlMath* and make bougie lattes. It's the best job in the world.

The most popular drink is the number thirteen: *The Swiftie Latte*, which has mocha and hazelnut syrups. Then I top it with whipped cream and chocolate drizzle. It's Mallory's favorite, which is why she begged me to name it after her favorite pop star. She's Mrs. Hollis's thirteen-year-old niece who moved in with them after her parents passed away a few years ago, and since Noah's my best friend, she's become like a little sister to me, too.

"Mornin', gorgeous." Landen's thick drawl snaps me out of my thoughts, and I immediately perk up.

Tripp stands next to him with his arms crossed and rolls his eyes at Landen's over-the-top flirting. I'd eventually admitted to Landen that I had a crush on Tripp and since he treats me like an annoying little sister, Landen likes to put on a show anytime Tripp's around for pure amusement.

Hell, it's what he gets for all the mixed signals he sends me. Years of hoping he'd finally see me as more than his little sister's best friend.

Not that I blame him one hundred percent. Stupid me took my ex back shortly after Landen's and my date, but I finally broke up with Travis for good two years ago after he drugged Noah and me at my birthday party. We were on and off again through high school and shortly after graduation, but never again. Now, I'm thriving and living my best life with my own business, ready to focus on my future.

"Good mornin', gentlemen." I smirk, glancing between them. They're wearing Wranglers, boots, and worn-out ballcaps. I prefer cowboy hats, but they only wear those when they're riding on hot days. It helps the sun stay off their necks and faces, but it feeds my fantasy of a real-life Rip Wheeler. Now that it's October, the hot days are few and far between.

"Well, it is now." Landen winks.

I know he's only playing around—it's something we do—but Tripp's annoyance never goes unnoticed. If he has a problem with men flirting with me, then he should do something about it instead of staying *just friends*.

"What can I get ya?" I lean my elbows on the counter. It's not very big since the trailer was built for one person, but it gets the job done. There had to be room for a decent espresso maker, a fridge, syrups, and all the supplies that come with serving drinks.

"I'll take a number sixty-nine with extra cream," Landen says, pulling out his wallet.

Folding my arms, I shake my head. "Does that line actually work for you?"

"Wouldn't you like to know," he muses, and I give him a pointed look so he'll tell me what he actually wants. "I'll take a regular coffee with two creams and one sugar."

"And for you?" I direct my attention to Tripp, who's burning a hole in the side of Landen's head.

"Same for me," Tripp grumbles.

I grab two large cups and pour the coffee. Then I add in the creams, a packet of sugar in each, and sprinkle cinnamon on top— my signature ingredient for the upcoming holidays.

"That'll be ten dollars," I say, setting down their cups.

"For *two* coffees?" Landen asks.

"Yeah, but I threw in the attitude for free." I smirk.

They know I'm overcharging, but they won't call me out. Being their little sister's best friend and an honorary Hollis means I get to charge double. I took out a business loan to buy the trailer and supplies, so I have to pay it back somehow, and what better way than to make *them* pay extra.

"This better be the best damn coffee I've ever tasted." Landen slaps down a twenty and Tripp takes one of the cups.

"I've never had a complaint." I take the money and put it into my register without handing back any change. "Thanks for the tip."

"That better get me a free coffee next time." Landen points a warning finger at me.

I point one right back. "That's for that sixty-nine comment."

He rolls his eyes, testing his drink.

"Why's this taste like Christmas in a cup?" Tripp asks after taking a sip.

"I may have added a little somethin' extra."

Landen tries his next. "Mm. I like it."

"I knew you'd like the cinnamon. It's my fav—"

"*Cinnamon*? I'm allergic!" Landen starts coughing and a wave of panic rises up my throat.

I rush out of the trailer and toward him, panicking at his struggle to breathe.

"Why…why're you tryin' to kill me?" Landen gasps as if he can't suck in enough air.

"I didn't know!"

Landen hands his cup to Tripp, who just stands there, unfazed. Why isn't he doing something?

"What do I do?" I shout as Landen's face turns red. "Oh my God."

Landen points to his lips. "Mouth to mouth…" he manages to spit out.

Tripp snorts, grabbing my attention, and that's when I realize Landen's a lying sack of shit.

No wonder Tripp isn't reacting.

I shove his chest with all the strength I have, but he only moves back an inch. "Mouth to mouth, huh? How about *knee to balls*?"

Landen squirms back, out of my reach, and covers his junk. "Damn, okay. Don't be threatenin' the jewels. I wanna have kids someday."

Stomping closer, I smack his arm. "You made me think I killed you!"

He grabs my wrists, holding me tight to his body, and leans down until his mouth is near my ear. "I was tryin' to help you out. Figured Tripp would lose his shit if he saw you kiss me."

I pull back slightly and catch his devious smirk.

Ever since I told him I liked Tripp, he's found ways to try to make him jealous by openly flirting with me. But apparently, he thought we needed to take it to the next level.

"At this rate, I don't think it's gonna happen," I say quietly so Tripp can't overhear.

"It will once he gets his head outta his ass." He gives me a look that hints at what he's talking about. Between losing his best friend seven years ago and dealing with internal guilt, Tripp's primary focus has been work. He dated in between the times I was with Travis, but he's never had a long-term girlfriend. It's like he refuses to allow himself happiness no matter how much he deserves it.

"Can you two make up later so we can get back to work?" Tripp's annoyed tone has me taking a step back.

I arch a brow at Landen. "See?"

He gives his head a little shake, then grabs his cup from Tripp.

"See ya later, Mags," Landen calls out as they walk toward his truck.

Tripp stays silent, but a few moments later, I catch him glancing at me over his shoulder.

Nothing reminds me of how single I am more than watching my best friend plan her dream wedding.

I'm happy as shit for her and Fisher, but goddamn, some of us are ready to be God's chosen one for once.

Dear Lord, would it kill you to send me a six-foot-three-tall cowboy with dark hair, brooding eyes, and a free use kink? I'm not askin' for much here…

"Can you go with my brothers to their suit fitting? My dad has a meetin' that day, and I need someone to keep their asses in line."

Noah gives me a pleading look through the mirror, brushing her wet, long, golden blond hair.

"And where will you be?" I tease, lying on her bed and flipping through one of her bridal magazines.

She tosses me her planner, and as soon as I read through it, I regret asking. The monthly spreadsheet is covered in ink. Not that I'm surprised because Noah's a professional horse trainer and doesn't know how to take a damn day off—except when she fractured her ankle and broke some ribs, then she was forced to. But she hated every minute of it. Hell, I wouldn't be shocked if she worked the morning of her wedding just to get a few hours in before the ceremony.

"Fine, I'll go. Just tell me when and where." I skim through a few more pages of gowns and destination honeymoon landscape photos before stopping to admire a gorgeous dress covered in lace.

I came over after work since she had a gap in her schedule and Fisher was still working. It's rare I get her to myself since the lovebirds are attached to each other's hips, so I took full advantage when she texted and asked me to come over.

"Friday, two o'clock at Murphy's."

I pause. *That's in three days.*

But she's my best friend, and as her maid of honor, I can't say no to her.

"Got it." I program it into my phone calendar, then ask, "Anything else comin' up? I wanna make sure I don't miss it."

She's been planning this wedding since they got engaged four months ago. Now they're only one month out and close to the wire of getting the final touches done.

"Final dress fitting is in two weeks, so if you're gonna lose or gain weight, do it now or prepare to suck in your gut."

I snort at the memory of our last fitting. "I told the seamstress to make it super tight. The *girls* will be on proper display." Sitting up, I wave a hand over my chest and arch my back.

Noah shoots me a glare, but the corner of her lips curls up, so I know she's not mad.

"What?" I shrug. "I haven't been laid in over a year. Sue me."

"*Over a year*? Goddamn."

"Tell me about it. I'm desperate."

"No, you're not. You're beautiful, smart, funny, and a successful businesswoman. Any man would be fuckin' lucky to have you. Don't you dare settle for anything less than perfection."

"Not *any* man..." I murmur.

"Tripp's dealin' with his issues and one day he's gonna realize what a good thing he missed when you're plannin' your dream wedding. It'll be too late, and he'll have to wallow in his consequences."

It's not that I haven't tried with Tripp. I've given him so many signs throughout the years about how I'm interested in him, but there comes a certain point where I have to protect my dignity and stop chasing a man who doesn't want to get caught.

At this rate, it's just embarrassing.

I've tried to accept it and move on, but my heart still flutters like a teen girl crushing over a boy in middle school. If he'd stop stealing glances and staring at my lips like he wanted a taste, I'd believe he didn't want me, too.

For whatever reason, he just won't allow himself to give in to what we both want.

"Have you started writin' your speech?" she asks.

"I have to give a speech?" My brows rise to my hairline.

"You're my maid of honor, so yes. Damien will give a best man speech, and then you'll give yours."

I grab my phone and click on my notes app that's filled with other silly moments, then start typing out more with a chuckle. "This is gonna be so good. You'll be sorry you reminded me."

"Magnolia..."

Her warning tone doesn't scare me.

"This is twenty years of friendship in the makin'. All the dumb shit we've done and have been through. It's gonna be the most epic speech."

"It's supposed to be about me and Fisher," she reminds me, but I wave her off.

"Yeah, yeah. I'll throw some of that lovey-dovey soulmates crap in there, too. But the real fun will be all the embarrassing shit you did before you met him."

She walks off with a groan. "You're fired."

"You wish you could…" I taunt. "Now, should I begin with the nipple piercing story or the time you got drunk and begged a random guy on the street to tattoo your ass?"

"MAGNOLIA!" she screeches from the bathroom.

"Is that your *orgasm* scream? Goddamn, I felt that one all the way downtown. No wonder Fisher was obsessed with you since the first night."

A hairbrush comes flying past my head and smacks the wall behind me.

"Missed," I muse, unfazed by her chucking things at me.

"You won't miss my boot up your ass if there's anything I haven't approved beforehand."

"Can I at least mention the first time you rode the mechanical bull and face-planted on the mat afterward?" I quirk a brow, and she shoots me a glare from the doorway. "Hey, it's that or when you went to buy condoms for the first time, then tripped and the entire display collapsed to the floor. Pick your poison."

She groans, stalking toward me with a scowl. "I hate that you know all my embarrassing stories."

"Bestie privilege!"

She opens her closet and rummages through her options. "Just remember, whatever you say about me, I'll get you back twice as much when it's your turn."

"Go ahead. We'll be eighty before that happens, and both suffer from memory loss anyway."

"Remember when we were like thirteen and promised to get pregnant at the same time so our kids could grow up together?"

I laugh at the random question. "Yeah, but I'm pretty sure we were also supposed to marry brothers so we could become sisters. You ruined our plans."

"If I recall, you're the one who told me to go talk to Fisher at the rodeo. So you only have yourself to blame."

"How was I supposed to know he didn't have a hot, younger brother for me?" I scoff. "And since I can't marry one of your brothers, we're never gonna be sisters now."

"I have four brothers, so never say never."

"Tripp doesn't want me, and I already went on a date with Landen, so that leaves me with the double-trouble twins? Don't think so." I pause, quirking up the corner of my lips. "Although…"

"No," she says firmly. "They're definitely not ready to settle down."

"I could change that…"

Noah snorts, finally pulling out the clothes she wants to wear. "Says every woman they sleep with."

I fall back on her bed, groaning. "Well, don't wait for me to get pregnant, then. Go get knocked up, and I'll just be the cool aunt who gives them money and candy."

She throws a blanket over me, making the room go dark.

"You have plenty of time, drama queen."

"If I'm gonna die sad and alone, just start sizin' me for my coffin now." I stretch out my legs and arms. "But make it comfy and spring for the high-thread-count pillow."

"If you don't stop wallowin', I'm draggin' your ass to the Twisted Bull"—she whips off the blanket, hovering above me— "and makin' *you* ride the mechanical bull."

"It'd take a keg and a half to get me on that thing."

"Don't tempt me." She grabs my hand and yanks me to my feet. "Now c'mon. I'm takin' you for food. Maybe that'll fix your hangry attitude."

Chapter Five
Tripp

"*G*oddamn, I'm a sexy motherfucker." Wilder stands in front of the mirror, smug as shit, sliding his palms down his tux coat.

Magnolia stands next to him with her arms crossed and rolls her eyes, but I see a hint of a smile at his obnoxious antics.

Landen snorts as our idiot brother struts around the store like he's hot shit. Meanwhile, I'm dreading my turn.

I'm happy for my sister and Fisher, but watching them plan their wedding brings back unwanted memories of Billy from high school. We'd joke about growing old as best friends and being each other's best men when we finally settled down. I can't even imagine going through another major milestone without him. I already had to graduate high school without him by my side, and celebrating that felt like a knife to the gut.

Knowing it'll never be possible to share these types of special moments with him as I get older has my chest tightening in what I know is an oncoming anxiety attack. I focus on my breathing so my heart slows down.

"Tripp, hello?" Landen kicks my boot with his. "You're up."

I blink up at him as if he'd been calling my name and see Magnolia studying me with concern.

"Doing okay?" she asks.

I shake my head, set my hands on my knees, and stand. "Great. Where do I go?"

"Shannon's waitin' for ya in the back. She'll take your measurements and grab you some options," Magnolia explains.

"And she's a fuckin' fox." Wilder comes over and nudges me. "I already got her number, though, so don't even think about askin' her."

My eyes dart to Magnolia and she flinches at his words. And to fuck up my life even more, she looks even more gorgeous than usual.

Her long brown hair is pulled back into a braid that wraps around her shoulder, with loose hair pieces framing her face. She looks goddamn adorable. A forbidden temptation I've spent years keeping my distance from.

"Thanks for the heads-up," I murmur to Wilder, then follow Magnolia to the back.

"Hey, you alright?" she asks when we fall into step.

"Yeah, why?"

"You just seem like something's on your mind. You dazed out back there."

I shrug dismissively. "I'm fine. Just thinkin' of all the work shit I gotta do later."

"Oh really? Landen said y'all finished for the day."

My shoulders are tense as I silently curse how much she talks to Landen. They've become close friends over the past couple of years, and I swear they gossip more than she and Noah.

But I don't want to lie to her, so I need out of this conversation as soon as possible.

"I promised my dad I'd help him with some maintenance at the retreat cabins."

Technically, it's not a lie, but it's not the truth either. Dad asked me to stop by after dinner to discuss some tasks we needed to focus on this weekend, and I know one of them is about the cabins.

"Noah told me he couldn't come today because he has a meetin' this afternoon."

The hint of suspicion in her voice has my throat going dry. If she wasn't so perceptive of how I was acting differently, she would've never asked me if I was okay, and I wouldn't be scrambling to get my foot out of my mouth.

I force out a cough. "Yeah, he does. We talked about the tasks he wanted me to do earlier."

"Oh, okay. Well, this shouldn't take too much longer."

When our eyes meet, the corner of her lips pulls up into a sweet smile reserved just for me.

I almost give her one back.

Shannon greets me in one of the back rooms and explains what to do. I zone out while she takes my measurements, then leaves to grab a tux and shoes in my size. The minutes pass, and my heart beats harder. Blood rushes to my ears. My fingers twitch as I sit and my leg shakes up and down, desperate for this to be over.

"Alright, here we go." Shannon walks back into the dressing room with a handful of hangers. At least ten random items are displayed as she explains what Noah and Fisher picked out for us. "If you need help with anything, please holler. I'll have you do the squat and bend test when I'm back."

"The what now?"

"Gotta make sure the pants aren't too tight when you sit or bend over. Fitted suits can be a little snug, and you wanna make sure nothin' rips or gets...*pinched*."

"Excuse me?"

She giggles at my horrified expression. "I'll also bring some underwear options. Silk boxers are usually preferred, but if you prefer briefs..."

"Noah specified our underwear?"

It's bad enough her wedding colors are olive green, copper, and peach. We're gonna look like a Thanksgiving floral bouquet.

"No, but it's one thing men don't think about, and then they end up uncomfortable. So I mention it during the fitting. Wilder opted to go commando." She giggles, and a blush covers her cheeks. "I told him that wasn't recommended but…"

I shake my head. "Yeah, not surprised. I'll do the silk pair if that's what you suggest."

"Great. Just come out when you're done."

Once the door closes, I look at all the items spread out. Suspenders? And a *bowtie*?

God.

But I love my annoying little sister, so I push down the anxiety and get dressed. As soon as I get the black slacks and white button-up situated, I start to sweat, and my body overheats. The last time I wore something this fancy was for senior prom. Billy and I thought we'd look like top shit in matching suits, black cowboy boots, and Stetsons. We drove into the school parking lot in my truck with the music cranked, a six-pack hidden in the back seat that we stole from the twins for the after-party, and walked through the doors like badass motherfuckers.

We took a million photos that night. Laughed nonstop. Danced like morons to every fast song. And made enough memories to last a lifetime.

Well…a lifetime that was cut way too damn short.

This shirt's itchy and way too tight, nearly cutting off my air circulation. Yanking at the collar, I attempt to loosen it, but my shaking hands make it impossible to grasp the button properly and loosen it.

"Fuckin' piece of shit," I mutter, staring in the mirror and lifting my chin. The material digs into my skin, and my breaths come out short and fast.

"Tripp? Doin' okay in there?" Shannon asks from the other side.

No, I'm not okay. I need out of this goddamn shirt.

Finally, I manage to get the top one undone, but I'm too impatient to do the rest. With two hands, I yank down the middle and pop the buttons off with one hard pull. They fly across the room, hitting the wall and floor with a clatter. It does nothing to alleviate the anxiousness consuming me in the stark white room.

"Tripp?" Shannon's knocking grabs my attention, but when I open my mouth, nothing comes out.

Fuck. It's been a while since I've had one this bad.

I kneel next to the wall and tilt my head back, then I close my eyes and count.

One, two, three, four, five…Billy, breathe!

Six, seven, eight, nine, ten…Exhale.

I picture my hands on Billy's chest as I performed CPR, begging his heart to beat. Begging him to breathe. If I'd gotten there faster and not stopped at Miller's first, I would've found him sooner. He wouldn't have gone so long without oxygen and had a fighting chance. Those missed minutes could've saved my best friend's life. Or hell, maybe if I'd just told him I was coming instead of arguing, he wouldn't have gotten behind the wheel at all.

So many fucking regrets.

More knocking echoes throughout the room, but I can't move or speak.

I should be focusing on something else to help me get through the anxiety instead of what's causing it, but sometimes I can't help it.

"I'm comin' in."

This time it's Magnolia speaking.

Her sweet, sultry voice always puts me in a better mood.

Swallowing hard, I open my eyes and see her crawling under the door.

"Tripp, what happened?" She kneels in front of me and grabs my hand, worry lines forming across her forehead. "You're shaking."

"It'll pass," I say roughly. "Just need…a minute."

Her palm flattens against my half-open shirt. "Your heart is racin'. Take some deep breaths and focus on my voice."

I nod, slowly filling my lungs.

"You're clammy." Her hand moves to my cheek before she wraps her fingers around mine. "What do you need? Water? Fresh air?"

A time machine.

Her hand to never leave mine.

A world in which I'm allowed to touch her.

"Tell me a stupid joke or a story," I murmur.

"For real?"

"Distract me. Say anything."

"Okay. Um…Old Man Terry stopped by for a coffee this mornin' and as he was walkin' away, he dropped something, so when he bent down to grab it, I saw his whole ass. Worse than plumber's crack. Looked like Sasquatch. I nearly threw up my breakfast."

I cough out a laugh. "Who hasn't seen his ass at this point? I swear, the man doesn't own a belt."

"Or underwear."

I dig my nails into my palm while focusing on her brown eyes. She's so close and yet not close enough. "What else ya got?"

"Hold on, lemme think."

My gaze moves to her lower lip when she bites it.

"To no one's surprise, Wilder's out there makin' a whole ass of himself in front of Shannon. Flirtin' so damn hard and completely blind to the fact Shannon's not only *uninterested*, but she's dating a woman."

Now that does make me laugh because that sounds just like him. *Oblivious.*

"She's tryin' to be professional and polite, but I can tell she's about to tell him the truth and break his poor heart."

"*Poor heart?*" I scoff, feeling some relief in my chest, the weight of an elephant releasing. "He'll forget her name by the time he leaves the parking lot."

"That's probably true." She chuckles and studies me. "You're startin' to look better."

I lean my head back with my eyes closed, embarrassment

flooding in that Magnolia is witnessing this. "Thanks for distractin' me through the worst of it."

"Happy I could help. Does this happen a lot?" she asks softly.

Little does she know, she's calmed me several times throughout the years. I'd feel one coming on during a family event or when we'd go out to the bar, and the moment I'd find her, a wave of calmness would surface.

"It hasn't in a while. Right after Billy…yeah. But stayin' busy helped. Kinda annoyin' it still affects me after all these years."

When she grabs my hand and interlocks our fingers, my eyes whip open.

"Grief doesn't have a time limit, Tripp. Some days it can feel like it was forever ago and at the same time, like it was only yesterday. Did being here trigger something?"

"Yeah." Instead of elaborating, I abruptly pull back and get to my feet. I've already humiliated myself and now have to ask Shannon to bring me a new shirt. The last thing I should be doing is letting Magnolia get too close.

She stands, adjusting her jeans and top while avoiding my gaze. I can't even blame her. For so long, I kept her at arm's length but was always tempted to take that leap. Losing Billy was a level of grief that consumed me for so long. I know I could never survive that type of pain again. Getting involved with Magnolia would be a risk that'd affect everyone. Not just my heart but my sister and how weaved into our lives she is. If I fucked up or she went back to Travis at some point, I'd never be able to escape her.

It'd be worse than losing my best friend because she'd still be around, taunting my broken heart and reminding me of the guilt I already harbored.

But there's a part of me that thinks the risk could be worth it…

If only I'd be brave enough to take the leap.

Chapter Six
Magnolia

"How's my favorite farrier?" I grin at Fisher when he walks up to the counter. I haven't seen him since the tux fitting two weeks ago. He stopped in after Tripp's turn to sign some paperwork and see how everything was going.

He smirks, pulling out his wallet from his back pocket. "I'm the only farrier you know."

"Perhaps but even so." I shrug. "What're you doin' in town?"

On Fridays, I park downtown and grab the early morning crowd, then stay through the afternoon for the after-work crowd.

"Pickin' up some things for the honeymoon. But shh, it's a surprise. Noah thinks I'm meetin' Jase for lunch."

I feign a shocked gasp and clutch my chest. "You want me to *lie* to my bestie? Hmm. That may cost you extra…" I tilt my head toward my tip jar.

He shakes his head, grabs a twenty, and shoves it in. "That enough for your *silence*?"

"That'll do it. Now what can I getcha?"

"A regular coffee with caramel and two creams."

"You know what'd pair great with this?" I grab a cup. "A blue-choco-berry muffin."

It's a new thing I'm trying. Baking, that is. Customers have been asking for food options, so I'm starting small. With the weather getting colder, I'm spending more time inside and figured I'd give it a try.

Plus, it helps keep my brain busy so I don't overthink how I'm going to be a single cat lady for the rest of my life. Well, as soon as I get some cats. It's worked for Taylor Swift.

But I'd probably forget to feed it.

Or maybe I'll get a hamster. I'm ninety percent sure I could keep a hamster alive.

"A *blue-choco* what?"

"I mixed blueberries and chocolate chips with a hint of cinnamon," I explain, making his drink. "It's an orgasmic explosion for your tastebuds."

His brows rise with amusement, but he doesn't tell me no. Fisher's too sweet to make fun of my random concoction.

Too bad he doesn't have a brother. Preferably one closer to my age, rich, and single.

"How many do you have left?"

Once I put the lid on his cup and hand it over, I look over at my tray. "Three. Sold five this morning."

"Okay, I'll take the rest." He smiles wide, pulling out more cash.

"All three? Better not let those Hollis boys see you with these. They'll fight ya for one."

"Pfft. They're too scared of their sister's wrath to mess with me."

I laugh because it's true. Noah's the youngest sibling, but she holds the reins on her brothers. Now that Fisher's joining their family, he gets auto-protection.

After the muffins are bagged, he hands me a fifty and tells me to keep the change.

My jaw drops. "Are you sure? That's like a thirty-percent tip."

"Consider it a gift for everything you're helpin' Noah with. Especially when it involves her brothers." He winks.

I put the change in my tip jar and thank him. "Yeah, four hot, rowdy cowboys. Definitely a hardship."

He smirks, then takes a sip of his coffee. "This is good, Magnolia."

"You doubted me?"

"Never. Just givin' you a compliment. I'm sure the muffins are equally delicious."

I put my hands on my hips and stare at him. "Why do I have a feelin' you're butterin' me up for something?"

He barks out a laugh. "You caught me. I need a favor…"

I sigh. "What?"

"This is another one of those times where you can't tell Noah."

Rolling my eyes, I cross my arms. "Of course it is."

"I have some items on hold for Noah, but I wanna make sure they'll fit her comfortably." His voice is hesitant, nervous even, and it makes me narrow my eyes. I grab my iced coffee and suck it down as he continues. "Thought you could maybe go look at 'em and if you think they'll fit. Or if you think she'll hate them. They're at Lacey's."

Before I can catch myself, icy liquid spurts out of my mouth and spills across my countertop. I cover my mouth and choke the rest of it down.

"Shit. You okay?" He hands me a napkin from the dispenser.

"Did you say Lacey's? As in…the *lingerie* store?"

"Yeah. Sorry, I shouldn't have asked. That's probably weird, right?"

"Well…" I dab my chin and clean up my mess. "No weirder than me knowing where Noah hides her vibrator. Did she say she wanted lingerie?"

"Yeah, we talked about it. She thought it'd be sexier if I picked it out versus someone gifting it to her from the bachelorette party. I found some sets, but I want her to love them and fit correctly. There's so many options. And pieces. And clips. Hence where you come into this very awkward picture."

His cheeks are red as he scrubs a hand through his shoulder-length hair. I'm pretty certain there's a line of sweat along his forehead. It's kind of adorable.

Noah's a little curvier than me, but we have the same size chest. So it couldn't hurt to at least see what he found. Might be fun to play dress-up even if no one besides me will see it.

"Alright, I'll do it. What's your budget?"

He snorts. "Um…a hundred bucks?"

"That's it? That'll get you a thong and an overpriced scrunchie." Lacey's is known for their luxury lingerie lines. They're pricey, but you won't find better quality anywhere within a hundred miles.

"Per piece, Magnolia. I'm not *that* cheap."

I chuckle in relief and shake my head at the irony. "And to think *I'm* the one who told her to go talk to you and now y'all are havin' hot sex while I'm"—I wave out my arm around my small trailer—"makin' coffee and bakin' muffins. Alone."

He sucks in his lips as if he's stifling a laugh at my dramatics. "Did I ever thank you for that, by the way?"

"You're about to when I find myself a really cute set and add it to your tab. Ya know, for psychological damages."

He slides over his credit card. "Here. Get the ones you think Noah will like that I put on hold. And nothing over a hundred for your…extras. I'm not cheap, but I'm not loaded either."

I play with the card in my fingers. "Pff, you're marryin' into the Hollis family."

"Magnolia…" He pins me with a warning stare.

"Fine, fine. Do you want pics?"

"Of what?"

"Me. To get a visual of how they look."

"Jesus Christ, no. You tryin' to get me divorced before I even walk down the aisle?"

A laugh bubbles out of me as I pocket his card. "Calm down, cowboy. Just messin' with ya."

Noah wouldn't believe anything was going on between us anyway. She's smarter than that.

"I need that back when you're done." He points to my shorts pocket.

"I'll bring it with the secret stash." I wink as if we're dealing hardcore drugs. "Secret's safe with me."

He blows out a breath. "I'm regrettin' this already."

I've never worn lingerie before, but it wasn't hard to find what I liked. After trying on and approving the sets and pieces Fisher picked out, I went shopping for myself. Fisher has good taste, so I grab similar items to try on. Where he got blacks and whites for Noah, I opt for blacks and reds for me. They look sexy against my tan skin and dark hair, if I say so myself.

But the truth is I have no one to wear it for. So I'll wear it for me.

I take a mirror selfie with each outfit change so I can remember how good they look on me since I can't purchase them all. I don't want to bankrupt Fisher since I actually like the guy, so I'll stick to the hundred-dollars-per-piece rule.

The black corset with the garter belt paired with a push-up bra and see-thru lacy panties is my favorite. Since I can't ask Noah's opinion without her getting suspicious, I have to resort to my only other friend who will tell me honestly.

MAGNOLIA

Need your opinion on something. You free?

LANDEN

Just ridin' with Tripp checking fences. What's up?

> MAGNOLIA
>
> I'm trying on lingerie and want your opinion on which one to get. Can I show you the pics?

> LANDEN
>
> Of you in your underwear? You never have to ask permission for that. Show Daddy.

> MAGNOLIA
>
> OMG, you perv! I'd text Noah if I could, but I'm helping Fisher out with something so you're all I've got. Maybe this is a bad idea...

> LANDEN
>
> Calm your titties. And then show 'em to me.

He sends a devil emoji, and I'm regretting this already.

But I really do want his thoughts on which one is the most appealing to a guy. Who knows if the one person I want to show will ever see them, but better to be prepared.

> MAGNOLIA
>
> No inappropriate comments!

> LANDEN
>
> I can't promise that...or thoughts.

With each lingerie change, I took a handful of mirror-length selfies from the front and back. I attach the best ones to our message and hit send.

My heart races while I wait for him to respond. Two, three, five minutes go by without a word.

Shit. I probably look stupid.

I can't wait any longer.

> MAGNOLIA
>
> You better not be jerking off to my pics.

LANDEN

> I'm definitely sporting a boner. Thanks for that.
> Painful as fuck in these jeans while I'm on a
> horse, btw. Sydney's gonna end up pregnant by
> the end of my shift.

I roll my eyes. And cringe at the image.

Landen and I are good friends, so I felt comfortable enough showing him, but he's not the one I want to impress.

MAGNOLIA

> Which one do you think Thor would like the best?

I giggle at our fake nickname for Tripp. Ever since I told Landen about the crush, I made up a name to use when we text. The last thing I need is Tripp seeing them and feeling like a fool. Since I wanted the name to start with the same letter as Tripp's, I picked the hottest character played by the hottest man in Hollywood—Chris Hemsworth.

Landen teases me for it, but I feel better knowing I can talk about him in secret.

LANDEN

> Uh…literally all of them. There's not a straight
> man in the world who wouldn't give up one of his
> senses for a shot to be with you.

Guilt crashes into me, worried that maybe Landen's crush on me isn't as over as he says it is. He's always trying to find ways to get Tripp and me together or to make him jealous, so if he does, he's not made it obvious to me.

MAGNOLIA

> I can only buy one. So tell me which is your
> favorite?

LANDEN

The third one. It's sexy without revealing everything. Lets me use my imagination while still being teased.

I smile because that's mine too.

MAGNOLIA

Thanks. I appreciate your input. Now delete these photos!

LANDEN

Why the fuck would I do that? That wasn't a condition for helping you.

MAGNOLIA

Because I don't want anyone else to see them!

LANDEN

Don't worry, they're in my private folder labeled SPANK BANK.

MAGNOLIA

OMG, you're disgusting! Delete them. Now.

LANDEN

You should wear it underneath your dress at my birthday party tomorrow night. Then you can let me see it in person instead ;-)

I groan, knowing the shit is going to taunt me with these until I threaten him with bodily harm.

MAGNOLIA

Then I either get a dick pic or get to dick-kick you for being a creep.

LANDEN

Hell nah.

MAGNOLIA

Fair is fair. You got tits and ass pics of me. So...
send me a dick pic for insurance you'll never
show mine to anyone.

LANDEN

I wouldn't do that, Mags.

MAGNOLIA

It's small, huh?

LANDEN

You're such a brat. Go ask Thor for his instead.
Oh, wait. You're too chicken shit.

MAGNOLIA

Asshole.

I take the final set to the register and have the woman ring me up with Noah's. Once I've paid with Fisher's card and grabbed the bag, I walk out to my Honda CR-V. Sadly, I had to trade in Big Red when I got the trailer so I could tow it from place to place. The trailer isn't super large, but I needed something stable for the investment I put into building it.

Once I'm buckled in, I grab my phone and shoot a text to Fisher.

MAGNOLIA

I've secured the goods. Let me know where you
want me to drop them off.

FISHER

I'll stop by for coffee on Tuesday. Bring it then.

MAGNOLIA

Aye aye, captain. Wanna see pics of me wearing
the white Teddy?

I'm totally messing with him since I didn't take any of the ones

67

that are for Noah. But making him uncomfortable and annoyed is part of my best friend duty.

> **FISHER**
>
> Please, no. Send them to Thor instead.

My eyes bulge out of my head, and my jaw drops.

> **MAGNOLIA**
>
> How do you know that name?

> **FISHER**
>
> Your best friend is my fiancée.

That little snitch.

> **MAGNOLIA**
>
> That was a secret!

> **FISHER**
>
> And it's safe with me.

Then he sends a cheeky smirking emoji.
Not helping.

> **MAGNOLIA**
>
> If I'd known you two were swapping more than spit, I would've bought myself two sets.

> **FISHER**
>
> Thanks for your help. I do appreciate it.

I sigh, unable to stay mad at the guy who's making Noah the happiest I've ever seen her.

> **MAGNOLIA**
>
> Are you sure you don't have a brother?

> **FISHER**
>
> Sorry.

Stay With Me

And that's when I decide. Landen's birthday party is at the Twisted Bull, and I'm going take a few shots for courage, dance as if my life depended on it, and get Tripp's attention once and for all.

Chapter Seven

Tripp

The sun is brutal today, even if the heat isn't as bad as it has been, but enough to warrant my Resistol hat instead of my preferred ball cap. It usually gets the out-of-state guests excited to see a "real cowboy," so it's not a total waste.

In between working at The Lodge in the afternoons and training with Noah in the mornings, Landen and I work on various tasks on the ranch, such as riding horseback around the ranch's perimeter to check the fences and for anything else out of place. With his birthday party tomorrow night, we need to get most of our shit done today since he'll be spending his actual birthday on Sunday nursing a hangover.

"Guess who's comin' to the Twisted Bull?" Landen flashes a shit-eating smirk, and I can only imagine the response I'm going to get. "The Marrow twins! You can thank me later. Lydia's already foamin' at the mouth for a taste of you."

Gross. My entire body breaks out in hives.

Lydia's a cockroach who tried to trap her ex into having a baby he wasn't ready for. Poking holes in the condoms and going off her birth control without telling him.

But then she cried to anyone who'd listen to her that he broke up with her for "no reason."

"You remember what she did to Ashton, right?"

He shrugs. "Well, double wrap it for extra security."

I scoff. "No, thanks. I'm not that desperate."

"You can still be nice and dance with her. Just tell her hands above the belt at all times." He smirks over his shoulder, and I want to smack that cocky look off his face.

"Why do I have to be *nice*? I don't even like her. You're the one hot for her sister."

"Exactly. Quinn won't pay attention to me if she's worried about Lydia. So ya gotta do this for me. Just keep her occupied so I can keep Quinn...*occupied*."

He waggles his brows, and I nearly throw up in my mouth.

"Dude, c'mon. Don't ask me that."

"It's my *birthday*..." His taunting voice tells me he's not going to quit until I agree to this ridiculous plan. But that doesn't mean I have to stick to it. He's turning twenty-seven, and if he can't get women without a wingman, that's on him.

"Whatever," I grumble.

"Yes! I'll owe ya one."

"You always say that. I think you're up to three hundred and twenty-two IOUs."

He barks out a laugh. "You're keepin' count?"

"Educated guess. All the times I drive your drunk ass home. All the shifts I cover for you when you're hungover. All the chicks I dodge in town askin' why you ain't callin' 'em back." I scowl at his proud grin. "Oh, by the way...not your fuckin' secretary. Break up with them like a normal person."

"Nothin' to say. I'm never exclusive. It ain't my fault they always want more than I can give. Guess it's my natural wit and charm."

I snort, then dig my heels into Franklin so he catches up to Landen, and we can stop shouting to hear each other. He's my four-year-old Appaloosa, and I ride him everywhere on the ranch. He's an easy, calm horse when he's not next to Landen's quarter horse.

As soon as we're side by side, Franklin releases a loud whine.

"You're alright." I pat his neck. "Settle down."

"He's such a finicky bitch." Landen laughs.

"Sydney's a tease," I remind him. We've caught them many times trying to bite each other when we put them in the pasture to muck their stalls. No idea why, but they clearly have beef with each other.

"Don't listen to him, baby," Landen says in a sickly sweet voice. "You just don't take shit from a man, right?"

Rolling my eyes at the irony, I give Franklin another kick so we can hurry this along. When we get up one of the hills, I go right, and Landen goes left so we can cover more area quicker.

We check the fences every quarter, usually around season changes or after we get hit with lots of rain or wind. The ground shifts and that affects the fence line.

By the time I meet back up with Landen, he's grinning like a fool at his phone.

"Who're you chattin' with?" I ask.

"Just Mags."

Jealousy slices through me at how close the two are. Talking about only God knows what.

My mind's distracted as I catch up to him and end up too close to Sydney. Franklin's high-pitched whine scares her, and she bucks.

"Oh, shit. None of that, Syd." Landen tightens his hold on the reins and his phone goes flying from his grip. I manage to catch it before it drops to the ground and the screen with his text messages appears.

The conversation with Magnolia.

I shouldn't look, but when I glance down briefly, my eyes catch a name I don't recognize. Thor. *Thor?* Who the fuck is that?

Scrolling up to see if there's an explanation for this "thunder-god," my jaw drops when I see several photos of a half-naked Magnolia in barely there lingerie.

And fuck me, she's drop-dead gorgeous.

I blink the images away, feeling like a creep for sneaking a peek. Then I quickly read the rest of their messages. The way Landen talks makes me wonder if he's still crushing on her.

"Dude, good catch," Landen says once Sydney's settled.

"Yeah, here." I extend my arm until he reaches it. "Who the fuck is Thor?"

He snorts so goddamn loud, I almost wonder if it came from Sydney.

"Saw that, did ya?" He shoves the phone into his pocket.

"You gonna tell me or what?"

We continue riding toward the family barn as he shrugs. "It's…nobody."

I roll my eyes at his lack of an answer.

"You still like her, don't you?"

"Only as a friend."

"Sure about that? I read the messages."

He barks out a laugh as we ride side by side, with more room between us this time. "You fuckin' snoop."

"Why's she sendin' you nudes then?"

"Jesus Christ, Tripp. You her boyfriend or somethin'? What's with the third degree?"

"Because I know you."

He whips his head at me in offense. "What's that supposed to mean?"

"You're not lookin' for anything serious. You just said you don't do exclusivity," I remind him. Landen hasn't been in a serious relationship since high school.

"And Magnolia is?"

That I'm not sure, but I do know he'd hurt her. And then I'd have to kick my brother's ass.

"When're you gonna finally ask her out, man?"

"What're you talkin' about?" My stomach coils at him knowing the truth. I haven't told a single soul about my feelings for Magnolia. How could he possibly know?

"I'm talkin' about you mannin' the fuck up, admittin' you like

73

her, and askin' her out instead of"—he waves his hand out in a circular motion toward me—"pretendin' like she doesn't exist."

"I don't do that."

His amused chuckle pisses me off, but I don't exactly have an excuse to defend myself. So I shut my mouth before he can give me more shit.

Neither of us talks the rest of the way to the newly built family barn where all of our personal horses are boarded. It burned down last summer, but we had a team clean up the aftermath and started rebuilding as soon as possible. Luckily, all of our horses were saved when Fisher risked his life to get all of them out after he was nearly knocked unconscious.

The barn's close to our parents' house, which is the main house on the ranch. Landen and I moved out earlier this year into one of the duplexes on the ranch hand quarters. He took the top level, and I moved into the bottom. We each have two bedrooms and bathrooms of our own space, which is nice after sharing a house with my brothers, Gramma Grace, and my cousin Mallory, but sometimes I miss the chaos. It gets lonely living alone, but at least we meet up every Sunday night for family supper.

"Wanna hang out tonight?" Landen asks once Sydney and Franklin are brushed and back in their stalls.

"Nah. I need to mentally prepare for the hell tomorrow night's gonna be."

His palm smacks my shoulder. "You mean the most epic party ever."

"Right. Some of us still have to work this weekend."

"You have cabin call. Big deal."

Big deal? Says him.

Every afternoon, I work in The Lodge with the receptionist when the guests check in. Everyone who stays in the equine retreat cabins and wants to go trail riding must use the same horse during their stay. My parents wanted a curated experience for each guest, and they get a horse based on their riding knowledge and age. It's my job to pick the right horse for them, and then I call Waylon so he can get the right ones ready.

"I also train in the mornings," I remind him, although Landen trains too during the off-breeding season.

"Complain to me when you're jerkin' off horses all summer."

Landen loves to throw it in everyone's face that he manages the breeding operation, which keeps him busy all summer. During the off months, he takes care of the stallions and is in charge of booking mares for the following year.

"You're the one who volunteered for that position," I remind him.

"Well, yeah. Who else gets to say they sell sperm for a livin'?" He waggles his brows and his tongue flicks between his lips.

"You're so fuckin' weird." I shake my head on my way to my truck.

"Don't forget you're my DD bitch tomorrow night. You can drive Quinn and me back and then bring Lydia back to your place for a nightcap."

"Pfft. I'm always your bitch. And I'm not bringin' Lydia to my house, so she better have another ride home."

"Aww, don't be like that. Just occupy her for a few hours and then Quinn and her can Uber home."

"No."

"It's my *birthday*..." The taunting way he sings those words makes me want to punch his pretty boy face.

"Imma get wasted just so I don't have to take you or the twins home. I'd rather pass out in the alley than bring her to my house."

Landen shoves me into the driver's side door before he goes around to the passenger's side. "You wouldn't dare."

He's right, and I hate that he is.

If I'm not in the safety and comfort of my house or my parents', I'm not drinking.

Just the thought threatens an anxiety attack.

"You're a dick." I hop in, then buckle up.

I'm in hell.

No, this is much worse.

Lydia won't keep her hands off me and Landen's so obsessed with Quinn that he doesn't even bother to come rescue me.

I spent the day finishing up work chores and then got ready to come out. Waylon and Wilder were jacked up and ready to party hours ago. My brothers and I met up at Landen's to pregame — well, I drank water — and then I drove everyone into town. We hit up a Mexican restaurant first to get food into their stomachs and then walked to the Twisted Bull where I'm currently burning in hell's flames.

Wilder signed everyone up to ride the mechanical bull, including Fisher, who doesn't even need to hang onto the horn. Noah's staying close to Magnolia, but when I see her asshole ex show up, my hands ball into fists, ready to take him out.

I haven't seen him around much since he reported me to the sheriff two years ago, and I ended up with a hundred hours of community service. Since I had witnesses to claim the actual events of what happened, I was able to make a deal that kept me out of jail. I stayed away from Travis and worked at the homeless shelter and food bank all summer.

Magnolia volunteered to work the hours for me, nearly begging the sheriff to let her since she felt at fault, but I told her absolutely not. I'm the one who punched and kicked Travis and fuck him, I'd do it again if it meant he left her alone.

But for some reason, the universe is punishing me. He's here tonight when I can't escape Lydia and her clingy fingers to keep an appropriate watch on Magnolia.

"Do you wanna get a drink?" she whispers in my ear much too loudly as we sit at a bartop table.

"I'm only drinkin' water. But feel free to get a refill of yours."

I glare at Landen across the table, whose tongue is currently bobbing for apples inside Quinn's mouth. *Fucking asshole.*

"Wanna come with me?" Lydia asks sweetly.

Turning to face her, the guilt creeps in at how harsh I'm being. It's not her fault I've been tasked with babysitting her, but I also hate leading her on.

"Sure," I say.

When we approach the bar, Noah and Magnolia are also there getting shots.

"Hey, Tripp. Wanna recreate my birthday party BJ shot?" Magnolia's halfway to drunkville, which makes me even more worried about Travis being here.

"I ain't drinkin' tonight," I tell her, then look at Noah. "Fisher drivin' y'all home?"

"Yeah, he's our DD."

I nod, appreciating that she'll be looked after.

Her mentioning that night has my chest vibrating. It was the first and only time our lips touched, and I was tempted to do it again as soon as she pulled away. Travis glared like he wanted to murder me, and if it wasn't for him being there, I actually might've kissed her for real.

Consequences be damned.

"Oh, c'mon!" Magnolia pleads, bouncing on her tiptoes as she inches toward me. "It's one shot."

At her closeness, Lydia slides in next to me, wrapping her hand around my arm. *Squeezing*, rather. She glares at Magnolia. "And who are you?"

"That depends. Who are *you*?" Magnolia pretending not to know makes this even more hilarious. Sugarland Creek is a small town of only two thousand people. Everyone knows everyone, but the Marrows are Landen's age, so although they're four years apart, there's a low chance they've never heard of each other.

"Lydia Marrow...his *date*."

Fire burns in Magnolia's eyes when she scowls at me. "Tripp doesn't date."

"Apparently, he does because here I am." Lydia's silky sweet voice has Magnolia grinding her teeth.

Magnolia's gaze finds mine and a sinister smile forms on her face. "Be careful or you'll become a daddy…and not the sexy *Daddy* kind."

Oh, fuck. She's heard the rumors, too.

I'm too busy focusing on Magnolia to react when Lydia steps forward and gets in Magnolia's face.

"Excuse me? What'd you just say, little girl?" Lydia's taller by a few inches, but that's never scared Magnolia off before. "You're one to talk…*slut.*"

Without a word, Magnolia reaches up and pulls a chunk of Lydia's hair.

"GIRL FIGHT!" Wilder shouts from behind them.

Remind me to kill him later.

Luckily, Noah beats me to it and smacks him across the head.

Quickly grabbing Lydia's arm, I yank her back before there really is a *girl fight* in the middle of the bar. It's not to protect Lydia but to keep Magnolia out of trouble.

"Don't talk to her like that," I warn Lydia.

Her jaw drops as she motions toward Magnolia. "She just pulled my hair! Didn't you hear what she said about me?"

"I don't give a shit. You don't call anyone a slut, especially *her*, around me." I set my jaw, narrowing my eyes so she understands my warning won't be repeated.

Before another word is muttered, Travis walks up behind Magnolia, and my vision goes black.

This motherfucker.

"There a problem, Hollis?" The arrogance in his tone makes me want to deck that smug smirk off his face.

"There will be if you don't mind your own damn business." My eyes zoom into how close he's standing to Magnolia.

"Lookin' to add a second round of community service to your

résumé?" His arm drapes around her shoulders in a familiar way, and it makes my hands itch to smack his hands off her.

"Fuck off, Travis. This doesn't involve you...for once," I spit out.

"Sure it does. Your little girlfriend there is getting in my Maggie's face. So you either stop her...or I will."

"Shut up, Travis," Magnolia scolds him with an elbow to his gut.

Good girl.

"Baby doll, I'm just protectin' you."

"Well, I don't need it," she hisses, walking around him and shoveling through people to get away.

I give Travis a cocky smirk just to piss him off that he's not getting Magnolia's attention tonight either.

Chapter Eight
Magnolia

*F*uck me sideways, what have I done?

 The beige walls with the posters of naked women are all too familiar and make me dry heave, the memories of last night playing in a loop. Of all the men in the world, why did I have to end up at Travis's place?

I was in recovery! Two years of no Travis. Two years of not going back to him.

Two years down the drain.

Over…just like that.

Alcohol-infused IV straight into my arm and my dumbass ends up back here.

God, I'm pathetic.

The moment I saw Lydia Marrow—besides wanting to vomit on her shoes—I wanted to flick her long claws off Tripp's arm. If the rumors are true, she tried to trap her ex-boyfriend into having a baby, and as soon as he found out, he dumped her. Whether she did or not, I don't trust her. Especially with Tripp.

And it made me get absolutely wasted.

Noah and I danced nonstop and continued drinking. I took shot after shot, hoping to wash the image of Lydia fucking Tripp out of my head. I did my best not to pay attention to them, which was easy enough since my brothers hung out in the back to play pool and darts. When Noah and Fisher were ready to go, I was still partying with a couple of our other friends, so I told them I'd Uber home since I only live a few blocks away. There's no way I planned to drive, but somehow between scheduling my ride and the exit, Travis convinced me to go home with him.

"Maggie…" He groans, tightening his hold on my stomach. "Ride me before I lose my mornin' wood." He grinds his cock into my ass, and I gag.

I could not be more dry.

Shuddering at the thought of him touching me again, I slide out from under the sheet and search for my clothes.

"It's *Magnolia*," I tell him for the thousandth time. "And this was a mistake."

"You don't mean that. C'mon, we can shower together, and you can suck me off."

"I was drunk, you moron," I remind him, grabbing my dress and panties, then sliding them on.

"We're good together, doll. I've changed, and I promise this time—"

"There's no *this time*. You and me, never happenin' again."

A cocky smirk flashes across his bemused face as he crosses his arms behind his head. "You said that last time."

Finally finding my shoes, I swipe them off the floor and scowl at him. "Lose my number."

Once I grab my phone and bag, I aim for the door and am relieved when I see the disposed condom on the floor. At least he managed to get one on.

"You'll be back! You always are…"

If I wasn't in such a hurry to wash last night's regret off me, I'd march back into his room and stab him with my high heel.

It's Sunday morning, which means downtown's quiet except for the church bells. All the shops are closed, and Ubers are limited.

I decide to do the walk of shame down the five blocks to my

apartment. Living in a small town means nothing's too far away, but it also means Travis is too close.

Ugh. I hate him.

But more than anything, I hate myself.

After a scalding hot shower and brushing my teeth, I go through my messages to make sure I texted Noah that I was safe and sound.

NOAH
> Text me when you're home!

MAGNOLIA
> *thumbs-up*

Two hours later…

NOAH
> You better not be dead in a ditch. Are you home?

MAGNOLIA
> I'm fimee motor

I cringe at my drunk texting skills. Thought I was getting better at that.

NOAH
> You're wasted AF. Please get home safely.

Then I sent her a drunken selfie with a cringy-as-hell smile and one squinted eye.

Jesus. I'm a mess.

Her most recent text was from an hour ago.

NOAH

Morning, drunky. Hungover?

Instead of texting out a response, I send her a selfie with my middle finger.

Thank God Sundays are my days off because I'd be drinking more of the coffee than serving it.

Once I hit send, I look through my other messages and see Tripp's name. We hardly ever text because he never responds anyway. And apparently, I sent him a message at two o'clock this morning.

MAGNOLIA

Tripp Clark Hollis! Actually...I don't think that's your middle name. It starts with a C though, right? Chad? Chuck? Chattanooga? Well, whatever it is...I hate that chick. LYDIA?! Out of all the single women in town, you date her? Please tell me you aren't taking her home. Your balls will shrivel up and die if she touches them. RIP Tripp Chattanooga Hollis's balls.

Oh. My. God. I smack my forehead and pray for a quick death.

It's not the first time I've drunk texted Tripp, but this is at the top of the most embarrassing things I've said to him. Now that I'm aware of how badly his anxiety still affects him, I feel even worse for acting completely out of pocket.

What's even worse is Tripp responded at seven this morning when he was probably getting up for work.

TRIPP

It's Cameron.

Tripp Cameron! Shit, I knew that.

But what the fuck kind of response is that? He doesn't even acknowledge the Lydia or balls comment or the fact that I was drunk off my ass. Tripp's already hard to read in person, but over text, he comes off like a robot.

So if he's not going to mention the elephant in the room, then I won't either.

It's hours later, and he's probably still working, but I can't help wanting to get any kind of response from him.

MAGNOLIA

Hmm...Chattanooga has a better ring to it.

To my complete surprise, the jumping dots appear on the screen right away.

TRIPP

I'll make sure to edit my birth certificate right away.

And as per usual, I can't tell if he's being a sarcastic asshole or awkwardly flirty.

MAGNOLIA

You should. Then we can name our firstborn son after your middle name and make his Tennessee.

TRIPP

Chattanooga Tennessee, huh? That's borderline child abuse.

My smile widens at how the mention of a child isn't what he focused on but rather the name of said child.

MAGNOLIA

We'll call him Chatty for short.

TRIPP

If he's anything like his mama, he'll talk nonstop, so I guess it's perfect.

Stay With Me

I'm sorry...Did he just...Excuse me while I pick up my jaw off the floor.

MAGNOLIA

> Glad you agree. Guess it's time for you to knock me up, cowboy.

I hit send before I can word vomit another sentence because *oh my God* did I really just text that?

It's the hangover making me feel brave or the filter from my brain to my mouth is broken.

To absolutely no one's surprise, Tripp doesn't text back, and I spend the rest of my day obsessively *not* checking my phone.

It's the Monday-est Monday I've had in a long-ass time. My espresso machine is having a full-on hissy fit, and my paper delivery is delayed until Friday, which means I'm going to run out of cups and lids before more arrive. Since I woke up late, by the time I arrived at my trailer parked downtown, I already had a line waiting for me.

All I want to do is eat four massive tacos and take a six-hour nap.

After I finish serving my final customer of the day at three, I lock up and walk to the Mexican restaurant down Main Street. Landen texted earlier and said he'd be in town, so I invited him to meet me here for an early dinner. Whether he could or not, I had no problem sitting alone to sulk about my poor decisions and karma's way of smacking me across the face.

As soon as I take a large gulp, Landen walks up and leans into my ear.

"Knock me up, cowboy?"

He chuckles and I slap my palm against my mouth to keep my drink from spewing all over the table. When he sits across from me, I swallow it down and glare at him.

"I hate you."

"Is that any way to talk to your future kid's uncle?"

I kick him in the shin under the table.

"Not funny, Landen!" I grit out. "He's never talkin' to me again."

He opens up the menu and scans the options. "I wouldn't say that…"

"Wait…I'm surprised he told you."

"He was actin' weird all mornin' until I finally asked him what was going on because he kept zonin' out every time I said something." He snags a chip and dips it into the salsa, then bites into it with a loud crunch.

"How desperate does he think I am now?"

"Quite the opposite. He was so shocked by your message that he contemplated for three hours how to respond. He kept typin' out replies to be funny or flirty, but it was like he couldn't get his head out of his ass long enough to come up with anything, so he just gave up. Now he's hyper-fixated on how to start up another conversation. Personally, I woulda gone with *Get your sexy ass over here right now* and *spread those baby-making legs*, but he was all about playin' it casual."

I reach over and smack his bicep. "This is why you're single."

"Single by choice, thank you very much."

I roll my eyes, knowing he's full of shit. When the right woman comes along, there's no way he'll be able to resist being obsessed with her.

"So he doesn't think I'm a complete weirdo?" My heart pounds so hard I can feel it beating in my ears.

"Nah. But I do think he's at war with himself about givin' in to his feelings. For whatever reason." He steals two more chips before sucking them down with the water I ordered for him. He has to go back to work after this, so I knew he couldn't drink and operate heavy machinery. It's why I am because he can drop me off on his way back to the ranch.

"Did you know he has anxiety attacks? I found him on the floor at the tux fitting fightin' through one."

"He was? I knew he'd experienced them in the past, but I didn't know he still was. Kinda surprised he didn't tell me." His brows etch together in concern, but if I know Tripp, he's not one to ask for help or share what he's going through to avoid inconveniencing others with his issues. It makes me sad to think of how many times he's suffered alone.

"He and Billy talked about being each other's best men, so being there was triggerin' to those feelings."

"Shit. I shoulda known that. He'll never not feel guilty for what happened, no matter how much time has passed. I know he misses him and it was traumatic to watch his best friend die, but I'd hoped it was gettin' easier for him. I hate knowin' there's nothing I can do to fix that."

Me too.

"Do you think that's why he doesn't date much? Well, besides this past weekend." I roll my eyes, taking a long sip of my margarita.

He snorts, but before he can respond, Miss Maria comes over. She's been the owner of Maria's Kitchen for as long as I can remember and serves the best food in town. Landen orders like he's going into hibernation for a month, and I get the taco platter with rice and beans.

I might've also told her to bring me a refill with my food.

"You know he ain't really datin' her, right? He was playin' wingman," Landen explains.

"What're you talkin' about? Why would *you* need one of those?"

"I wanted to hook up with Quinn, but I knew we wouldn't get the chance if she was too busy worrying about Lydia all night, so I asked Tripp to keep her *entertained* for me so I'd get all of Quinn's attention."

"And I'm sure it was such a hardship for Tripp to *entertain* Lydia all night."

"Soundin' a little jealous, Magpie."

"Ew, don't call me that." I throw a chip at his face. "And I'm not jealous. But Lydia?"

"For what it's worth, I guilt-tripped him into it since it was my birthday. But it didn't work anyway because after your little scuffle with her, the girls left."

I sit up straighter. "So he didn't take Lydia back to his place?"

"Nope. I knew he wouldn't sleep with her because he's basically a monk, but I didn't think she'd start a fight. So now they're both written off in my book."

"What do you mean? How come?"

"Because Quinn took Lydia's side and you're my friend." He shrugs like it's no big deal. "And my future sister-in-law."

I lean over the table and smack his arm. "Stop sayin' shit like that. It's gonna give me hope for something that'll never happen."

"Never say never, Maggie Mae. Just have patience. I think Tripp's comin' around to the realization he deserves to be happy and lettin' himself admit what he wants."

"Why can't anyone just use my name? Are y'all allergic to it or something?"

"Yeah, it's pollen season."

"Cute." Grabbing a chip, I drown it in the salsa before taking a bite.

"You let him call you Sunflower or Sunny," he argues.

"I don't *let* him. He's just done it forever. There's no point in scoldin' him each time."

"Ya know…he only has a nickname for you. That's gotta mean something."

"I figured it was because I'm Noah's best friend and he saw me like an honorary annoyin' little sister."

He shrugs as Miss Maria returns with our plates. We thank her, and I dig in once she walks away.

"Maybe in middle school, but I think when y'all got older and hung out more, something shifted. You weren't exactly subtle about your crush, but you kept going back to Travis, so he probably thought he'd never have a chance."

My shoulders tense at the mention of my ex.

I hate that Landen's right, too. Over the years, I've had a bad habit of giving him multiple second chances. And now I'm living with the regret that I slept with him a couple of days ago because I thought Tripp was dating Lydia.

Finding out it wasn't even legit has me wanting to throw up my food before I even digest it.

Chapter Nine
Tripp

S ince I haven't been able to sleep much the past few nights, I'm up earlier than I need to be and decide to stop at The Lodge for breakfast. Usually, I stick to a protein drink or a granola bar, then load up at lunchtime. But I need the distraction.

It's been two days since Magnolia's last text and the longer I go without responding, the more awkward it's going to be the next time I see her. She's always flirted with me in a casual kind of way that I never took for more than that's just how Magnolia is, but when she saw Lydia hanging on my arm, something in her eyes flared with a level of jealousy I'd never seen before.

I was more than happy to get Lydia away from me when she and Quinn announced they were leaving. Though I was ready to leave, I had to wait for the birthday boy and our brothers so I could drive their wasted asses home.

The next day when I got up for work, I was shocked as hell to see a text from Magnolia. It was clear she drunk texted me, but I decided to respond anyway. I didn't expect her to actually reply hours later, but she continued the conversation like no time had passed.

It was silly and fun until she hit me with her last text—*guess it's time for you to knock me up, cowboy.*

How do I even respond to that?

I tried like twenty times to think of something witty and nonchalant, but that's never been my style. It brought on a different type of anxiety than I was used to and that gave me anxiety about feeling anxious. It was a never-ending cycle as I attempted to get my head on straight.

Once I told Landen, he came up with a bunch of inappropriate and lame responses.

Doggy or cowgirl?

Don't threaten me with a good time. When and where?

My place or yours?

As long as you wear those high heels while I bend you over my bed, I'll knock you up twice.

Along with many more cringy ones.

Yeah, I wasn't about to send any of those and have Noah show up at my door with a knee to my balls for inappropriately sexting her best friend.

After eating, I drive to the family barn to get started on morning chores. We have four new family check-ins today, so cabin call will be extra busy this afternoon.

Noah works with the competitive horses, and we manage the other boarders who need basic work and exercise. Last year, she nearly killed herself doing trick riding when a snake in the arena made the horse freak out. It dragged her around before stomping on her ribs and making her break a few of them. She fractured her foot and had to stay off of it for six weeks. During that time, Landen and I took over her clients, but since she's more qualified —or rather *gifted*—some of those horses would only listen to her no matter what we tried.

But it's why most of us are equipped to do several tasks around the ranch and retreat so we can easily take over for each other if we need to.

I take Sydney and Franklin out first but put them in separate pastures so I don't have to deal with them biting each other. Since we muck their stalls daily, I could easily pick up their droppings with them still inside, but it's good for them to get out.

Once I grab the wheelbarrow and shovel, I blast some music to drown out my thoughts.

At some point, Landen walks in, overly cheerful and singing the wrong lyrics to the song currently playing.

He raises a curious brow. "You're early."

"You're late."

"Hardly. I didn't even get the chance to stop for coffee. You should go to Magnolia's and grab us some since it's Tuesday."

My shoulders tense at the mention of her name, but I know what he's doing. He's not good at hiding his amusement.

"You just want me to embarrass myself."

He dramatically gasps. "I'd never."

I ignore him and continue working. He grabs fresh straw and spreads it out in each one as I finish. He fills up their food buckets and I refill their water. We work like a well-oiled machine for an hour until we have each one done.

"Be good, Franklin." I pet him goodbye before we jump into my truck.

Landen's glued to his phone with a smirk on his face, which means he's talking to a chick.

"So now that Quinn's out of your contacts, who's makin' you giggle like a middle schooler?" I ask as we drive to the stables.

He snorts. "Magnolia."

My gut turns at the mention of them texting. I know they're *just friends*, but I hate that he's closer to her than I am. Though according to Landen, I have no one to blame for that but myself.

And I hate even more that he's right.

When we get to the barn, Landen hops out and gets on a call. Then he mumbles something, walking away.

Weird, but not out of the norm when it comes to him.

Noah's talking to one of the ranch hands, Ruby, and I notice a large pink box on the table behind them. Gourmet donuts.

Hell yeah.

I slide in between them, grab one with Oreo crumbs dipped in frosting, and shove it into my mouth.

"Oh. My. God."

Noah and Ruby go silent as they stare at me.

"Can you keep the moanin' to yourself?" Noah scowls, her brows pinching together in disgust.

"That was hot. Do it again." Ruby smirks.

Noah nudges her and wrinkles her nose. "Gross."

"Did someone say donuts?" Landen shouts, yanking one with Cap'n Crunch pieces on it.

"The good kind too," I confirm.

"What're we celebratin'?" he asks around a mouthful.

"My birthday, thank you very much." Ruby smiles.

Landen obnoxiously sings her happy birthday as we each grab a second donut.

"Boys...watch the sugar." Noah smacks our stomachs with the back of her hand. "Y'all need to fit in your tuxes in a couple of weeks."

"Rock-hard abs, baby! Rock. Hard. Abs." Landen lifts his shirt and dances around like he's on a horse.

"This is why I show up to work every day..." Ruby playfully fans herself, staring at Landen.

"Should I tell Nash about your little crush?" I tease her about her long-time boyfriend.

She waves her left hand. "Until there's a ring on this finger, I'm leavin' my options open."

"You couldn't handle me, Ruby." Landen drapes his arm around her. "I'm still sowin' my wild oats."

"I don't think you can say that at your age anymore," Ruby argues.

"Can't tame me, *baby*!" Landen lassos his arm over his head and skips down the center aisle.

The dumbass is so insufferable he doesn't even realize when his phone falls out of his back pocket. He's still hooting and hollering as I grab it off the ground and immediately see his messages with Magnolia on the screen.

I shouldn't look. *I'm not looking.*

MAGNOLIA

> Thanks again for having lunch with me yesterday
> and talking to me about Thor. I was thinking of
> texting him later, but I'm worried he'll think I'm an
> obsessive psycho.

LANDEN

> Nah, no more than usual. And you're welcome,
> Maggie Magpie.

MAGNOLIA

> Sometimes I really wonder why I'm friends
> with you.

LANDEN

> Because I'm the brother you never had and the
> only one who tolerates you.

MAGNOLIA

> Noah tolerates me just fine.

LANDEN

> Then why aren't you bothering her with any of
> this?

MAGNOLIA

> Because she's in full wedding mode. The last
> thing she needs is me distracting her with my boy
> problems. Plus, she's too goddamn happy and
> will ruin my self-loathing mood.

LANDEN

> Wow, I'm glad I could be your second choice.

MAGNOLIA

> Technically, Thor would be if he was an option...

> LANDEN
>
> So I'm your THIRD? What the fuck? In that case, I'm about to go tell Thor everything...

MAGNOLIA

Landen Michael, you wouldn't!

> LANDEN
>
> LaLaLa...can't hear you.

MAGNOLIA

Real mature.

> LANDEN
>
> I'm very mature. Have you seen my eight-pack?

MAGNOLIA

Oh look, Ellie's coming for some coffee. Hope I don't accidentally let any of your secrets spill out...

> LANDEN
>
> Woman. I am begging you...

Goddammit, who is Thor?

Her mentioning Ellie must be why he was so quick to call her when she didn't respond.

But what does she know about Landen that I don't know? I was under the impression we told each other everything.

Then again, there's a lot I haven't told him recently.

Ellie's a professional barrel racer that our sister's been training for the past couple of years. She's even younger than Noah, so this is an *interesting* discovery.

But I still can't get my mind off who the fuck this Thor guy is and why Landen wouldn't tell me who he was when I asked him the first time.

"Hey, Skippy!" I shout, grabbing his attention as I hold up his phone and shake it.

He pats himself down, realizing he dropped it. "Shit. Thanks."

"I'm gonna ask you one more time...who's Thor?"

His face splits into a shit-eating grin and it pisses me off. "Again, it's nobody."

When he reaches for the cell in my palm, I grip it tighter and pull away. "Then why don't you tell me about Ellie? Or should I ask her for myself..."

"Dude, what the fuck? What'd I do to you?" He quickly yanks it from my grip, and I let him keep it this time.

"I wanna know. She talks about him with you, so he must be important."

Landen gives me a look that resembles pity, and I hate it.

"Yeah, he is important to her," he clarifies.

My heart stops. "Oh."

"Why don't you finally tell her you like her instead of being a little bitch?" Landen crosses his arms, pinning me with a stare I don't like.

"Sounds like I'm too late."

"For fuck's sake." He rolls his eyes, then shoves me back. "Go ask her out. She's parked at the retreat until three. Tell her you're doing guest services this weekend and managin' the Halloween party. And don't forget to wear a costume."

It's Landen's weekend, so I guess that means we're swapping. All of us siblings and some of the ranch hands rotate karaoke and square-dancing nights for the guests at The Lodge, but since Halloween is Friday, we're doing a special themed dance party for the kids with lots of candy surprises. At first, I was relieved it wasn't my turn, but I'll take any opportunity to spend time with Magnolia.

"And what if she laughs and says no? Or goes back to Travis? She already saw me freak out in the tux shop. Why would she wanna be involved with someone like that?"

And what if I'm no good at dating? Hell, I've never really done it.

Or worse, I fuck it up and ruin everything.

Landen pulls me in for a hug, something I hadn't anticipated, and my shoulders tense before they relax against him. "Anxiety attacks aren't a freak-out, Tripp. She'd never think less of you for them. You gotta know that. She's liked you for a long-ass time. She told me after our date. That's why we agreed to be just friends."

"She did?" Their date was over three years ago.

"You're the one who's been pushin' her away and giving her mixed signals. Not the other way around."

I blow out a breath and nod because yeah, he's right about that too.

"So you really don't have any feelings for her anymore?"

"Nope. As soon as she told me she wanted to ride your dick to pound town, all my feelings immediately vanished."

"Dude." I bark out a laugh and push away. "So wait, who's Thor, then? It ain't Travis, is it?"

He shakes his head at me as if I'm missing the punch line. "You are, dumbshit. It's your secret code name. In the event you saw our messages"—he shoots me a glare—"or overheard a conversation, you wouldn't know we were talkin' about you. But hey, now that the cat's outta the bag, you can finally go ask her out, *Thor*."

I almost choke when I think back to what those messages said.

"So those texts about the lingerie and you teasin' her about being too chicken shit to tell Thor were actually about me?"

"Yep." He smacks my shoulder and squeezes. "Guess I was being *your* wingman all along."

"And hers."

"That's true." He brushes off his hands before he starts walking toward the tack room. "Y'all owe me. Landen Michael would make a great name for your firstborn considerin' y'all already talkin' about gettin' her knocked up!"

"*What*?" Noah squeals from somewhere behind me.

"Thanks, asshole." I wave my middle finger at him.

"What was that about?" She walks up and shoves me with her elbow.

"Nothin'. Landen being intolerable as usual."

I'm not about to tell her a damn thing. She's just as loud and gossipy as he is.

"You good to exercise some of the horses today? I'm dealin' with a new boarder, who's a handful and a half. Kinda like you." She pats my arm with a smirk.

"Cute."

"I know. Then tell Landen he can deal with the new mare. She's a spitfire."

"Oh, kinda like *you*?" I throw her words back in her face and she laughs.

She punches her fist in the air. "The one and only!"

Rudy, Ayden, and Trey are the ranch hands for the stables, so they're in charge of mucking stalls and feeding. Luckily, Landen and I can swap and rotate if we're needed elsewhere.

For the next hour, I lunge June in the corral and ride her to the training center and back, all while trying to ease the nerves settling into the pit of my stomach.

After she's groomed and back in the barn, I decide it's now or never to go visit Magnolia. The lunch rush will keep her too busy and the longer I wait, the more time for my anxiety and self-doubt to talk me out of going.

I freshen up in the bathroom so I don't completely smell like a barn, but at least she's used to it. Once I'm in my truck, I think of a memory that makes me happy. One of the coping mechanisms I found online when I feel anxious is to think back to a time when I wasn't.

Most of those memories revolve around my family and friends, so it's usually not hard to focus on one, but right now all I can think about is doing something I've wanted to do for years.

But I always made excuses.

Landen likes her.

Travis being in and out of her life.

Suffering from anxiety and the fear of not being good enough for her.

But not today.

Today, I'm breaking those barriers down and pushing through the wall of self-doubt.

Chapter Ten
Magnolia

I love working at the retreat because it's a constant flow of customers who tip exceptionally well for coffee and muffins. The guests beam about my cute little setup, and the staff comes for an extra special treat to break up their week.

When I got approved for a small business loan, I bought an old horse trailer and hired a contractor to help me build it out. After months of researching, I had a vision board and knew exactly what I wanted—white and bright with blue accents and lots of greenery vibes. Some of the final touches were adding fairy lights through the vines secured above the wheel hubs and adding a turf wall to the trailer door with a neon sign of my business name.

It screams cottagecore single girl aesthetic who makes frou-frou lattes, and that's exactly what I was going for.

In the summer, I could wear cute sundresses or rompers each day and keep fresh flowers on the counter. Now that the weather is cooling down, I wear leggings with boots and long sweaters to stay warm.

Just as I shove half of a muffin into my mouth, I hear someone approaching and turn around to greet them. I nearly choke when I see Tripp...and *only* him. He never comes by himself.

"Tripp, hi." I cough, forcing myself to swallow the food down without tasting it. "Came alone today, huh?" I scrub my hands down my apron, wiping off the crumbs.

"Yeah, Landen's stuck at the stables gettin' his ass whipped by Summer, so figured I'd come to see you and get a caffeine boost."

My gaze scans the length of him, always looking like a Southern dessert—tight jeans, scuffed work boots, and a white T-shirt under a plaid flannel—with a metaphorical flashing "no eating" sign across it. He's not wearing a hat today, but the top of his head is messy like he's been threading his fingers through his hair.

"That okay?" The lingering in his voice snaps me out of my obvious staring.

"Great. Perfect. Your regulars?" I stammer, grabbing two cups.

"Actually...what do you recommend? I've yet to try anything besides coffee."

"Oh." This is new. "What're ya in the mood for?"

He shrugs, and I almost direct him to the menu, but I like having all of his attention on me.

"What's your favorite?" he asks.

I feign an exaggerated gasp. "So cruel. That'd be like askin' me to pick a favorite child."

He shoves his hands into his pockets. "Well, it'd obviously be Chattanooga Tennessee."

My face gets impossibly hot as my heart thumps faster.

That's how he's going to bring it up after not responding to my texts?

"Of course. How could I forget our beloved firstborn, Chatty?" I smirk, swallowing down the nerves from how flirty he's being today. But then tomorrow he'll be closed off and ignore me. His MO since I was in high school. "But if you insist I choose, I think you'd like the Hot Mess Express Latte."

His head tilts with a cocked brow. "That's an interestin' name."

"It might've been self-inspired."

He laughs. "What's in it?"

"White chocolate and tiramisu syrups with coffee bean powder on top of whipped cream."

"That sounds delicious, actually. I'll take that for me and Landen's regular for him."

"Did you wanna add a muffin? Today's special is Razeberry Delight."

"*Raze*-berry?"

"Raspberry and blackberries. I wanted to give it a more fun name than just mixed berries or whatever," I explain.

"Alright, I'll get two so Landen doesn't steal mine."

I smile, knowing he would do just that, too. "You got it."

Once I pump the syrups into his cup, I pull the espresso shots and then froth the milk. My back's turned to him, but I feel his heated gaze on me. Normally, I have small talk with my customers while making their beverages, but our conversation hasn't turned awkward like it usually does, so I'd like to keep it that way for as long as possible.

"Any plans for Halloween this weekend?" He breaks the silence, and if I didn't know any better, there's a hint of nervousness in his voice.

I glance over my shoulder and watch him wipe a bead of sweat across his forehead.

"Just Noah's bachelorette party on Saturday. What 'bout you?"

"I'm managin' the Halloween party at The Lodge on Friday."

I could've sworn Landen told me he was in charge of that. He mentioned it a couple of weeks ago when he was looking at costumes.

"That'll be fun with all the kids," I say, wiping down my machine before putting the espresso shots into his cup and then pouring the milk on top. "What're you gonna dress up as?"

"Not sure…"

The hesitation in his voice has me meeting his gaze over my shoulder before I add the finishing touches to his drink.

Then he adds, "Maybe a Marvel character. What do you think?"

My heart threatens to beat right out of my chest as it races against my rib cage at the mention of Marvel ideas.

It's just a coincidence. Calm down, Magnolia.

"Yeah, I could totally see you in some Spiderman tights."

He coughs out a laugh as I put the lid on his cup and then pour Landen's coffee before adding in his cream and sugar.

"You should come with me." He says the words so casually I don't let myself read into them, but Tripp's never invited me to tag along with him anywhere.

"Why? You need an MJ?" I ask, referring to Spiderman's love interest. "Not sure I could pull off the red hair."

"What about blond?"

"Mm...maybe?" I shrug, putting two muffins in a bag and then setting everything down in front of him. "Who has blond hair?"

"Jane."

I freeze in front of the cash register at the familiar name. "Who's she with again?"

And if I remember correctly, I'm not going to like his answer.

He swallows hard, his stare penetrating me. "Thor's."

My teeth grind together as I contemplate my next move.

This is no coincidence.

"You okay?" he asks when I don't speak.

"I'm gonna kill him." I grab my keys off the counter, then storm out of the trailer toward my SUV.

"Sunflower, wait." He grabs my arm, and I freeze at his gentle touch. The urgency in his voice has my nerves on fire. Then he pulls me back until I'm standing in front of him.

I blow out a nervous breath. "Whaddya know?"

His eyes soften, lowering to my mouth. "Enough to know you have a code name for me."

"You weren't supposed to know about that."

"It's not his fault. I saw the texts and blackmailed him into tellin' me. The first time I saw it, he dismissed me completely. It wasn't until I thought *Thor* could actually be a threat that I snapped."

My tongue peeks out, and I lick my lips. "A threat to what?"

His hand cups my cheek and his face splits into a wide smile. "Takin' you from me."

My throat goes dry, and when I open my mouth, nothing comes out, which isn't like me.

Finally, I manage to speak. "I'm gonna need some context here."

I feel like I missed a few chapters.

How'd we go from him barely acknowledging me to him asking me to go with him to the party? Oh God, how much of Landen's and my messages did he read?

Then his calloused thumb brushes muffin crumbs off my cheek when he adds, "I *like* you, Magnolia. And I want us to hang out on Friday."

Magnolia?

I shake my head, wondering if maybe I'm in a dream state. Did I hit my skull on something and suddenly wake up in my fantasies?

If that's the case, I never want to leave here.

"You do?" I squeak out embarrassingly.

He nods with a grin. "I have for some time."

And he couldn't have told me like I don't know…*a few years ago?* Or at the very least, before last weekend happened when my stupid self made the worst decision of my life.

"So all this time…" I blink, still trying to wrap my brain around this news because I've been waiting for this moment for as long as I can remember and now that it's happening, I'm taken off guard.

All because he thought I liked another man and was at risk of losing his chance of telling me?

His tongue peeks out and swipes along his bottom lip as he leans forward to my ear. "I can hear your mind going a million miles an hour. Say you'll go with me to the Halloween party, Sunny."

He has no clue—or hell, maybe he does—that whispering in my ear in that seductive tone would have me doing just about anything he asked.

"Okay," I finally manage to answer. "But do I really have to go as Jane?"

He chuckles, sliding his hand down my arm until it captures my fingers. "You can go as anything you want."

Maybe Noah will let me borrow her yeehaw clothes, and I'll go as a cowgirl. Not an original idea, but it's the best I can do on short notice. I'll have to be sneaky about it, though, or she'll ask me a hundred questions, and I'm not ready to add that level of pressure. It's bad enough Landen knows, but as soon as it's out there in the open, everyone else will add in their two cents and get in my head.

"Is this a date?" I ask because I'm done second-guessing when it comes to Tripp. If he likes me, then he should want to take me out on one.

"I wanna say yes, but I also don't want our first date to be at The Lodge surrounded by a dozen little kids singing Disney songs."

I chuckle. "Fair enough."

He steps an inch closer, grabbing a piece of loose hair and twirling it around his finger. "But just so you know, when we do go on one, you won't need to ask for clarification. You'll know."

Then he fucking *winks*.

I want to give him shit for how overconfident he sounds considering how long it took him to even admit he likes me—some Ross and Rachel from *Friends* style bullshit—but then a throat clears behind us and we break apart.

Smiling apologetically at the woman waiting to order, I quickly turn back to Tripp.

"You better go before y'all's drinks get cold," I tell him.

"Right. I still gotta pay," he reminds me as he follows me back. "Do I still get the *double* price discount?"

"Just for that, I'm *triplin'* it."

With a smirk, he pulls out a fifty. "Shoulda known nothin' would change."

"When it comes to givin' me cash? Never. I'm not one of those women in rom-coms who won't spend the billionaire's money. You wanna add my name to your account?" I toss my thumb over my shoulder. "Let's go to the bank right now."

His chuckle sends shivers down my spine.

But then I swear he lowers his hand to adjust himself beneath his jeans.

When I hand him back his change, he immediately puts it into my tip jar. "Good. Don't change, Sunny. I like how unapologetic you are and everything else that makes you, *you*." Then his panty-drenching smile returns with another wink.

Goddamn him.

And goddamn the customer standing behind him for interrupting our moment.

"Landen Michael Hollis!" I pound my fist on his front door, knowing he's inside because the asshole locked it and he never locks it. It's like he knew I'd come for him. "I will kick this down if I haveta!"

Finally, I hear the deadbolt turn and the sound of the lock unclicking. Then he whips it open with an amused grin. "You'd break your foot tryin'."

"Fine, then I'll kick you instead." I glare, then lower my gaze to his crotch.

He quickly cups himself as if that'd stop me. "What for? I

thought everything went well. Tripp returned all smiley and said you two were going to the Halloween party on Friday."

I shove my finger into his chest, stepping inside and forcing him back. "That doesn't wipe out what you did. You broke the code!"

He holds up his hands in mock surrender. "It was either tellin' him the truth or lettin' him think you were interested in someone else. Then he woulda never confessed his feelings. So actually... you owe *me*. You're welcome. Do I get free coffee for life now?" He waggles his brows.

I roll my eyes because he's right, but that still doesn't take away his betrayal.

"Well, let's hope you feel the same way when I see Ellie this afternoon."

"Joke's on you. She just left for a competition."

"You little stalker. I'll have to look up her social media to see if she's with that really cute barrel racer...what's his name?" I snap my fingers. "Elliott? Evan? Either way, I bet they're gonna be spendin' lots of time together. Especially in those really small campers...probably only one bed, too."

He puffs out his chest and crosses his arms. "*Easton* is too scrawny for her anyway, so who cares?"

"Oh, so you've looked at her pages already." Chuckling, I pat his chest before turning toward the door. "Who says that's not her type? A lanky Southern gentleman who wouldn't think twice about lettin' her cross the finish line first..."

He leans against the doorframe. "Just shush that big ol' mouth of yours, Magnolia," he warns, but a hint of panic tinges his voice.

"But why? Wouldn't you rather tell her the *truth*..." I mimic his words back to him.

His gaze narrows in on me. "Might wanna wipe that smug little smirk off your face or I just might let it slip that I saw you cozyin' up with Travis last weekend..."

My stomach bottoms out as I stare at him, wondering if he's bluffing or if he really did see us. After my scuffle with Lydia, he occupied himself with another chick to even notice what I was doing, so there was no way.

"Nice try. Your tongue was down Stacie's throat after the Marrow twins left. The only thing you saw were her eyelids."

He snorts. "A little birdie might've seen something. Is it true?"

"Who I did or didn't cozy up with is none of your business. Neither is my sex life." I make my way down the stairs toward my SUV before my face gives me away. The coffee trailer's already connected since I'll be parked downtown for the next couple of days.

"You're the one tryna ruin mine!" he calls over the balcony.

"I'd hardly call it that when Ellie can't even stand you!" I laugh at his pitiful expression.

A part of me wants to tell Noah about his little crush because I know she'd get a kick out of one of her brothers liking her client, but then she'd tell him she's off-limits and that'd only make him pursue her more.

I can't even blame him, though. Ellie's a knockout with long, thick, blond hair. She's so tiny, and I always wondered how she doesn't get yeeted off her horse when he's rounding barrels at high speeds.

But what's really amusing is how Ellie's six years younger than him and Landen would still be too immature for her.

"That's what they all say until they get up close and personal with —"

"Do not finish that!" I hold up one hand while I open my car door with the other.

Thank God Tripp isn't home to hear us shouting at each other. Though it'd probably be nothing new since we're always giving each other shit.

"A secret for a secret, Magpie!"

"Too bad I don't have one!" I taunt, then get in the driver's seat and shut the door.

I wait until I'm halfway home before I allow the panic to settle in. If someone saw me leave with Travis, that means it could only be a matter of time before it gets back to Tripp. If what Landen said is true and Tripp worried he'd never have a chance with me because I always went back to my ex, him finding out we slept together last weekend could ruin everything before it even begins.

Though I don't want to lie to Tripp, the truth would only hurt him and add to his anxiety.

It could make him look at me differently or he could change his mind about me.

And after years of waiting to hear he likes me too, I'd be devastated if he walked away now.

Chapter Eleven
Tripp

I look like a tool.

Why I let Landen talk me into this, I'll never know, but I was desperate for any opportunity to ask Magnolia out. At the time, I didn't consider I'd have to dress up.

And now I'm standing in front of her door dressed in a light and dark green dinosaur onesie.

When my mom and Gramma Grace found out I was taking over the Halloween party for Landen, they were hell-bent on my costume being kid-friendly. Considering the short notice, the stores in town had extremely limited options. It was this or a pink and orange Trolls costume. I picked the lesser of two evils.

When the door whips open, her eyes widen, and her mouth falls open.

"Don't even say it…" I warn her before she can get a word out.

The bubble of laughter that escapes her is iconic even for her. Full belly wheezing as she grips the doorframe and nearly falls over at my expense.

"Are you done yet?" I cross my arms, fighting back a smile because her laugh is contagious.

Tears stream down her cheeks, and now I know this was the worst idea of all time.

"Wh-what're you wearin'?" She finally manages to speak between catching her breath.

"You're lucky this isn't a date because I'd leave your ass here."

"Liar." She steps forward and tugs on one of the dinosaur spikes. "You look adorable."

"I'm twenty-five. I don't wanna look *adorable*."

"The kids are gonna love it," she reassures me.

I finally take a moment to look at her outfit. Tight red dress with a slit and a garter around her thigh. Black heels that make her a few inches taller. Chunky gold bracelets and hoops in her ears to finish off the look.

Fuck, she looks sexy.

"Betty Boop?" I confirm.

"Good job, cowboy. I was gonna ask Noah to borrow some of her stuff, but I figured seein' me in your sister's clothes might be a boner killer."

Chuckling, I nod. "Thanks for that."

"You're welcome. Oh, shit. You're gonna need a new nickname now. Thor doesn't quite suit your look anymore." She pauses and steps back to analyze my humiliation. "Barney's too old-school. I'm thinkin' Pebbles."

My face drops at the seriousness of her tone. "Pebbles?"

"Yeah, you have these little polka dots on your tummy that look like pebbles. Plus, it sounds like a sweet and gentle giant's name."

I groan as I contemplate ripping off the damn thing. "First you call me adorable, and now sweet and gentle? You're fucking killin' my ego here."

"C'mon, Pebbles. We're gonna be late!" She smiles wide and shuts the door behind her, then takes my hand when she leads us to my truck.

"Does this mean I get to give you a new nickname?" I ask

when I shift into gear and then blurt out my next words before I chicken out. "Like *Mine*?"

Her brows shoot to her hairline. "You wanna call me *yours*?"

I nod once, then reach over and grab her hand. "I know this is new, but I don't wanna do casual with you. I'm all in. I've made us wait long enough, don't ya think?"

"My inner sixteen-year-old self is freakin' the fuck out right now."

Lifting our hands, I bring my lips to her knuckles and brush a kiss over them. "I am too. Trust me." Then I place her palm flat across my chest so she can feel how hard my heart is pounding.

"You're nervous?"

The shock in her voice causes a laugh to bubble out of me.

"Always when I'm around you, Sunny."

"I think that's sweet. Even though you have no reason to be. We've known each other a long ass time."

"Exactly. Now I gotta find new ways to impress you and this dinosaur costume ain't helpin'."

She gasps dramatically. "I disagree. You just went from brooding cowboy to sexy dino. It's gonna be impossible to keep my panties on all night."

When her eyes drop to my groin, I quickly readjust myself and she giggles.

"Sunflower, that's not funny. You can't say shit like that, especially when I'm drivin'." This erection is already getting out of hand and painful beneath my jeans I'm wearing under this ridiculous costume.

"I thought you had a new nickname for me?" Her tongue teases her bottom lip like a temptation I'm constantly craving. It's hard to focus on driving when all I want to do is stare at how beautiful she looks.

"You'll always be Sunflower and Sunny to me."

"Is it true you don't give them to anyone else?" she asks.

"Yeah, I liked the attention you gave me whenever you'd call me out for sayin' them, so I kept doing it. But after you told me they were your favorites, I stuck to them because I thought they fit you best, too."

"Why's that?"

"Because they reflect your energy and the way you light up a room every time you walk in. Made me smile each time I thought of you. Like a warm, sunny day before the hurricane storms enter and cause destruction."

She snorts. "You just had to add in the hurricane part."

I laugh, but it's true.

She's sunshine mixed with a little hurricane.

Unpredictable but loyal.

Wild but steady.

The best kind of storm to curl up and fall asleep to.

"It was either that or a wildfire of suffocation."

"Tripp Chattanooga." She shakes her head as I crack a smile at the made-up middle name she's given me. "You know how to make a girl swoon."

I flash her a wink. "I decided it was finally time to tell you these things."

She sighs, and the blush that covers her cheeks is almost too cute not to tease her about.

The Lodge parking lot is nearly full by the time we arrive. The party doesn't start for ten minutes, but kids from all over Sugarland Creek are coming. The special events aren't just for the guests. They're extended to the community, too. My parents, Gramma Grace, and Mallory are coming as well, so I already know it's going to be chaotic.

Why limit my embarrassment to kids? Of course my family would be here.

I open Magnolia's door, and instead of easing her to the ground, I pick her up behind the knees and carefully set her down. But not before appreciating her body molded against mine for those few seconds. Her dress is skintight, and there's no way she can move in that thing.

"Always the gentleman," she coos, adjusting herself once she's on the sidewalk.

"Were you expectin' anything less from a dinosaur?" I hold out my arm so she'll take it. "Southern manners are ingrained into us from birth."

She snickers, squeezing my bicep. "Tell that to your brothers."

"Oh, they're straight-up gremlins."

Speaking of which, from the moment we enter, it's chaos. Tiny kids in costumes are running around everywhere. They're already high on sugar from trick or treating, and now they're chasing each other.

"This is nuts…" Magnolia whispers next to me as we stare in shock at the pandemonium before us.

"Is it too late to run away and hide?" I murmur.

She nudges me. "C'mon, you can do this."

More like I have no choice. The place is already set up with a DJ booth in one corner, a prize table in another, and lots of activities sprawled out in between. The ceiling is dripping in fake spider webs and sparkly fairy lights. Decorations litter every inch of the space. It's no wonder the Halloween stores were basically sold out. My mom bought them out.

"Tripp, finally!" Mom approaches with sparkles in her eyes. She holds out her arms and then wraps me in them. "The kids are so excited."

"Hi, Ma. This is a bit more than I expected," I tell her truthfully.

"Well, ya know. Once Gramma Grace and I got started, we couldn't help ourselves. Plus, it makes the little ones happy!"

I grin at her enthusiasm. Mom was always in charge of the parties at school when we were younger and for good reason. She goes all out.

"Magnolia, sweetie." My mom moves over to her and kisses her cheek. "Landen said you were comin' to help. You look amazing!"

"Thank you, Mrs. Hollis. I'm glad to assist in any way I can."

"Magnolia!" Mallory squeals, then grabs her arm and drags her away. She's in some kind of cheerleader uniform that looks way too short and tight for her age. But I'm guessing that's the whole point. My parents raised all boys until Noah came along and even then, she was more of a tomboy than a girly girl all through school. Mallory's the complete opposite, and I think Mom is just happy to have a girl in the house who will wear dresses and bows in her hair without a fight.

When Mallory moved in with us, Noah and Magnolia took her under their wings. They have scheduled weekend sleepovers, and we've all taken part in giving her horseback riding lessons. Now at thirteen, she's full of attitude and dark eyeliner.

"Well, let's get started!" Mom leads the way as Dad grabs the microphone and announces the event is officially beginning. Squeals and screams echo throughout the room as they jump around.

The next two hours consist of me flailing in the middle of the makeshift dance floor, singing along to Kidz Bop songs with over a dozen children hanging on me. I explain how to play each game, hand out prizes to the winners, and throw out candy like a piñata. The parents sit and drink cocktails as they take photos and gush about how cute everything looks.

Mom and Gramma Grace made dozens of sweet treats: bars, cookies, and cake pops. All spooky-themed, of course. The punch is a mixture of soda flavors with orange sherbet ice cream floating around. If it wasn't for the fear of getting into a diabetic coma, I'd be splurging right along with them.

Finally, we get to the final event of the evening—the costume contests.

Magnolia offered to judge earlier and now gets to make the announcements.

"Are y'all ready to hear the winners?" she asks, and they erupt in screams. "Okay, there's gonna be three prizes for the most creative, most unique, and best-dressed costumes. Ready?"

Magnolia dramatically announces the first two winners with

the best expressions to get the kids really excited. She tells each one they have to do a fashion catwalk to show off their costume. They giggle and circle around the dance floor with Magnolia strutting next to them, holding their hands and twirling them around.

"And now for the final award for the best-dressed costume…" She unfolds a piece of paper as if she didn't write them all down herself. "Oh my goodness, it's a tie!"

Mallory kneels to the ground and smacks her palms against the floor, and soon all the kids follow suit as a drumroll beat echoes throughout the room.

"Carrie Lopez as Wednesday Addams and our very own Tripp Hollis as Pebbles the Dinosaur!"

Cheers erupt and I shake my head in her direction. That little sneak.

Magnolia takes Carrie on her victory walk and makes sure she gets the appropriate amount of attention, then leads her to the prize table. After that, she grabs my hand, and I reluctantly let her pull me into the center.

"I think this is cheatin'…" I whisper.

"How so?"

"I had an *in* with the judge. They're gonna call me a phony."

She pats my arm with faux sincerity. "I wouldn't worry much about that. They're the ones who told me you needed to win something."

"They did?"

"Yep. Now go strut your stuff, *Pebbles*." Her teasing tone has me smiling as she encourages me to do my own victory walk. After a minute of being silly and getting laughs out of the kids, I go back to Magnolia and yank her toward me.

"You walked with the others. Don't leave me feelin' left out."

Her heated gaze lowers to my lips as she smiles. "Can't have that now, can we?"

She takes my dino paw in her palm and leads me around the dance floor as music fills the air. The kids jump up and down to an old remix, but my attention is on Magnolia. Her long dark hair is halfway pulled up, with curls spiraling down her back. That red garter on her thigh has me grinding my molars and wishing I could tear it off her body with my teeth.

Ever since I confessed I liked her a few days ago, we've been texting in between our work schedules and throughout most of the evenings. I still can't wrap my head around this being a reality, but I'm done questioning it. I spent years giving excuses and getting into my own head about my feelings.

But now, I'm ready to go all in and see what happens. During one of our texting sessions, we agreed to explore things between us privately before announcing it to everyone. We both know how obnoxious my family can be, and I'd rather not have their unsolicited input until Magnolia and I decide we're ready to go public. I never considered how Noah would react because I didn't think Magnolia was an actual option for me. Whether or not we dated, our lives are forever intertwined because of hers and my sister's friendship. If I fuck this up, Noah would never forgive me, and I'd never be able to escape the heartache of losing her.

I push down the familiar overwhelming tightness in my chest as my dad thanks everyone for joining us tonight. It's after nine and most of the kids are crashing from their sugar highs as their parents load up their things and slowly drag them outside. Overall, it was a successful event. I'm glad Landen talked me into this even if he knew all along Magnolia liked me, too.

"You two did wonderful!" Gramma Grace approaches me with a hug. She's at least a foot shorter than me, so I envelop her in my arms.

"Thanks. It was fun."

"Magnolia's a natural. The kids love her."

"That she is."

Whereas I'm mostly introverted, Magnolia's an extrovert when it comes to being social and spontaneous. Never afraid to blurt out what's on her mind or threaten to sock you if you say something inappropriate. I've always liked that about her.

"You should bring her to family supper on Sunday."

"Why's that?" I ask cautiously.

"Well…if she's gonna be a part of the family, she should be included."

One could argue she's already part of the family considering how long she's been in Noah's life, but by the suspicious twinkle in Gramma Grace's eyes, I don't think that's what she's referring to.

"What're you sayin'?" I keep my expression blank so I don't give any of my own secrets away, but if I've learned anything over the years, she's always aware of things before everyone else.

She gives me one of her knowing smirks and shrugs. "Don't let her get away now that you finally have her."

I blink a few times as if that'll change the words she just blurted out. Maybe tonight it could've been a little obvious we were acting a bit friendlier than usual, but how in the world does she know I've wanted her? I'd never told anyone and pretty sure it wasn't *that* obvious if Magnolia didn't even know.

Before I have the chance to ask her, Mallory comes over and asks her questions about the leftover desserts, and then they leave to put them away. My eyes scan the room for Magnolia, who's chatting with my dad and laughing.

"Can I get out of this costume now?" I grumble to my mom, who's sweeping. I could hardly drive in it, let alone help them pick up this mess.

"Oh, lemme grab a picture for the scrapbook first! Magnolia, Mallory! Stand next to Tripp."

Just great. Now there's going to be photographic evidence of this humiliation.

They stand on each side and wrap an arm around me before Mom instructs us to smile. Once she's gotten a few shots, I stare down at Magnolia. A bright smile is plastered on her face as she tightens her fingers on my waist. After a few more clicks of the camera, she looks up at me, and her smile widens even more.

"Perfect! Can't wait to get these printed!" Mom gushes, and Mallory nudges me before walking off.

"I'm gonna change out of this, and then we can go once everything's cleaned up," I tell Magnolia.

"Sounds good."

I give her arm a little squeeze before moving toward the bathroom. Luckily, I was able to wear jeans and a T-shirt underneath, so I didn't have to bring any extra clothes with me.

Once I help Dad put away the DJ booth and tables and The Lodge is put back together, we say our goodbyes. Magnolia and I didn't make any plans beyond the Halloween party, so I rack my brain for what to do before taking her home.

"You wanna go for a drive?" I ask before shifting my truck into gear.

"In the dark?"

"You afraid?" I muse.

"No, just…cautiously aware. There are murderers in the dark."

I grab her hand and pull it close to my mouth before dropping a kiss along her knuckles. "I promise to keep you safe."

Chapter Twelve
Magnolia

E very inch of my body is on fire as Tripp holds my hand and drives us out of town. I had the best time tonight even if we couldn't really talk. It was still fun to see him interacting with the little kids and being playful. His dinosaur costume was a huge hit, and I couldn't stop laughing at how silly he looked. It's a side of Tripp I haven't seen in a long time, and I hope it stays. The go-with-the-flow and letting loose parts of him that initially attracted me to him are why I crushed on him so hard in high school. Add to that his little flirty comments and how he always got me out of sticky situations, it's no wonder I was a goner for him.

But then Billy died, and those parts of him did, too.

I knew the real Tripp was still inside him somewhere, and I'd wanted to be the person to bring him back to life if he'd let me.

"Thanks for bringin' me along tonight," I say after a few minutes of silence. Darkness surrounds us, but the dashboard lighting reflects off his eyes. "It was a ton of fun even if those kids could run circles around us."

His face softens with a smile and he squeezes my hand. "Thanks for sayin' yes to going with me."

Before I respond, Tripp pulls his truck over to the side of the road. There's no oncoming traffic, but being surrounded by dark shadows makes me nervous.

"What're we doin'?" I glance around, making sure the door is locked. On a normal day, I'm positive I could take on a sociopathic murderer, but I'm in a short dress and heels, so tonight I'd be at a disadvantage.

"Figured it was time to teach you how to drive a stick shift." He adjusts the bench seat, moving us all the way back.

My lips curve up in surprise. "Wait, what?"

"You don't know how, right?"

"Well, no."

"And you mentioned at one time wantin' to learn, so..." He pats his thigh. "Saddle up, Sunny." My heart races in anticipation of sitting *on* Tripp for the first time.

I'm so used to him avoiding eye contact, so when our gazes meet, my breathing stalls. For what feels like the first time, he doesn't glance away, and having his full attention gets me flustered.

"You remember me sayin' that from five years ago?" I ask, stunned. "And wait...didn't Landen say *you don't let chicks drive your truck*?" I quote the exact words he'd said in my best deep, manly voice.

He barks out a laugh. "Yep, you'll be my first." Then he leans over and brushes his thumb along my jaw. "I remember everything about you, Magnolia. Especially the drunken moments."

I groan at the embarrassing things he's witnessed over the years. "You coulda just left it at that first sentence."

He tilts my chin, and my breath hitches at his proximity. Technically, we've kissed before during my birthday BJ shot, but this is different. This is private. No drinking game, no pressure, no audience. Tripp wants this as much as I do. I've pictured this moment for years, and now that I'm here, my nerves are getting the best of me.

"I should warn you…I don't kiss on the first date," I blurt out before our lips touch.

The corners of his mouth lift as it brushes against mine and he whispers, "Then it's a good thing this wasn't a date."

And just like that, I'm putty in his hands.

He closes the tiny gap between us and my entire life changes. Tripp doesn't just kiss me.

His tongue intimately dances with mine in tender strokes as he cups my face. Soft, eager lips mixed with his rough facial stubble hold me hostage to his intimate touch. One hand slides behind my neck and pulls me impossibly closer until his chest presses to mine. Then I fist the fabric of his shirt, holding him to me and never wanting to let him go because I think I'm still in shock that this is happening.

The rough edges of his calloused fingers mixed with the tenderness of his hold have every inch of my body burning hot. Shivers soar down my spine and butterflies pool in my stomach. His touch is nothing like I've felt before, and I'm eager to keep it as long as possible.

A deep, guttural moan releases from his throat as my heart thunders inside my chest because this man, one I never dreamed would reciprocate my feelings, is ruthlessly fucking my mouth with his tongue. And I never want him to stop.

"Sunny…" He pants out like his resolve is seconds away from snapping. "Fuck, you taste so good."

"Then why're you stoppin'?" I whimper when his lips feather down my jaw and neck, sending tingles down to my core.

"Because if I don't," he whispers in my ear, "I'll keep you hostage in here all night long."

"Then I'd be a willing hostage."

He chuckles and brings his lips back to mine. "I think that's a contradiction."

I shrug, loosening my grip on him. "Then so be it."

He pants against my mouth as he kisses me once more. "You have no idea how long I've wanted to do that."

"What was holdin' you back?"

Instead of being guarded like I half expect him to, he rests his forehead on mine. "A lot of shit. Mostly anxious thoughts about not being good enough or how I don't deserve to be happy that got into my head. But I'm tired of lettin' those fears get in the way of puttin' myself out there. I think you and I deserve a chance to see what this could be without that gettin' in the way."

My heart is beating out of control at his raw emotions. Tripp's been reserved for so long that every word out of his mouth is taking me by surprise. But it fills me with warmth that he trusts me enough to be open and honest.

Pulling back, I cup his face until he meets my eyes. "I agree, and I hope you know you can always share those fears with me. You don't have to go through shit alone if you don't want to. I'm here for you to get through it, whether that be talking it out or just sitting with you and holding your hand until it passes. Anxiety gets to me too, just in a different way."

Like how scared I am to lose him now that I finally have him.

How being together changes everything.

What will Noah really think when she finds out?

Landen knowing is one thing since he's been in on the secret for a while, but Noah's my childhood best friend and is protective of me in a different way than she's protective of Tripp, but I'm still worried about how she'll react. She knows my past and what her brother's gone through, so our dating could cause tension in our friendship even if she's always encouraged me to tell him. She wouldn't want either of us to get hurt, and if there were a fallout, she'd be stuck in the middle.

The last thing we need is other people's thoughts and opinions to bring in more anxiety and concerns about whether we can actually be in a relationship. Neither of us has had success in that area, but I'd like to think Tripp's and mine could be the outlier.

His thumb strokes over my hand. "You're really amazing, you know that?"

"You better keep that thought when you try to teach me how to drive this thing."

His face splits into a wide grin. "It'll be good practice for when I teach Mallory in a couple years."

My jaw drops in offense. "I better be easier than a thirteen-year-old!"

"Well…let's find out." He sits back and motions for me to come over.

"Are you sure about doin' this in the dark? Is it safe?" I ask, positioning myself on top of him.

My legs sink in between his thighs and he pushes the steering wheel up so we have enough room.

"Don't worry, I know these roads like the back of my hand. I'll work the clutch and pedals for now and keep an eye out for deer. You focus on steerin' and shiftin'."

Relief swarms through me at not having to multitask at a time when Tripp's groin is directly under my ass. I can barely breathe as it is with his chest pressed to my back.

Has he no clue what he's doing to me right now?

He grabs my right hand and puts it on top of the shifter, then jiggles it around. "Get comfortable with how it feels so you can get used to the feeling of switchin' gears."

The only thing I'm focusing on is how his dick is only two fabric layers away from my bare skin.

"Okay?" he prompts when I forget to speak.

"Yep. One hand on the wheel, one hand on the stick."

His laughter makes his chest shake. "Precisely, yes."

Then he explains what each letter and number mean and when to shift into those gears. Seems basic enough, but considering my mind is elsewhere, it's a good thing we're on an empty country road.

"Okay, now we'll shift into first and you can turn back onto the road," he commands.

Tripp keeps his hand over mine, and when he accelerates, he talks me through shifting into second and then again into third.

We're still going under the speed limit driving, but it helps to get me used to the feeling of when to change gears.

"You're doin' good…just keep drivin' straight, and I'll go a bit faster so you can feel when to upshift again."

The roar of the engine vibrates as he speeds up. My breathing also increases when he removes his hand from mine and moves it to my upper thigh.

After he presses the clutch, I move us into fourth. When I feel him let off the gas, and he clutches again, I shift into fifth.

"Fuck, that was hot."

"If I didn't know any better, I'd say you're gettin' a little excited," I taunt, wiggling my ass against his erection beneath me.

"Sunny…I wouldn't do that if I were you." His taunting voice echoes in my ear and stills my movements.

I ground my hips and sink lower against him as I move back and forth.

Instead of scolding me, his fingers tease over my thigh, pushing up my dress and exposing more bare skin.

"There's a stop sign ahead…and it seems my hand is occupied, so you're gonna have to shift to neutral when I tell you to." He skims his finger along the seam of my thong and my breath hitches.

He presses down on the clutch and brake, and I struggle to concentrate with how he's touching me.

"Now." Tripp's hoarse voice whispering in my ear as he gets closer to my pussy nearly has me steering us into the ditch.

"Good girl. And now you'll shift to first while my foot's down."

My eyes roll to the back of my head at the *good girl* comment and I do what he says. "You ain't playin' fair."

His finger peeks underneath my underwear and brushes over my clit. "Stay focused. There's headlights ahead."

"Then you better stop distractin' me."

"I dunno what you're talkin' about…" His tongue glides up my neck and his teeth graze my earlobe. He presses on the gas, and I instinctively shift into second once he speeds up.

When the pads of his fingers rub harder, I rock against him faster.

Two can play this game.

"I think you're gettin' the hang of it. You ready to try the clutch?"

"I don't think I can reach it." I stretch out my legs and my heel just barely touches it.

"Sit up a little."

As soon as I do, he moves the seat forward and then palms the outside of my thighs, guiding me back down on his lap while sliding my dress up to my hips.

"Now put your foot on the pedal and shift."

"You want me to do both?" My hand-eye coordination is questionable on a good day but trying to focus when his hands are on me?

He pulls his feet back to give me room. Headlights in the rearview mirror make me panic.

"Tripp, someone's behind us."

"Then you better drive, Sunny. Once you press on the clutch, let the gas pedal come up naturally without takin' off your foot. Then shift into second and let up on the clutch as you give it more gas."

He might as well be speaking to me in French.

But I comply and when I hear the engine choking, I know I need to shift again.

"You're doing so good," he says, coaxing his fingers along my slit and making me melt against him.

My anxiety can't handle the pressure of focusing on driving and his hand inside my panties. He's going to make me crash into a tree if he continues torturing me.

"Oh shit." The truck makes a weird noise when I fuck up the clutch-gas-shifting trifecta.

"You've got this. Just stay focused."

"That'd be a lot easier if you weren't rubbing my pussy," I say with a shaky breath.

He slides a finger inside, and I gasp at how deep he penetrates me.

"Do you want me to stop?" he asks while his thumb circles my clit.

I'm driving at a steady speed, so I only have to focus on staying on the road at this point.

Instead of responding, I rub my bare ass against his erection.

He growls against my neck, then teases me with a second finger. I moan until my head falls back and he cups my throat with his other hand.

"Eyes on the road, baby."

My God. The way that word just shot tingles down my entire body as his fingers tighten under my jawline.

"I think it's time we go to my house," I beg him, wanting to drive us back toward town.

"Take a right up here. Press the clutch and release the gas as you downshift," he reminds me, lowering one hand to the crease.

By some miracle, I do exactly that without grinding the gears and smoothly accelerate back up to speed once I've rounded the turn.

Now that I can pay attention to where his hands are touching, I'm close—*insanely close*—to losing control with the way he's teasing me. Fingers pinch my nipples and the steady rhythm on my clit paired with his deep thrusting is driving me to the edge.

"Tripp…I'm—" The rest of the words die on a heavy exhale.

He removes the hand that was on my breast and takes the wheel as the other stays on my pussy.

His nose brushes my skin. "I've got you. Come on my hand, Sunny."

And I do just that.

My body spasms, my head falls back against him, and his lips hover at my ear.

"Downshift, sweetheart. We need to pull over."

Blinking roughly, I shake off the afterglow and palm the

shifter. His fingers continue playing with me as my body shivers through the aftershocks.

"That was the hottest fuckin' thing I've ever experienced," he whispers.

"I coulda killed us," I remind him.

He chuckles as we get his truck to the side of the road and park.

His fingers slide out from my panties, and when I glance over my shoulder, he sucks them between his lips.

"But what a way to die, huh? With the taste of you on my tongue."

Rotating my body the best I can, I palm his face and slam my mouth down on his.

I wanted Tripp Hollis like this for as long as I can remember, and I'm done holding back.

"Lemme take care of that for ya…" I beg, rubbing over his erection, and he groans at the friction.

"There's no rush, Sunny." He captures a piece of my hair and wraps it behind my ear. "I'm not going anywhere."

I sit up slightly until I can look into his piercing brown eyes. "You promise?"

Though I hate that I sound like a whiny, needy child, I'm terrified to lose him now that I finally have him.

He grips my chin, gazing deep into my soul. "I swear on our firstborn child."

I snort out a laugh. "Not Chatty!"

He smirks, palming my face, and presses tender kisses to each of my eyelids. "I should drive you home before someone calls the sheriff for suspicious activity."

Sighing, I nod. "And I'd hate for you to have to do more community service on my account."

"You'd have to do it with me this time." He winks. "But kickin' Travis's ass that night…was so fuckin' worth it."

Chapter Thirteen
Tripp

Witnessing my three brothers drag their asses into our parents' house for Sunday night supper is amusing. With the amount they drank at Noah and Fisher's joint bachelor/bachelorette party at the Twisted Bull last night, it's no surprise they're still feeling it.

The guys went to dinner at Antonio's Seafood House first, while the girls had their own dinner celebration. Once we finished eating, we hopped on the party bus, picked them up, and then went to the bar.

Since Magnolia and I are keeping quiet, we acted the same as we normally do so no one suspected anything. I held her drinks while she danced and resisted touching her every time she was within arm's length. Except when she left to use the bathroom, I waited in the dimly lit hallway and then stole a kiss when no one was around.

But as I watched her from across the bar, I felt this strong urge to text Billy and tell him all about how I finally confessed my feelings to Magnolia. Although I hadn't outright told him, he made comments about how I looked at her and nudged me to ask her out even during the years she was on and off with Travis. Even he knew her ex wasn't good enough for her and part of me wished I'd listened. But the other part wonders if we would've been too young and immature to know how to make our relationship work back then. Perhaps we were meant to wait until we were at the same stages of our lives to put in the right amount of effort to have a real one.

"Hello, boys!" Noah nearly shouts as they approach the table. "So nice of you to join us!"

"Dude, lower your voice." Wilder winces, covering his ears.

"What's the matter?" I match Noah's volume, leaning back in my chair with a smug grin.

Fisher chuckles as Noah and I taunt them. Although they're the future newlyweds, they didn't get crazy drunk. However, they both took a turn on the mechanical bull last night, and I'm halfway surprised Noah didn't show up with a concussion after face-planting the mat.

At least I didn't have to worry about Magnolia in that area because she refuses to get on it. Since I wasn't getting drunk, there was no way I was riding it either, but we all enjoyed watching my brothers act like dumbasses.

Once everyone's seated at the table, Gramma Grace and Mom bring all the food platters to the table, and Dad carries the pitcher of sweet tea.

"Surprised y'all showed up for work this mornin', to be honest," he says, pouring drinks.

"Didn't know it wasn't an option not to," Waylon mutters.

Even though the twins are almost thirty years old, they still party like they're twenty-one. One of these days, it's going to catch up to them. After countless beers and shots, I had to nearly carry them out of my truck and walk them to their doors. They live in one of the ranch hand duplexes next to Landen and me, so at least it wasn't out of my way, but goddamn, I thought they were gonna nosedive on the sidewalk and choke on their own vomit they were stumbling so much.

"It ain't," Dad confirms.

Mallory giggles as Waylon makes a sour face at his response.

Not every day is a full workload, but each morning we're expected to muck stalls and feed the horses. Guests stay at the retreat seven days a week, so there's always a full staff on board and plenty of chores to be done.

"Let's say the blessing," Mom says once she takes her seat next to Dad's.

Gramma Grace offers to say it, and we bow our heads. She blesses the food, each family member, and Noah's upcoming nuptials. Then she takes us all by surprise when she ends it with, "And let there be a new baby in the family before the end of the year. Amen."

"Gramma Grace!" Noah scolds, but she's grinning.

"What? I didn't specify any names." She shrugs innocently, and my mom smiles. I'm sure she'd love nothing more than to be a grandma.

"Let us enjoy being married first."

It's still a little weird to me that she's marrying her ex's dad, who's literally twice her age. If they have a kid soon, that means his oldest child and his youngest will be twenty-five years apart. *Weird*.

But as long as they're happy and he treats my sister the way she deserves, I wouldn't care if they had ten babies.

Assuming she doesn't ask me to babysit every weekend.

Although I probably would since it'd be better than playing DD bitch to my brothers.

I'd just have to learn how to change diapers, feed a baby, and about everything else that comes with taking care of one.

And of course, I'd be the favorite uncle.

"Callin' dibs on godfather!" Landen shouts randomly after we've all filled our plates with homemade macaroni and cheese with fried steak and gravy. My dad's favorite.

"You can't do that!" Waylon flings a roll at his head. "Plus, it's tradition the eldest brother gets that title first."

"What?" Wilder gasps. "You're older by like two minutes! I should be an option."

"Too bad, I already called it." Landen gloats like the idiot he is.

"I'm not giving any of you that title to my *unconceived* child." Noah rolls her eyes.

Fisher laughs, joining in on the fun. "I just imagine our little girl growing up with a much older brother and four uncles. God help her."

"And me!" Mallory chimes in. "I get to be godmother, right?"

"You'll haveta fight Magnolia for that title." I chuckle. Considering she's the maid of honor, there's no way those two haven't already decided on everything else growing up. I wouldn't be surprised if they have their baby names picked out, too.

As if she heard me say her name from her apartment twenty miles away, my phone vibrates in my pocket and her name pops up on the screen with a text message. We're not supposed to text during supper, but seeing as everyone's occupied with a baby that doesn't exist, I keep my phone in my lap and click on the screen.

MAGNOLIA

> Hope you're having fun at supper with your family. Meanwhile, I'm over here ALONE just thinking about how wet you made me the other night. I've gone through four pairs of panties just today.

Jesus Christ.

TRIPP

> Sunny! I'm literally at the table with them right now. And my GRANDMOTHER.

MAGNOLIA

> Oh sneaky. Don't let them catch you texting me. Or the boner you're trying to hide.

Goddamn her.

TRIPP

You did that on purpose.

MAGNOLIA

I'm horny, so sue me. Would you rather I text someone else instead?

Just the thought of that has my hand balling into a fist.

TRIPP

Don't you even dare.

MAGNOLIA

I have some new lingerie pics to show off...who should the lucky man be?

TRIPP

Do you make it a habit to send other men half-naked pics of you? Now I have to smash Landen's phone. And his temporal lobe.

I know they're only friends, but that doesn't mean I want him to have access to those photos anymore.

MAGNOLIA

Only when the one person I want to show ignores me.

TRIPP

This uncomfortable erection you've given me should make it very clear I'm not ignoring you.

MAGNOLIA

Good, because I'd rather show you in person.

We've already discussed hanging out again this upcoming week, but now I'm tempted to ditch early and drive over to her place.

But I can't because we're all being forced to stay for scrapbooking after we eat. It's a tradition Mom and Gramma

Grace started a while ago. Usually, my brothers and I get out of it, but lately, I've been staying since I don't see them as much anymore. With all the wedding planning, the second annual fundraiser our family hosted this past summer, and keeping busy with ranch work, we've all been scattered.

TRIPP

How about Tuesday night?

With tomorrow being Monday and traditionally the most chaotic of the week, I know I won't even get home until seven or eight.

MAGNOLIA

You want me to wait forty-eight whole hours to relieve this ache between my thighs?

I can't help the goofy smile that spreads across my face at how needy she sounds. I know we should be taking it slow, but we already know so much about each other. The time couples take for the talking stage and getting to know each other has long passed for us. Even if I don't know every little detail about her, I'm excited to find out more each time we hang out.

TRIPP

How about we FaceTime later, and I help you with some of that tension while you give me a little early preview of your lingerie?

MAGNOLIA

I'm sure I can arrange that. Hope you like black lace.

Before I can respond, she sends a photo that shows off the top of a see-through lacy bralette and the bottom half of her face. She's biting down on a finger with a smirk around it.

That little fucking tease.

TRIPP

You just wait, Sunny.

MAGNOLIA

What're you gonna do, cowboy?

"Is your food okay, Tripp?"

I snap my head up and catch Mom glaring at me and my still-full dinner plate.

"Yeah, it's great." I grin, grabbing my fork and diving in.

As quietly as I can, I slide my phone back into my pocket and focus on eating. Magnolia's about to be tortured from waiting for my response. But considering she has me sitting with a boner at the table surrounded by family, she can suffer right along with me.

Once we finished dessert, Noah and Mom grab the bins, and we get started.

Typically, I work on whatever book my mom needs me to, but tonight I decide to start a new one for me. *And Magnolia.*

But no one has to know that yet.

"Only six days until y'all say I do!" Mom smiles wide as a spread of scrapbooking supplies covers the table.

"Which means you still have time to run!" Wilder tells Fisher.

Noah whips a roll of washi tape at his head. "Dude!"

Wilder ducks just in time and laughs.

"You're in the weddin', moron. Though I'm not sure why." Noah groans.

I swear, those two have always fought more than any of us did growing up. Though it's no secret they're complete opposites.

Noah's a stickler for schedules and planning while Wilder's set on causing destruction wherever he goes.

"Because I'm your favorite brother." Wilder gloats, but the rest of us laugh at his delusional thinking.

"Between you and my ex as part of the groomsmen, I'm already nervous, so don't make it worse!" She scowls at him.

"Me?" Wilder feigns offense. "Y'all should be worried about Landen. He's the one who punched Jase in the face. Wouldn't be surprised if a brawl takes place at the reception."

"That was over a year ago," Landen reminds him. "He learned the hard way that I have brass knuckles, and I doubt he'd need a reminder."

I shake my head at his arrogance. The only reason that fight started in the first place is because he was yelling and pushing Noah. The four of us immediately jumped in to get him to back off.

"We have the best family conversations," Waylon muses as he continues decorating pages.

"You sure you wanna join this, Fisher?" I tease.

"Well, they always say you don't just marry your spouse. You're marryin' their family, too. So I knew what I was gettin' into before I proposed." He smiles at Noah like she's his whole world.

A week ago, that look would make me roll my eyes.

Now, I can't wait to scream from the rooftops that Magnolia and I are dating so I can have that same look.

"Aww…you two are gross." Landen mimics a gagging noise.

"They have the best love story ever!" Mallory chimes in as she fights with a piece of ribbon glued to her fingers. "Just like the Taylor Swift song."

"That's right." Noah grins at her. "Get ready to dance to her music all night long."

"*What*?" All four of us brothers shriek in unison.

Noah barks out a laugh as Fisher keeps his expression flat. I have a feeling he didn't have much say in the music options or he simply doesn't care as long as Noah's happy. But if I know Fisher and have witnessed enough of their relationship over the past year and a half, it's definitely the latter.

"Please tell me it's an open bar," Wilder says, groaning.

"It is for everyone *except* my brothers."

"Liar." Wilder snorts.

Noah blows out a frustrated breath as she focuses on her book. "Maybe we shoulda eloped," she tells Fisher.

"Don't worry, sweetheart." Mom pats her hand. "Damien and your dad will keep an eye out on your brothers. If they get too rowdy, they'll be escorted out."

This is obviously news to us, but Wilder and Landen gawk at the announcement. Damien's Fisher's childhood best friend, a scary-looking detective, and has about a hundred pounds of muscle on us.

"I think not," Wilder demands. "When everyone's bored from your sad-girl music and sappy love speeches, you'll be thankin' me for bringing the party to the dance floor with my moves. Plus, think how good I'm gonna look in a suit, too. All the chicks are gonna want some."

I snort at how confident he sounds. "And every one of 'em you'll be related to, dumbass."

"Swear word!" Mallory shouts, then holds out her palm.

A few months ago, she started making us pay her five bucks anytime she caught us cussing.

I'm at least fifty bucks in the red.

I dig in my back pocket for my wallet and then hand her a twenty. "Here, I'm paid up for three more."

Dad scowls in my direction, but I ignore it considering the twins are in the hole enough to practically buy her a car.

"I won't be related to *all* of them," Wilder defends. "And who's to say you can't find your soulmate with your second or third cousin?" He laughs because even he knows he sounds ridiculous.

"My great-aunt Polly married her cousin," Gramma Grace says, and we all snap our gazes toward her.

"Who?" Mom asks, clearly unaware of this, which makes it even more entertaining.

"Uncle Freddy. They were second cousins by blood. Got married and went on to have seven boys," Gramma Grace explains.

"Well, see, now that explains a lot about the bloodline." Noah chuckles, then adds, "Because it only affected the double X chromosomes."

"God, our family is weird." Landen shakes his head. "First, Gramma Grace married her pastor-teacher twice her age and now we learn we're all incested."

I snort at his dramatics, but it is funny. Especially seeing Mom's horrified expression.

Last year, Gramma Grace shared the story of how she met our grandfather and it's safe to say we were all surprised. And even more when it came out that Noah and Fisher were dating. History was practically repeating itself in the forbidden love department.

"We're all linked in one way or another," Gramma Grace says. "It wasn't unheard of for members of wealthy families to marry and reproduce to keep the bloodline strong. Especially in royal families."

"Well, we're neither billionaires nor royals, so…" I stare pointedly at Wilder. "No baggin' a cousin."

He scoffs, and Mom shakes her head, clearly giving up on scolding us.

"What if it's by marriage?" Waylon asks as if he's a hundred percent serious in his question. "There's no bloodline crossing, then."

Dad blows out an exaggerated breath, obviously so done with the five of us. But he sticks around and listens to our antics.

"That's a good loophole!" Wilder exclaims. "So where's this guest list of yours, Noah? I need to see who my options are ahead of time."

We laugh at the way she glares at him, and he continues to taunt her until we finally pack up and call it a night.

"Thanks for dinner, Ma." I give her a hug before kissing her cheek. "It's gonna be an interestin' week, huh?"

"A nerve-wrackin' one, yes. I'm marrying off my youngest baby." She wipes her cheek. "It's gonna be emotional, but I'm so happy for them."

"If it helps, she'll probably be the only one of us who gets hitched." I smirk because she knows I'm only teasing. One of the twins will be drunk enough to wake up married someday.

"Oh, don't play coy with me."

I furrow my brows. "What's that mean?"

She rolls her eyes as if I should know what she's talking about, but I honestly don't.

Once I say goodbye to everyone else, I head to my truck and then fish out my phone. It's been at least two hours since I've responded to Magnolia, and I'm expecting a full-on freak-out text.

Except when I see she's sent me a photo with her hand in her panties, I'm the one having the freak-out.

MAGNOLIA

I had to finish without you. What a shame.

TRIPP

My grandma was in the same room as me! I couldn't step away.

MAGNOLIA

yawn Sorry, who is this?

Two can play this little game.

Instead of FaceTiming her when I get home, I strip off all my clothes and stroke my cock until I'm rock-hard. As I lie in bed, I continue getting myself off until I'm close to finishing. Then I hit record and moan her name over and over until I come all over my stomach.

After I've cleaned myself up, I attach the video to our text thread and hit send.

Less than five minutes later, she responds.

MAGNOLIA

> A freaking VIDEO, Tripp Hollis? I sent one cutesy photo, and you make a video of you growling my name as you come?

At first, I worry I've overstepped.

It was too soon.

I came on too strong.

She thinks I'm a creep.

But then, she sends a second message in all caps, and my whole chest shakes with laughter.

MAGNOLIA

> PAYBACK'S A BITCH, THOR.

And then my phone vibrates with a FaceTime call.

Chapter Fourteen
Magnolia

My panties are still drenched from our sexting FaceTime session on Sunday night, and not being able to see him until tonight has been torture. We talked and teased each other for two hours until he was close to falling asleep. I knew he had to get up early for work as did I, so we called it a night. Then we did the same thing last night, except he only made it an hour before his yawning took over and I told him to go to bed. Tripp works a lot, so that's nothing new, but I'm finished with work by three or four since my targeted customers are early birds.

But tonight, I plan to stay glued to him for as long as he'll let me.

I've waited long enough to get Tripp like this, and I'm not wasting time now that I have him.

Luckily, he'll be off work earlier than last night, but I still have two hours until he picks me up so I can take my time getting ready. He won't tell me what his plans are for our "first official date," but I picked out a pair of jeans and a sweater since the weather's cooling off.

Since it's Tuesday, he stopped by for a coffee this morning, which gave me a chance to quickly kiss him. I feel bad not telling Noah, but the last thing I want to do is to outshine her special weekend by talking about Tripp and me. We're only four days away from the wedding, and then she goes on her honeymoon. Once she's back, I'll tell her everything.

When my phone chimes with a text message, I smile in anticipation of seeing Tripp's name, but once I tap my screen and see it's from Travis, I frown.

TRAVIS

Maggie, baby. Come over tonight. I wanna see you.

My stomach turns at the thought of seeing him in person ever again.

MAGNOLIA

I thought I told you to lose my number.

TRAVIS

Don't play hard to get. We had fun last time, so come over and we'll have a repeat.

MAGNOLIA

For the last time, that was a MISTAKE. It's never happening again, so stop texting me.

TRAVIS

That's not what you were saying when I was fucking that slutty pussy of yours.

God, I hate him so much.

MAGNOLIA

I'm blocking you now.

And then I do what I should've done earlier and block his number.

Just the memory of his hands on me makes me want to claw it out of my brain.

When Tripp texts and says he's on his way, I can hardly

contain my excitement. Tonight's the only night we can hang out this week since I'm booked with wedding stuff with Noah. I already told her I'd be at her beck and call, so Tripp and I will have to stick to texting and FaceTiming until we can be alone again.

A knock on the door has me fleeing across my apartment. As soon as I open it, Tripp scoops me up in his arms and crashes his mouth down on mine. I wrap my arms and legs around him as he steps inside and then kicks the door shut behind him. Then he spins us around and pushes me back into the wall.

"Fuck, I've missed you." He presses harder into my body as he slides his tongue between my lips, and his erection poking into me confirms just how much he has.

"I can tell," I taunt, arching my back against him. "You been walkin' around with that weapon all day?"

With a laugh, he leans back and cups my cheek with one hand while the other palms my ass.

"That's just from finally gettin' to see you, Sunny."

I lower my face to hide my blush. "Wow. That's quite a talent."

He tilts my chin and presses a tender kiss to my mouth. "Are you ready to go on our first date?"

"I still think you teachin' me to drive stick shift was a date. I mean, there was a happy ending after all."

"We'll consider that the prequel to the real one because tonight you're also gonna learn something new for the first time."

When he lowers my feet to the floor, I pout. "You're educatin' me on another thing? Why do I feel like you're gonna give me an exam by the end of the month?"

"Trust me. You're gonna like it."

"Mm-hmm. I'll see about that." I grab my bag, slide on my boots, and take his hand as he leads us out the door. "And if you did give me an *exam*, I'd pass it with flyin' colors."

"Because you'd be naked?" He lifts his brow with amusement on his face.

I nod once. "That's right, cowboy."

Tripp drives us out of town. Though I love Sugarland Creek for its charm and epic mountain views, there isn't a ton of stuff to do. But when he parks in front of an unfamiliar place with a big picture of an axe on the window, it's the last thing I expected.

"What's this?" I ask when he helps me out of the passenger's side.

"Axe throwing."

"You think I have enough arm power to throw an axe?"

He threads his fingers through mine and walks toward the door.

"Not sure, but it'll be fun watchin' you try." He winks as he motions for me to go inside.

"Tripp Chattanooga! You brought me here to embarrass myself."

"I've seen plenty of your embarrassin' moments. But this allows me to stand behind you and *help* you."

"If you wanted to touch me from behind, all you had to do was ask," I tease and enjoy the way his face turns red.

The place is packed, but he must've reserved a spot for us ahead of time because we're shown right into an empty stall. We're required to wear protective glasses, but he opts in for us wearing hard hats until he sees me throw one.

That earns him a glare.

There's a bar at the other end, and I don't know why it makes me laugh, but a place that is loaded with axes shouldn't be anywhere near a place with alcohol.

"Alright, you ready to try?"

I exhale harshly. "I'm fairly confident I can throw it right in the center of his heart."

There's a wood target several feet away, and we had the option of a traditional bull's-eye with point markers or a paper silhouette of a man. I asked for the paper because I like the visual, but also in my mind, it's Travis's body, and he's going to finally get what he deserves.

Tripp chuckles, then hands me the axe. "Let's see what ya got."

I grip the handle with both hands, squint my eyes as I slowly aim it toward the chest, then stretch my arms behind my head.

"Do you want help with your aim?" Tripp asks.

"You better step back," I warn him confidently.

I want to at least try on my own before I succumb to his *help*.

He chuckles, moving farther away. With as much force as possible, I whip the axe in front of me, and then we watch it fly. Even I'm surprised when the sound of it hitting the wood target reaches my ears.

"Ya nailed him!"

"Did I get his heart?" I ask eagerly.

"His neck."

I bark out a laugh and give him a high five. "Even better."

Tripp goes next and, to no one's surprise, gets him right in the chest. "Bull's-eye."

"Imagine if I could get the crotch."

His eyes widen as he adjusts himself. "Aim low."

And so I do. Although there are only a few inches of wood beneath the photo where the cock would be, I focus as best as I can and throw it right at the groin.

"Goddamn!" Tripp cheers with an enthusiastic clap.

I cross my legs, wave out my arm, and bow. "Thank you, thank you."

"I bet you'd love archery."

I furrow my brows and grimace. "Let's not get ahead of ourselves. My arm already feels like it's gonna fall off."

My dad didn't teach me any outdoor activities, and a part of me wishes he had, but he was too busy trying to keep my mom alive and basically raise me as a single dad. My parents weren't prepared for me at all. They weren't exactly trying for kids either. My mom got pregnant with me in her forties, and by that time, she was already diagnosed with bipolar disorder.

She also suffers from depression, sleepwalking, and has had episodes of self-harming. I love my parents and never resented my

145

upbringing, but as an only child, I spent most of my time at home, alone in my room.

Even though I've been best friends with Noah since we were kids and she lives on a ranch, I was never into riding horses and four-wheelers. I only got out of the house when Mrs. Hollis picked me up, and I slept over at the ranch on the weekends.

Noah and her brothers tried to get me to do outdoorsy stuff, but I couldn't find it in me to try.

Part of me was too scared to get hurt so my dad didn't have a second person to take care of on top of a full-time job.

Mom couldn't work. She never left the house, so I hung out with her after school until Dad came home and made supper.

In the mornings before school, he'd make a pot of black coffee, and we'd sit at the table before Mom woke up and talk about anything and everything. It became our tradition even though I hated the taste.

When I was old enough, I found a job at a coffee house so I could learn to make coffee I liked. Once I saved up enough money, I bought an espresso maker and practiced making drinks at home. Dad always taste-tested them for me.

Every one I made for him got his thumbs-up of approval.

When I was working on my coffee menu, I decided to name a latte after him, Bless Your Black Heart. Although he's the sweetest man you'll ever meet, that was his favorite Southern saying anytime he talked about someone being cold or cruel.

"Hey, you okay?" Tripp asks, and I blink away the daze.

"Yeah, I'm good. Is it my turn?"

"Not yet. I'm thinkin' of where to get him next."

I glance at our half-mutilated silhouette.

"The eyes," I tell him.

"Savage. I love it." He laughs, then gets into position.

"Should we make it interesting?" I ask before he throws.

"Such as?"

"Whoever throws the most times in a row without missing gets something from the other."

He arches a brow, licking his lower lip. My gaze traces his mouth as he contemplates my offer.

"Hardly seems favorable for you, but okay, I'm all ears."

"Rude." I smack his flexed bicep. "Whoever loses is at the mercy of the other person's request."

"And what would yours be?"

"Oh, that's the best part. We don't tell each other until there's a winner."

He shrugs as if he's got this in the bag. "Alright, you're on. But, Sunny?" He cups my chin, inching closer, but not quite touching. "Don't think I'm gonna take it easy on ya."

I reach between us and palm his dick over his jeans. He's not hard but chubbed enough for me to feel the outline of his length.

"Good. Because I never said I played fair."

Stepping back, he blocks my hand from touching him. "No way. I'll end up with an axe in my foot if you distract me."

"That wasn't in the stipulations."

He playfully glares. "I wasn't aware I needed any."

"Ah, well, better to remember for next time." I lift my shoulder, then remove the gap between us and drag his mouth down until it reaches mine. I kiss him like my life depends on it, sliding my tongue between his lips and moaning as he squeezes my ass. My body grinds against his erection, and once he's rock-hard, I pull back and pat his chest. "Best of luck to you, cowboy."

"I'm callin' a foul."

"No such thing."

"You're ruthless, ya know that?" He adjusts himself as he groans at me.

"You're up." I hand him the axe with a sickly sweet smile.

Instead of giving him room to throw, I kneel in front of him, unbutton his jeans, and lower his zipper. Then I remove my glasses and hard hat.

"What're you doing?" he whisper-hisses, glancing around us and removing his own hat.

"No one can see me down here." I lower his boxers just

147

enough to pull him out. Tripp's hard and thick in my hand, with angry veins pulsating against my palm. It's so much hotter in person than on a screen.

"*Magnolia*. We're gonna get caught."

I ignore his panicked tone and laugh to myself at how he thinks using my real name will stop me.

"Our stall is private, and I'm hidden under a wooden table. The only ones who could potentially see are the ones watching the surveillance cameras behind you. So if you don't want them to see what I'm about to do to you, I suggest you stand still." Then I give him a long, hot lick up his shaft.

"Jesus Christ." His head falls back as he keeps his feet planted. "You're in so much trouble."

"Don't forget your axe," I tease before wrapping my tongue around his crown and then push him into my mouth.

He cups the back of my head with one hand and white-knuckles the edge of the table with his other. "I can't throw with you gaggin' on my dick, Sunny."

His hushed voice has me smiling with pride.

I release him with a pop. "Told you payback's a bitch."

Then I deep-throat him as I stroke his length over and over. Saliva covers my fingers as I keep up with my pace. There's no time to go slow or tease him, so I need to bring him to the edge as fast as I can.

"Holy fuck. I'm gonna come." His fingers tighten against my skull as if he's fighting back his moans. Between the music and people chatting in the other stalls, no one would hear him anyway.

When he bites his lip and holds his breath, I feel his body tense against me. A deep, guttural groan vibrates through him, and I know he's close. I open wide, stick out my tongue, and hold his shaft as he unleashes in my mouth.

He finally exhales and his entire body relaxes.

"That was insane." He smacks his tip against my tongue, and I laugh.

Once he puts himself back in his boxers and zips up, he whips off his glasses, grabs my hand, and helps me to my feet. I expect him to scold me or threaten punishment, but he lifts me up on the table, stands between my legs, and devours my mouth.

"That was the second fuckin' hottest thing I've ever experienced," he says against my lips. "And so damn risky."

"I thought you were a risk-taker," I muse, lifting a brow.

"Not usually in terms of public sex, but I'll try anything once." He smirks. "We should go before I eat your pussy right here for all those creepy security guards to watch."

"Don't haveta tell me twice."

Tripp helps me down, but then I quickly grab his hand to stop him. "Wait. Does this mean I won?"

Closing the gap between us, he holds my chin and tenderly rubs the pad of his thumb along my jaw. But then a devilish smirk spreads across his face. "Who said we were done playin'?"

I'm left speechless as Tripp drags us out of the building, and when he opens the back door to his truck, he motions for me to climb in.

"Lie down, sweetheart. I'm about to take back the victory."

Thank God for bench seats.

I do as he says while he closes the door, and then he rests one knee between my legs.

"Good thing it's already pitch-black out because the thought of someone seein' you spread out half-naked through the window would drive me crazy." He grabs the button on my jeans and flicks it open before lowering my zipper.

"I like this possessive side of you." I'm already panting as I help him drag my panties down.

"It's always been there. I was just good at hidin' it from you." He leans down, spreads my legs open, and then brushes his nose along my slit.

The warmth of his breath has me lifting my hips, desperately seeking his touch.

"You want me to taste your pussy? Make you scream my name while you come?"

"No, I'm panting like a dog for funsies."

He barks out a laugh, shaking his head at me. "Then say it, Sunny. Tell me what you want me to do to you."

"Bury your face between my legs until I'm close to passin' out from lack of oxygen. But don't stop until I'm coming all over your lips."

"Jesus fucking Christ," he hisses, blinking up at me. "That goddamn dirty mouth of yours."

I shamelessly lift a shoulder. "You shoulda known what you were gettin' into."

He stretches his body over mine and leans down until he's half an inch from my mouth. "Hope you also know what you got yourself into, sweetheart. Because I've spent years fantasizin' about tastin' your sweet cunt, and I ain't stoppin' until every inch of you is shakin' beneath me."

A shiver runs down my spine at his promise. I'm already breathing hard, and he hasn't even started yet.

Tripp repositions himself, lifts one leg up to rest on the back of the seat, and then *finally* covers my pussy with his hot mouth.

His tongue laps at me in between sucking my clit and thrusting his fingers inside me. The roughness of his facial hair scratches my bare skin and the sensation of it all drives me wild.

"Yes, right there. Oh my God." I arch my back and squeeze around his digits when he slides back inside.

My hand finds the top of his head, and I pull at his hair while he tightly grips my hip. His movements drive me closer to the edge, which seems impossible because I never come this fast. Even when I do it myself, it takes more effort and time. But Tripp's tongue lapping on my clit as he twists his wrist over and over is the perfect rhythm to set me off.

"Shit, I'm so close. Don't stop," I pant out in harsh breaths.

He slides his hand underneath my ass, lifts my hips, and then slams his fingers against my G-spot.

"Tripp! My...I'm —" The complete lack of oxygen makes my words come out inaudibly as a wave of pleasure hits me so damn

150

hard, my eyes roll to the back of my head, and white stars take over my vision.

But then I feel it.

Wetness pools between my thighs as I squirt around his fingers that continue to thrust in and out of me.

My God. *That's never happened before.*

"Holy shit, did I just…" I stammer out as I attempt to blink away the static in my eyes.

Tripp clamps his lips down on my clit again and the sensation is too intense to handle.

"I can't…" I thrash my arms to grab his head, but he remains a statue as he pushes my thighs apart. "Tripp, it's too much!"

He shakes his head, and my body caves into the second wave of pleasure that has me unraveling once again.

Harsh breathing resounds within his truck as he finally climbs up my body and brushes his hand over my cheek. "That's now beat out first place for the hottest thing I've ever experienced. And I'm pretty sure *I* win now."

I pant out a laugh. "I hate you."

"Your pussy doesn't." He cups my chin and kisses my half-open mouth. "Next time, you'll be bent over so I can eat you from behind and bury my face in your ass."

Is it possible to squirt a second time from only his words?

Because I'm pretty sure I just did.

Chapter Fifteen
Tripp

Three days after taking Magnolia on our first official date, I'm still riding the high of tasting her sweet cunt on my tongue and the very public display blow job she gave me.

Making her come in the back of my truck wasn't only a fantasy but a *need*. I was desperate for her. I've wanted this for so long and finding out she's always felt the same had this uncontrollable urge to claim her right there in my back seat.

I can still taste her on my tongue, but I want more. Again and again. I'd never get sick of being around or talking to Magnolia. The intimacy is just a *very nice* bonus.

Tonight's Noah and Fisher's wedding rehearsal. Magnolia looks stunning in a skintight, strapless, baby pink dress, but I hate the way Wilder ogles her. He's never voiced being attracted to her, but Wilder will sleep with any woman with an ass and tits. Even if he did know about us, that wouldn't stop his lingering gaze.

"Dude, quit staring." I nudge his elbow with mine when I catch him for the third time focusing on her tits.

He leans over, his eyes never wavering as he whispers, "She's right across from me. I can't help it."

I smack his cheek to knock him out of his trance. "Well, help it. You're being rude and a creep."

Finally, he snaps out of it and flashes me a devious smirk. "As if you haven't been undressin' her in your mind since we've arrived? Gimme a break. I know a sneaky groin adjustment when I see one and you've been doing it all night long."

Goddammit, this asshole.

"It's these damn pants!" I defend. "You know I don't wear dress slacks. They're itchy and keep ridin' where they don't belong."

Not a complete lie, but my dick has been attentive since the moment I laid eyes on Magnolia walking through the church doors like the brunette bombshell she is. I knew within two seconds I was in deep shit.

Tan legs on full display with white leather ankle boots.

Long, dark hair curled in waves and pulled back behind her ears with clips.

Dark red lipstick staining her delicious mouth.

Fuck, I'm such a goner.

It'd be impossible not to notice her.

But still, I'm not giving Wilder a pass when it comes to Magnolia. *He's* supposed to think of her as a sister, not a woman available for him to gawk at.

He snorts as his gaze wanders back to his plate still half full of food. The rehearsal went as one would expect with four unruly brothers not wanting to accept their little sister is getting married before any of us. But besides the taunting and cackling at Noah's expense, it went great.

As I eat a piece of Gramma Grace's famous peach cobbler — Noah's favorite — Dad stands and demands our attention. He gives a fatherly speech about how blessed we are to have everyone here to celebrate his little girl finding love. The room is filled with family and friends, too many to fit in the main house, so they hosted the dinner at The Lodge in one of the private conference rooms.

Gramma Grace and Mallory went to town on the decorations since the gift opening brunch will be here Sunday morning. But if

Noah thinks any of her hungover brothers are going to make that, she's more delusional than Wilder, who's currently winking at Magnolia and thinking she'll reciprocate.

"Dad, that was so sweet!" Noah has tears in her eyes as she stands and hugs him. He kisses the top of her head and looks so proud. It's funny to think how if he hadn't hired Fisher to be our farrier, the two would've never met.

"My turn!" Mom speaks next, making most of us laugh at how Gramma Grace told her the two were sneaking around and how she secretly hoped they were because of Fisher's charmingly good looks.

And then Mallory decides she needs to add to the torture and recites all her favorite Taylor Swift songs that she swears are Noah and Fisher coded.

After fifteen minutes of reading off lyrics, Mom finally motions for her to wrap it up.

"That was perfect, Mal. Thank you." Noah wraps her arms around Mallory, and she grins wide.

Mom says the final goodbye, and we gather for a group photo before everyone breaks away.

I try not to watch Magnolia's every move, but it's so damn hard when she's so close, and I can't touch her. Her head falls back with laughter at something Landen says, and I hate that he gets that reaction out of her. But I've vowed not to get jealous of their friendship anymore, which means I need to stop worrying. If she wanted him, she had her chance to date him when he liked her.

"Say good night to your fiancée. I'm stealin' her for the night so you don't see her before the weddin'," Magnolia teases Fisher.

Fisher frowns at Noah, who giggles at his reaction.

"You'll have fun father-son time with Jase tonight. It's just for one night, babe. Then we'll have two weeks of *uninterrupted* newlywed time."

The suggestive way she says those words has me cringing. I don't want to think of my sister like that.

"Gross." Landen peaces out before he can hear Fisher's response. "See y'all tomorrow!"

I say my quick goodbyes and leave before I'm tempted to steal Magnolia for myself. Tomorrow's going to be nonstop busy, and although I'm looking forward to it, I want to spend time with her without sharing her with everyone else.

"Hey, cowboy!" I hear her shout across the parking lot as I walk to my truck.

When I spin around, she leaps into my arms, and I quickly catch her. Her bare legs wrap around my waist, and I turn until she's pressed against the driver's side door.

"What're you doin', troublemaker?" I smirk, inching closer to kiss her. Luckily, it's already pitch-black out, but the parking lot lights beam enough that if you walked by us, you'd be getting a free show.

"Ooh, is that a new nickname?" she teases and then grabs my lower lip with her teeth.

Cupping her face, I brush my mouth against her ear. "Depends how often you plan to be one."

"In that case, all the damn time."

I pull back just enough to capture her lips in a searing hot kiss. She digs her nails into my neck and my erection pokes against her thigh. Heat forms between us as she rocks into me, and I palm her breast when she moans.

"You're evil." I growl, trying to adjust myself. "I'm gonna haveta take care of this by myself now."

"If I had more time, I'd help ya out, but bridesmaid duty calls."

The little smirk on her face as I lower her feet to the ground tells me she did this on purpose.

"What're you and my sister doin' tonight anyway?"

"Facials while we watch Taylor Swift's new tour movie with Mallory and Serena. So they'll be dancin' and off-key singin', of course. Then we'll eat snacks until the sugar crash hits and pass out."

I grab her hand and kiss her knuckles. "Well, if you get a

break between the dancin' and sweets, text me. I'll be up for a while since I have to start tomorrow's chores tonight."

"I'll do my best. Those girls are nosy as shit anytime I'm on my phone, so I'll have to sneak around."

Serena's eleven now and Mallory's best friend. She moved here two years ago when Ayden, the boarding operations manager, found out he had a daughter he knew nothing about. His former high school sweetheart spent years looking for him, and after they reunited, she moved here, and they got married last fall.

I press my lips to hers once more. "Have fun. Save a dance for me." I wink, then release her when Fisher and Noah walk out of The Lodge.

"You know I will, cowboy."

"By the way, you look gorgeous tonight. Nearly had to pluck Wilder's eyes out for staring at you so hard."

"Well, it's nice to know if one Hollis brother doesn't work out, I have options."

My smile drops, and I scowl. "Cute."

She pats my chest with a cheeky grin. "I know."

After she meets up with Noah and drags her to her car, I hop in my truck and drive home so I can change out of my dress slacks and into jeans and a sweatshirt. Then I go to the family barn to check on the horses. Ayden and Ruby will take care of the boarders tonight, so it shouldn't take me too long.

"Hey, Franklin buddy." I pet his nose and he grunts at me. He's not used to seeing me at night since I muck their stalls first thing in the morning. "Gonna lemme come in for a few minutes? I'll even put your favorite songs on."

I reach into my pocket to grab my phone and notice a text from Magnolia.

MAGNOLIA

Imagining you wearing your cowboy hat tomorrow already has my panties soaked.

TRIPP

Hm...let me see.

But then I furrow my brows.

TRIPP

Wait, who said I'm wearing a hat tomorrow?

MAGNOLIA

Noah. She said she wants y'all to wear them for groom pictures because it'd pay tribute to Fisher's bull riding days or some shit like that. But either way, I wholeheartedly agreed so all the guys are supposed to bring their black Stetsons.

Then I notice our sibling group text thread is going off where Noah's telling us the same exact thing.

TRIPP

Why do I have a feeling you highly encouraged this change?

MAGNOLIA

I may or may not have mentioned it was a fantasy of mine to get railed by a hot guy wearing one and how she was lucky she had Fisher to fulfill that for her. Then one thing led to another and now y'all are wearing them.

TRIPP

I'm gonna need you to repeat that for me, sweetheart.

MAGNOLIA

I didn't mention the hot guy being you but it's not like she's not aware of my crush to put two and two together ;)

My dick gets hard at the very non-subtle way she mentions having sex.

Franklin whines and abruptly jerks up his head, nearly knocking the phone out of my palm.

"Easy, boy." I give him another pet. "You finally get to date the woman of your dreams and you'd be distracted, too."

TRIPP

> I'll have you know that Franklin and I are having a very awkward conversation as I try to clean his stall with an erection.

MAGNOLIA

> You poor baby. Wish I could help with that but you're just gonna have to take a long shower tonight.

TRIPP

> Oh don't worry…already planned on it.

MAGNOLIA

> And if you want to make another video for me, I wouldn't be mad about it.

TRIPP

> Is that so? What will I get in return for said video?

MAGNOLIA

> Depends what you want, cowboy.

Her. All the goddamn time.

TRIPP

> Tell me a secret no one else knows.

The jumping dots appear, and then after a few seconds, they're gone. Maybe I ruined the moment by asking a serious question. Or she had to put her phone away before one of the girls saw. Either way, I'm anxiously waiting as I keep my phone propped up while I muck Franklin's stall.

MAGNOLIA

> I'm not as strong as I try to portray. Rather, I feel like I have to be so I'm never dependent on anyone else.

My heart shreds at the words on the screen. I know exactly how that feels and hate that she does, too. I know how she grew up. Noah's told me things over the years, but Magnolia's never talked about it. Anytime her parents were brought up, she'd smile and say everything at home was great. I had a feeling it wasn't and that she didn't want anyone to know the truth, so I never pushed her for more.

TRIPP

> You are strong, baby. Even when you're not trying to be, I see it in you. I'm always here if you want to talk about it. I know a thing or two about not wanting to look weak but you never have to worry about that with me.

MAGNOLIA

> Be careful, Tripp Hollis. I just may fall hard and fast if you insist on melting my heart with words like that.

I can't help the stupid grin that fills my face.

TRIPP

> I'd love nothing more.

Chapter Sixteen
Magnolia

"It's with great honor and privilege to introduce for the first time ever, Mr. and Mrs. Underwood! Fisher, you may now kiss your bride."

I grab the pastor's arm and yank him toward me so he's not in the picture. He chuckles as I shrug at not giving him a warning ahead of time, but I've taken all my maid of honor duties seriously. When Noah made it clear she didn't want him in their first kiss photos, I took notes.

Fisher cups Noah's face, leans in, and dips her before crashing their lips together. The guests hoot and holler, cheering loudly and whistling. When they shared their vows, there wasn't a dry eye in the room. Fisher's mentioned how much his life changed after meeting her and how she gave him a second chance at happiness. Noah gushed about soulmates and how when you know, you know. There was no second-guessing he was the love of her life. Then when Noah promised him forever and always, he teased her about slipping in a Taylor Swift song reference.

I snuck as many secret glances at Tripp as I could during the ceremony, and he looks so good in his sleek suit and black Stetson hat. While they were gathering the groomsmen outside for photos, the bridesmaids peeked out the window and cat-called them.

When Tripp looked up and winked at me, I resisted the urge to blow him a kiss in front of everyone. The video he sent me last night of him in the shower is still living in my head rent-free, and I can't wait to get him alone again to hear his moans in real life.

As I follow the couple down the aisle, I mentally prepare for madness to ensue. After everyone goes through the wedding party receiving line, it'll be time for photos. While we're doing those, the space will be converted for the reception with a DJ, bar station, and buffet. The white tent is already beautifully covered in lights, tulle, and vines.

Noah's dream was an intimate country fall wedding on the ranch and that's exactly what she got. Even though it's early November, she lucked out with the weather. It's sixty-five degrees and there's not a cloud in the sky.

We spent the morning at the main house drinking mimosas and getting our hair and makeup done. Gramma Grace baked goodies for us to snack on and Dena tried not to cry at Noah's first full look.

"Hope you're ready for my maid of honor speech," I tease Noah as I stand next to her.

"As long as it doesn't embarrass me, I can't wait."

"That wasn't in the agreement."

She glares. "Be nice."

I feign shock. "Aren't I always?"

Damien stands next to me and chimes in, "I wasn't aware of the *being nice* stipulation, therefore I will be roastin' Fisher in my entire speech."

I bark out a laugh as Fisher scowls at his best friend.

"I'll say nice things about Noah, though." Damien smirks.

"I like him," I tell them with a cheeky grin. "He should come 'round more often."

"Don't get any ideas. He's too old for you," Noah warns in a hushed whisper.

I motion toward Fisher, who's literally twice her age. Not that I'm after Damien, but I don't like the hypocrisy.

"That's different." She shrugs.

"Just for that, my speech will now be going as planned."

When I lean back and look down the line, my gaze catches Tripp's, who's also leaning back to look at me. He holds my stare before slowly lowering his gaze down my body and biting his lip. Once our eyes meet again, he mouths, *"Mine."* Then flicks his gaze toward Damien with a scowl.

I hold back laughter and smile at his jealousy over a man I have no interest in. But just to fuck with him, I arch a brow and mouth, *"Prove it."*

His eyes darken as if I just gave him a dare he refuses to back out on. But then people start coming down the line to congratulate the newlyweds, and I focus on greeting everyone. A few minutes pass, and I hear a faint, "excuse me, comin' through," and notice Tripp walking behind the wedding party as he makes his way toward me.

What the hell is he doing?

"Noah?" Tripp grabs her attention, then hands her a mini water bottle. "Don't want ya to get dehydrated being out in the sun."

"Aw, thanks." She gushes as she takes it from him.

Then instead of making his way back, he squeezes between me and Damien. "You mind if I stand here?" he asks him.

"Sure." Damien's brows pinch together as he shimmies over to make space.

Tripp's all broad shoulders and puffs out his chest as he presses close to me. Then the arrogant asshole smirks down at me and winks. "Hey, Sunny."

I shake my head as I look away so he doesn't see my smile.

God, that was hot.

But I'm not admitting that to him.

It takes a good twenty-five minutes for everyone to go through the line. Although the guests consist of mostly close friends and family, they chat our ears off congratulating the couple and gushing about how beautiful the ceremony was. While

I agree, standing in these heels without moving gets uncomfortable.

"Nicely played," I finally tell him when we're free to break away from the tent. "Where'd you get that bottle anyway?"

"One of the guests gave it to me because, and I quote, 'was lookin' a little flushed.'"

I snort out a laugh. "Better quit starin' at me or you'll be gettin' that comment all night long."

"Can't help it." He leans in closer as we walk side by side and then whispers, "You look so fuckin' beautiful."

My heart ramps up every time he says those words to me, but right now it's in overdrive.

We have a good twenty minutes to kill while Noah and Fisher get their photos taken, so I grab his hand when we're out of view and pull him toward the family barn. It's the closest private spot and beggars can't be choosers.

"What're you doin'?" He smirks as I lead us to the tack room.

"Stealin' you for a few."

"You know, we could just tell everyone, and we wouldn't haveta hide," he suggests.

"But I like keepin' you to myself. Plus, sneakin' around is kinda hot." I lower my hand to his zipper and feel his growing erection. "And I think you like it, too."

"That's just from you, sweetheart." He groans when I palm his cock. "But then I could at least claim you out in the open so handsy guys stay away from you."

Ah ha. So that's the real reason he doesn't want to stay a secret.

"Damien wasn't being handsy, so stop worryin'." I pluck the button open on his slacks and slide my hand inside his *silk* boxer shorts.

"Yeah, because I stepped in before he could." He releases a moan when I pull out his hard length and stroke him.

"Does it look like I'd let another man touch me when all I want is you?" I ask, increasing my pace, and he lowers his gaze to my hand that's jerking him off.

He grabs my waist and pulls me in closer until our foreheads are touching. "You're gonna ruin me, Sunny. I've never been feral over the thought of someone else touchin' you and now the very thought makes me see red."

"You're tense, cowboy." I wrap a hand around his neck so I can yank his mouth down to mine, and then I kiss him. "Lemme help you with that."

"You know I want you for more than just this, right?"

"Obviously for my amazing axe-throwin' skills."

He huffs out a laugh at my inability to take him seriously when I have his dick in my hand.

"I'd beg you to fuck my face, but Noah will kill me if I mess up my makeup before photos."

At my words, his cock twitches.

"Goddamn, don't say shit like that right now. I'm already gonna explode and make a mess."

"Then you better have good aim," I tease, bringing his mouth back down to mine and sliding my tongue between his lips.

His hand moves underneath my dress until he finds my panty line and then slides a finger along my wet slit before thrusting inside my pussy.

"Oh my God," I breathe out. My eyelids flutter and my head falls back as he continues his delicious assault.

"I need you to come before me and we only have a few minutes before someone comes lookin' for us or notices we're both gone," he urges, pushing my panties to the side more so he can shove a second finger inside.

"Then you better start rubbing my clit because you've been edgin' me all day."

He chuckles. "How so? This is the first time I've touched you."

"I've been wet since I saw you in that cowboy hat. I had to go change underwear before we left."

"Fuck. Now I need a taste."

Before I can argue, he lifts me up by the ass and sets me down on the little wooden table. It's not comfortable by any means, but I don't even have the will to care when he hikes up my dress and slides my panties down.

"No screamin' or someone will hear you," is his only warning before he spreads my thighs and dives between them. He rests my legs over his shoulders as he rubs the pad of his thumb over my clit and tongue fucks my pussy so damn good, it's only a matter of minutes before I come on his tongue.

"Holy shit," I moan as quietly as I can, but if someone were in the barn right now, they'd definitely hear me.

Tripp finishes himself off with his free hand and comes right after I do.

"So fuckin' good, baby." He wipes his mouth with the back of his hand and then tucks himself back in.

"How am I supposed to stand for photos when my legs feel like jelly?" I sigh as he helps put my panties back in place.

"Just tell her you need to sit on my lap the whole time."

I playfully smack his chest as he lifts me down to my feet. Then he tenderly rubs his thumb along my jawline. "I wanna kiss you so hard."

"Soon. I have extra powder and lipstick in my bag, so once the photographer is done with us, it'll be fair game." I smirk when he chuckles.

"Deal." He takes my hand and presses a kiss to my knuckles. "Don't forget to save me a dance and no letting other guys touch you. Especially Wilder."

I bark out a laugh as we double-check our clothes are in place. "Since when is he a threat?"

"Since I caught him drooling over your tits."

Arching my back, I push out my chest. "Well, can you blame him? They're great tits."

His gaze narrows into a glare. "I don't want my brothers gawkin' at you."

"What about cousins?"

"*Sunflower,*" he grits out between his teeth and digs his thumbs into my hips as if his resolve is going to snap. Yanking me closer, he softly presses his lips to mine. "The moment we're public, I'm markin' you as mine."

"Hmm?" I muse. "What kind of markin' are we talkin' about here? Tattoo? Hickey? Teeth impression?"

"Yes."

I chuckle. "As long as I get to do the same to you."

"Fuck yes." He winks.

Tripp leaves first, checking it's clear, then I follow behind him and smooth my dress down as if it wasn't wrapped around my waist. He goes back toward where the guests are sitting, and I make my way toward my SUV to grab my bag.

Once I've reapplied my lipstick and powdered my face, I meet up with the wedding party just in time to be called for photos.

We spend an hour taking photos and then the photographer has Noah and Fisher move to different locations for more couple pictures. Now we're waiting under the tents for happy hour.

"Such a gorgeous day." A man I don't recognize stands next to me.

"It truly is." I smile politely, sipping on a glass of wine.

"You are too, by the way."

My stomach bottoms out at the nonchalant way he comes on to me. I casually take a step away from him.

"Thanks. Didn't get to pick what I wore, though," I say with a smile that hopefully tells him I'm not interested.

"That shade of green is really your color."

This time I just nod, purse my lips, and look away.

My gaze meets Landen's at the bar, and I widen my eyes and signal to the stranger next to me. Then I mouth, *"Help."*

He's talking with someone but finally gets the hint and struts over.

"Hey, Kyle. How's it goin', buddy?" Landen makes his way in between us and directs his attention away from me.

"Good. Been a while since I've visited the ranch. Lookin' nice. *Very* nice." The way his tone changes makes my skin crawl because I imagine his eyes on me.

Landen laughs, but it's not his real one. More so to humor this guy.

Then I see Landen smack Kyle's shoulder and lean in. "Just between you and me, you're not her type."

I'm full-on eavesdropping even though they're whispering.

"How do you know?" Kyle asks, sounding offended.

"Because she rejected me and told me she prefers younger men with mommy issues." Landen shrugs, and my hand balls into a fist, tempted to whack him over the head.

"She's a cougar?"

Landen sighs as if he feels bad telling him my secret. "Yeah, she likes 'em fresh outta high school. Kinda weird if you ask me, but figured I'd tell ya before you get embarrassed like I did."

Oh my God. I'm going to kill him!

"Got it. Thanks, man."

Landen claps his shoulder again. "No problem. Good to see ya."

Kyle walks away with a quick glance over his shoulder at me and this time he stares with disgust. *Fucking great.*

"Are you insane? Like seriously, you need your brain checked out!" I grit out between my teeth.

"It was either tellin' him that or the truth…" He arches a brow, challenging me to stay mad at him for saving my ass.

I huff, crossing my arms. "You couldn't come up with anything better than makin' me sound like a predator?"

"I implied they were of age!"

Scowling, I smack his arm and then chug the rest of my wine. "Never askin' you for help again."

"Oh, c'mon, Mags." He wraps an arm around my shoulder and pulls me into his chest. "I'm your favorite and we both know it."

"Be careful. Tripp nearly pushed Damien out of the way when he was just standin' next to me in the receiving line."

He laughs. "Is that what that was? What a loser."

I elbow him in the ribs and he backs away. "Pro tip, women like men who aren't afraid to claim what's theirs."

"My bad. I wasn't aware y'all wanted to be treated like property."

"Geez, you're dense. This is exactly why you'll never have the balls to ask Ellie out. You think she should come to you because you're God's gift to women."

"Not true. Although I could be, but that's not why I'm not askin' her out."

"Mm-hmm. She's here somewhere. If you're such an expert on women, go ask her for a dance later."

His shoulder lifts. "Fine. No problem. I will."

His rambling causes me to smile. He's so going to chicken out.

"And are you gonna dance with your boy toy in front of everyone?"

Little does he know I already planned to.

"If that's what it takes for you to stop being a little bitch and tell Ellie you like her."

The fact that she hates him makes this so much better.

He huffs at my *little bitch* comment. "Deal."

Chapter Seventeen
Tripp

By the time we get to the dance, my brothers are well on their way to tipsy. Wilder's made it his mission to be as rowdy as ever and constantly have a drink in his hand. Waylon and Landen are close behind and dancing like their asses are on fire. Although I don't have to drive and can walk home, I don't overdo it with drinking. My eyes are laser focused on Magnolia and witnessing guy after guy hit on her.

I watched from across the room as Landen got Kyle away from her. I'm not sure what was said, but at least it worked. He's our second cousin, so we only see him during family reunions, but he's made his way to the bottom of my favorite cousins list.

"Wouldn't it just be easier to ask her out?" Noah's voice next to me makes me jump. I didn't even notice her coming my way.

"I dunno what you're talkin' about," I deadpan.

"Oh, really? You haven't been pining over my best friend for seven years? Or hell, maybe it's been longer."

Shrugging, I break my gaze from staring at Magnolia and take a sip of my warm beer.

"You aren't concerned that if we date and break up, it'd make things weird between y'all?" I ask because even though we're sneaking around, it's been a genuine concern about going public.

"Maybe. It could. But it could also be a forever kind of thing. You'd have to risk more than your heart to find out…"

"And I suppose you're the expert now, huh?" I tease.

She waves out her hand. "Well, I mean…exhibit A, your honor. We're at my wedding."

"Is this where I make fun of you for not being able to find a man your own age?" I flinch in anticipation of her smacking me.

"Ha! I'm not breakin' a nail to hit you. But I could get Landen to do it for me."

I snort and then decide it's a good time to throw him under the bus so she stops focusing on me. "A little birdie told me he's into Ellie. You hear anything 'bout that?"

Her jaw drops as her eyes widen in surprise. "Not uh! Are you just sayin' that so I stop buggin' you about Magnolia?"

I make a face that neither confirms nor denies. "It's just what I heard."

"He's too immature for her. Plus, last I knew, she couldn't stand his annoyin' ass. Told me that herself."

"Isn't there a lovey-dovey phrase that goes with that? Something about there being a thin line between love and hate. Maybe her *hate* comes from liking him."

She bellows out a laugh. "Okay, Mr. Romantic."

Smiling, I look at Noah in her wedding dress. "You look really pretty, by the way. Not used to seein' you without dirt on your face and clothes. You clean up nice."

She tilts her head as if she's contemplating scolding me or thanking me. "Well, I guess that's better than Wilder's, *'Hey, sis, you look bangin'*" comment." She deepens her voice to talk like him, and I bark out a laugh.

Of course that dumbass would say something inappropriate.

"Imagine the day Wilder walks down the aisle," I muse. "He'd probably be loaded before the ceremony started."

"I seriously can't. He's gonna be a bachelor until the day he dies."

We laugh at his expense even though he's nowhere to be found.

"May I steal my wife for a final dance?" Fisher approaches with his hand out and Noah takes it.

"You absolutely can, my husband."

I make a show of rolling my eyes at their flirting. "God. How long are we gonna hear that now?"

"Probably the next forty or fifty years?" Noah lifts her head and presses her lips to Fisher's.

"And that's my cue to go."

"Go ask Magnolia for a dance, chickenshit!" Noah arches her brow as if she's daring me to deny I want to.

Before I can come up with a witty response, Fisher drags her away.

Well, at least now I won't have to be anxious about asking Magnolia.

I find her near the bar with Landen, Waylon, and one of our other cousins, Harrison. She's gripping a drink that's half empty, but she's been sipping it for the past hour. They're laughing at something, but I invade their group circle without a second thought.

"Dance with me," I tell Magnolia, standing in front of her and holding out my hand like I watched Fisher do.

She gives me a hesitant expression, purses her lips, and circles her gaze around us as if to ask, *"are you sure?"*

I nod once.

"Um...okay." She grins, placing her hand in mine.

"Wait." Harrison's voice interrupts. "She told me she broke a toe and couldn't put too much pressure on it."

Magnolia's eyes widen at getting caught lying. I hold back a laugh at Harrison's butthurt tone.

"That's why I plan to hold her up the whole time," I tell him.

"You can't be serious," she mouths.

I wink, then step closer until I can pick her up just enough for her shoes to lift off the ground. She wraps her arms around my neck as I settle my hands below her ass.

"Let's go, Sunny."

She pouts as I make my way to the opposite side of the dance floor and hopefully out of view from Harrison.

Then I slowly lower her feet to the floor.

"That was obnoxious," she hisses.

I chuckle, pulling her to my chest and wrapping her back in my arms. Lowering my mouth to her ear, I say, "Noah caught me staring at you and basically told me to stop being a coward. Then said I should ask you to dance. She's gonna freak out when we tell her we were already together."

She laughs and gazes up at me. "If she wasn't leavin' for her honeymoon first thing Monday, I'd tell her now, but her finding out we're dating will require a full girls' night of juicy details while eating cookie dough and watching *Dirty Dancing*."

"That's oddly specific."

She lifts a shoulder and grins. "We have our guilty pleasures and Patrick Swayze in the eighties is one of 'em."

"As long as no one tells her before you or I do, I think she'll be happy for us," I say honestly. "When I asked her if it'd make things weird between us in the event we broke up, she said it'd be a risk I'd have to take."

"And to think all this time you coulda asked me out in high school."

I scoff. "You were jailbait, Sunny. Getting on Sheriff Wagner's bad side once was enough."

"You're only older by two years!"

"Doesn't matter. Why do you think Landen waited a couple years to ask you out on a date? He wasn't about to do time for you either."

She rolls her eyes as we sway to a song that is surprisingly not a Taylor Swift one. I'm pretty sure they've played every single one of hers tonight, which has kept Mallory and Serena happy.

"By the way, I loved your speech. You had everyone in the

palm of your hand by the way they were glued to you and laughing, especially when you recapped Noah fallin' in horseshit on Fisher's first day on the ranch. That was epic."

"Right?" She beams. "Totally funnier than Damien's."

"Obviously."

"Oh, that reminds me. I bet Landen if we danced together, he had to ask Ellie out."

"There's no way she's gonna say yes."

"Exactly. That boy could use some humbling."

We laugh, and I inch as close as I can without making it obvious I'm dying to kiss her.

"You should stay with me tonight," I whisper, breaking the silence. "After everyone leaves."

"I wish I could." She pouts, sticking out her lower lip that I want to pull between my teeth and suck on. "But the gift opening brunch is tomorrow morning, and I'm in charge of bringing all the presents over and then making sure everything's set up properly. While they're opening, Noah wants me to keep track of who they're all from so they can send out thank-you notes."

"Damn. That's a lot."

"I know. And, well, if I come over, I have a feelin' there wouldn't be much sleeping involved, and I'd be a zombie in the mornin'."

My cock twitches at the vision of her in my bed all night long.

"At least your schedule will open up once it's all over." Though mine never slows down.

"Thankfully. I need to put together a holiday menu soon. Care to be my drink taste tester?"

"Are you gonna charge me twenty dollars a cup?" I muse, sliding my palm down to discreetly pat her ass.

"What can I say? I'm a smart businesswoman."

My face splits into a huge grin at how unapologetic Magnolia always is. Never tries to impress me by being anything other than herself.

"I'd love to try anything you make. Within reason."

She wrinkles her nose. "What's that mean?"

"I can only handle so much caffeine in a day."

"What if I make it worth your while?" The corner of her lips curls up suggestively.

"I'm listening."

She pulls my shoulders down until her mouth brushes my ear. "For every drink you sample, I remove a piece of clothing. Including the black lacy lingerie set I'll be wearing underneath."

I inhale sharply through my nose at the image of her in that sexy piece.

"That's a fuckin' deal."

When the song ends, she tells me it's time to make Landen eat his words.

"There's the lovebirds," he mocks when Magnolia approaches him at one of the tables. "Takin' off?"

"Not yet. You haven't asked Ellie to dance. The DJs gonna be packin' up soon, so you better hurry."

His eyes nearly cross when he gazes up at us. "I don't even know where she is." He scoffs with a drunken slur in his tone.

Fuck, this is gonna be interesting.

Some of the guests have already left, but there is still a good chunk of people here. I scan my eyes over each table and the dance floor until I spot Ellie sitting next to Mallory and Serena.

"Found her," I blurt out, then point in her direction.

"Perfect." Magnolia smirks. "We danced in front of everyone, so now it's your turn to buck up, cowboy."

Landen stumbles to his feet and flattens his palms down his dress shirt. His suit coat and tie are long gone, with his sleeves rolled up to his elbows. "Fine. But after this, I don't wanna hear you shit-talkin' about it again."

"Yeah, we'll see." Magnolia snickers.

We follow him as he maze-walks through the tables and when we get close, Magnolia and I break off so we're within listening distance but not invading. We find a table nearby and sit as if we're just taking a little break.

"Landen!" Mallory exclaims.

"Hey, Mal." He nods at her, then turns toward the woman he's been avoiding. "Um...Ellie?"

With a huff, she turns and meets his eyes. "What, Landen?"

The snappiness in her voice has me flinching for him. It's not only if her looks could kill, it's her tone, too.

"Would you wanna dance? Um, with me. On the dance floor. Together."

Magnolia palms her forehead as Landen struggles to piece together a full sentence. I resist laughing at his expense, but goddamn, am I gonna give him shit for this when he's sober.

"Awww..." Mallory and Serena coo in unison.

Landen gives her a lopsided grin.

"Sorry, I broke my toe and can't put pressure on it."

This time I don't conceal the chuckle that bubbles out of me because she just gave him the same excuse Magnolia gave Harrison.

Landen's jaw tenses at her words, presumably aware she's full of shit.

"Didn't look broken to me when you were dancin' earlier to 'Lover'?" Landen calls her out and Magnolia's eyes are locked on them as if a telenovela is unfolding right in front of us.

"That's because it just happened. Someone stepped on my foot when I was dancing, and I was just about to get some ice before it swelled up."

Landen slowly nods, his lips in a flat line and fingers gripping the chair in front of him as if he's about to snap it in half. "I'll get some for you then."

But Ellie doesn't take the bait. She crosses her arms over her chest and deadpans, "No, it's okay."

"Why not? I'd hate for it to fall off and your barrel racing career tanks because you're down to nine toes."

"Fine," she grits between her teeth.

"Be right back." Landen flashes her a cheeky grin that has Ellie rolling her eyes.

We watch as Landen walks toward the bar.

"Can't say he's a quitter." I laugh.

Magnolia shakes her head in disbelief. "She's gonna give him a run for his money."

"And I can't wait to see him get knocked to his knees."

She playfully smacks my chest. "Be nice. At least he's puttin' in the effort."

I know that's a jab at me for waiting so long, but I can't even be mad to tease her back when I finally have her now.

"So after tomorrow, when can we see each other again?" I ask while we wait for Landen to return.

"I'll be at the retreat Tuesday and free once I close up at three."

"Good. What about Wednesday?" I ask.

"Same, except for working downtown."

"And Thursday?"

"Same thing."

"Friday?"

She smirks. "For the unforeseen future, I work until three and then I'm free the rest of the evening."

"Geez. Get some friends, Sunny," I mock.

She leans over and twists my nipple.

I'm too slow to smack her hand away. "Ow! That's attached."

She scowls. "Then don't be rude!"

I laugh, capturing her hand and pressing my lips to it. "Just pencil me in for every night."

She yanks it out of my grip. "No. According to you, I need *friends*. Maybe I'll go ask Harrison to hang out. Or Kyle. I mean, you weren't specific on only *girl* friends."

"Do that and you'll find out very quickly how fast a fight can break out."

"Over me having friends you told me to get?" she challenges.

"I don't want my girlfriend hangin' out with guys who want to get into her panties. And I'd hope you'd feel the same way about me being around chicks who make suggestive comments about ridin' my dick."

She stares at me. "Did you just call me your *girlfriend*?"

"Yes."

The silence lingers as Landen returns with a baggie of ice for Ellie and the anxiety of her not responding surfaces up my chest and neck until I can no longer take it. The hives are making me itch and even if she's messing with me, I need to clear the air now.

"Have I not been clear that we're together and a *thousand percent* exclusive?" I ask, no longer watching Landen ice Ellie's fake broken toe.

"Hmm. I guess I don't remember you askin' for my hand in girlfriend-boyfriend matrimony."

My hand lowers beneath the table and when I find her thigh, I squeeze it hard between my fingers. She releases a little yelp and flashes a smart-ass grin at getting me worked up.

Yeah, she knows exactly what she's doing. The little shit.

Leaning closer until our shoulders touch and my mouth brushes her ear, I decide to fully give in to her little game and make her eat her words. "I still have the taste of your sweet pussy on my mouth from when you came on my tongue this afternoon. The photo of you in that little lacy number is all I see when I close my eyes. The first thought I have when I wake up at five in the morning is wondering when I'll get to talk to or see you again. And the first time I took a woman out on a real date or let drive my truck has only ever been you. But if you need me to drop to my knees and propose girlfriend-boyfriend to you, then just say the words, sweetheart. I'll do it right now."

Her throat moves and her body stiffens when I lean back in my chair. Ellie has apparently dismissed Landen after he brought her ice. And considering it's melting on top of the table confirms she gave him a bullshit excuse to avoid dancing with him.

Magnolia turns toward me, neither of us seemingly worried about who could be watching us right now, and I arch a brow as she noticeably struggles to speak.

"Something you wanna say, Sunny?"

Her eyes narrow into a glare and my lips curl up in victory.

Finally, she swallows hard and straightens her shoulders. "No. I think I'm good."

With a wide grin, I nod once. "Glad we're on the same page, then."

Chapter Eighteen
Magnolia

The urge to straddle his lap in the middle of the reception was so strong, I had to remind myself why I couldn't.

I spent an embarrassing amount of time getting myself off in bed that night. Pretty sure I wore out my vibrator's batteries and they were a fresh pair.

Goddamn him and the hottest words I've ever had whispered in my ear.

It's not that I wanted to put any doubt in Tripp's mind, but our relationship over the years has been built on giving each other shit, teasing, and taunting at any given time. Mostly because I just wanted his attention even if I thought my feelings weren't reciprocated. It's hard to just turn that off when I'm still in denial that he wants me the way I've always wanted him.

Physically, I know we're compatible. There's no doubt about our connection and chemistry in terms of being attracted to each other. But there's still a little nagging voice in the back of my mind that's telling my brain there's no way he'd want a commitment. He's never had a serious relationship. What makes me think he can have one with me?

It's stupid, honestly. He's given me no reason to think otherwise. But hearing him confirm what I knew deep down to be the truth knocked that little nagging voice right out of my head.

Tripp's with me because he wants to be. He likes me as more than just his little sister's best friend.

He's my *boyfriend*.

And isn't that the weirdest thing on the planet to say when I was about to give up on ever thinking he would like me back.

The gift opening brunch went smoothly, and everyone had fun. We took tons of photos, and I ate more than my fill of food.

Tripp, Landen, and Waylon helped load the presents and delivered them to Noah and Fisher's cottage. After cleaning up the room with Dena and Gramma Grace, I helped Noah pack for her honeymoon and said one more final goodbye before they flew out the next morning.

Once the sun set, I was ready to sleep for the next twenty-four hours, but my maid of honor duties still weren't over. I collected all the groomsmen's tuxes so I could return them to the rental place on Monday and since Wilder didn't show up to The Lodge, I had to track him down at his house and play hide 'n' seek with his clothes scattered across his floor.

By Tuesday, I'm still not fully recovered from the insanely busy weekend, but I'm excited to finally get Tripp alone tonight. We texted throughout yesterday and he helped me get Wilder's tux when I came looking for it, but I still miss him.

It's silly, I know.

This is so new, and I shouldn't be this head over heels already, but I can't help it. No guy has ever made me feel as special or important as Tripp does, and I crave his proximity every time we're apart.

MAGNOLIA

> Are you visiting me today? Or do I need to find me a new cowboy to overpay for coffee?

It's almost three and he hasn't stopped by yet. Landen showed up at eight for his usual, but he said Tripp was too busy to leave.

TRIPP

> So you admit you make me overpay?

MAGNOLIA

> Don't think I ever denied it.

TRIPP

> I think it's time I make you pay for once.

MAGNOLIA

> What for??

He doesn't respond, which only makes me more anxious that he won't make it in time before I close. I know he's busy, so I shouldn't give him shit, but I was hoping to see him even for a few minutes.

MAGNOLIA

> Tick tock, cowboy. Trey's offer to hang out later might be one I need to revisit.

Trey Mitchell's one of the ranch hands at the stables and an overall nice guy, but not one I'd ever be interested in. He also never asked me to hang out, so I might be throwing him under the bus a little to make a point. I know I'm playing with fire by mentioning him, but I'm hoping it's what lights a fire under Tripp's ass to get here.

But still, no response.

A few more customers arrive, who order the last of the muffins, and when I finish ringing them up, it's time to close. I bring in my *Pay with Cash and it's Free #GirlMath* chalkboard sign, unplug all the fairy lights, and fold up my counter window.

Once I clean my espresso machine, put everything back in its place, and wipe it down, I close out my register. I go to the bank every couple of days to deposit money and then send my accountant quarterly receipts and business expenses. I've never been good at numbers, so to stay on track with my bills, I keep a close eye on what I'm making and spending.

Just as I'm counting my inventory in the fridge, a body presses against my back and a single rose appears in front of me. I smile wide as I press my nose into the center and inhale the floral scent.

"You're late," I scold, taking the stem and spinning around in his arms so I can kiss him.

My eager smile immediately falls when my eyes land on Travis.

"Oh my God! What're you doin' here?" I shove away from him, creating much-needed space.

"You blocked me. What was I supposed to do?"

"Um…get the hint that I don't wanna speak to you!"

"Maggie, c'mon…" He holds out his arms, steps closer, and I move back as far as I can.

"Don't call me that. And. Get. Out!" I point toward the only exit.

Instead of listening, he invades my space, caging me against the wall with his broad arms. "We're not done, Mags. I love you and you know we're supposed to be together. So quit being a stubborn bitch and unblock me."

He's close enough that when I forcefully raise my knee, it drives right into his groin. As soon as he keels halfway over, I use the heel of my boot to shove him down the rest of the way. His arm flails as he tries to catch himself, but he ends up smacking his wrist against my counter instead.

"*Fucking. Cunt*," he spits out between labored breaths.

I set the rose down and lean over him. "I warned you, Travis. Leave me alone or it'll be more than your balls going up inside your body."

"You're a psycho." He squeezes his eyes as if he's trying not to cry out in pain.

Instead of leaving it alone and letting him suffer in silence, I take my boot and step on the wrist he smacked with as much force as I can add.

He hisses when he tries to jerk out from underneath my heel.

"You've not seen anything, Travis. It'd take one phone call to get the Hollis boys to dig me a hole six feet deep and then push your body inside it."

Okay, maybe that was a bit much threatening murder and all, but I'm not letting my asshole ex ruin my relationship with Tripp now that I finally have him. The moment he'd see Travis near me, Tripp would lose his shit before I even had time to explain I already took care of him.

"You bangin' one of 'em now, ain't ya? Fuckin' whore."

I finally ease off his wrist and allow him to get to his knees.

"Wouldn't you like to know? Maybe I'm sleeping with all four of them. Wouldn't be any of your business even if I were."

"And you wonder why everyone calls you a slut," he spits out when he stands to his full height.

"Is this where you expect me to say *it takes one to know one?*" I mock with an eye roll. "Grow up."

"Fuckin' watch that mouth, *Magnolia*." He walks toward the exit, and I exhale a full breath for the first time in five minutes.

"No, you watch yourself because I won't hesitate to use my taser next time." I quickly reach for it out of my bag and click the two side buttons that make it zap. "And trust me when I say, I'll be aiming low."

"Bitch," is the last word I hear him mutter when he finally walks out and into the parking lot.

With the taser gripped in my hand, I rush to the door and lock it shut.

My chest rises and falls as I sink to the floor and attempt to steady my breathing. I shouldn't let him get to me like this and even though I fought back, my anxiety is through the roof. Travis is a giant compared to me. He played football in high school and continued to bulk up after graduation. He could've hit me if he wanted, but that's never been his MO. He's all about mental control and emotional whiplash. A gaslighting pro. And a delusional idiot.

Several minutes pass before I manage to get to my feet and finish counting inventory. When my phone goes off with a text, I jump and lose my breath all over again.

TRIPP

> I'm so sorry. Cabin call took longer than expected. There was a guest mix-up and Rachelle got flustered trying to fix it. Are you still here?

Rachelle's one of the receptionists at The Lodge and though I feel bad there was an issue, I wish she had been able to figure it out herself so Tripp could've been here. But maybe it's a good thing he wasn't. Having to explain why Travis is suddenly interested in getting back together would bring up what happened between us a couple weeks ago, and I'm not ready to have that embarrassing conversation.

MAGNOLIA

> That's okay. About to leave.

TRIPP

> Wanna go for a horseback ride? One of Landen's stallions got loose and he's picking up hay a few hours away so I was about to go look for him.

I pause when I read his words. It's only in the fifties today, and I'm not dressed for something like that. Not to mention, I haven't been on a horse since Noah convinced me to try riding years ago. But I want to spend time with him even if it's doing something that terrifies me.

MAGNOLIA

> Sure, but I'll probably kill myself.

TRIPP

> We'll ride together, baby ;) We have a special
> saddle for two.

MAGNOLIA

> Okay, where do you want me to meet you?

TRIPP

> I'll pick you up. I'm a minute away.

For the first time since Travis invaded my trailer, I smile in excitement. I don't want him to think anything's wrong, so I try to shake off the jitters my asshole ex left me in.

As soon as I lock up the trailer, I hear Tripp's truck pull up.

He swoops me up in his arms, and I melt against him as I inhale his bodywash scent mixed with sweat and leather. I bury my face into his chest and my breathing steadies.

"You okay, Sunny?" he asks when I don't release my grip on him.

"Yeah, just missed you. And a little scared of what I agreed to."

He chuckles, brushing strands of my hair behind my ear. Then he tilts my chin and crashes his mouth down on mine. Warmth invades me as he consumes my body and thoughts, and the fear of losing him increases.

"Don't worry. I won't let anything happen to you. I'm bringing an extra rope so I can bring Rocky back, and he likes females, so he won't hurt ya." He winks at his cheeky comment.

Of course a stallion would like girls.

"Prepare for me to hang on for dear life."

He takes my hand and leads us to the passenger side of his truck.

"Oh no, you clingin' onto me. What a hardship."

I playfully roll my eyes as he helps me up into my seat. Then he leans over and buckles me in.

"I'll give you my jacket so you stay warm. If he's where I think he is, it shouldn't take too long to bring him back."

With every sweet gesture, the guilt chips away at my heart for not telling him the truth about what happened the night of Landen's birthday party.

I know I need to, and I will.

Just not right now when I'm falling so damn hard for him.

It's selfish of me to wait, but I finally have everything I ever wanted, and I don't want to lose it.

Or break his heart.

Chapter Nineteen
Tripp

"You're gonna get us in trouble." Magnolia pants between her words, and I love the sound of her losing control around me.

"You're the boss," I remind her, thrusting my fingers deeper toward her G-spot. "Who do you think is gonna catch us?" She's already done for the day, so the counter window and door are closed and locked.

"I-I dunno. The health inspector because this most definitely violates a few codes."

Considering her ass is perched up on the counter and her thighs are spread wide for me, I can't disagree. But it's been three days since I've seen her in person, and I was desperate for a taste before we go on our date tonight. With Noah away on her honeymoon, the rest of us are picking up her slack with the boarding horses and making sure they get exercised, which has meant working later and less time to see Magnolia.

After we rode around looking for Rocky, I found him up the mountain grazing and the little bastard ran as soon as he saw Franklin. It took a little sweet talking to convince him to trust me and not take off. Once I was able to swing the rope around his neck, I led him back to the breeding operations barn and put him in a stall. The pasture he was in has a broken fence post, and I stayed busy helping Landen fix it for the past couple evenings.

Magnolia and I text each day and stay in contact, but it's not the same as getting to touch and kiss her. She even gave me a little striptease over FaceTime as she was undressing before she got in the bath. So as soon as I was able to come to the retreat after her shift today, I was ready to devour her.

"Shit, I'm so close." She digs her nails into my hair as I kneel in front of her and hike one of her legs over my shoulder.

My tongue flattens along her slit before I capture her clit between my lips and suck until she goes breathless. I drive my fingers faster into her sweet cunt and when she nearly screams through her orgasm, she squirts all over my hand.

And I lick every last bit.

"Fuck, Sunny. You had some pent-up tension to release." I shoot her a wink and she blushes.

"You've been teasin' me all week."

Between the daily sexting, FaceTime calls that eventually turn sexual, and being insanely obsessive over her, I don't blame her. My palm's gone raw over abusing my cock each night.

Grabbing her leggings off the floor, I stand and grab her foot so I can slide them back on.

"Forgettin' something?" She arches a brow when I pull them up.

"No."

"So you're just gonna pretend you didn't steal my panties and shove 'em in your pocket?"

Her taunting voice has me smirking as I avoid her gaze, concentrating hard on making sure I get her clothes situated properly.

"That'd be correct."

"Then I get something of yours," she says once I lift her off the counter and onto her feet.

I tease the tip of my tongue along my lower lip as I stare into her beautiful brown eyes. "Okay, whaddya want?"

"A T-shirt."

My brows pinch together in confusion because I was expecting something a lot more scandalous.

"Just any shirt?" I ask.

"One that smells like you. That night I stole one from your room, you made me give it back. And I'd like one to keep for when I'm alone in my bed and missing you."

The vulnerable sadness on her face has me cupping her cheeks and stepping closer until I capture her mouth. My tongue slides between her lips and she opens hers to let me in. This kiss isn't rushed or filled with desperation but rather sweet and tender. Her arms wrap around my waist, pulling me tighter until we're gasping for air.

"I'm sorry I took it from you." I rest my forehead against hers. "You can have my entire closet, Sunny. It's yours."

She chuckles, tilting up to meet my gaze. "This one will do for now."

"You got it." I pull back and yank it over my head. I left my jacket in my truck, but I don't mind the cold because as soon as her eyes land on my chest, fire burns in her eyes.

"Is that—" She squints, leaning in closer. "A sunflower tattoo?"

She brushes a finger underneath Billy's inked name and confusion covers her face.

"I don't remember seeing that before."

"The birth and death dates written underneath his name had the wrong years, but I didn't realize it until after it healed. So instead of trying to get it fixed and risk it turnin' out worse, I decided to just cover it up with something better."

"With a *sunflower*..." Her baffled expression is adorable. She really has no idea how long I've liked her. "When did you get it?"

I brush a finger down her cheek. "About two years ago, after you told me that Sunny was your favorite nickname from me."

She swallows hard as she continues examining the design. A

189

bouquet of sunflowers lies below Billy's name like a decorative signature.

"I liked what you said about sunflowers and how they were a sign of positivity, happiness, and hope. Figured I could use some of that in my life." I shrug.

She finally meets my eyes. "You never told me."

"I didn't tell anyone."

"Not even Landen?"

"Nope."

"I can't wrap my head around this, Tripp. Why would you get my favorite flower tattooed on your skin? And two *years* ago? I still thought you could hardly stand being around me or only put up with me because I was Noah's best friend."

"That was me tryin' to keep my distance because you were on and off with Travis, and I knew Landen liked you, so you were off-limits. I thought if I stayed guarded and put you in the friend zone, you'd stop flirtin' with me, and I'd stop liking you." I smirk, plucking her bottom lip between my thumb and finger. "My feelings never faded, though."

Something passes in her eyes, almost like a flinch, but she quickly recovers, so I don't question it.

"Even after you thought we'd never have a chance, you still did it?" she asks.

I hold her face in my hands and smile down at her. "Yeah, Sunny. No matter what did or didn't happen between us, I liked the thought of having you close to me."

"Tripp Hollis." The corners of her eyes well with tears, and I quickly brush my thumb across her cheeks before they can fall. "That is the sweetest thing I've ever heard. And now I kinda hate you for it because how am I ever gonna compete with that?"

With a grin, I dip down and capture her pouty lips. "You could get a tattoo of my handprint on your ass cheek."

"I won't be able to show anyone if it's there."

I cock a brow. "Exactly."

"Please tell me you aren't takin' me to some archery place. Because I really think axe-throwing was my limit on arm strength."

I glance over at her in the passenger seat and chuckle. "No, don't worry. That's more of a fifth date kinda thing."

"Oh good, remind me to be sick that day."

Leaning over, I squeeze her thigh. "You're such a brat."

"I thought you liked that specific trait of mine," she muses with a cheeky grin.

I cup her chin while keeping one eye on the road. "Only if I'm allowed to give out punishments for said *trait*."

"Hmm…well, how else would I get your handprint on my ass for that tattoo?"

My eyes darken at the thought of someone else seeing her there. "Yeah, I change my mind. No one sees your bare ass except me."

"Tattoo artists are professionals. They pierce dicks and vaginas all day long. I'm sure my one little ass cheek wouldn't even faze 'em."

I snort. "Is that so?"

"Well, I dunno, but I'm sure they've seen it all. They're practically doctors and are immune to that stuff."

"Right…" I drawl out, still not convinced.

"So I'm guessing if I tell you I've been thinkin' of gettin' my clit pierced you'd be against it?"

My cock jerks beneath my jeans, and I have to adjust myself before it rubs uncomfortably along my zipper. She catches me and grins.

"No talkin' about your pussy while I'm drivin'."

"Okay, what about nipples? I could pierce those."

"Sunny…" I warn. "Unless you want me to pull over and take you right here, I suggest you stop talkin' about all your body parts I wanna devour."

"Not sure that's as much of a threat as you think it is."

I shoot her a side-glare as I continue fighting with my erection.

"Ya know, I could help you out with that…" She nods toward my groin.

"That's dangerous while I'm behind the wheel."

"More than finger-fucking me while teachin' me to drive?" she counters. The gloating smirk that covers her stunning face tells me she knows she's got me there.

Before I can argue, she flips off the chest strap of her buckle and crawls toward me on the bench seat. I pop the steering wheel up so she doesn't smack her head and widen my legs.

"This is a bad idea," I say as she undoes my button and zipper.

"You just focus on the road, cowboy. Leave me to it down here."

I scoff, death-gripping the wheel with one hand as she pulls out my hard length. "Yeah, sure."

My eyes are laser focused on the traffic in front of me. All it'd take is one nosy trucker to glance over and see Magnolia with my cock in her mouth.

The moment her hot tongue swirls around the tip, I'm fucking gone. She bobs up and down on my shaft like it's a goddamn Popsicle and when she makes gagging noises, it brings me closer to exploding down her throat.

"Sunny, I'm gonna come," I warn her, barely able to breathe. Not touching her the way I want to is torture, but I fist her hair so I can control her head if I need to. I wouldn't think twice about moving her over if there was a threat of an accident happening.

As if she can feel my entire body tense, she hollows her cheeks and sucks harder until my spine tingles and vibrations rock through my balls.

"Holy fuck," I breathe out as she swallows me down.

Her tongue slides up and down, cleaning every ounce of me, but I need her to stop before I get hard again.

"You gotta stop now, baby."

She sits up and proudly wipes her mouth with the back of her hand, and I shove myself back in my boxers and rebutton my jeans.

"That was fuckin' impressive, Sunny." She's close enough to kiss, so I drag her mouth to mine for a quick one. "Now, please, sit and put your buckle back in place."

She mocks me with a salute.

My truck's never seen so much action, but I'm starting to like these bench seats more and more.

Ten minutes later, we arrive at our date location and as soon as she realizes what we're doing, her face lights up like a kid's on Christmas Day.

"We're seeing a movie?" Her mouth opens. "I haven't been to the theater in years."

Not surprising since her asshole ex wouldn't go with her and everyone streams at home now.

"It's why I wanted to take you. Thought it'd be fun to veg out on popcorn and snacks and enjoy their heated recliners for a couple of hours."

She tilts her head in confusion. "Whaddya mean? How'd you know that?"

"You might not remember because you were high on Molly, but you mentioned it that night."

"Oh my God. Either you have the memory of an elephant or you're utterly obsessed with me." Her tone is teasing, but she's not wrong. I have been for longer than I'd like to admit.

Instead of telling her that, I casually shrug. "I do have a good memory."

The corner of her lips hikes up with a smug grin. "Mm-hmm. I'm sure that's it."

"C'mon, let's go. The movie's gonna start soon." I open my door and she reaches for hers, but I grab her arm. "Wait."

Slamming mine shut, I sprint around my truck to her side. Then I pull her handle and hold out my hand so she can take it.

"Aren't you such a gentleman."

Once she steps down, I pull her flush against my chest and kiss the tip of her nose. "Oh, I have secret motivations."

"Hm...care to elaborate?"

"Nope. You'll find out." I wink, then lock my truck and lead us to the theater.

I already bought the tickets, so once we're inside, we hit the food stand. We order a large popcorn with extra butter, two bags of gummy worms, one red and one blue slushie to share, and then a box of M&M's to sprinkle on top of the popcorn.

"Anything else, Sunny, or is this enough of a sugar high for ya?" I tease before I give the girl behind the counter my card.

"I think this'll do until we get back to town."

She chuckles when I shake my head. I'm not a huge sweets person, but I could easily devour one of Gramma Grace's Butter Pecan pies.

"So what movie are we gonna see?" she finally asks, and honestly, I'm surprised it took her until now to ask.

While we wait to go in, I point at a banner of Patrick Swayze and Demi Moore behind her. Every month, they reserve a theater for a specific theme and when I saw they were doing the '90s and featuring a movie of his, I knew she'd enjoy it.

"*Ghost*?" She looks back at me in confusion with her lips parted.

"It's no *Dirty Dancing*, but it has your favorite actor."

Her mouth is still half-open in surprise. "I've never seen that one."

"Good. Then you'll actually pay attention to it and won't spend the whole time tryin' to tempt me."

"Except there's a loophole in your well-crafted plan."

I look down at her devious grin and furrow my brows. "And what's that?"

She licks her lips. "I'm a *master* multitasker. Years of working in customer service help me focus on more than one thing at a time."

Instead of giving in to her devious attempts to seduce me in yet another place we could get caught, I bring my mouth to her ear. "Sweetheart, I deal with rowdy thousand-pound horses, overly needy guests, and unruly siblings on a daily basis. So if you think I can't handle your *loopholes*, think again. Because if I need to, I'll pin you down in that recliner with my fingers shoved in your wet pussy and edge you for a solid two hours before lettin' you come."

When I pull back, she's biting the inside of her cheek as her nostrils flare.

Probably to stop herself from giving me a verbal lashing.

A smug smile forms across my face as she tries to stay mad at me.

"Ready to go in?" I ask once I hand our tickets to the attendant.

She continues to shoot me death glares when we walk inside the first auditorium and climb up the stairs to find the best seats.

"What section do you want?" I ask over my shoulder. "The very top, or is the middle okay?"

"You sit wherever you want, cowboy. I'll sit down here so I don't *tempt* you." Then she parks her ass in the front row of the second level.

I chuckle to myself, put our drinks in the holders and the bag of popcorn in the seat next to mine, and march back down the stairs. When I stand in front of her, she purposely shifts her body to look at the blank screen behind me. The previews haven't even started.

"Excuse me, you're blockin' my view and everyone else's who'll sit behind me."

I make a show of glancing around the bare room. "Hmm…I think it's just yours, sweetheart."

"Well, you better go away so I can focus on Patrick Swayze's good looks and *only* his."

I have a suspicion she has no clue what this movie's about.

"You can focus on *only* his next to me up there."

Without giving her a chance to respond, I pick her up and throw her over my shoulder like dozens of other times.

And she pounds her fists on my ass like she's always done. "Tripp! Put me down, you caveman!"

"Gladly. In the seat next to mine. Where you belong."

When I reach our chairs, I gently set her down and then sit beside her.

"That was unnecessary."

Reaching over to grab our popcorn, I hold it out for her with a grin. "Want some?"

She snatches it from me and shoves a mouthful in. "I'm not allowed to *tempt* you because there'll be other people around, but you can carry me like I'm a drunk sorority girl inside a movie theater?"

"It was that or shoutin' across the auditorium to ask if you wanted any snacks."

As if she can't feign being angry anymore, she laughs and flicks a piece of popcorn at my face. "You're insane."

"All for you, baby." I wink and she rolls her eyes.

When the lights dim and the previews start, she looks around and notices no one else is in here.

"Is it normal for these themed nights to be empty?"

I lean over with a smirk. "I figured we'd want our privacy, so I bought every single ticket for this showing."

Her mouth drops open. "You sneaky shit. This whole time…"

"Don't get any ideas, Sunny. We're watchin' the movie."

She rips open the M&M's box and dumps it on top of the popcorn. "Then there better be some man ass in it to keep me entertained."

Fuck. She hasn't a single clue what she's about to experience.

Chapter Twenty
Magnolia

I'm in awe of this man who bought out this theater so we can spend it completely alone. I know it couldn't have been cheap and even though the Hollises are wealthy, it's the thought behind it that's making my heart melt.

But also now I don't have to feel bad about talking through it because although I've heard of this movie, I haven't a single clue what it's about. But Tripp doesn't seem to mind my commentary as we drink our slushies and eat popcorn and gummy worms.

"Oof, the quality."

"You'll get used to it," he reassures me.

These recliners are super comfortable, and my ass is toasty warm, so I have no complaints.

"Ooh, she makes pottery."

"Demi is so beautiful, but that haircut is not it, bestie."

"It was on trend for the late eighties and early nineties," he counters.

"I guess. She can really pull off any look, but I love her long hair."

A dreamy sigh escapes my lips when a bare-chested Patrick enters and sits behind her. "He's so classically handsome. I just wanna thread my fingers through his golden strands and give them a little tug."

Tripp glances at me with an arched brow.

"What? Am I not supposed to appreciate good hair?"

He smirks, shoving more gummy worms in his mouth. This is why I requested my own bag.

"Holy shit, that's hot." My eyes are glued to the screen when Patrick starts kissing Demi's neck while her hands are covered in clay. Even though he's supposed to be helping her, he accidentally destroys her vase, and they begin making out instead.

"You should get me a pottery wheel so we can recreate that scene. Except I don't wanna get all messy. We'll just skip to the good stuff."

He barks out a laugh. "Duly noted."

"So this *is* a spicy movie." I giggle when Patrick slides his hand underneath her oversized shirt and palms her bare ass.

"Dear Lord, look at his abs." I mimic licking up an ice cream cone and Tripp shoots me an annoyed side-eye. "You're the one who brought me here to watch a Patrick Swayze porno."

He inhales a sharp breath as if he's regretting that decision.

"Fine, no more commentary on his looks." I mimic zipping my lips closed.

Now they're walking in some dark alley. Could never be me.

"Wait, who is that guy?" I sit up when some rando demands Patrick's wallet.

Demi's screaming at Patrick for him to just hand it over, but when the mugger shoves her, Patrick loses his shit.

As he should.

My heart's racing as I watch the scene unfold and when the gun goes off, I jump.

"Oh my God. Who got shot?" I grip the armrest and sit up.

Then Patrick's chasing after the guy, and I blow out a relieved breath.

"Oh whew, he's okay." I palm my chest over the pounding inside my ribcage.

Ten seconds later...

Patrick's watching Demi cry out for help, and I'm just as confused as he looks.

"Wait, what? He got SHOT?" I squeeze Tripp's arm when we see a bloody Patrick in Demi's lap. "No way he dies. Right?"

I gasp when the realization hits me that it's Patrick's ghost watching the scene unfold.

"I can't believe he dies," I choke out. "Why would you take me to this?"

"Why do you think it's the title of the movie?" he asks carefully.

"I dunno! I wasn't thinking of it *literally*." I frown. "So now what? He's gonna haunt her until the murderer is caught?"

He takes my fidgeting hand and threads his fingers between mine as we watch the funeral scene.

"If we get to attend our own funerals from the afterlife, everyone better be cryin' over me and only showin' off my best photos."

I frown when Demi screws up her vase. "Aww. I hate seeing how sad she looks. She can't even enjoy makin' pottery anymore."

My heart aches at the grief I can feel on her behalf.

We continue watching as he learns how to go through walls and kick cans, and then the realization of how things are going to continue hits me when Whoopi Goldberg shows up.

"Whoopi's the psychic medium in this?"

"Technically, she's a fraud until Patrick shows up, which is why she's freakin' the fuck out."

I snort.

Tripp continues holding my hand and we eat popcorn with our free ones. I'm glued to the screen to find out how the hell this progresses now that someone can hear him.

"Oh, hell no. I see a penny sliding up a door and floating in the air, I'm fuckin' gone. How is she so chill?"

"Well, if someone showed up after I died and knew private

details about us no one else would know, you wouldn't stay to hear her out?" Tripp asks.

"See, that'd never happen because you're not allowed to die on me now that we're finally together. But if you did and were murdered, I'd fully expect your ghost to harass a psychic until she agrees to talk to me so we can figure out how to catch the murderer."

He grins. "Okay, deal."

The scenes where Patrick makes Whoopi pretend to be Rita Miller to get back at Carl are thrilling. I want that bastard to rot.

And when the broken window pierces Carl's chest and he's taken over by some weird black smoke, I smile wide in victory. It was much more satisfying than Willie's death, even though he's the one who actually shot Patrick. Carl was the mastermind behind it.

"Thank God. No one schemes to kill my Patrick and lives to tell the tale."

Tripp grins. "Just wait now…"

"Ugh, my heart can't take any more," I say when we watch the light shining above Patrick and he's saying goodbye to Demi and Whoopi.

My throat burns as I hold back tears, but when I can no longer keep it together, I let them fall.

And then I wonder how watching this is affecting Tripp with his own personal experience of losing his best friend.

When the final scene ends with Patrick fading away to his new home, Tripp leans over and wipes my cheek with the pad of his thumb.

"So did you like it?"

I glower at him.

"I'll take that as a…*maybe*."

"Of course I did, but goddamn. It was heart-wrenching."

"Yeah."

"Are you okay?" I ask when the lights return and notice how red his eyes are.

"I'm good. Just made me think of Billy and how I wish I had the chance to say goodbye."

"I wish you did, too."

"But it was nice not having an anxiety attack like I normally would at thinking about him. I think you being next to me helped."

"Really?" I squeeze his hand. "Guess that means we can't ever be apart."

He smiles. "Patrick's character and I do have one thing in common, though. When he talked at the beginning of the movie about whenever something good in his life happens, he's afraid he's gonna lose it. That's exactly what it feels like being this happy. Like I don't deserve it and it's gonna get ripped away from me."

His words slice through me and shatter my heart all over again from what I just experienced. His raw honesty makes my gut somersault at the thought of Tripp getting hurt and me being the cause of it.

"I'm not going anywhere," I promise, cupping his face and pulling him in for a kiss. "No one's gonna stop us from being together and happy."

Noah will be over the moon once I tell her the news and their parents already love me, so it's only a matter of keeping Travis away from us for good.

"Am I taking you home or do you wanna stay at my place tonight?" he asks as we walk hand in hand through the parking lot.

"Sleepover? Uh, yes, please!" I beam at the thought of curling up to Tripp all night. Though I should be nervous since we've never done that before, but I'm excited to spend more time with him.

He chuckles and when we get to his truck, he smacks my hand away when it touches the handle. When he opens my door for me, I burst out laughing at his aggressiveness in not allowing me to open it for myself.

"Surprised you let me walk," I tease when he hops in on his side.

"I figured hauling you over my shoulder again would be frowned upon."

"Well, just for future reference, the only circumstance it's accepted is when I'm naked and you're throwing me around like a rag doll. Then by all means, throw me over your shoulder."

A deep growl escapes his throat as he grips the steering wheel with both hands. "You know it's a forty-minute drive to my house, right? Must you make me drive with a hard-on every time we're in my truck?"

I shrug with a smug grin. "Oops."

But I know better than to mess with him now that it's pitch-black out. The country backroads can be dangerous if deer jump out or when other drivers aren't paying attention and suddenly swerve.

As we drive back to Sugarland Creek, my stomach starts to turn, and nausea hits me as we go down a winding road.

"You alright?" Tripp asks when I press my cheek against the cool window.

"Just feelin' a little queasy. I think I ate too much sugar."

"Oh shit, do you need me to pull over?"

I shake my head. "No, I should be fine once we're not driving."

"I'll slow down. These roads can be twisty and give you motion sickness."

Part of me wants to tell him to speed up so we get home faster, but as soon as he lets off the gas, it settles.

"Better?" he asks when I sit up.

"Yeah, that was weird. I think it passed."

He takes my hand and kisses my knuckles. "I have meds at home that should help."

Finally, we arrive at the ranch and once he parks, I wait for him this time to grab my door.

"Good girl." He winks as he takes my hand and helps me down.

"You better watch it. Those words are known to make panties disappear."

"Oh, I already have yours from earlier."

I laugh at his cocky grin. "And where exactly did you put 'em?"

After our little moment in the coffee trailer, I drove home and changed before our date and replaced the ones he stole. But I wouldn't be opposed to him ripping off another pair and keeping those, too.

"That is my little secret and only for me to know."

I scoff as he unlocks his front door and motions for me to go inside first.

"If I know you as well as I think I do, they're in one of two places. Your nightstand drawer that's most likely filled with condoms and lube or your truck's glove compartment. Damn, I shoulda checked before!"

"Wrong and wrong."

"In one of your dressers."

"Nope."

I walk farther into his apartment. Technically, it's a duplex, but Landen lives upstairs, so close enough. I've only been in here a few times but never had the opportunity to really look and snoop around.

"Wait...I know." I help myself to a tour and walk down the hallway, past the master and guest rooms before I find the right door.

"Where're ya goin'?" He follows behind.

"If I find 'em, I get to steal 'em back."

"I don't think so! I stole those fair and square."

When I enter the bathroom, I whip open the shower curtain and bark out a victory laugh.

"HA! You little perv." I swipe them off the showerhead.

Tripp snatches them from my fingers and holds them above my head. "Don't think so, Sunny. These are mine."

I raise my arm, but it's no use even if I could jump ten inches high. "Is that so? Because I hardly think sheer pink is your color."

"No?" He holds them up to his scruffy face. "I think they go well with my complexion."

"Oh my God, you're an underwear freak, aren't you? Do you have a bunch of random women's panties stashed in your drawers?"

I reach for them once they're within my arm's length, but he's too quick and yanks them over my head again.

Just as I attempt a second jump, the queasiness returns.

"I think I'm gonna be sick," I tell him and turn around toward the toilet.

The moment I lift the lid, my stomach wretches and all the popcorn, M&M's, gummy worms, and the slushie come out.

"Oh shit, Sunny." Tripp kneels beside me, grabs my hair, and rubs my back as wave after wave slams into me.

Ten minutes later, I wonder how I have anything left in me to release, but it doesn't stop. The pain is so intense, I swear I pop a blood vessel in my eye.

"I think I'm done." I groan, and he helps me stand.

"Sit, and I'll get you some water."

I put the lid down and lean back.

When he returns, he hands me a pink bottle and a glass of water.

"Do you feel any better now that it's all out of your system?"

I open the bottle and take a long chug, then chase it down with the water.

"Not really. Throwing up in front of you is like number one on my ick list, so ya know, glad we got that outta the way early on." My elbows rest on my knees as I wait for the queasiness to vanish.

"C'mon, I'm tuckin' you into my bed and I'll put the trash can next to it in case you feel sick again."

He scoops me up in his arms as if I'm weightless, and I rest my head on his chest as he carries me to his room.

When he puts me on my feet, he pulls the comforter and sheet back, then tells me to sit. "I'm gonna grab you a T-shirt to sleep in."

Every little movement feels amplified, and I groan as he lifts my arms and takes off my sweater. Then he slides an oversized shirt down and helps me out of my leggings to pull the shirt down to my knees.

"You can keep this one, too." He winks. "Wanna try lying down now?"

I nod, although I think it might make me feel worse.

He tucks the blankets all around me and repositions my hair so it's out of my face.

I pout. "This is not how I envisioned you puttin' me in your bed for the first time."

"Don't worry, Sunny. We'll schedule a make-up sleepover when you're back to feelin' better." He cups my cheek, then leans down and kisses my forehead. "Be right back with your water and bucket."

I fall asleep somewhere between him setting my phone down on his nightstand and then him crawling in behind me and rubbing my back.

When I wake up sometime in the middle of the night, there's a lamp glowing, and I hear soft snores next to me. Turning around toward Tripp, I study his features up close and personal. The scruff covering his sharp jawline. The light dusting of freckles on his cheeks that are only visible if you're looking for them. His dark eyelashes that are somehow longer than mine. And his perfect lips that I never want to stop kissing.

I still can't believe that after all this time pining over him, he's finally mine.

Now I just need to make sure my past stays in the past, and I don't lose him.

Chapter Twenty-One
Tripp

Waking up with Magnolia in my bed and in my arms is a wild dream come true. I hate that she got sick from all the sugar, but I enjoyed holding her all night.

It's also the best night of sleep I've had in years. Typically, I have anxious thoughts and my mind doesn't shut off for hours. But last night, I rubbed her back until her breathing evened, and then I passed out moments later.

Unfortunately for me, I have work, so I sneak out from under the blankets as quietly as possible. She typically opens for business at the farmer's market downtown on Saturday mornings, but I'm not sure if she'll be up for it, so instead of waking her to ask, I leave her a note.

Sunny,

I put a fresh glass of water on the nightstand for you and a couple Tylenol in case you have a headache. Call me if you need a ride home or feel free to stay as long as you want and make yourself at home. I work until 4 and then if you're up for it, I'd love to hang out again tonight. I know I'm probably not as fun as Noah, but we can stay in and watch Dirty Dancing if you need another Patrick Swayze fix ;) No sugary foods, though.

Then I spend more time than I'd like to admit trying to figure out how to end it.

Love, Tripp

-Tripp

Always yours, Tripp

After several minutes, I say fuck it and just leave it without anything. She'll clearly know it's from me.

When I arrive at the family barn, I'm surprised when Dad greets me. He's usually at the retreat or The Lodge first thing.

"Hey, old man. What's goin' on?" I slide on my gloves and grab a pitchfork to get started on stalls.

He leans against a stall, looking exhausted. "It's Sydney. Been up with her half the night waitin' on the vet."

"Oh, shit. Does Landen know?"

He shakes his head. "Hasn't answered my calls or texts, so figured he's been sleepin'. Not much he can do anyway until we know what's wrong. She won't eat or drink. Hasn't had a bowel movement in twenty-four hours. Pretty sure she has a fever, too."

I look over the door and see Sydney lying down. My heart crushes seeing her in pain. Even though she's a little shit toward Franklin, she doesn't deserve this.

"She's probably constipated. I can give her a natural laxative."

"Tried that already..." He checks his watch. "Six hours ago."

"Damn. He's gonna have to go in and manually clear out the blockage before she gets worse."

"Should be here within the hour to check her, but yeah, it ain't gonna be a quick and easy fix. Even Franklin's been worried."

I chuckle at that and then, as if on cue, he releases a loud whine. Looking over at his stall, his head pops out and he lets out another one.

"It's alright, buddy." I go over and pet his nose, then check his stall to make sure he has droppings. He does, which means whatever Sydney has is most likely an isolated incident.

While we wait for Dr. Weston, I take a few of the horses out to the pasture and start on their stalls. When Landen finally shows up, Dad gives him a recap and then Landen sits with her until he arrives.

I stay out of the way, mucking stalls, and then refill their food and water buckets, but I can overhear mostly everything. Landen's worried sick as he rattles questions off and Dr. Weston tries to reassure him that he'll do everything he can to help Sydney.

After an initial check-up, Dr. Weston decides to do an enema first and then give her some pain meds for discomfort. When she's finally able to go, her stall is going to be a disaster, but I'd rather deal with that than have her go through more extreme measures like surgery.

"Doing okay?" I ask Landen when he walks over to a stall I'm sprinkling fresh straw in.

He lifts a shoulder as if he doesn't really know. "I hate feelin' helpless, and I'm low-key annoyed. We provide top-tier care and feed 'em the best. She gets daily exercise, fresh water, and routine exams. I don't understand how this happened. Especially if it turns out to be a parasite." He blows out a frustrated breath, lifts his cap, and brushes his hand through his hair before replacing the hat. I've not seen him this worked up in a long time.

"She could've eaten something that's causin' it. Shit, who knows what blows into the pasture that she ate. Could be a piece of twine or anything else. Doesn't mean we don't take proper care of 'em," I tell him, clapping his shoulder. "C'mon, let's talk about somethin' else to get it off your mind. Have you seen Ellie since the wedding reception?"

He shoots me a death glare, and I chuckle.

"Guess not."

"She hasn't been here since Noah left. She has a competition next weekend, so I assume she'll be back soon to train on her own."

"You memorized her schedule?" I taunt, laying down the last bit of straw for this stall.

He crosses his arms as he stands across from me. "Are you really in any position to give me shit about being an obsessive asshole?"

I flash him a lopsided grin. "But at least my obsessiveness paid off."

"Easy for you to say. Magnolia never despised you. I don't even know what I did to piss off Ellie. That's what doesn't make sense. I've been nothin' but nice to her."

"You constantly tease her when she's trainin'," I point out. "Every interaction I've witnessed with you two has been you makin' fun of something she was doing wrong. Her stance. Her *almost* knockin' down the barrel. Her timing being too slow. Or you taunt her on her outfit. Her hat and boots being *too* sparkly. You callin' her Pippi Longstocking because of her cowgirl braids. Maybe you could give her a compliment for once."

The corner of his top lip perches up in confusion. "But I say them in a flirty way! Not like I'm bullyin' her. And it's part of my job to critique her. If I kissed her ass and told her how amazing she was, she wouldn't push harder to get better."

"Noah's her trainer, not you," I counter.

He rolls his eyes. "Doesn't mean I don't have valid points when I watch her practice. And Noah usually agrees with me anyway."

I give him an easy shrug. "She clearly ain't feelin' your flirty vibes, so maybe try talkin' to her about something other than her career. I'm sure there's more to her personality than being a barrel racer. Ask her what other things she's interested in."

"Don't matter anyway if I did. After I gave her that bag of ice at the reception, she told me I wasn't invited to sit at the table with her and to go away. So even if I tried makin' conversation, she wouldn't be interested."

I laugh at his pitiful expression. "Damn, she's so under your skin."

He groans and then walks back toward Dad and Dr. Weston.

By the time I finish taking the horses out to the pasture and mucking stalls, Landen prepped all the feed and water buckets for me to distribute. He can't do anything about Sydney except wait, so at least he made himself useful.

I'm about to leave to go to the stables when my phone vibrates with a text, and I smile when I see who it's from.

MAGNOLIA

> I think you have the cleanest house of any guy I know. Haven't found a speck of dust or any expired food in the fridge. And yes, I checked every item.

I snort at her ability to easily brag about snooping.

TRIPP

> You're giving me shit for not having a filthy place? That has to mean you're feeling better.

MAGNOLIA

> Yes and no. My throat feels raw from throwing up, and I woke up with some heartburn. But I haven't gotten sick again, so silver lining, I guess.

TRIPP

> I'm sure you already found it but I have Tums in the medicine cabinet.

Stay With Me

MAGNOLIA

Okay now I'm gonna give you shit for having a medicine cabinet. What are you, 50?

TRIPP

Responsible adults have those, Sunny. You're telling me you don't keep meds or vitamins in your apartment?

MAGNOLIA

Well I guess if you consider birth control pills and a couple random blue ones I found.

TRIPP

I'm realizing now why your self-inspired latte is called Hot Mess Express.

MAGNOLIA

Don't say you weren't warned.

And then she sends an emoji of a smiley face sticking out its tongue.

TRIPP

Oh I fully knew what I was getting into with that mouth of yours.

MAGNOLIA

Speaking of mouth, you left without giving me a kiss :(

TRIPP

I didn't want to wake you, baby. I wasn't sure if you were getting up for work so I figured I'd let you sleep in.

MAGNOLIA

Mm-hmm. I'm sure it had nothing to do with my vomit breath.

TRIPP

I wasn't even thinking about that so shush.

MAGNOLIA

You could come home and make it up to me.

I groan as I contemplate doing just that. Landen's already going to be useless today, and I haven't even seen the twins out yet.

I send her a few kissy-face emojis and then add...

TRIPP

That'll have to do for now because I'm heading to the stables and we're already behind. But I promise when I get home, I'll give you more than a kiss ;)

Instead of responding, she sends a selfie from inside my shower. Fucking naked.

Goddamn her.

Shaking my head, I make a U-turn and drive toward the ranch hand quarters. *Fuck it.* I've covered the twins' asses enough times that they can handle the stables on their own today.

Once I've slammed my truck into park, I sprint into my house and start undressing as I make a beeline to the bathroom. Steam and the scent of my body wash smack me in the face when I open the door and then remove my socks and boxer shorts before opening the curtain.

"Change your mind, cowboy?" She smirks and my gaze falls down her body on full display for me. *Fucking beautiful.*

I step inside, close the curtain behind me, and then cup her damp face. I crash my mouth down on hers and shove my tongue between her lips, capturing her breathy moans. Her hands roam over my body as my fingers slide up into her wet hair, and I push her to the wall so the stream of water hits my back.

When she wraps her palm around my shaft and begins

stroking, I inhale sharply and try to gain some semblance of control. Magnolia and I have fooled around a lot these past couple of weeks, but we've never been completely naked together. Her body is unbelievably out of this world, but it's the way hers responds to my touch that gets mine hot.

"Fuck, Sunny. You're too good at that," I hiss through the pleasure I'm trying to refrain from taking over. I come way too fast when she's touching me.

I slide my hand down her leg and hike it up around the top of my thigh until I can reach her pussy from behind. As I rub her clit, her head tilts back, and I suck her neck.

"Careful," she breathes out. "If you mark me, I get to do the same to you."

At this point, I don't care who knows we're together even if we're waiting until Noah gets back, I'd proudly admit it if someone asked.

I chuckle, sliding my tongue up to her ear. "You forget I've already marked myself for you. There's no question who I've always belonged to."

She releases a gasp when I thrust a finger inside her cunt.

"Ain't that right, my Sunflower?"

Her lips part and she nods, but no words come out.

"Say it, baby. Who do I belong to?"

I add a second finger and drive in deeper as she squeezes my cock harder.

"Me," she finally says. "Only me."

"Goddamn right, Sunny. And you're *mine*."

I slam my mouth down on hers again and work her pussy until she writhes against me.

"I'm so close. Don't stop," she pleads.

"Hang on." I kneel between her thighs, place her leg over my shoulder, and suck her clit while my fingers fill her cunt.

"Oh my God, Tripp." Her fingers thread through my hair as I devour her sweetness. She tightens around me, and I know she's almost there, so I twist my wrist and reach for her G-spot. "Yes, right there."

Her heavy breathing fills the shower, my lips sucking and flicking her clit until moments later, she unravels with an ear-piercing scream-moan. The taste of her orgasm consumes my mouth, and my painfully hard cock can't take it anymore. Giving it one long stroke, I come undone with a loud groan.

Tilting my head up to her stare, I smirk at her little pouty expression. "Feelin' you come on my face had me losin' control. Sorry, sweetheart." I stand and kiss her lips. "You can finish me off next time."

She reaches between us and takes my cock in her hand. "This is *mine*. You don't touch yourself when I'm around."

I chuckle at how serious she sounds. "All yours, sweetheart."

When I notice she shivers, I move her underneath the water and turn it on as hot as it'll go. Instead of rushing to go back to work, I take my time washing her hair and lathering soap all over her body. I spend extra time massaging her breasts and playing with her hard nipples. With her back pressed to my chest, she leans against me, and I continue working her perfect tits and kissing her neck.

"I wish we could stay here all day." She smiles up at me when I towel-dry her hair.

"Me too, love." I kiss the tip of her nose. "But I gotta finish muckin' stalls and then check on Landen and Sydney."

"Oh no, what happened?"

I explain everything that I know so far while we get dressed and then she says she's going to visit her parents today since she skipped the Farmer's Market.

"How're they doing?" I ask because she rarely brings them up and it's always seemed like a topic she didn't want to discuss.

"Well, after pleading with my dad for the past few years, he finally moved them into an assisted living home. He doesn't need it for him, but it became a safety issue anytime he left my mom alone. She'd turn on the stovetop and forget she was boiling a pot of water or turn the oven to five hundred degrees and burn the food. He'd return from work with the fire department out there. There's been a few occasions where she'd run a bath and never turn off the water, so it'd just flood into the rest of the house. Every time he calls, I anticipate him tellin' me the house burned down or worse, Mama accidentally killed herself."

"Wow, Sunny. I'm sorry. Are things better now that they moved?"

"Yeah, I think so. They have sensors and alarms for everything there. And Dad added cameras so he can watch her while he's at work. They started hiding her meds in her food or she'd refuse to take 'em, so I'm hoping today's a good day for me to visit."

My chest aches at how much she's dealt with on her own. I remember Noah begging Mom to let Magnolia sleep over every weekend and she'd basically live at our house over summers.

I didn't understand then how rough it was, but seeing her now as an adult, I'm amazed at how far she's come.

I grab her hand and pull her closer. "I'm really proud of you, Sunny."

She wraps her arms around my waist. "For what?"

"Given the circumstances, you could've easily taken a different path to deal with your problems, but instead you worked your ass off to get what you wanted. That takes courage and a lot of strength. You should be proud of yourself, too."

She's silent, and I tilt her chin until her eyes find mine. "And even if you don't wanna hear it, I'm gonna say it anyway because you deserve to know. You have a heart of gold, you're stronger than you realize, and loyal to a fault. I adore your ability to just go with the flow and not take shit from anyone. And if anyone asks how I got someone like you, I'll fully admit you're the catch in this relationship, and I just got lucky."

Tears well in the corner of her eyes as she sucks in her lips. I know it's way too soon to tell her how hard I'm falling for her, but it shouldn't be a secret at this point. My little high school crush turned into a full-on obsession long before I was ready to admit it.

"That's honestly the sweetest thing anyone's ever said to me, and I'm not quite sure how to take it." She closes her eyes and the tears fall down her face.

I brush the pads of my thumbs over her cheeks before pressing my lips to hers. "You don't have to say anything, Sunny."

She wraps her arms around my neck and pulls me in for a hug. I hold her tight as she buries her face in my neck, and we stay like that for several minutes before she exhales a deep breath and steps back.

"Are you sure you have time to take me home?" she asks.

"Yep. I'll text Waylon and make sure they cover me until I'm back."

She's silent on the drive into town but squeezes my hand. When I pull up to her apartment building, I jump out and open her door.

"Thank you."

I pull her in for a kiss and am tempted to get lost in her lips, but I know we both have shit to do.

"Text me later if you wanna hang out and watch a movie," I tell her.

"I might need a couple hours to decompress after I get home from visitin' my parents, but I definitely will let you know."

I give her a final peck and then watch as she walks toward her door. Then I honk twice and wave before driving away.

My phone rings when I pull out of the parking lot. It's Landen.

"Yeah?"

"It's Sydney. Dr. Weston's preppin' her for surgery."

"Oh fuck. I'm on my way back to the ranch from Magnolia's. Be there in fifteen."

Chapter Twenty-Two
Magnolia

I give Tripp a final wave before walking toward my apartment. Since I've already showered, I just need to put on clean clothes and eat something. I snagged the shirt Tripp let me sleep in and added it to the other one he gave me. It's overwhelming how strong my feelings have grown for him in such a short time, and it's obvious he has the same ones for me, which is why I froze after he told me the sweetest words I've ever heard. I'm not used to having a boyfriend who showers me with kindness and isn't afraid to tell me exactly what's on his mind.

And how fucking sad is that?

It took me off guard how easy it was for him to tell me how proud of me he was. I don't think my own father has even said those words to me. Though it's not because he isn't. He just isn't a man of many words.

But it's nice to hear them once in a while.

After I change and stuff a granola bar into my mouth, I text my dad to let him know I'm on my way.

When I get to my SUV and see something under my windshield wipers, I stop dead in my tracks. I've seen enough videos on social media talking about various traps for human trafficking that include distracting someone outside their vehicles with money or flyers on their car so they can grab you from behind.

Not today, Satan.

I grab my taser from my bag and hold it in my hand while I circle around to check my surroundings. A few of my neighbors are outside smoking and another is walking their dog. It's the middle of the day in a somewhat busy parking lot, so I'd hope if anyone hears me screaming, they'd come to rescue me, but again, I'm not depending on anyone to save me.

Hesitantly, I get closer to my car and keep my taser stretched out in my hand. As I step toward the windshield, I notice a single-stem rose and a folded piece of paper.

Son of a bitch. That better not be from who I think it's from.

Yanking it out from underneath the wiper, I grab it and quickly unlock my car to jump inside.

I toss the rose onto my passenger's side, and although I don't give a shit what he says, I want to make sure it's not from some random creep.

I'm sorry for what happened the other day. I just miss you and wish you'd give me another chance. I know I was part of the problem in the past, but I've changed. I want us to live together and plan our future.

Please forgive me.

-Travis

Did he honestly write he was *part* of the problem?
Oh, you stupid fucker. You're the whole-ass problem.
His level of delusion is honestly astounding. I've got to give it

to him, though, for not giving up after I kicked him in the balls
and threatened him with bodily harm.

It's one thing to be a shitty partner, but Travis has literally
tried gaslighting me over what my own eye color is. He claimed
they were green like lima beans, and I looked him dead in his eyes
and said, *they're brown*. He went on for ten minutes about how they
were in fact not brown. I almost considered he was color-blind
before realizing he just couldn't handle being wrong.

I crinkle up the paper to throw in my back seat, but then I
think better of it. If he continues harassing me after I've already
told him no and I need to get a restraining order, I'll need proof
for the courts. So instead, I flatten and fold it up and then set it
down next to the rose so I'll remember to take it into my
apartment with me.

As I drive through town, the sheriff's SUV and fire
department's truck block the corner of Main and First Street. It's
usually blocked off for the farmer's market, but that should be
over now. This looks like something else completely.

I reroute and go down another street toward Sage Meadow
Homes. It's been a month since I've visited and no matter how
often or not I come, I always feel a bit nervous.

"Hi, sweetie." Dad opens the door, smiling around his long
salt-and-pepper beard that matches his shaggy hair.

"Hey." I walk in and give him a hug. "How're things today?"

He shrugs with a frown, closing the door behind me. "She no
's in a depressive cycle."

I nod, understanding what that means. It's the version I saw of
her the most growing up. Sometimes we'd just sit together while
she watched TV and she'd randomly talk to me about the
characters in her show as if they were real people. I've seen
random *Grey's Anatomy* episodes, never in order, but I could tell
you every single main character's name and what their specialty is
based on how much my mom talks about them. Alex and Meredith
are her favorites. And according to her, screw Dr. Burke.

219

"I put a pot on. Want some?"

Considering I haven't had an ounce of caffeine, that sounds perfect. "Yes, please. Do you have—"

"Sugar-free hazelnut creamer? Just grabbed some from the store for ya this mornin'."

I smile as I sit down at the little kitchen table. "Thanks, Dad."

He brings over two mugs and the creamer. Then he sets out a little platter of strawberry Fig Newton's with a scoop of peanut butter for dipping. It's been our thing for as long as I can remember. It tastes like a mini PB&J.

"How come you didn't work downtown today?" He takes the seat across from me, dips his cookie, and then dunks it into his mug.

"I was sick last night and slept in."

"Are you feelin' well now?" he asks.

"Better, yeah. I ended up eatin' popcorn, candy, and a slushie in a two-hour period, so it upset my stomach. Guess I'm not twelve anymore." I laugh, stirring in my creamer.

The scanner Dad always has on goes off and makes me jump. "Holy crap, that scared me."

"Sorry." He lowers the volume. "Been going off all mornin'. Brinkley's Jewelry got robbed last night."

My jaw drops. "That must be why Main Street was blocked off."

"Yep, they smashed a brick through the window and broke through all the glass cabinets. Must've been a speedy fella because the alarm company got the deputies out in seven minutes and they were already gone."

"Wow. How sad for the Brinkley family."

"Second robbery in town this month," he tells me. "The pawn shop got hit two weeks ago."

My brows shoot up because it's already uncommon to have one robbery in Sugarland Creek, but to have two? Nearly unheard of.

"Sounds like it coulda been the same person, then," I suggest.

"That's what I think, too. The guys at work and I were talkin' about it earlier this week, and it sounds like there was only one workin' camera in the pawnshop. But whoever it was kept their head down and had a mask over their mouth. We'll have to wait and see if there were any similarities with the jewelry shop, but considering the window got smashed in with a brick at the pawnshop, too...someone's on a robbery rampage."

"Well, that's concernin'. I park my trailer in the parking lot a few blocks away. Not that I keep cash inside the register, but they could break in thinkin' I do and trash it. Or take my expensive espresso machine."

"Not sure how valuable that'd be in terms of the black market resale. Sounds like they're hittin' the stores with bigger markups."

My mouth gapes open. "That machine cost nearly four grand!"

"Really? My coffee maker was on sale for thirty bucks." He smirks around the rim of his mug.

I snort. "Totally the same."

After Dad and I talk over coffee and cookies, he tells me Mom's in bed watching her shows. I head down the hallway and peek inside to make sure she's not asleep before walking in.

"Hey, Mama."

"Magnolia, sweetheart." Her face lights up when I sit on the bed next to her and wrap an arm around her for a hug.

"How're you feelin' today?" I ask, then sit back against the headboard, studying her over.

We share a lot of the same similarities, down to our dark hair and eyes. She looks much younger than her mid-sixties age, but she's never been one to wear makeup, smoke, or stay out in the sun for hours.

"Oh, I'm okay." She grins softly. "Woke up with a crick in my neck, so I'm gonna soak in the bath after supper."

"Do you want me to massage it? I can try to rub out the knot."

She turns back toward the TV. "No, you don't have to. I'll be okay."

I nod, feeling awkward. Sometimes she's in a chatty mood and other times we just sit in silence.

"Have you read any good books lately?" I ask when I notice the stack of hardcovers on the nightstand.

"My eyes aren't so good anymore, so your dad's been readin' to me an hour each night before bed."

"Aw, that's cute. I'm sure Daddy loves doing that for you."

"Sometimes I listen to the audiobooks," she says, keeping her focus on the screen.

"I love listening to podcasts when I'm at home cleanin' and stuff. Makes it go by faster. Maybe I'll try an audiobook next time. Any recommendations?"

She lists off two book titles I've never heard of before.

"Oh, I'll have to look them up. Might be better than listenin' to the Wines and Crimes podcast before bed now that there's a criminal on the loose." I chuckle lightly although it's not at all funny.

I stay for two more episodes of *The Big Bang Theory* before Dad pops in and brings Mom her afternoon snack. I suspect it has her meds in it, which is why he's adamant she eats it.

After a few more minutes, I kiss Mom's cheek goodbye and promise to visit her again soon.

Dad and I walk out of the bedroom and toward the kitchen where I left my bag.

"Forgot to tell ya. I ran into that ex-boyfriend of yours a few days ago at the gas station. He stopped to say hi, but I pretended I didn't hear him and walked away. Don't like that boy."

I snort. "Join the club. He wants to get back together."

His brow arches and concern flashes across his face.

"I'm not interested, don't worry. Actually, I'm dating someone else now."

He tilts his head. "Do I know him?"

"Technically, yes. But I don't think you know much about him."

"Well, out with it. Who is he?"

Nerves settle into my gut as I say the words aloud. "It's one of Noah's brothers, Tripp."

He folds his arms over his beer belly. "That the goofy-lookin' one who always looks like he's tryna solve a math problem?"

"*What?*" I bark out a laugh. "Who is that?"

Probably Wilder.

He lifts his shoulder. "So which one is Tripp?"

Instead of trying to describe him, I find a photo of him on my phone from Noah's wedding.

"Nice-lookin' fella. He treatin' ya right?"

"Better than any man could, Dad. Literally the sweetest guy I've ever met."

He nods once. "Good. I'd like to meet him, then."

"I'm sure you will. I haven't told Noah since she's on her honeymoon, but as soon as we're public, we can plan a lunch."

Once I grab my things and hug him, he walks me to the door. "Take care, sweetie. Come back soon, okay?"

I lean up and kiss his cheek. "I will, Dad. Love you."

After I get to my car, I check my phone and see several unread messages.

TRIPP

> Sydney's in surgery. Landen's a mess. Maybe you should try texting him because he won't talk to me.

My heart drops at the thought of Landen losing her. I know how much he loves that horse, even if he acts too big and tough to have feelings.

MAGNOLIA

I'm leaving my parents' right now and can come over. How are you doing?

TRIPP

Keeping busy.

MAGNOLIA

Where is he?

TRIPP

Sitting at our parents' house with Mom.

MAGNOLIA

Okay, I'll drive right over.

It's a fifteen-minute drive out to the ranch, and once I park in front of the main house, I hop out and knock on the front door. The Hollises live in a Southern dream. A wraparound porch, flowers on the windowsills, and rustic vibes all through their home. I loved visiting every weekend and daydreaming of having a home like this when I got married and had kids.

"Hi, sweetie. Come in." Dena opens the door for me, and I enter, then give her a hug.

"Hey. I heard Landen was here."

"In the kitchen with Gramma Grace and Mallory."

I follow her until I see a sad Landen chugging a beer.

"Want some sweet tea, dear?" Dena asks.

"Yes, please. Thank you."

I set down my bag and then pull out the chair next to Landen. Instead of pressing him to talk, I curl my arm through his and lean my forehead on his bicep. There's no denying we love giving each other shit and messing around, but he's also one of my closest friends. Seeing him hurt makes me hurt, too.

"Any update?" I ask softly.

"Not yet," Mallory answers. Her eyes are red as if she's been crying.

I reach over and squeeze her hand.

She loves horses as much as Noah does, but she's only lived here for a few years, so I don't think she's had to experience the pain of losing one. I remember they lost one back in high school and Noah cried for days.

The worst part now is Noah's at an unplugged resort, so we can't even get ahold of her to tell her what's going on. I like the idea of her getting away for two weeks to enjoy spending time with her new husband without interruptions, but it sucks when there's an emergency.

Gramma Grace brings over a pan of Brookie bars and a handful of plates. I grab two, put a bar on each, and then set one in front of Landen. Dena pours the drinks and we eat in silence.

When the front door creaks open, we sit up straighter in anticipation. Landen's dad appears, and he's wearing a frown.

"Any news?" Dena asks him.

"She went into shock. Her heart's strugglin' to keep up, but Dr. Weston cleared out the blockage and has her sedated for now."

"Why can't her heart keep up?" Mallory asks the same question I was wondering.

"Not sure, sweetheart. She may have a genetic heart condition. We'll do some testing once she rests a few days."

"What's the recovery rate?" Landen's harsh tone blurts out.

Garrett shrugs. "Too hard to know for sure. Shoulda been an easy procedure, but considering there were complications tells me there's something else going on."

"I don't want her to suffer. When it's time, we should..." Landen chokes on his words as if he's holding back tears. "We just shouldn't let her suffer, is all."

Garrett circles the table and claps Landen's shoulder. "We won't."

Chapter Twenty-Three
Tripp

The past few days have been hell for Landen, and even when I try to talk to him about something else, he either ignores me or grunts out a response. I haven't seen him this way since his ex broke up with him in high school. Landen's not one to process his feelings with words. Instead, he's hiding out in the middle of the woods with a case of beer and an axe.

I'm not sure how long he's been out here, but it's safe to say we have enough chopped wood to last the retreat for the rest of winter.

"It's gettin' cold out here," I say, approaching him delicately so he doesn't whip the axe at me.

"Then take your scrawny bitch ass back inside."

His tone is crude and harsh, but I bark out a laugh at his ability to insult me so easily.

He slices through another chunk of wood and the pieces go flying.

"C'mon, man. Let me take you home. Magnolia's worried about you. She keeps askin' why you aren't responding to her texts."

"Because I have nothin' to say."

Another chop.

"I know you're in pain, but drunk wood choppin' is just gonna send you to the ER."

He ignores me and cuts through another stump. "Do you remember when Noah helped me rescue her? She was just skin and bones."

I nod because that day was absolutely nuts. We don't make it a habit of stealing horses, but it was obvious Sydney was neglected. Her owner couldn't afford the cost, and instead of giving her away to someone who could take care of her, they just left her in a barn to die. Landen got a tip from a neighbor, and one night, he and Noah snuck into the barn. Our sister is basically a horse whisperer, which is why Landen dragged her along. But when the flashlights and break-in spooked Sydney, it was not Noah she wanted. Landen held out his hand and spoke softly to her, telling her they were there to help her. She immediately warmed up to him and came up to him. Once she was close enough, he was able to slide the halter around her neck and get her inside the trailer.

Once she was ours and got a full health check, we realized she had a laundry list of health issues from being malnourished and having overgrown hooves. Landen took her under his wing and even paid for all her treatments himself. He trained her for riding, and eventually, she was healthy enough for ranch work too. He was so proud to have Sydney as his own and kept up the responsibilities of making sure she got all her vaccines and annual physical exams.

"You gave her a good life," I tell him when he stays silent. "She woulda died much sooner if it wasn't for you."

"I should've kept a closer eye on her," he mutters. "Then I'd have seen the signs before she got worse."

"You couldn't have known, Landen. A genetic heart condition isn't easy to diagnose. The signs weren't obvious enough to know we needed to do those types of tests."

"It's fuckin' bullshit." He raises his arms over his head and then slams the axe through another block. "She coulda had so many healthy years left in her had she been on meds for it."

There's nothing more I can say to change the outcome or how he feels about it. We didn't know Sydney was sick before we approved her for the surgery. There was no way to know it'd be too hard on her heart and she'd go into a cardiac shock. When there was no improvement after forty-eight hours, Dr. Weston said it was only a matter of time before her heart would stop completely. Instead of letting her suffer, Landen demanded he give her the meds to let her go peacefully.

My parents and siblings stood around Sydney's stall as Landen sat next to her. She lifted her head just enough to look at him before Dr. Weston injected her with the sedation and then seconds later, the euthanasia drug mixture.

After she was confirmed gone, there wasn't a dry eye in the barn. Magnolia kneeled behind Landen and rubbed his back as silent tears fell down his cheeks. And later when we were alone, I pulled her into my arms while she let out her own.

A loud engine roaring breaks me out of my memories. Two loud, rowdy voices echo in the distance, and soon, Wilder and Waylon are charging through the woods to us.

"Y'all havin' a woods party without us?" Wilder scoffs, carrying a twenty-four pack of beer. "Now the real fun can begin."

Waylon grabs a can and sits next to me on one of the trunks. "He doin' okay?" He nods toward Landen, who's still chopping away.

"Whaddya think, asshole?" I shake my head. "And no party. We're just...hangin' out."

"Sounds fuckin' boring." Wilder cracks open his beer and sits next to Waylon. "Where's the music? The chicks?"

"Probably at the bar," I murmur.

We sit in silence as we watch Landen. None of us know what to say or do to make him feel better, so instead of forcing him to talk, we continue drinking, and I keep a close eye on him. Even if he doesn't want our company, he's getting it anyway.

"So what's up with you and Magnolia?" Wilder blurts out to no one in particular, and I can't grasp if he's asking me or Landen.

"What're you talkin' about?" I finally ask when Landen continues his silent treatment.

"Wonderin' if he still has a crush on her or if she's open season." When he waggles his brows, I crush the empty beer can in my palm and fight the temptation to throw it at his face.

"Fuck off. She's not a piece of meat," I say instead.

"Told ya." Waylon smirks back at Wilder as if they're in on some twin secret.

"Told him what?" I ask.

"You're the one who wants her, not Landen. And that reaction proves I'm right." Waylon points at Wilder. "Cough up my money."

"Y'all made a bet?"

"Wilder was so sure that she and Landen were foolin' around, but I bet fifty bucks that it was you she was after," Waylon explains.

"That doesn't prove anything," Wilder argues. "Tripp's always defended her. So until I see it with my own eyes, I'm not payin' you shit."

"Dude! You're such a cheap ass." Waylon shakes his head, sucking down the rest of his beer.

I neither confirm nor deny helping Waylon win his money. It serves them right for always getting in my business and being nosy fuckers.

"I'm not datin' Magnolia," Landen speaks minutes later. He finally drops the axe and shakes out his arm. "But I know who is. Does that mean I get money from both of ya?"

I glare at him, but he's not looking at me. Is he honestly going to throw me under the bus for a hundred bucks?

"You're bluffin'," Waylon says. "You don't know."

"She's one of my best friends. Why wouldn't I?" Landen counters, opening a new beer.

I'm happy he's finally talking, but I could've done without the topic of my girlfriend.

"He's gotta point," Wilder says. "Okay, so tell us. Who's her new guy? And can I kick his ass?"

Waylon howls out a laugh. "Magnolia wouldn't date you even if she were single."

"No, I think even if he were the last man on Earth, she'd still reject him." Landen laughs at Wilder's expense, and I stay frozen, waiting to hear where Landen takes this.

Wilder stands and swings his arm around in a roping motion. "She couldn't handle all this anyway."

Waylon tosses one of the empty cans at him and then brings his attention back to Landen. "So are you gonna say who it is or not?"

Landen briefly catches my gaze before snapping it back to Waylon's. "Nah. Bestie code."

"Motherfucker!" Wilder tosses up his arms.

I bring my beer to my lips to hide the smile spreading across my face. Five minutes later, and the twins are already talking shit about something else.

But the mention of Magnolia has me missing her even more. It's been an emotional week and all our free time has been spent in the barn with Sydney or in the house with Landen. We continue to text and FaceTime, but I'm dying for Friday to roll around so we can have our sleepover redo. She's bringing over her holiday drinks so I can taste test and if all goes right, she'll be stripped down to nothing before the evening ends.

I check my phone as my brothers continue shooting the shit and getting wasted.

MAGNOLIA

How are things going with Landen?

TRIPP

Well, he finally stopped chopping and is now drinking with the twins.

Stay With Me

MAGNOLIA

> He's gonna hurt for a while. It's good y'all are spending time with him. Keep his mind busy.

TRIPP

> I'm trying. The twins brought up your name, and I had to resist blurting out that you were mine, and they better stop getting ideas.

MAGNOLIA

> So damn possessive.

Then she adds a blushing smiley emoji.

TRIPP

> Protective. And okay, maybe a little obsessive.

MAGNOLIA

> Just a smidge...

TRIPP

> Speaking of, where are you?

MAGNOLIA

> Taking a bath. Wanna see?

TRIPP

> Yes, but I really don't need a boner with my brothers around.

MAGNOLIA

> I'm sure you can use your imagination, cowboy.

TRIPP

> You have no fucking idea. I don't think I can wait two more days to touch you.

MAGNOLIA

> Don't worry, baby. I plan to make the wait so, so worth it ;)

I can hear her sweet, seductive voice in my head, and that's all it takes for my cock to wake up.

Fuck.

Her calling me baby is new. *And I like it, a lot.*

Landen decides he's done and asks me to drive him home. Wilder and Waylon opt to stay and have a wood-chopping contest.

"You morons better not call me in ten minutes because someone chopped off a foot," I warn before leaving them behind.

It's times like these Noah would be the logical one and take the axe away from them, but I'm not in the mood for a fight. If they wanna be dumbasses, then by all means.

Landen climbs in my truck and slumps against the door.

"No throwin' up in here," I taunt.

He scoffs. "I don't get sick from beer."

"Last night, you were doing shots of tequila, so at least beer's a step away from a cry for help."

He lifts his shoulder. "Whatever numbs the pain."

I know that feeling all too well.

"It's a temporary fix, Landen. I know you're hurtin', but alcohol won't solve your problems."

"Maybe not, but it sure as hell beats the overwhelming sadness."

I blow out an uncertain breath, white-knuckling the steering wheel as we get closer to home. "I think Franklin actually misses her, too. He was snippy with me all mornin'."

"They were in the makin' of their own enemies-to-lovers romance story."

My lips part as I bark out a laugh. "What do you know about romance books?"

"I was listenin' to Noah and Magnolia talk about one they were reading."

"You mean eavesdropping."

"A man's gotta learn somehow." The corner of his mouth teases a smile. "There was some knife to the throat scene they were going feral over."

My brow etches up in interest. "Who was holdin' the knife?"

"The chick and then when the guy leaned forward with a smirk, they squealed like a bunch of seagulls."

I laugh at that because that definitely sounds like Noah and Magnolia.

"Sounds like it could be your enemies-to-lovers moment between you and Ellie."

"Pfft. She'd take the knife and just stab me in the heart with it."

"You sure? She did give you a condolence card."

"That just means she's not a heartless bitch. Doesn't mean she *likes* me."

"Ya never know." I shrug. "Crazier shit has happened."

When I park in front of our duplex, I look over, and he's frowning.

"Wanna hang out for a bit and play GTA?"

He shrugs but then nods. "I wouldn't mind kickin' your ass."

"So overconfident of your skills." We jump out of the truck, and I follow him up to his place.

Even though I rarely play video games and admittingly suck at them, I'll deal with losing if it means Landen doesn't spend the night sulking alone.

Chapter Twenty-Four
Magnolia

This Friday's busier than it's been previously at the retreat, and I can hardly keep up as customers form a line at my trailer. It's a good problem to have, and I'm grateful for the business, but I'm so damn anxious for this weekend I can hardly focus.

It doesn't help that this week has been an emotional rollercoaster, and I've felt a bit off. But I've been waiting for tonight with Tripp for the past several days and am not letting anything get in the way now.

I hand off a customer's latte, and when I see the man standing behind her, an uneasy shiver runs through me.

He stands tall in an all-black suit, with his hands in his pockets and a sly smirk on his lips. His gaze lowers down to my chest and then back up again. Sugarland Creek's population is two thousand, and most of the locals are ranchers, work on one, or own a small business. And he doesn't look like any of those. He's even too dressed up to be one of the two lawyers in town.

Assuming he's staying at one of the cabins here, he still sticks out like a sore thumb. Most of the guests come for horseback rides, mountain biking, fishing, or any of the other numerous outdoor activities they offer.

"Hello, welcome to Magnolia's. How can I caffeinate you this mornin'?" I continue with my usual introduction to new customers.

"Good morning. Can I assume you're Magnolia?" His little flirty tone has me eager to reach for my bag where I not only keep my taser but my new pepper spray and brass kitty knuckles. Even if they're pink and sparkly, they could cause real harm when I need them to.

"Yep, the one and only."

"That's a beautiful name for a beautiful woman."

Without sounding dramatic, I'm certain my breakfast just came up my throat, but I force a smile and swallow it down.

"Thanks. How can I help you?"

"Just a black coffee, please." He reaches into his suit coat and takes out his wallet. "Actually, those muffins are calling my name. I'll get one of those, too."

I smile because I spent three hours last night baking my new double-choco pumpkin-flavored muffins. At least the creepy stranger has good taste.

"Good pick. They're perfect for the fall season, too."

Even though Thanksgiving is next week and the town will turn into full-on Christmas mode, I'm holding onto these muffin fall flavors as long as I can.

Once I have his coffee and bagged pastry on the counter, I input his order into the cash register.

"That'll be seven-fifty, please."

He hands me a twenty. "Keep the change, *Magnolia*."

I don't like the way he says my name or holds onto the bill a second too long before releasing it. And I especially don't like when he winks at me as if I'm in on some creepy secret.

But for the sake of staying professional, I thank him and put the rest in my tip jar.

"Have a great rest of your day," I say, hoping he gets the hint to walk away.

When he finally does, I help the customer behind him but subtly watch as he goes to his blacked-out Denali.

Yeah, he's definitely not from here.

By the time I finish work, take an everything shower—where I exfoliate, do a hair mask with avocado oil, extra moisturizer, and shave every inch of unwanted body hair—get dressed with my new black lingerie underneath, pack an overnight bag, and collect all my coffee ingredients, it's after six before I get to Tripp's place. He's freshly clean and looking even more delicious than usual.

"I've missed you." He captures my lips before I even step inside.

"Mm...I've missed you more." I lean into the kiss as he cups my cheeks and then I slide my hands around his waist. "I have a couple bags to bring in."

"Stay here. I'll grab 'em for you." He pecks my lips once more before going out to my car, and I wait for him at the breakfast bar.

I watch as he effortlessly carries in my mini espresso maker from home, my bag of syrups, milk, and toppings, and then my overnight bag.

"I can't believe you brought this all in with one trip."

"I'm used to liftin' two hay bales at a time for a solid hour. This was nothing."

He flexes his biceps as if to prove his point, and I laugh at how confident he looks.

"Oh, would you mind grabbin' my purse for me, please? It's on the passenger seat."

"Yep." He kisses my temple as I stand and start organizing everything.

My espresso maker from home isn't as precise as my expensive one in the trailer, but it'll do for taste testing. I have three new flavor combos I want him to try and maybe a fourth if he still hasn't stripped me down to nothing.

"Magnolia."

Tripp's deep drawl using my real name has an icy shiver running down my spine. When I meet his eyes, they're lethal as he holds up the rose and note from Travis I was supposed to take into my apartment last weekend. The rose is withering from days without water, but all I can focus on is Tripp's tense jaw and tight grip on the piece of paper.

"What is this?" He slams them down on the counter. "And what the fuck did he do to you that he's apologizing?"

I flinch at how angry he sounds. Telling him about him coming into my trailer will get him even more fired up.

"What aren't you tellin' me?" he prompts when I stay silent. When I struggle to get out the words, he steps closer, grabs my hand, and then tilts my chin until our gazes meet. "Sunny, tell me. *Please.*"

Finally, I blow out a hesitant breath and nod.

"He's been beggin' me to take him back, and when I blocked his number, he showed up when I was closing. When he wouldn't leave, I kicked him in the balls, stepped on his wrist, and threatened him with my taser. Then I might've said something along the lines of the Hollis boys digging me a six-foot hole and helpin' me push his body inside."

"Jesus Christ," he mutters with a breathy laugh. "When was this?"

"Last Tuesday when you got held up at The Lodge."

"That motherfucker." He scrubs a hand over his jaw. "Why didn't you tell me?"

"The last thing I want is for you to get in trouble again because of me. I didn't want you to get involved because Travis is nothing to me and he's not worth going to jail for."

He cups my face and plucks my lower lip out from my teeth. "Stop worryin' about me and feelin' guilty about what happened last time.

Even knowin' I'd have to do a hundred hours of community service, I'd do it all over again if it meant keepin' you safe and away from him."

"He's just lookin' for trouble and if you give him a reason, he'll fight you. I don't wanna see you get hurt either. So it's better if you stay away from him."

He barks out a humorless laugh. "No, sweetheart. It's better for *him* to stay away from *me*. And most importantly, away from *my* girlfriend. Perhaps he needs a reminder not to touch what's mine..."

I groan at his implications. "See, this is exactly why I didn't tell you."

With a brow arched, he asks, "Have there been any other unwanted visits or letters since then?"

"No. I was only keepin' the note in case of a restraining order, and I'd need proof for the sheriff."

"Save everything." He grabs my hands and holds them to his chest as he closes the gap between us. "If he does anything else, you need to tell me. Promise, Sunny."

Reluctantly, I nod. "I just got pepper spray and kitty knuckles too. So you shouldn't be too worried about me. I took care of him by myself."

"But you shouldn't have to nor do I want him around you. If he can't get over you breakin' up with him over two years ago, he's unhinged at this point."

My chest tightens at the words trapped in my throat. The ones where I confess we hooked up four weeks ago and that's what prompted his obsession to get back together.

But the truth would only hurt him, especially seeing his reaction to Travis being near me. Tripp would want to kill him for real if he knew we'd slept together. And he'd most likely hate me for it, too.

"I can take care of myself," I remind him. "But I don't think he's gonna bother me anymore, so there's no need to worry."

He takes my mouth and delivers the most delicious harsh kiss

I've ever experienced. Tongue lapping at mine, strong hold on my cheeks, moaning between breaths. My fingers dig into his hips as I cling to his body, desperate for more.

After breaking our kiss, he leans his forehead against mine. "I'll always worry when it comes to you, Sunny. Even though I've witnessed you makin' grown men cry—hell, women too—but that doesn't mean I want you dealin' with assholes on your own. We're a team now. If someone's giving you shit, I wanna know about it. Got it?"

Grinning, my heart flutters at him calling us a *team*. I've never depended on anyone else except Noah, and even then, I don't like her being involved in anything regarding Travis drama. I'd rather forget he exists.

"Okay, deal." I wrap my arms around his neck and slide my fingers into his hair. "As long as that goes both ways and I get to know if any chicks are after you."

"With you on my mind every second of every day, I don't even pay attention to anyone else to know if they are. You never have to worry about that, baby." He grips my chin and pulls my lips to his. "But in the event I get a stalker, you and your kitty knuckles will be the first to know."

A laugh bubbles out of me at his smart-ass comment. "Don't underestimate the knuckles until you see how much pain they can cause." Then I lower my hand to his groin and palm the outline of his cock. "Especially here."

His eyes widen and he shakes his head, grabbing my wrist. "I don't trust you with sharp objects near my junk."

I snicker. "Good, then you know to be scared of me and my weapons."

"Cute." He lowers his hand to my ass and gives it a little smack. "Now, didn't you promise me a lingerie strip show?"

"Ha! After you taste test my drinks. Then if you're a good boy, I'll give you a personal viewing."

Tripp buries his face in my neck and growls in my ear,

pressing his erection into my stomach. "Then you better make it fast."

I'm seconds away from saying screw it and tearing off his clothes before he backs away, then sits at the breakfast bar. I stare at how sexy he looks in his plain T-shirt and backward baseball cap. It's basic, nothing special, but he wears it like a professional country boy model. And I'm tempted as hell to climb into his lap.

"What's the first one?" he asks, knocking me out of my trance.

"Um...well, it's a traditional peppermint mocha, but in mine, I put a pump of vanilla syrup for added sweetness and top it with whipped cream, dark chocolate drizzle, and candy cane pieces."

He grins. "Sounds pretty good."

"I hope so."

He updates me about Landen while I set up my espresso machine. I feel terrible for what he's going through, and I've tried reaching out, but he's not wanted to talk. Watching him cry over Sydney was one of the saddest moments I've ever witnessed him go through.

After I steam the milk, I grab one of his mugs and line it with the dark chocolate. Then I pour the hot milk over the syrups and espresso and stir it up real good. Once it's mixed, I swirl the whipped cream on top, add the drizzle, and sprinkle the peppermint pieces until it looks perfect.

"That's quite the presentation," he muses when I set it in front of him.

"Hopefully, it tastes as good as it looks," I say, prompting him to try it. "Oh, wait, let me take a picture. I'm tryin' to grow my social media pages."

I snap a few without him in the photo and then steal a couple as he holds it up.

"Am I good to try it now?"

"Yep, dig in."

As he takes a drink, I snap a few more.

I chuckle when he lowers the mug. "The whipped cream on your nose is what's really gonna sell it."

"Such a little smart-ass." He smirks, wiping off his face.

Laughing, I dip my finger into the cup, swipe more whipped cream, and then smear it over his mouth. "Here, let me get that for ya."

I lean in and brush my tongue over his lips, tasting the mix of him and the sweetness of the coffee. He moans as our mouths fuse together in a heated kiss.

When I pull back, he yanks me between his thighs and cups my ass.

"Mm...better be careful or you're gonna get addicted," I taunt, wrapping my arms around him as he kisses my neck.

"You've already infected my veins and you consume all my thoughts, Sunny. Addicted would be an understatement."

As much as I planned on teasing him and slowly revealing the lacy black lingerie I'm wearing underneath my clothes, I'm not sure I can wait much longer. His hands and mouth on my body have my skin on fire, and the more he touches me, the more I want to rip off his clothes.

"I think I'm owed a piece of clothing," he muses, flirting his fingers along the hem of my sweater. "And I'm choosing this."

Raising my arms, he slides it up and off. His gaze goes to my chest, and he licks his lips.

"Goddamn, baby. This is so much sexier in person." The pad of his finger glides down in between my breasts, around the corset lace, and then traces around my hard nipple. "I wanna rip this off you right now."

"Tsk, tsk." I step back out of his grasp. "No touchin', cowboy."

He pouts. "Since when?"

"That was the deal. For every drink you sample, I lose a piece of clothing. Nothin' about getting handsy."

Although I very much want his hands all over me, that's not part of our little game.

He arches a brow and crosses his arms. "Then I want to revisit the terms of this contract before the next drink..."

"Sorry, *oral* contracts cannot be altered." I smirk, then go back behind the counter and start on my next latte.

Although I'm not focusing on him, I can feel his gaze on me — specifically, my chest. But I love having his full attention on me even if I'm being my own personal cock block.

"You know, my eyes are up here."

"I'm aware, but your nipples stared at me first."

I snort at how serious he sounds. "And all this time, I thought you were an ass man."

"That's where you're mistaken, love. I'm a *Magnolia* man who's obsessed with everything about you."

My cheeks heat as I fight the urge to say *fuck it* and jump into his arms. But I'm not folding this easily just yet.

"Are you ready for the next one?" I top this drink with sweet, cold foam and cinnamon.

"That looks like dessert in a cup."

"Pretty close. I'm gonna call it the Cinnamon Roll Latte."

He takes a sip, licks the cold foam off his lips, and then tastes it again. "Very sweet, but I like it."

"Too sweet? I could add less syrup."

"Maybe a little, but honestly, it's still good."

"The sweet, cold foam on top adds a layer of sweetness, so maybe I'll put less syrup in the cup so it's not so overwhelming." I grab my phone and write myself a note for the next time I make it. "Okay, that was good feedback. You've earned another piece of clothing."

"Hmm..." His tongue teases his bottom lip as his gaze lowers down the length of me. "Jeans."

Just as I figured. He's going to die when he sees the see-through lacy panties, garter belt, and black stockings.

I flick open the button before he stops me. "Do I at least get the honor of removin' it for you?"

"If you think you can handle keepin' your hands to yourself," I tease and stand between his legs.

"Turn around," he orders, and I put my back toward him.

He wraps his arms around my waist, lowers the zipper, and then oh-so-slowly slides my jeans to my ankles.

"Boots?" he asks.

"Depends if you want 'em on or off..." I glance over my shoulder and see him contemplating.

"On...for now."

I kick them off so he can remove my jeans, then I slip the boots back on.

"Fuckin' hell. You're stunning, baby." His labored breathing tickles my neck as he stands behind me. "Not touchin' you is torture."

I turn around so he can appreciate the full look and his eyes grow to saucers at what he sees. His arms are behind his back as if he has to physically restrain himself from reaching for me and that level of respect from a man isn't something I've ever had. I teasingly tell him no touching and he's ready to cuff his wrists back so he doesn't cross the boundary I set.

When his heated gaze burns me from the inside out, I've never wanted his touch more than I do right now.

"I'm about to get on my knees and beg you to let me kiss you right now."

The desperation in his voice has me cracking. I wrap my arms around his neck, pull his head down, and crash our mouths together. His needy hands circle my waist, and he yanks me flush against his body with a relieved moan. The hardness beneath his jeans pokes into my stomach and my heart hammers at the anticipation of finally giving all of myself to him.

Tripp lifts my ass and my legs wrap around him as he settles me on the counter. Our mouths stay glued together as his hands explore my body, cup my breasts, and wander down to the garter piece.

"As beautiful as you look in this, I want to rip it off and kiss every inch of your skin."

"Just don't ruin it. Fisher paid for it."

243

Tripp freezes mid-touch and kiss. Welp, shouldn't have let that bit slip.

The corners of my lips tilt up as I wait for him to process what I just said.

Finally, he swallows hard. "Not sure I like the idea of another man payin' for my girlfriend's lingerie."

"To be fair, I wasn't your girlfriend at the time he did." I shrug as if that's explanation enough.

"And why exactly did my sister's new husband buy it for you?"

I chuckle at his serious tone. "Are you jealous?"

"*Sunny.*" His fingers dig into my hips as he pulls my ass to the edge of the counter. "I'm holdin' back every ounce of restraint not to go all caveman on your ass, so you better just tell me before my imagination runs wild."

Lowering my hand between us, I rub my palm over his erection and he groans. Then because I want him to very much lose control, I tell him the truth about Fisher asking me for help and letting me pick out my own.

"I probably didn't need to know you helped him pick out pieces for my sister."

"You asked." I smirk as he pinches the bridge of his nose. "That's what you get for being an obsessive, jealous addict."

He yeets me off the counter, throws me over his shoulder with one arm, and then walks out of the kitchen.

"Oh my God, Tripp!" I shriek as the whiplash has my hands reaching for something to hang onto and end up holding on to his back pockets.

His calloused palm connects with my bare cheek, and I squeal at the hard crack that ripples through me.

"You're gonna pay for that," I tell him in my most serious tone.

He tosses me on the bed, then hovers over me. "Such a devious little Sunflower. How shall I punish you?"

"Hmm..." I pretend to contemplate my answer, teasing my foot up the side of his leg. "You could fuck me six ways to Sunday and make me scream in ten foreign languages."

"Fuckin' hell. I don't know how I'm gonna survive you and that dirty mouth of yours." He tosses his hat, reaches behind his neck, and then yanks off his shirt.

About goddamn time.

Tripp's body is all tan skin and muscles with a light feathering of chest hair. I can't wait to drag my tongue all the way down his happy trail and that perfect V that hides beneath his boxer shorts to his thick erection. I'm going to make a whole meal out of this man's cock.

"Guess you'll have to keep my mouth busy then." Sitting up on my elbows, I reach for him, and he slips his tongue between my lips.

"Before we go any further, I need to make sure you truly want this. There's no rush, and I don't want you to feel pressured."

Damn. God knew what he was doing when he created this man for me. So sweet and perfect.

With the ability to melt my heart and body with just his words.

I really don't know what I did to deserve him, but I'm soaking in every minute he's mine.

Cupping his face, I bring his forehead to mine. "I want you, Tripp. In any way you want to give me, I'll take, but never worry I'm not right where I wanna be when we're together. In case you've somehow missed it, I've been crazy about you for some time..."

His cheeks stretch with a smile. "I'm glad you meet my level of obsession or this could get awkward."

A laugh bubbles out of my chest. "You mean more awkward than me tellin' you to knock me up in a text?"

His dick visibly twitches against me and my eyes lower to the noticeable bulge in his jeans. He quickly adjusts himself, clearly turned on by my words, and I grin at him liking it.

"Are you..." I laugh at the cute blush spreading across his cheeks. "Do you have a breeding kink I should know about?"

He grins with a shrug. "Or a Magnolia kink. Maybe both. Take it out and see for yourself, Sunny."

Licking my lips, I reach between us until I can pull him out and appreciate every solid inch of him. I wrap my fingers around his shaft, stroke the velvety skin, and watch as he squeezes his eyes.

"Time to test my theory." I continue my movements, increasing my pace as his breathing hitches.

Let's see how turned on he gets when I tease him.

"You wanna fuck me and put your baby-making seed inside me? Fill me over and over, own my body, and make me your good little breeding hole?"

His eyes roll to the back of his head. "Jesus Christ. You're gonna kill me."

Thank you, Noah, for introducing me to alien breeding smut because it just helped me seduce your brother.

"Too much?" I ask, but then pre-cum spills from his tip, and I smile with pride at getting him so easily worked up. "Guess not."

"Not at all. My cum is all yours, baby."

"In that case..." I rub the pad of my thumb over his crown, making him a mess for me. "Knock me up, cowboy."

Chapter Twenty-Five
Tripp

I pride myself on being level-headed and having decent self-control. I've held my feelings back for Magnolia when Landen liked her and even after they decided to only be friends, I'd kept my restraint. It wasn't until I learned she's liked me all along too that I finally gave myself permission to go all in, even as obsessive and addictive as it made me. Now that we've opened Pandora's Box, there's no going back.

But now hearing Magnolia's words, nearly naked beneath me, a new wave of possessiveness hits. It's bad enough I wanted to immediately find Travis and introduce him to my fist when I found that note in her car, but the thought of her pregnant with my baby makes me feral on another level I've never felt before.

The need to *possess* her.

Maybe I do have a breeding kink, but only with her.

She's the only woman I'd trust with my whole heart.

And although it'd be too soon for us to even think about starting a family, my cock got impossibly harder at the thought of knocking her up. I know she's on birth control from our medicine cabinet text conversation, so it's not something we'd actively try for right now, but the idea of it has me wanting to come deep inside her over and over.

"Say it again, Sunny," I demand once I shove my jeans and boxer shorts off the rest of the way and climb between her legs.

She holds my stare with a devious smirk. "Fill me up and own every inch of me. Oh, and don't forget your Stetson." She tilts her head to my nightstand where it sits.

A desperate growl releases from deep in my throat at how much her words turn me on. I love how unashamed she is to play into this fantasy and her fascination of having me wear a cowboy hat while we're having sex is one I'm all too happy to do for her.

Even if I'd rather see her wearing it while naked on top of me. *Next time.*

I lower my mouth down to her chest, cup her breast, and kiss the exposed skin around the lacy bralette. It pushes up her tits perfectly for me to taste and touch. They're so soft and firm, and I want to dig my teeth into her hard nipple.

She wraps her legs around me, pulling me tighter, and I chuckle at her eagerness.

"I want to devour all of you, Sunny," I tell her, lowering the bra cup. "No rushin' me."

She wiggles beneath me, arching her back to get even closer. "I've been waitin' years for you. This has been the longest game of foreplay in the history of ever."

Capturing her lips, I lie next to her and pull her on top of me. "Okay. Take the reins, Mama. I'm all yours."

She goes still, her lips parted slightly. "Did you just call me what I think you did? Because that's *hot.*"

Good to know I'm not completely sucking at this breeding dirty talk.

"Mm-hmm."

She plants her palms on my chest, straddles my waist, and rocks against my hard length. After she's thoroughly teased me, she lowers down my legs and takes me into her mouth. I curse as she hollows her cheeks and sucks me deep into her throat.

"Fuck, Sunny. Now who's torturin' who?" I cup the back of her head as she sucks the life out of me. Her hot tongue glides up my shaft before she swirls it around my crown, over and over the slit that triggers a full-body reaction. Between her sucking and licking, my willpower is seconds from snapping, and I'm not about to come inside her mouth when she has a little fantasy to play out.

"You better stop that," I warn, tightening my hold on her hair. "Get up here."

She looks up at me with a sultry look in her eyes, knowing exactly what she's doing to me. "Low stamina, huh?"

My jaw twitches, and I grab her chin. "You better hang on, darlin'. You're about to find out just how much I have from years of ranch work."

Before she can react, I twist my leg out from under her and use it to flip her body until she's on her back. I climb on top of her, pin one of her wrists to the bed, then wrap my other hand around her throat and hold her down.

Her eyes widen as if she's still processing we've just reversed positions. "How the hell did you do that?"

I smirk, squeezing her throat tighter. "I learned to hogtie at four years old. Still think I can't handle you?"

She rocks her pussy against my erection. "So what're you gonna do with me now that you have me?"

"Payback's a bitch, remember?" I tease my tongue along her bottom lip, then lower one hand between her legs, shove the fabric of her thong to the side, and find her wet slit. "No coming until I give you permission, *Mama*."

I thrust two fingers deep inside her tight pussy and she gasps, lifting her hips. When my thumb circles her clit, she moans so loud I'm tempted to give in and let her come right now.

"There we go. Let me hear you."

With a twist of my wrist, I drive deeper toward her G-spot and when she screams, her back nearly flies off the bed.

"That's my girl. *Louder*."

Her head falls back as her lips part and a delicious string of lyrical moans releases from her throat.

"I'm so close." She palms her breast and squeezes the nipple through the fabric.

I bury my face in her neck and kiss under her ear. "Then you better start beggin', sweetheart."

She digs her nails into my shoulder, thrusting up into my hand as I continue working her cunt. "Please, Tripp. I'm almost there."

Sucking on her soft flesh, I can feel how tense her body is and know it's only a matter of seconds before she falls off the edge.

"Not until I taste you on my tongue, baby."

"Tripp!" she squeals when I release her and move down her body. "You're the devil."

I kneel between her thighs, spread them wider, then lean over without touching her. "Then you better pray for mercy, baby. I'm about to devour you whole until your throat goes raw from screaming."

She gasps when I slide my palms under her ass, pull her up to my mouth, and give her one long lick. Capturing her clit, I flick it over and over before giving the rest of her pussy attention.

Magnolia thrashes under me, moaning and crying out each time she almost gets there, but then I pull back.

"I'm dyin' here..." she whines, trying to push my head back down when I blow cool air against her swollen pussy. "Please, please, *please.*"

I smirk against her hot cunt. "Mmm. Beggin' like the good girl you are. Hope you're ready..."

Without warning, I thrust against her G-spot and suck her clit in a steady rhythm. It only takes seconds until she's shaking beneath me, clasping her thighs around my neck, and screaming.

She comes hard and fast, and I lap up everything she gives me.

When I look up, her chest rises and falls as if she can't catch her breath, and a sense of pride rolls through me. I love that I'm the one who gets to make her feel good and give her the pleasure she deserves. And if I wasn't obsessed before, seeing her body respond this way would've sealed the deal.

"You okay?" I ask, partly teasing, partly concerned.

She nods once.

Crawling up her body, I tilt up her chin and brush my lips over hers. "You taste so fuckin' good I couldn't stop."

"What do I taste like?"

"Like sweet fuckin' paradise." Then I crash my mouth to hers and roll her on top of me. She gasps at the sudden movement, and I laugh as she situates herself comfortably on my hips.

Reaching over to my nightstand, I grab my Stetson hat and place it on my head. I smirk when her cheeks redden and she stares wildly at me.

"I'm wearin' the hat. Now time to ride the cowboy."

Chapter Twenty-Six
Magnolia

About goddamn time.

He looks even sexier than I imagined he would in nothing but a black cowboy hat.

Solid, broad chest I want to mark with my teeth.

Six-pack abs my fingers are itching to claw.

Thick, hard cock I'm desperate to take.

I'm tempted to tease the fuck out of him the way he did me, but I think my pussy would cry out in protest if I stalled for one more minute.

I'm still in my lingerie set, so I lift off his hips, move the fabric to the side, and then take his cock in my other hand. I slide his tip along my wet slit and his palms flatten on my stockings, squeezing my thighs in anticipation.

With my heart pounding in my ears and my breath unsteady, I slowly glide down his length. His gaze remains locked on mine as he fills me so full, I need a minute to adjust.

"You okay?"

I nod, widening my hips as his cock penetrates me. Every inch of my body is fueled with nerves that this is finally happening between us, and I want it to be as good for him as I know it'll be for me.

"Sunny, get out of your head." He sits up and cups my ass, pressing our chests together. "I'm supposed to be the anxious one between us." The corner of his lips curls up, and I smile at his ability to comfort me so easily.

I wrap my arms around his neck and slowly thread my fingers up into his hair without bumping the hat. "I've never been nervous during sex before, so I dunno why I am now."

"It's just me and you, baby. I'm giving you all control."

I rock against him and my stomach clenches at how full I feel in this position. The pleasure lights me up from the inside out, and when he digs his fingers into my ass cheeks, it prompts me to move faster.

"You're takin' me so good." He skims along my jawline as he continues to palm my ass with one hand and massages my breast with the other.

The wetness between my legs makes it easier to slide up and down his shaft and when the friction of his body against mine rubs my clit, my head falls back in pleasure. "Oh my God. That's intense."

He gives my ass a little smack, and I yelp.

"Do that again, but harder."

And he does, *twice*.

"Fuck, you feel unreal, Sunny. Squeezing and riding me like this, I'm gonna fill you up so full."

His words make me so wet, I'd be surprised if we don't drench his bedsheets.

Between him holding me in place and my hips grinding down on him, we find a perfect rhythm that has us both close to losing control. He kisses me until I can no longer focus on moving my lips and then sucks on my neck, purposely leaving a mark on my skin.

"I'm...so...close," I pant out, lifting up and then grinding down against him harder.

"Squirt all over my cock, Mama. Let me feel you come undone."

Moments later, I do just that.

My back arches as I chase the high of an orgasm ripping through me and shooting pleasure down my spine.

"Such a good girl riding me so fuckin' perfect. But I'm not done with you," Tripp murmurs in my ear as I ride the high.

Without a warning, he flips me on my back, loses the hat, and slides back inside me. My thighs wrap around his waist as he ruthlessly fucks me. He goes so deep when he slides my leg up to his shoulder, I swear he penetrates my cervix.

"Holy shit. Yes, yes, yes..." My eyes roll back as my fingers fist the sheets and hang on for dear life. He's thrusting into me so hard, my head's going to get a concussion from smacking the headboard.

I'm barely able to catch my breath and he's hardly breaking a sweat as he gives me everything he has. That's what I get for doubting his stamina because I'm about to tap out and beg for mercy.

"Tripp, I—"

"Give me one more, sweetheart."

"I can't."

"Yes, you can," I demand. "You're takin' my cock so well. Just one more. Then I'll reward your needy cunt with my cum."

I nod, biting my lower lip.

He rolls his hips and hits that sweet spot against my G-spot. Arching my back, I claw his arms as the room spins around us, and I soar through the intensity. The pleasure hits me so hard and fast, I scream louder than before.

"Oh my—" Words fail me as he buries his face in my neck and his body stills above me.

I squeeze his cock as he releases inside me and groans in my ear. A wave of satisfaction hits me at how hard he came because of me. Warmth settles in my chest at how content and happy I feel for the first time ever during sex.

"Sunny, *goddamn*." His growl vibrates my skin and when my fingers dig into his back, he fully relaxes on top of me. "I think you're tryin' to kill me."

My arms fall to the side like two boulders. "Me? You were hip-thrusting me into my grave. And now you're tryna break off my oxygen supply."

He coughs out a laugh as he lifts his chest off me. "Shit, we can't have that. We've got big plans for Chatty in our future."

My brows rise as I contemplate laughing or panicking. Now I can't tell if he's being serious or not.

Then he adds, "I'm thinkin' Willow if it's a girl, though. Y'know, Sunflower and a Willow tree. It'd be kinda cute."

"You're fuckin' with me," I say, needing to hear him say it.

"Don't like it? Maybe Ivy, Lily, Daisy? *Belladonna*?"

His tone is dead serious, and he's not breaking character, so I smack his chest back to reality.

Finally, he cracks a smile. "You're still too easy to rile up, Sunny."

He captures my mouth for a tender kiss before lying next to me on the bed.

"Says the one who wants to name our child after a *poisonous* flower."

Facing me, he sits up on his elbow and grins. "Remember who picked Chattanooga Tennessee."

"A solid Southern boy's name." I nod firmly.

"Until the kids at school make fun of him and call him Noogie."

I move to my side and mimic his stance. "Aww, that's cute. Baby Noogie."

He snorts, capturing my wild, loose strands and brushing them behind my ear. "At least he'll have a tough-as-nails mama to beat up all his bullies."

I can't help losing my serious expression and chuckling at how he effortlessly plays along no matter how ridiculous the topic.

"I'm sure they'll all be too scared of his lethal little sister, *Belladonna*, to mess with him."

"Of course. And then when *Foxglove* comes along, everyone will be afraid of the deathly trio."

I burst out with laughter. "Hell, I would be, too."

The smile on my face is permanent at this point, and I wouldn't be surprised if my cheeks hurt tomorrow.

Being able to play in the safety of our inside jokes, knowing we trust each other with our desires and fantasies without fear of scaring the other is something I've never had before.

Tripp rubs his thumb along my flushed skin, looking at me like I'm the most precious thing he's ever seen. "Be careful, Sunny." His voice is just above a whisper and it sends my pulse into overdrive.

My face tilts in confusion. "With what?"

He plucks my bottom lip, tracing over it with his fingertip. "My heart. I know it's quick, but it's all yours. And well, maybe it's not that fast because it's been yours for a long time. You just didn't know it."

My pulse has officially flatlined.

This sweet, brooding man is pouring his feelings out to me, and all I want to do is cry.

It's overwhelming to have someone like him be so genuine and tender after fucking my imprint into the mattress. The most perfect words I'd wished to hear for years and now he's telling me I own his heart.

It'd be impossible not to fall for this man.

I flatten my palm against his bare chest and feel it beat rapidly. "You've had mine since I was fifteen when I realized these weird feelings I was having were actually more than you just being my best friend's brother. Flutters in my stomach that I didn't get for anyone else, so it's safe to say mine's been yours for a long time, too."

Even in between all the times Travis and I were dating on and off, I was never fully his. I'd known Tripp for years at that point, and he always watched out for me. Anytime Noah and I got into sticky situations, we knew we could rely on him. He'd come and even help us in the middle of the night, no matter how inconvenient it was for him.

Most of my middle and high school memories involve him in one way or another.

And then I add, "So I'll gladly take yours if you promise to protect mine."

He thumbs my chin, bringing my lips toward his, but he doesn't close the gap. "I would take a bullet for it, Sunny," he whispers so earnestly.

Tears form in the corner of my eyes and before they fall, I wrap my arms around him and crash my mouth to his.

After several moments of getting lost in each other, he breaks the kiss. "As much as I'm enjoyin' the view of you in the sexiest lingerie I've ever seen, I need to clean us up. Take a shower with me."

"As long as you carry me. All my limbs feel like Jell-O."

He chuckles and then winks. "I think I can handle that."

Instead of lifting me up in his arms like I presume, he sits on the edge of the bed with his back facing me, grabs his hat off the floor, and then looks at me over his shoulder with the hat pointed at me. "Hop on, cowgirl."

A laugh bubbles out of me as I move closer and he sets it on my head. I climb on his back and hang on for dear life. "Don't drop me."

He secures his hands behind my knees and stands. "Doubtin' me over the simplest of tasks is gonna bruise my ego."

"It was just a statement, like *drive safe* or *break a leg*," I defend as he walks us toward his bathroom.

"Mm-hmm, right. Guess I'll have to show you just how strong I am by pinning you against the shower wall and fuckin' you into the tile."

"Keep threatenin' me with a good time, and I'll make sure to rip apart your masculinity next."

"Ouch, Sunny. Low blow."

He sets me down on the counter when we enter and then he spins around between my thighs. "Can I rip this thing off you now?" His dark gaze lowers down my body.

"Like rip *rip*?"

"Yes. The only lingerie I want you wearin' is ones I buy you."

"You're really possessive of my wardrobe," I taunt, licking my bottom lip in anticipation of him kissing me again.

"Just the ones another man paid for."

My cheeks heat at how deep and serious his tone is.

"Okay, cowboy. Do your best."

I spread my legs wider, giving him room to do whatever he wants.

In true Tripp fashion, he torturously teases me first, gliding his featherlight touch down my arms and thighs before grabbing my thong and literally tearing it off my skin. The garter belt and stockings go next. Then he puts one bra strap between his teeth, glides it down one arm, and does the same to the other.

He takes the cowboy hat off my head, and without missing a beat, he unclasps the back with one hand in a single flick.

Looking smug as if he's satisfied by his handiwork, he removes it completely and then tosses it to the pile on the floor.

Sitting completely naked now, his heated gaze rakes over every bare inch of my body.

As he stands between my legs, he traces over my lips and stares deep into my soul, grinning. "So fuckin' beautiful, Sunny. Inside and out."

I squeeze his hips to tug him closer. "I could say the same about you, or rather, handsomely beautiful."

His lip curls in disapproval. "Sexy? Masculine? Strong? Perhaps one of those."

I roll my eyes and push him back so I can hop off the counter. "Ego-driven, stubborn, clueless would be better options."

Before I can stop him, he hauls me over his shoulder and opens the shower curtain.

"Tripp!" I smack his bare ass, but it doesn't faze him in the least.

He holds my legs with one arm, and I hold on to him with a death grip.

"Sunny..." He chuckles, turning on the water. "I'm not gonna drop you."

"Oh, sorry for not being overly confident while I'm hangin' upside down with a hard floor beneath me."

He palms my ass and squeezes. "Trust, baby."

"I will when I'm facin' upright."

Once he steps inside and closes the curtain, he pulls me back up and positions me against the wall with his hips pinning me in place.

"Jesus, talk about whiplash." I firmly hold on to his shoulders and shiver under the cool air.

"The water should heat up in a second. Until then, my cock can keep you warm."

I look between us, notice he's hard again, and smirk. "Well, I'm not gonna knock myself up."

Chapter Twenty-Seven
Tripp

Sharing a breeding kink with your girlfriend is all fun and games until the risk of your dick falling off becomes a real concern.

I've lost count of how many orgasms Magnolia's had and the masculine pride in me is beaming like a smug bastard, but every part of my body is on fire. Coming from someone who's pulled many twelve-hour shifts doing bitch work on the ranch, that was nothing compared to the stamina of a woman who's making up for lost time. Of course, after bragging about the level of my own, I couldn't let her one-up me.

After the shower where I thoroughly fucked her against the wall, we took a dinner break, and I suggested we watch *Dirty Dancing* since we couldn't before with Sydney's emergency surgery. But halfway through the movie, her mouth ended up wrapped around my cock, and that led to round three.

Once we were ready for bed, she asked to borrow a T-shirt, and the moment I saw her in it, my dick was hard again.

Round four ended up with me bending her over and taking her deep and hard as she stuck out her perfect, round ass for me.

Admittedly, it's the first time I've ever experienced marathon sex, and now my calves are paying for it.

But it was so fucking worth it.

Holding Magnolia as she slept and being able to touch her is still surreal.

Thank God I have Waylon covering for me this morning. Since there are no new check-ins today, I don't have to worry about cabin call this afternoon. That means I can go with Magnolia while she works at the farmer's market. She mentioned some strange guy stopping by yesterday while she was at the retreat and considering I don't remember checking in a man with his description, I don't like the idea of some rando stalking my girlfriend.

But before I take her home to get ready, I decide to make her some food since we no doubt worked up an appetite.

I plate the eggs benedict, fill a glass with orange juice, and then bring it to her in bed. She's still passed out with wild dark hair covering half her face and my marks on her neck.

She looks so damn sexy.

"Sunny," I say softly, kneeling next to her after I set everything on the nightstand. "Wake up, baby. I have breakfast for you."

"Mm." She hums, shifting slightly, but then her eyes pop open. "What's that smell?"

The panic in her voice has me immediately on alert.

Before I can answer, she sits up, covering her mouth, and then throws off the covers before she rushes past me.

Standing in confusion, I follow as she goes into my bathroom. She hunches over the toilet, emptying her stomach, and I rush over.

"Shit, baby." I pull her hair off her face and hold it in my fist. She continues violently throwing up, and I rub her back as I stay behind her.

After the last round, she sits back, breathing heavily. I grab a washcloth and drown it in cold water, then pat it over her cheeks, forehead, and neck.

"That was terrible. I think I threw up my whole stomach."

Stay With Me

"Think you can handle some water?" I ask, taking her hand and helping her to her feet.

She nods and lets me bring her back to my bed.

"Stay here, and I'll grab some." I take the plate of eggs and orange juice, then go to the kitchen. I hate that she's feeling sick again. She must've caught something, which means I'll probably have it soon, too.

When I return with her water, she's lying down. "Sunny, sit up and take a drink."

I help push her up when she struggles and put the cup to her mouth. After a few seconds, I set the glass down and tuck her back in.

"Do I have to call anyone to let them know you won't be there today?" I ask when she closes her eyes.

"No, I'll just lose out on the vendor fee. But there's no way I can serve drinks while vomiting, so it's better for everyone if I don't go."

The sadness in her voice makes me frown. I know she especially relies on her Saturday sales to help pay her bills, but she needs rest more than anything. Mr. Waters is the president of the town committee who manages the farmer's market and since he owes me a favor from when I helped bring his escaped cattle back to his ranch, I'll ask him to waive her fee.

"Sleep as much as you need. I'll be here when you wake up." I kiss the top of her head and click off the light.

I clean up the kitchen, tidy up the living room, and do a load of laundry. When I check on her two hours later, she's still snoring softly, so I strip down to my boxer shorts and climb in next to her. She doesn't even startle when I wrap an arm underneath her and pull her into my side.

My phone vibrating on the nightstand wakes me up. It's a group text chat with my brothers.

> **LANDEN**
>
> There was a robbery at Phil's Grocery and a car exploded in the parking lot five minutes later. Downtown is blocked off with a dozen squad cars. Shit's getting crazy.

Jesus. That's the third robbery this month.

It's obvious it's the same person behind the recent crime spree in town. The first two times were small family businesses on Main Street. Looks like they evolved to bigger places with more cash.

> **TRIPP**
>
> They announce any suspects?

> **LANDEN**
>
> Well until I see Wilder and Waylon in the next five minutes, they're my first two guesses.

I snort.

> **WAYLON**
>
> Hey! I've been covering Tripp's ass all day. Definitely wasn't me.

> **TRIPP**
>
> Yeah, appreciate you doing that.

> **WILDER**
>
> I'm not dumb enough to hit a grocery store in broad daylight.

> **LANDEN**
>
> Dumb enough to hit one at night though, huh?

WILDER

> Well if I was gonna...yeah. The only thing I'd take is the fancy beer.

WAYLON

> What the hell is fancy beer? You bougie fucker.

WILDER

> Oh it's not bougie when you're stealing it from my fridge?

WILDER

> Wait, where the hell is Tripp? What's Waylon covering you for anyway?

I roll my eyes at his comment and look at the beautiful girl next to me.

TRIPP

> None of your damn business.

WAYLON

> You didn't even tell me. Where are you?

TRIPP

> You didn't ask.

WAYLON

> Well I'm asking now!

LANDEN

> Yeah, Tripp...what are you doing? Or should I be asking...who?

Motherfucker.

TRIPP

> Why don't y'all worry about yourselves seeing as you're on your phones instead of working?

WAYLON

You're really one to talk about work ethics.

TRIPP

Oh fuck off. I take one day off.

WILDER

...to rob a grocery store?

TRIPP

Yeah, figured I needed the thrill.

WAYLON

Hold on. Is that Magnolia's car in your driveway?

Should've known that was coming. The nosy bastard.

Noah returns from her honeymoon tomorrow, so it's not like they weren't gonna find out soon anyway.

But just to fuck with them, I play dumb.

TRIPP

How do you know what her car looks like?

WAYLON

Because she's here all the time. You fucker. I'm covering your ass so you can get laid? The hell.

I hold back laughter, envisioning his shocked face.

WILDER

WHAT?! Are you fucking kidding me?

This time I can't control it. The poor bastard really thought he was going to win her over.

LANDEN

Well that went as well as expected.

WILDER

You knew!

WAYLON

You didn't tell us?

TRIPP

Later, assholes. Keep me updated if you hear anything about the robberies. I have an alibi.

Then I send a middle-finger emoji and put my phone on do-not-disturb mode.

By the time Magnolia wakes up, it's well into the afternoon. Once her stomach feels better and she's ready to try eating, I make her some peanut butter toast to see how she handles it. She manages to get it down, and I notice she's not as pale as she was before.

"Hopefully it's just a twenty-four-hour bug or something," I say, sitting next to her on the couch after I grab her a fresh glass of water.

"I hope so. I've not felt this exhausted in ages. But I can't keep skippin' work."

"Want me to go for you?" I muse, grinning. "I can't make lattes or bake muffins, but I could pour a mean coffee."

"Do you know how to use the coffee machine?"

"Do I not just press the *on* button?"

She snorts. "Yeah, after you grind the beans, measure them out, and insert the filter."

"Hm. Guess I'll stick to the ranch." I chuckle, circling my arm around her shoulders. "If you need some cash to make up for your missed days, I—"

"Don't offer me money because I won't be able to say no."

I smile at her blunt honesty. "Then why wouldn't I offer it?"

267

"Because I started my own business so I didn't have to depend on anyone else. I just didn't consider sick days. Which is stupid, I know."

"No, you're still a new business and it's understandable you'd be worried about taking time off. But you can't control when you get sick, so if you need help, at least take it from me. We're a team now."

She rests her head on my shoulder and closes her eyes. "You're too damn nice to me, Tripp Chattanooga," she mutters like she's going to pass out again.

I kiss her hair and hold her closer.

If only she realized I'd do literally anything for her.

Chapter Twenty-Eight
Magnolia

"I'm baaaaack!" Noah singsongs into the phone when I answer it.

"About goddamn time! Do you know how long two weeks is? You were gone forever!"

"I know! I've never been disconnected for so long, and although it was so nice, I feel like I've missed so much."

That'd be an understatement.

"I can't wait to see you! I have so much to share," I say as I stare at the boxes of pregnancy tests on my counter. After being sick all weekend and having a bad reaction to the smell of eggs, I need to double-check I'm *not* knocked up for my own sanity before I see Tripp again. "Speaking of, have you heard about the robberies in town?"

"Yeah, I came back to a dozen texts from my brothers about it and some random car explosion. What the fuck was that about? I hope they catch him soon because now that everyone's on alert, they'll be keepin' their shotguns close by and loaded."

I chuckle because it's true. "Hittin' stores at night is one thing because you're racing against time before the cops show up, but doing it in broad daylight when people are shopping is just askin' to get shot."

269

"Exactly what I said!" She laughs. "I can't wait to show you all the photos I took. Even ran into a group of hot college guys and showed them my single bestie's photos. Might've gotten some numbers for ya."

I snort, picturing her doing just that. "And were any of 'em local?"

"From France, but their *accents*..." Her dreamy sigh has me giggling.

"You just want me to marry a French man so you can listen to him talk all day."

"Duh." She laughs and then continues telling me about a few of the things they did on their honeymoon. As much as I missed her and want to talk, the possibility I could be pregnant has my mind too distracted.

Considering Tripp and I only had sex three days ago, I know it wouldn't be his.

And that would be fucking devastating.

My birth control is for a three-month supply at a time, and I take them religiously on time every morning before work. The only times I've taken them late are when I was sick and slept in. And since that was after Travis and I had sex, that'd mean the condom Travis used either broke or was expired. Even though the pill isn't a hundred percent effective, the condom should've been a solid backup. Knowing how irresponsible and cheap he is, he probably got a condom from a quarter vending machine.

"Mags? You there?" Noah's voice beams in my ear, and I snap out of it.

"Yep, sorry. Just, uh...cleaning and watching *Hart of Dixie*." I lean back on the couch and prop my feet up on the coffee table.

She gasps. "Without me? How dare you?"

"As if we haven't seen it eighty million times. Plus, it's just on in the background while I get shit done around the house."

"Forever Team George."

I scoff. "You mean Team Wade. I know you like 'em older and all...but no. Bad boy underdog for the win."

"Oh my God. George ain't *old*."

I snicker at how offended she sounds. "Guess I shouldn't tell you I was blastin' a Taylor Swift playlist earlier and baking muffins."

"Magnolia Sutherland! You're doing all our favorite things without me." Her sad, pouty voice makes me laugh.

"Well, I gotta get shit done! Not all of us can go on a two-week honeymoon to the island of bumfuck nowhere. Plus, when I'm home, it gets lonely, so I needed Taylor and Wade to keep me company."

"Are you at least rememberin' to feed yourself?"

The thought of food makes me want to throw up. "Mm-hmm."

"More than girl dinner snacks?"

"Froot Loops is totally an acceptable dinner," I say, knowing she's going to scold me. "Oh, and Hot Cheetos."

She snorts. "Glad nothin' changed while I was gone."

"Hey, cookin' for one person is hard."

"You can eat at The Lodge on the days you're workin' there."

"By myself?"

"I'm sure you could convince Landen to go with you. He eats like eight times a day."

"He really does! And where does it all go?" The man has muscles for days.

"No clue. Have you seen him lately? How's he doing since Sydney?"

"I haven't seen him since that night, and he's not replying to my text messages. So I don't think very well."

"I feel awful that I wasn't here. He loved her so much. Tripp said he went into the woods and just started chopping wood." The sadness in her voice mimics how we all felt when it happened.

"He usually visits me when I'm at the retreat, so I'll try to talk to him tomorrow. Speaking of, when do I get to see my best friend again?"

"I'm unpacking and doing laundry today, and then I train in

the morning, but I'll stop by to see you in the afternoon when you aren't as busy. Plus, I miss my specialty Magnolia coffee."

"You better not have been cheatin' on me while you were away."

"Never! It was a strict diet of alcohol and greasy foods."

At the mention of *greasy* food, my stomach rolls, and I swallow down whatever just threatened to come up. Either I suddenly have an aversion to food or some*thing* is making me nauseous all the damn time.

"Hey, my dad's calling, and I wanna make sure everything's okay," I say.

"No problem. I'll see ya tomorrow!"

"K, love you."

"Love you, bye!"

I quickly click over to the other line. "Hey, Dad. You alright?"

"I was callin' to ask you the same thing."

I sit up straighter on the couch. "What'd ya mean?"

"I just heard on the scanner that a bunch of cars got broken into this afternoon off Second and Sheboygan."

That's only a few blocks from me.

What the fuck is happening around here?

"No, I haven't heard anything. But I can see my car from my front window..." I walk over and peek through the blinds to double-check. "Yeah, looks fine from here. Not that they'd find anything except some empty coffee cups and like twenty-three cents in change."

"Good. Don't leave anything valuable inside. You might wanna consider getting extra locks for your trailer."

My heart drops at the thought of someone breaking into it. "Yeah, that's a good idea. I'll grab a couple from the hardware store after work tomorrow."

I hate that I can't park it in my apartment complex lot, so I have to trust leaving it parked downtown for now.

"So anyway, how're you and Mama doing? I was thinkin' of visiting on Sunday. Would that be okay?"

Stay With Me

Even though Thanksgiving is this Thursday, we haven't celebrated together in years. I always go with Noah to The Lodge with her family, where they host a feast for the staff and guests.

"That'd be great, sweetie. I can make us lunch. Fried catfish, extra crispy how ya like it, and a side of asparagus and slaw."

Oh no.

Rushing to my kitchen, I dry heave in the sink until I finally get it out of my system and empty my stomach. I really need people to stop talking about food. If I'm pregnant, there's no way I'm going to survive nine months of this.

"Magnolia? Sweetheart?" I hear my dad's voice echoing from my phone.

I put him on speaker. "Sorry! Dropped ya."

"You okay? It sounded like you were at death's door."

"Nah, I'm fine. Totally fine."

The line's silent for a beat as if he's contemplating asking again, but when he doesn't speak up, I make up an excuse to get off the phone.

"I gotta finish up my laundry, Dad. I'll see you Sunday?"

"You got it, kiddo. See ya then."

After we say goodbye, I down a glass of cold water and swish out the bad taste in my mouth.

The boxes of pregnancy tests stare at me, and I can't take it anymore. I bought three different brands but grab the digital one first since it'll tell me a simple yes or no instead of trying to decipher one or two faint lines. Although it suggests waiting to test first thing in the morning, I'm doing it now because at this point, I just want confirmation.

In the odd turn of events that I'm not pregnant, then I most definitely have some kind of rare parasite living in my body because I've never felt this on-and-off sickness before in my life.

Grabbing a paper coffee cup I brought home, I go to the bathroom and pee. I've been sucking down water all day, so hopefully I'm not somehow over-hydrated.

Once I'm finished, I dip the stick in the cup for a few seconds and then set it upside down on the counter. The box says it can take one to five minutes, so I wash my hands and set a timer on my phone.

Since it's Monday, I worked downtown and didn't get to see Tripp at the retreat. I didn't yesterday either since I came home to sleep and clean up my apartment. He worked in the morning and then had Sunday night supper with his family, so we've been texting. That's how I found out his brothers know about us, which means I need to tell Noah as soon as I see her. I know she'll be happy for us, but I have a feeling I'll be telling her even bigger news.

It's not even the being pregnant part that scares me. I'd be more excited about the prospect of being a mom if it didn't come with a lifelong sentence of dealing with Travis. Assuming he wants to be involved, there's no way Tripp's gonna be cool with the idea of his girlfriend being pregnant with another man's baby. If the roles were reversed and some chick showed up saying she was pregnant with Tripp's baby, I'd be devastated. Knowing she'd be in his life for the next eighteen years and he'd experience all the parent firsts with her and not me would make me an emotional wreck.

The timer goes off, and I jump. I was so lost in thought I almost forgot I set it.

My heart hammers in my chest so hard that I can feel it beating in my ears. My palms sweat with nerves and it takes me a moment to catch my breath. I don't know why I'm so nervous, considering deep down, I already know what it's going to say.

Instead of drawing it out, I grab the stick, flip it over, and read the screen.

Pregnant.

"Oh God." I stare at the one word that's just turned my life upside down. "I'm gonna be sick."

I turn toward the toilet and throw up for the third time today. What the hell is even left in my stomach at this point? Considering

Stay With Me

I vomited first thing this morning before I ate breakfast just proves it doesn't matter if there's food in there or not. Soon I'll be throwing up my organs.

Once the sickness settles and I brush my teeth again, I grab the other two boxes of tests and dip them in the cup of pee just to double-check. Even though the digital test is supposed to be ninety-nine percent accurate, so should've been my birth control and condom combo. I'm not trusting just one test.

Ten minutes later, I have two more positive tests staring at me. I'm not really sure how to feel, but at least I know for certain.

And now, I need to decide how I'm going to tell my boyfriend and crush his heart.

As it gets colder out, I stay bundled up as I work. A hat, two layers on top, and insulated boots. Even though the trailer blocks out most of the cold, it's the wind that sends a chill to my bones.

Tripp already stopped by early this morning with Landen, and I hate that I had to act like nothing was different. It feels like lying, but I'm not going to tell him through text or while we're both preoccupied with our jobs.

Landen seemed better than he was last week and even teased me for looking like a hibernating bear while he was just in a long-sleeved shirt. But I teased him back that he works up a sweat and I stay in one spot for hours.

NOAH

I'm coming over now!

As soon as I read her text, I start making her coffee. She's a basic bitch like me and it's how I came up with the Basic Witch

275

Spice latte name, which is just pumpkin syrup with extra whip and nutmeg on top.

When I see her walking up, I rush out of the trailer, and she sprints toward me. I burst out laughing when she crashes into me and we wrap our arms around each other.

"I'm so happy you're back!" I squeal into her hair.

"Me too."

"I have a lot to tell you," I say, going back behind my counter to finish her drink.

"Oh God, that sounds serious." Noah stands close, waiting for me to elaborate, but the pounding in my chest is making me feel like I'm going to pass out.

"I fucked up," I begin.

She arches a brow. "With what?"

I blow out a breath, trying to calm my racing heart. She's going to be so pissed with me.

"I might've hooked up with Travis a month ago..."

Four weeks and three days, to be exact.

Her jaw drops as she gasps. "Magnolia Sutherland! You did not! And why am I just now hearin' about it?"

"Because I knew that'd be your reaction," I tell her honestly. *And it's embarrassing as hell.*

"Well..." She shrugs unapologetically.

"I was drunk and horny. And very, very, *very* stupid," I try to explain, but honestly it was more than that. Stupid Lydia and her annoying ass being all over Tripp is also to blame. Might as well blame Landen too for making Tripp hang out with her in the first place.

"The start to every country song." She snorts as if she's trying to hold back laughter. "Okay, so are y'all back together now or what?"

I shudder and nearly gag at the thought of his hands on me.

"God, no. I told him to lose my number and blocked him. Drunk Magnolia ain't makin' that decision again."

"Good. You deserve better." It's comforting hearing that

because Travis tried so hard to tear me down and make me believe I wasn't worthy to be loved or respected. Not to mention, took advantage of me when I was drunk and drugged me.

I finish her drink with a healthy dose of whipped cream, then hand her the cup.

"I took a pregnancy test, Noah." *Well, technically three.*

When I see her expression, reminding me just how much I've truly fucked up, tears fall down my cheeks.

"It was positive," I confirm.

"Aw, sweetie." She walks around to the side, opens the door, and engulfs me in a hug. "I'm not sure if I should say congratulations or not but—"

"I dunno either," I admit as I continue to cry with her arms wrapped around me.

Pulling back, I wipe my face and fidget before I tell her the rest. "That's not the worst of it."

Her brows lift. "What's worse than being knocked up by your ex?"

I swallow hard and try not to word-vomit the hardest part about all of this.

"I slept with someone I really like after him, and now I've ruined any chance at a relationship." *Well, a long-lasting one.* "He'll never want me once he finds out I'm havin' another man's baby."

Her eyes widen and her jaw drops.

Yep, just how I thought she'd react.

"Magnolia! I leave you for a couple of weeks..." She laughs but in a sincere way. "You're sure he ain't the father? What happened to those Magnum XL condoms I gave you last year? Surely you didn't go through an entire pack already."

"Trust me, Travis doesn't need XL, but we did use one. It was either expired or it broke," I explain with a scowl. "And yes, I'm sure. I track my period and ovulation cycles on an app. By the time I slept with the other guy, I woulda already been pregnant. I just obviously didn't know."

"Alright, so who is it?"

Nervously, I lower my gaze to the floor. "It was Tripp."

"Wait..." She scratches her head as if she needs a moment to compute the words I just said. "My *brother*, Tripp?"

I wince at her raised voice.

She clears her throat as if she hadn't meant to sound so harsh. "Tripp, as in the guy you've crushed on for nearly a decade and has never shown interest in you, Tripp?"

Sucking in my lips, I nod. "Yep. Turns out he does kinda like me." *A lot* if his words and actions are any indication.

She takes a moment to process and then says, "If he truly does, he'll accept you and the baby. But he might not be ready for that, so you'll need to prepare yourself for that possibility."

"Oh, I am. I'm expectin' him to push me away and never speak to me again."

That's what I'd do if I were him.

She pulls me in for another hug. "Well, I'll be here for you no matter what. My little niece or nephew will be spoiled as hell."

I tighten my grip around her. "Thank you." And then, to lighten the mood, I bring up something we've joked about since we were in high school. "I can't believe you get to sit behind me and chant *push, push, push* durin' my labor before I get to do it for you. My hot girl summer just turned into fat girl winter."

"Oh my God." She bursts out laughing as we pull apart. "First, that was never gonna happen. Second, summer was over before your little one-night stand mishap, but if it makes you feel any better, we'll at least be fat together."

It takes me a second to understand what she's saying, and then I lower my gaze to her stomach. "*What?*"

No freaking way.

She nods with a contagious smile. "Yeah. Just found out this mornin'."

My jaw drops, and I smash her into another hug. "Holy shit! I never thought we'd be pregnant together!"

"Me neither. We weren't even tryin'!"

"*Damn.*" I step back with a smirk. "Daddy Fisher sperm workin' double time." I waggle my brows at the nickname I gave him last year, and she smacks my arm.

"I swear it was the water at that place. Either that or honeymoon sex works faster."

I lean against the counter and grin. Her being pregnant with me makes this so much better. "What if our kids grow up and marry each other? We'd be in-laws!"

She giggles. "You're nuts, you know that?"

"I do. These hormones are about to make it worse, too."

"Now we can annoy Fisher and my brothers together."

She grabs her cup of coffee and takes a sip. Considering we're going to have to limit our caffeine intake now, I don't blame her for taking advantage one last time.

"About that. I need you to keep this a secret, at least until I can tell Tripp myself."

"Yeah, of course. Are you gonna tell Travis?"

My top lip curls as I groan. "Eventually. I wish I didn't have to, but if he finds out before I tell him, he'll be even more immature about it. If it were up to me, he wouldn't exist at all."

"You know that ain't fair, though. He deserves a chance to be a father; if he chooses not to be, you can cut him out completely. Just don't let him back into *your* life, if you know what I mean."

It'll be an icy cold day in hell before that happens. I cross my arms and sigh. "Yes, *Mother.* I don't wanna anyway."

"Good. Then all you need to focus on right now is eatin' healthy, stayin' stress-free, and gettin' enough sleep."

"What 'bout you? Are you still gonna ride?" I ask.

"Yes, but I won't do tricks or stunts. I'm sure Fisher will try to ban me from all trainin', but it's literally my job, so he'll just have to deal with it. But otherwise, I'm gonna make sure I don't overdo it, either. We can be accountability partners."

My whole body warms at that idea. I won't have to go through this new scary journey alone.

"I love that idea. This is much more excitin' now that you're knocked up, too." I giggle and take out my phone.

"Happy to have forgotten my birth control for you," she deadpans.

"I downloaded this pregnancy app. You should get it, and then we can track our progress and milestones. It says my baby is the size of a lentil." I hold up my hand and make a tiny circle.

Once she's downloaded it, she inputs the date of her last menstrual cycle, and it reveals she's four weeks along.

"Mine is the size of a poppy seed." She shows me the photo. "Hm, Poppy. That's a cute name."

I shoot her a look of concern. "Sorry, but I'm not namin' mine Lentil." If that's where she's going with it, I'd choose Chatty or Willow first.

At the thought of Tripp's baby name idea, tears threaten to fall again.

Noah bursts out laughing. "Fair enough."

Per the app, I'm six weeks along, which means we're only two weeks apart and we'll go through a lot of our milestones together.

"I'm excited to go through my first pregnancy with you. Even if the circumstances aren't what you'd hoped for, you're gonna be a mom, and that's somethin' to celebrate," she says as I stare at the screen.

I nod. "You're right."

At the end of the day, regardless of the shitty situation I got myself in, a new life will be born in nine months and I'll be responsible for them. A baby that'll change my life forever.

"We'll plan a dinner and sleepover at my house this weekend. Whaddya say? I'm sure Mallory and Serena would love to come to a dance party.

I actually love that idea. We've been doing them for years, and when the girls came into our lives, we recruited them to join us. Even in our twenties, we act like we're back in high school again and have the time of our lives.

"Can you still have slumber parties when you're married?" I

tease, and when the tears I try holding back fall, I quickly wipe them.

"Um, duh. Fisher knows who he married. If he wasn't prepared for Taylor Swift sing-alongs and pajama nights, he shouldn't have proposed."

I'm so envious of their relationship but am so happy she has him. She deserves a great guy like him. That's the future I envisioned with Tripp, but now, that might be gone.

"You're so lucky to have each other. You won the husband lottery," I say.

"And you will find someone equally lucky to have you. I promise."

I already have...but he might not want me after he finds out the truth.

We chat for a few more minutes as she drinks her coffee. When a customer approaches, we hug goodbye and make plans to see each other on Thanksgiving in a couple of days.

For the next two hours, I have a steady line of people, so I don't have time to overthink, but as soon as three hits and I close up for the day, my brain spirals out of control again.

Maybe I should only focus on my business and pregnancy.

Maybe being in a relationship right now isn't the best idea.

Maybe I should let him go so he can be happy with someone else.

Tripp doesn't deserve the shitstorm I'm about to lay on him. Especially once Travis knows, he's going to be insufferable about us getting back together.

No matter what he says, promises, or does—that'll never happen. I'm stronger and have more self-respect for myself than when I was in high school. Plus, it's not only me I have to think about now. Another human is going to depend on me for everything and that alone is scary. How am I supposed to juggle dating into the mix?

I can't even fathom being with someone who's having a kid with someone else, so I can't expect that kind of understanding from Tripp. As much as I've wanted him for years and have been insanely happy these past few weeks, my life's about to flip upside down.

And that's not fair to him.

By the time I get home, I've made my decision.

Our now perfect little bubble is about to burst because I'm about to destroy everything we made.

Chapter Twenty-Nine
Tripp

November 26th can go fuck itself.

There are two dates that'll forever haunt me — Billy's death and his birthday — and each year, it hurts a little more than the one before.

He's forever eighteen while I continue getting older and living life without him.

I hate that finding joy in the little things is always followed by the guilt that I'm still alive. And lately, I've been happier than ever before, and although he'd want that for me, I can't help the little nagging voice in my head that drags me back into the dark.

It's your fault.

He's dead because of you.

Billy would still be here if you'd just agreed to go to the party.

Yes, I know he's at fault for his own decisions, but I'll never forgive myself for how it played out.

If my phone had been on silent, I would've never answered it in the first place and his little game of coming to get me wouldn't have happened.

I knew him better than anyone else. That's the worst part. That's what eats at me.

I should've seen the disaster ahead as soon as I picked up the phone.

The what-ifs, the if-only-I-had done this or that overwhelm my thoughts until they trigger an anxiety attack. Hell, sometimes a panic attack too in the middle of the night. I'll be sleeping and wake up with my heart racing and my chest so tight, I swear I'm having a heart attack.

But I haven't had a single one since Magnolia and I started dating.

Although they've been happening less and less as the years go by, sometimes it'll just hit. Noah's wedding was harder on me than I expected because it reminded me of how many important milestones he's not here to experience.

Regardless of how I feel on the day of his birthday, I always buy a birthday cake, a bouquet of flowers for his mom, and a handful of balloons. Then I get in my truck and drive to his parents' house for lunch.

Marissa answers the door with a smile, but her eyes are glossed over.

"Hi, sweetheart. Come in."

"Thanks, Marissa."

She takes the cake from me, and I follow her through the house. When we get into the kitchen, there's a spread of Billy's favorite food. William is already seated, and when he notices me, he smiles. Even after all these years of being divorced, they get together one day a year to celebrate their son's birthday.

"Tripp, hi." He stands to take the balloons and puts them in the middle of the table.

"How y'all doin'?" I ask, still holding the flowers.

"We're good. You?"

"Same, thanks."

When Marissa hands me a vase with water, I unwrap the flowers and place them inside. Then I set it down next to the balloons as per our tradition.

"Can't believe he'd be twenty-five this year," Marissa says as she cuts into the cake. "A fully grown man now."

I smirk at that. "I dunno. I have a feelin' he'd still be as rowdy as when he was a teenager. He'd just be old enough to know better."

"I like to imagine him with a girlfriend or wife and maybe a baby or one on the way."

Knowing how Billy was with girls back in high school, he would've had three kids by now.

"You just know the weddin' woulda been wild," I say, going along with her idea. There's no doubt he would've stood at the altar drunk off his ass with me by his side, trying to keep him awake.

Marissa sits down next to me after bringing the cake over. "Is there someone special in your life, Tripp?"

William begins scooping mashed potatoes on his plate, and I follow suit, grabbing a piece of fried steak.

"Yeah, actually, there is. It's new, but...she's the one," I say confidently.

"Really?" Marissa's whole face lights up. "That's so great."

"Happy for you," William says. "What's her name?"

"Magnolia." Saying her name aloud makes me chuckle because of how rarely I do say it. "But I call her Sunny. It's our little inside nickname."

"Sutherland?" Marissa asks.

I nod as I add more food to my plate. "Yeah, my sister's best friend."

"Oh, she's lovely. I stop by her coffee shop every Saturday at the farmer's market." Marissa smiles. "You picked a good one."

"Yeah, I did." I can't stop grinning as I think about her. We made plans for her to come over tonight, which is much needed after an emotional day. "I think Billy would give me so much shit for finally admitting I liked her after all these years."

"I'm sure he would, too." William smirks.

As we continue to eat, we discuss the recent crime sprees in town, share a few memories of Billy that pop up, and, overall, enjoy each other's company. This has been our tradition for years, long before he died. Every birthday, he'd invite me over for dinner with his parents, and after he passed, I didn't want his parents to spend it alone. So I continued to show up, bring cake, flowers, and balloons, and for a couple of hours, we sit, eat, and catch up.

Honestly, it's kind of nice. A day just for Billy. William and Marissa have always welcomed me into their home and treated me like their second son. It's one of the perks of growing up in a small town and having the same best friend since kindergarten. Your parents become theirs and vice versa.

"How're your folks?" William asks when we move to dessert.

"Great. Stayin' busy as usual. Already eager for the next wedding."

"Noah's was so beautiful. It was a lovely day." Marissa grins, but there's a hint of sadness behind her eyes. She'll never get to experience that as a mother.

"Yeah, it was. My sister just got home from her honeymoon a couple of days ago."

"Where'd they go?" she asks.

"Honestly, I'm not even sure. Some remote island where they had to disconnect and just...I dunno, drink and explore? I'm sure she'll tell us all about it tomorrow at Thanksgiving."

"Oh, how nice. I've always wanted to travel, but well, I can't go alone."

William keeps his head down.

"What about takin' a friend?" I suggest.

"Maybe one day. Right now, my job and takin' care of the home keeps me plenty busy."

I don't want to push it, so I nod and take another bite of my cake.

Once we're finished eating, Marissa brings out the photo albums like she does every year. Billy was their only child, so there are hundreds of pictures. We flip through every single page, reminisce, and share stories we've told dozens of times before, but it never gets old. Keeping his memory alive is what helps us get through the years without him.

"Thanks again for lunch." I hug Marissa at the door. "Remember there's an open invitation for y'all to come stay at the retreat anytime. Landen and I will take you horseback riding up the mountain and tell you all the dumb shit we did with Billy up there."

"Tripp Hollis!"

"We were kids!" I laugh when her jaw drops.

"Well, I'd love that. Maybe in the spring," she says.

"Sounds great. Just let me know."

Then I shake William's hand, give Marissa one more side hug, and walk out to my truck feeling a tad lighter than when I came here.

Every year after I have lunch with his parents, I drive to his gravesite and then tell him all about it. I like to imagine him waiting for me, ready to hear about the new town gossip.

"So there's some dipshit robbing businesses in town and breaking into cars. Probably some little punk with a death wish. I heard Sheriff Wagner's demand they add more cameras downtown and alert everyone to lock their doors. If you were still here, you'd be ready to hunt the bastard down." I laugh because it's totally something he'd recruit me for, too.

"Your folks think you'd be married by now. But based on your previous datin' history, you'd probably be on your second or third marriage by now because you woulda gone to Vegas for your twenty-first and married some random chick totally fuckin' blitzed. Then you woulda had a divorce party at the Twisted Bull, where you met your second wife and eloped after you knocked her up during your one-night stand." Chuckling, I picture all of this playing out in my head.

After a few moments, I decide it's time to tell him about Magnolia. He'd be lunging at me with excitement considering how much shit he used to give me.

"You're gonna flip out when I tell you Magnolia and I are

dating now. It's been almost a month. The best one of my life, honestly. Every time I see her, I forget the pain. The anxiety vanishes. Everything in the world is right again."

My heart races at just the thought of her and knowing she's coming over later.

"And I know you'd be threatenin' to kick me in the balls when I tell you I'm gonna marry her someday. She's the one. Hell, she's always been the one. Before I was ready to admit how much I liked her, I knew I could never love someone else the way I love her. Honestly, it scares me to give so much of myself to one person, but for the first time, it feels right. There's this overwhelmingly possessiveness I feel about her. The craving to be around her all the fuckin' time. It doesn't even matter what we're doing. We always have a good time. I'm so goddamn obsessed with her, it's surreal we're actually together now." The smile that takes over my face is downright embarrassing. "My only regret is not tellin' her sooner. But now that we're together, I wanna give her the world and protect her from everything bad in it."

The way I can see him rolling his eyes but then yanking me in for a hug.

"When I ask her to marry me, you're gonna be at the wedding, right? You promised to stand next to me, and I'm holdin' you to that."

I soak up the sun for a few more minutes before standing and letting the tears fall. Then I tap his headstone and repeat the words I say to him every time before I leave. "See ya next year, Billy. Don't party too hard up there."

By the time I get home, the emotional weight of today hits me. You'd think that after seven years the grief, it wouldn't be as heavy as it is during these moments. But then I look around and am reminded of how much older I am now than him. A grown man in his own apartment, responsible for myself, a full-time job, bills to pay. It's such a contrast to how things were when he died.

I haven't texted Magnolia since this morning and didn't tell her what I was doing today. She'd want to console me and sometimes I just want to sit with the pain. Use it as a reminder of how short life is and be grateful for what I have. Not take any of it for granted because it could be cut short at any given time.

Deciding I need a reset, I take a shower and then text her I'm available if she's ready to come over now.

MAGNOLIA

Okay, on my way.

I smile at getting to see her soon. Since I don't have anything planned for dinner, I'll probably suggest we go somewhere. With tomorrow being Thanksgiving, we'll be at The Lodge for lunch.

When I was at the store buying the stuff for Billy's birthday lunch, I grabbed an extra bouquet with sunflowers, orange roses, Magnolia leaves, Chrysanthemums, and Mums in a mason jar for Magnolia.

She knocks, and I immediately get up to open it for her.

"Hey, Sunny." I smile wide as she comes in. "I got you something."

She follows me toward the couch where I grab them off the coffee table.

Her eyes widen as she dips her nose to smell them. "They're beautiful. What're these for?"

I shrug. "They reminded me of you, and I thought you'd like 'em."

Something crosses her face, an emotion I wasn't expecting. A flash of sadness.

"You okay?" I set down the flowers and tilt her chin. "Feelin' sick again?"

She closes her eyes and exhales sharply. "I need to tell you something."

With her serious tone, anxiety surfaces in my chest, knocking against my ribcage. "Okay. Let's sit."

She follows me to the couch, and I face her, waiting.

"There's no easy way to say it, so I'm just gonna come out with it."

"Alright." I nod even though my heart is pounding and sweat is taking over my palms.

She meets my gaze with hesitation. "I'm pregnant."

Chapter Thirty
Magnolia

If it weren't for the fact that I can feel my pulse beating in my neck, I'd assume my heart exploded by the chest pains taking over.

Saying those two words to the man I wanted forever with should be an exciting occasion—if the baby were his. As painful as this will be for both of us, I have to tell him the full truth.

He clears his throat as if he's contemplating how to respond. "You're...jokin'. Right? Is this part of the breeding kink fantasy or something? You can't find out you're pregnant that quickly after sex, can you? It's been less than a week."

Five days, to be exact.

I shake my head, lowering my gaze because I can't stomach watching the pain I'm about to bring him.

"No. I was pregnant already when we had sex. I just didn't know it then."

"How's that possible?" He tilts his head as if he's trying to count how long we've been together. Uncertainty flashes across his face. "What am I missin' here?"

I meet his gaze, my hands shaking as I hold them in my lap. "Before you and I started datin', I had a one-night stand. We used protection, but when I kept gettin' sick, I realized it was possible I could be pregnant, so I took a test."

His lips twitch as if he wants to say a thousand things at once. "A-are you okay? I mean, that has to be a lot to wrap your head around."

"Physically, I feel sick twenty hours a day. Mentally, not great. This was unexpected and things between us were going so well..." I pause briefly, collecting my thoughts. "But this changes things."

He stands abruptly, wiping his palms down his jeans. "Whaddya mean?"

"I'm pregnant...with someone else's baby. I'm gonna be a first-time mom. How would that *not* change things?"

He tilts his head curiously. "Sunny. Who's the father?"

I don't want to say the words that'll crush his heart, but there's no getting around it. He'll find out the truth eventually.

"Tripp..." I hesitate, wishing I could change how badly this is going to hurt him. He looks at me like he already knows and is pleading with me not to confirm it. "I'm so sorry."

"Please, *please* tell me you didn't sleep with your ex. I need you to tell me that."

The desperation in his voice has me fighting back tears. Instead of trying to speak, I just nod.

With his jaw tense, eyes narrowed into slits, and hands balled into fists, he looks lethal. "Did he drug you again?"

I shake my head.

"Why would you go back to him?" He scrubs a hand over his pained face. "After everything he did to you, *why?*"

His voice isn't judgmental, but I hear the disappointment and disbelief in his tone.

A wave of dizziness hits me as my eyes gloss over. "I wasn't thinkin' clearly. It was the night of Landen's birthday party, and I thought you were gonna hook up with Lydia. Stupidly, I got trashed, and when he asked me to go home with him, I was too gone to care. I fell into what was familiar at a time when I felt really low about myself. I'm not proud of what I did, and I regret it immensely."

"That's why he started harassing you again about gettin' back together."

"Yeah. When I told him to lose my number and blocked him, that's when he showed up at my trailer and started leavin' me notes."

He scrubs a hand through his hair, pulling the strands and shaking his head. "Fuck, Sunny. I hate him so goddamn much. You have no idea. So many times over the years I was tempted to knock him out on his ass. That night he drugged and shoved you in an Uber, I was close to losin' it. If Landen hadn't been there to help me, I would've knocked his sorry ass out and not quit until he stopped breathing."

The vein in his forehead is throbbing and so red, I swear it's going to burst.

"I know, and it's why this makes things extra difficult."

"Wait..." He sits on the coffee table, caging my legs between his thighs. "Are you going back to him? Is that what you're tellin' me?"

Quickly, I shake my head. "No! God, no. I don't even want him to be the father. If I could hide my pregnancy and keep the baby a secret, I would. But there's no doubt he'll eventually find out."

"Tell him it's mine," he blurts, and my breath hitches at how easily he throws out that idea.

What is he talking about?

I'm in disbelief at his reaction to all of this. When I spoke to Noah yesterday, I was so certain he'd want nothing to do with me or be so angry he'd tell me to leave. But instead, he's ready to take responsibility for a baby that isn't his.

Though I could never let him do that.

"I wish I could, but I can't lie to him about his own child. I hate him just as much as you do, but it wouldn't be fair to him or the baby. He or she deserves to know who their biological father is, even if he's a piece of shit. I also can't put you in that position to have your family thinkin' it's yours when it's not."

"Are you plannin' to tell him right away?"

"Not if I don't have to. There's no legal obligation sayin' I have to involve him in my pregnancy. When he or she is born, then I'll tell him. But if he wants to see the baby, it'll be supervised. Knowing how he is, he'll be unreliable anyway, which is why it's even more important for me to get a plan in place."

He leans back slightly. "Whaddya mean by that? What kind of a plan?"

"Well, I'll be a single mom. I own a business and won't be workin' for a while after I give birth, so I need to figure out how I'm gonna support myself and the baby. I need to look into childcare and insurance. This was obviously unplanned, so I need to sort out how I'm gonna do this. Travis can't hold a job, so I can't rely on consistent child support."

Tripp looks at me as if he's staring into my soul, and I avert my gaze when the realization of what I'm saying hits him.

"You don't have to do this on your own, Sunny. I'm here. I'll help you. Just because I hate that motherfucker doesn't mean I don't wanna be involved or here for you. I want you, no matter what. You havin' his baby doesn't change how I feel about you."

Fuck me, he's so goddamn nice and a way better man than I deserve.

Why can't he just get mad and scream at me so I wouldn't feel like absolute shit for what I'm about to say?

"Tripp...you don't deserve to go through the shitstorm I'd push you in. You didn't ask for this responsibility. This is mine to figure out, not yours."

"Don't..." He shakes his head. "Don't you dare push me away."

"That's not what I'm doing. I'm protectin' you. You're not seein' the bigger picture right now because you want us to go back to how everything was before. If you think clearly for just a minute, you'll realize I'm right and that it'd be easier in the long run if we returned to being just friends."

"No," is his immediate response.

I cock my head at the finality in his tone. He's not acting at all the way I assumed he would, and it's throwing me off. How can he just talk like we'd be one big, happy family after that?

"Tripp, this isn't what you envisioned for your life. Being with a woman who's about to be a first-time mom, dealing with pregnancy sickness, numerous appointments, and labor. Not to mention the newborn phase. Then the infant and toddler stages. How are we supposed to be in a relationship when my life's going to revolve around raising a child?"

"You're so used to that asshole disappointing you that you've defaulted to thinkin' all men will fail you. I know you're strong and independent. You're used to only relyin' on yourself, but you don't have to anymore. You're scared I'm gonna let you down because that's all you know when it comes to relationships. But I'm not him, Sunny. I'm not going anywhere."

I hate that he knows me well enough to see right through me and although he's somewhat right in his assumption, I can't fold when I've already made my decision. Admittedly, it'd be so easy to give in to what he's offering. So damn easy to curl into his arms and say *okay*. Just like all the times I gave in and went back to Travis. That's how I know it'd be the wrong decision. For once, I'm not going to cling to safety and familiarity, not when it could also ruin Tripp's life.

Mentally, I'd prepared for yelling, anger, rejection, and disgust even. But this? I didn't expect his reaction to be so accepting and it's making it so much damn harder to explain why we can't stay together. This is for the best. He just doesn't see that at the moment.

"I'd never compare the two of you. But I can't allow you to take on this burden that's not yours."

"Don't I get a say in that? Shouldn't I get to decide what I wanna do?"

"It's much more than me being pregnant. It's dealing with Travis for the next eighteen years. It's the way people will make assumptions about you being with me and having his baby. It's the responsibility of taking care of a *child*. It's no longer about what *I* want. Being in a relationship seems selfish when a baby is going to be fully dependent on me. That's where my energy should go. We're already jugglin' our work schedules to make time to see each other. It'd be selfish as hell for me to expect you to accept second priority in my life. You deserve so much more than that."

His jaw twitches as if he's holding back screaming his lungs out at me. "You don't even wanna try after everything it took to get here?"

I wish it were that easy.

I swallow, choking back my emotions. "And prolong the pain when you inevitably get tired of only getting scraps of me? I want nothin' more than for you to find someone who makes you insanely happy. We'll always be a part of each other's lives because of Noah, but I won't get in the way of your happiness."

"You are right now."

Tears continue to well in the corner of my eyes, but I don't let them fall. I need to remain strong to get through this because right now I want to fold and accept everything he's offering. But I know I can't.

"I'm sorry. I truly am because this is not what I'd hoped for us. But it's better this way. You'll understand when the pain subsides that I did you a favor."

He flinches like I backhanded him. "Don't fuckin' do me any favors, Sunny. I'm not lettin' you go."

Of all the ways I predicted he'd react, this wasn't even in the top ten of how I thought he'd respond.

"Why do you want to drag this out? It'll hurt worse the more we invest into this and it ends up not working out. At least this way, it only lasted a month, and we can move on easier."

He crosses his arms stubbornly. "I don't wanna move on and

neither do you. We belong together. You want this as much as I do."

"But it's not just about me anymore. I have to also consider my baby's needs now and what's best for them." I'll be juggling so much as it is, I can't bring him down with me.

"And I couldn't play a role in that?"

He makes it sound so easy, as if being around Travis or a child who looks like him won't remind him every damn day what I'd done. As if his fear of me going back to Travis wouldn't surface and leave doubt in his mind.

"Of course you could, as a friend, but you need to move on. You have so much love to give and so much to offer the *right* woman. My focus will be on this new phase in my life and all the changes I'll be going through. I can't offer you what you need. Why're you making this difficult?"

He licks his lips and nods once like he's defeated from arguing. Then he stands, putting distance between us.

"Say whatever you want, but you're foolin' yourself if you think I'm just gonna walk away from you." He paces on the other side of the coffee table and my heart pounds in sync with every step he takes. Then he stops and stares at me. "You will always be the love of my life no matter if we're together or not. There is no *moving* on for me. There is and has always been only you."

This time, there's no stopping them. The tears I've held back fall down my cheeks and if I don't leave right now, I'm going to unravel in front of him. "I think it's best if I go."

When I move toward the door, he follows and then opens it for me.

Great, it's raining. *Just perfect.*

Before I leave, he leans in and brushes the pad of his thumbs under my eyes. He's so close that I can smell the familiar scent of his cologne.

"You sleep on what I said, Sunny. I'll see you tomorrow for Thanksgiving."

He cups the back of my head, presses a kiss to my forehead,

and when I close my eyes, I can almost imagine the life he's painted for us.

"Drive safe."

Unable to look him in the eyes, I lower my gaze to the ground. "Good night."

Driving home is miserable. I already hate driving at night, but trying to see in the dark on back country roads while it's raining and I'm crying is practically a near-death experience.

Deep down, I know I did the right thing. Tripp's too amazing of a guy to realize it's better this way. He deserves the kind of partnership where he doesn't have to deal with baby daddy issues or a child who isn't his. And right now, there's no way I can put my all into a relationship while also configuring my life around to have a child. He should find someone who can give him everything and more.

By the time I get to my apartment, my face is a mess, it feels like my heart's having palpitations, and I'm second-guessing everything. I just want to take a bath, text Noah an update, and crash. With tomorrow being a holiday, I won't have to get up early for work, but I don't know how I'm going to sit with their entire family and pretend everything's fine.

When I get out of my SUV, I cover my head with my bag and walk toward my apartment. It's not until I go to unlock my door that I realize it's already ajar.

What the fuck?

Looking around in circles, I don't see or hear anything, but I pull out my taser anyway. Then I push my door, and it creaks wide open. When I don't hear any other noises, I grab my phone for the flashlight and check to see if anyone's inside.

"Hello?" I call out and am greeted with silence.

Taking two steps inside, I flick on the light switch and gasp when I see the destruction.

My couch and coffee table are flipped over. Trash, shoes, and picture frames littered everywhere. My dining table chairs are broken. Shoes I had by the door are thrown across the room.

Stay With Me

I don't dare go any further and instead go back to my car and call the sheriff. The dispatcher said I'm the fourth break-in tonight. That does nothing to ease the fear flowing through me at feeling violated. Some stranger was in my home, touching my things, and going through my belongings.

I want to vomit, and this time it's not because I'm pregnant.

But because the one person I want to call is the one person I just broke.

Chapter Thirty-One
Tripp

After getting a solid two hours of sleep, I'm up earlier than usual to muck stalls and get a head start on chores before meeting everyone at The Lodge. I was tempted to text Magnolia all night, but I didn't want to suffocate her while she processed everything. She's acting on emotion and what she thinks she should do for my sake, but I'm hoping she'll come around. What we have is too special to walk away from.

Though I'm still trying to wrap my brain around her being pregnant with that fuckwad's baby. Not that it matters. It changes nothing.

Actually, that's a lie.

It has me feeling even more protective and possessive of her but not only her. The baby, too.

Even if she thinks I shouldn't be involved, it's too late. I'm not going anywhere, and she'd be better off accepting that sooner rather than later. But if I have to take the slow route to show her I'm in this for the long haul and keep her in my life, then I'll do whatever it takes.

Hell, I'd birth the kid for her if it were physically possible.

Just as I'm moving the wheelbarrow out of the barn, I'm hit in the face with something hard and knocked over. The load of horseshit I was wheeling topples over with me and covers my bottom half.

What the actual fuck?

Before I can get up to murder this asshole, Wilder's standing in front of me, doubled over, laughing.

"Good mornin', dipshit. Look alive next time."

I'm going to kill him.

Looking at the ground, I see what he threw at me. *A fucking bucket.* I'm about to use up all my pent-up frustrations and anger on him. "You better fuckin' run."

He cowers, holding up his arms and stepping back. "It's not my fault you didn't see that comin' a million miles away. If you weren't in lala land, you woulda had plenty of time to dodge it."

Getting to my feet, I use my gloves to brush off my jeans. "I wasn't lookin' in your direction, asshole."

"Goddamn. You're in a shit mood. Figured you'd be nicer now that you're gettin' laid regularly."

"My sex life is none of your concern. Go finish the stalls so I can start lungin' the horses."

With it being a holiday and a half-day of work, exercising times will be cut short, so I need to get as many done as I can before lunchtime.

Wilder comes over, gets the wheelbarrow upright, and then tells me he'll take over. A flash of pity crosses his face, and I hate how easily he can read me.

Landen hasn't stepped foot in the family barn since Sydney's passing, so Wilder or Waylon have been helping me with morning barn chores. Usually, the twins focus on the retreat barn, but for now, they've swapped.

I take Rocky out first and work him for twenty minutes before I switch him out and grab Denver. He's usually an easygoing quarter horse, but my mind's so distracted and consumed with thoughts of Magnolia being pregnant that I don't notice when a rabbit hops inside the corral until it's too late.

Denver stops galloping, retreats backward toward me, and ignores my commands.

"What're you doin', buddy? Let's go."

I prompt him to get back into position, but the closer the rabbit comes, the more fidgety he gets.

Denver releases a loud whine, stomping his front foot.

I push his butt back to the center while rolling my eyes at Denver, a thousand-pound horse, being scared of a two-pound animal.

"It ain't gonna hurt ya."

When the rabbit inches closer again, Denver backs up into me until I'm forced into the fence.

"You're gonna squish me, dude. C'mon, move." When he doesn't, I add, "You should be embarrassed."

Wilder jumps up on the post behind me, cracking up with laughter. "How's it goin'?"

I glare at him over my shoulder. "How do you think?"

Wilder whistles loudly, grabbing the rabbit's attention and scaring it off. Denver watches it go and then releases a whine as if to tell the rabbit off for disrupting him.

"What a little shit," I mutter.

"You're welcome," Wilder calls out as I get back into place.

Ignoring him, I resume working and continue rotating horses.

At eleven thirty, I head home to shower and get ready for the rest of the day. The only thing preventing me from blowing up Magnolia's phone is knowing I'll get to see her soon at The Lodge.

Once I arrive, I glance around the parking lot for her SUV, but she must not be here yet. Everyone else is inside the big conference room we use for parties, and you can tell Mom and Gramma Grace spent some time decorating it in fall decor.

I slap a smile on my face for my mom's sake and greet her with a hug.

"Happy Thanksgiving, sweetie."

"You too, Ma. Everything looks and smells great."

"Wait till you see Gramma Grace's new caramel apple bars she made."

At that, my stomach growls. "I better get there first before the others steal 'em all."

When Gramma Grace approaches, I greet her with a kiss on the cheek and then tell her how excited I am to try her new dessert.

"Where's Magnolia?"

At first, I'm taken aback that she's asking me. Normally, that'd be a question for Noah, which tells me she knows something.

"I'm not sure," I say hesitantly.

"Oh, I just thought she'd be comin' with you."

"Why?" I ask, then glance at my mom, who's grinning.

Crossing my arms, I blow out a breath. "What do y'all know?"

"Just that you finally put us out of our misery with your little will-they or won't-they games."

"Gramma Grace!" I laugh for the first time in two days.

She rolls her eyes as if me being shocked is ridiculous.

"So who's the rat?" I ask. Someone had to have told them.

"Oh, you foolish boy. I don't need snitches to find out what's going on 'round here," Gramma Grace says with a level of sass I usually get from Mallory.

"Alright." I laugh. "Then how'd you know?"

"She was a sleuth in her other life," Mom teases.

"Magnolia's car being here when Noah was away was my first clue. You being on your phone durin' family supper. The way you've been smiling like you had a hanger stuck in your mouth."

"Oh, and we saw you dancin' at Noah and Fisher's wedding. Y'all weren't as discreet as y'all thought," Mom adds.

Goddamn.

Leave it to the gossip queens to figure it out before we even formally announce anything. Too bad now I'm practically on my hands and knees, begging Magnolia not to walk away.

"Well, there's no use denyin' it." I shrug, though I wouldn't anyway. "But I'm not sure where she is. I was just about to ask Noah."

"Ask me what?" As if summoned from the ceiling, Noah appears between us.

"If you knew where Magnolia was," I say. "She's coming, right?"

"You don't know?" Confusion flashes across her face. Her gaze shoots to Mom and Gramma Grace as if she's not sure how much she should say around them.

I narrow my eyes at Noah, wondering how much she knows.

"Is someone gonna tell me?" Gramma Grace blurts when we stay silent.

Noah scratches her head as if she's conflicted but speaks up anyway. "Her apartment was one of the break-ins last night. She called me from her parents and is stayin' with them today."

"*What?*" My chest caves in and my heart threatens to stop beating at the unexpected news. I'd heard there were some last night but never expected she wouldn't call or text me if it happened to her.

I should've fucking texted her last night to make sure she got home safely.

"She didn't call you?" Noah asks.

Hurt and frustrated, my jaw clenches. "No."

"Oh, that's horrible!" Mom says, but I'm too pissed to look away from Noah.

"They'll catch him," Gramma Grace reassures.

"Yeah, there has to be cameras," Mom adds.

"Text me her parents' address," I tell Noah. If it wasn't for it being a holiday and special to my parents, I'd leave right now.

"Can't you just ask her yourself?" she asks.

"Yeah, but I have a feelin' she wouldn't tell me," I deadpan.

Without arguing, Noah pulls out her phone and sends it to me. Then she sends me a second text.

Stay With Me

NOAH

> What's going on with you two? Did she tell you...

Once we take our seats and say grace, I shoot her a reply.

TRIPP

> Yes, and then tried to break up with me.

NOAH

> What?! She didn't tell me that part. What'd she say?

Dishes are being passed around, so I set my phone down next to my plate and respond in between adding food to my plate.

TRIPP

> That we should return to being just friends. But I told her no.

NOAH

> You told her no? LOL

I hear her snicker from across the table.

TRIPP

> Yeah. I'm not letting her break up with me.

NOAH

> Gee, I wonder why she didn't call you with that caveman behavior.

TRIPP

> She's just scared and thinks that I wouldn't still want her. But I'm not going anywhere.

NOAH

> As chivalrous as that is, you gotta give her some space to process this. Don't go banging down her door and demanding she move in with you or something.

TRIPP

Well, now that you gave me the idea...

NOAH

Don't you dare.

TRIPP

She can't stay with her parents. Do they even have room for her?

NOAH

Not really. She slept on their couch last night.

TRIPP

Absolutely the fuck not. I have a guest room she can use.

NOAH

TRIPP! Do. Not. Overstep.

TRIPP

You're the one who gave me the idea, and it was a good one.

She sends me her infamous eye roll emoji.

NOAH

Fine, whatever. We're meeting at her apartment tomorrow afternoon. I'm gonna help her clean it up once the sheriff releases it. She's gotta report anything missing to her rental insurance company.

TRIPP

I'll come, too. Then she can pack some bags and bring everything she needs to my place.

NOAH

She's not gonna go for that.

TRIPP

Then help me convince her. You know she shouldn't stay there by herself with this criminal on the loose. What if he returns and she's home that time? If she's with me, I can keep her safe and be there to help when she gets sick or bring her whatever she needs.

NOAH

You don't think that'll be too awkward for her?

TRIPP

Not if I don't make it that way, which I won't. You act like I just wanna jump her bones. I've been nothing but respectful and waited years to even tell her I liked her. I'll wait as long as it takes for her to realize I'm not like her ex and not going anywhere.

Noah gives me a sappy, pitiful look, and I groan. Luckily, everyone else is chatting and not paying attention to our secret conversation.

NOAH

You're a good guy, Tripp. I truly think she's in love with you and is just doing what she thinks she should by letting you out of a complicated situation. It doesn't help she's hormonal and will be going through a lot of changes. Did she tell you about me?

Looking up from my phone, I furrow my brows at her.

TRIPP

No. Sorry to say your name didn't come up while she was breaking my heart.

I glance up just in time to see her roll her eyes.

NOAH

We haven't announced it yet, but I just found out I'm pregnant, too.

My eyes widen because that's the last thing I expected. Then I look at Fisher next to her, staring at her like she's his whole world.

TRIPP

Wow. Congrats?

NOAH

Yes, you dummy. We're married and happy about it. I wasn't planning to tell everyone until I had the first ultrasound, but I'll probably tell Mom and Dad tonight.

TRIPP

Don't be surprised if Gramma Grace already knows.

NOAH

Funny you say that because she does! After Magnolia and I talked, I went to Mom and Dad's to make Fisher a scrapbook to tell him the news and Gramma Grace was like, "You're gonna make a great Mom!" And I was like HOW? I just found out myself.

I smile at that because we've all been there with Gramma Grace knowing shit before anyone else.

TRIPP

I swear she's a psychic.

NOAH

Or a mind reader!

TRIPP

Probably both. She knew about Magnolia and me before I even said anything.

NOAH

> At this rate, I'm surprised she hasn't revealed who's been doing the break-ins.

TRIPP

> Me too. Get the FBI on the phone and tell them to hire her for the job.

She giggles.

"What are y'all texting about?" Fisher asks, leaning over Noah's phone and she holds it out for him to read.

After a few minutes of him scrolling through our messages, he arches a brow at me.

"Don't give me that look. You slept in the bed of your truck outside of Noah's place after she broke up with you, and she was injured at the time," I remind him. "So you better be on my side about this."

Fisher nods, then gives Noah a shrug when her jaw drops in disbelief that he'd agree with me.

"Well, she *is* pregnant..." he whispers, but leave it to my nosy-as-shit family to overhear.

"Who's pregnant?" Mallory blurts from four seats over, and everyone goes silent.

Noah freezes, and I do, too. It's not exactly our business to share with everyone that Magnolia's pregnant, but considering most of them know we're together, they'd assume it's mine. Since she doesn't want them to think that, it makes announcing it a bit tricky.

"Um..." Noah swallows, and I watch as her mind spins.

Then she glances at Fisher, and he gives her a smile of approval.

"Well...I am. We just found out."

"Oh my goodness!" Mom nearly flies out of her chair, rushing over toward them.

Next, the rest of the family takes their turn giving hugs.

"Good thing I already called dibs on godfather, huh?" Landen smirks when everyone gets back in their chairs.

"Nice try," Noah says.

"Oh, come on. I've been really sad lately, and this would bring happiness back into my life." Landen sticks out his lower lip, laying it on thick.

"That's pathetic!" Waylon shouts.

"You can't use the dead horse card!" Wilder argues.

I wrap my arm behind Waylon to smack Wilder in the head. "Dude, shut up."

Wilder's brain-to-mouth filter is defective on a good day, but Jesus Christ, he really has no sense of aptness.

"Just for that, I *should* get to be." Landen shoots a shit-eating smirk in Wilder's direction.

Waylon and Wilder argue with him before Dad clears his throat.

"Boys," he barks, grabbing our attention. "Back to your food."

Noah chuckles at us getting scolded, and Waylon kicks her underneath the table before we get yelled at again.

If this is how they act with Noah's pregnancy announcement, they're going to lose it when they find out about Magnolia. But I don't give a shit what they think or say. I'll shut down each and every one of their inappropriate comments if I have to.

Chapter Thirty-Two
Magnolia

After forcing turkey and pie down my throat, I slept for twelve hours straight. The emotional toll from telling Tripp I'm pregnant and then finding my apartment got broken into quickly caught up to me. I missed going to the Hollises for Thanksgiving, but I didn't have it in me to socialize even if for a few hours.

Additionally, I told my dad about the baby after he found me bent over the toilet.

His eyes lit up until I told him who the father is. Disappointment flashed across his face, and even though he doesn't like Travis, he said he was thrilled for me.

Then he asked how Tripp took the news, and I had to explain that I ended things and why. Though he didn't say it with his words, I could tell he disagreed with my decision.

When I told my mom, she hugged me for the first time in a year, and I cried for a solid thirty minutes.

Now it's Friday, and I need to get my shit together so I can mentally prepare to clean out my apartment. There's no way I can live there in its current condition, but at least Noah will be there to help me. Sheriff Wagner told me to document everything and figure out what was taken. At first glance when I flicked on the lights, it didn't look like any of my big stuff was gone, just thrown around. The TV, my laptop, iPad, and even my espresso machine were still there.

Since my dad's off for the holiday weekend, he offers to come and help with the clean-up. When we get there, the crime scene tape is gone, but it still feels weird to go inside. The sheriff's deputies dusted for prints, but from what they said of the previous break-ins, they weren't finding any that didn't belong to the residents. They most likely wore gloves.

The next step is getting security footage from the apartment buildings and other residents who have doorbell cams. But again, if it's the same person from the previous break-ins, they wear all black and keep their heads down.

"Hey!" Noah runs up to me before we walk in.

I pull her in for a hug. "Thank you so much for comin'. You don't know how much I appreciate this."

"Of course, Mags. I'm here for whatever you need. Always." She smiles, and I'm tempted to cry again. God, these hormones should be criminal.

"It seems weird they'd pick your apartment with it being so close to the parking lot," Dad says as we approach my door. "You'd think the ones in the back would be more private and less risky to get caught in the act."

Noah glances around and nods. "Yeah, unless they just hit the first one that looked vacated, but then again, if it's the same person doing the robberies, they're not very smart."

"Smart enough not to get busted," I retort, inserting my key and twisting the doorknob.

"They will," Dad says reassuringly. "Or someone's loaded Glock will."

Turning to face him, he opens his coat and reveals his gun holster. "Geez, Dad."

His only response is a wink.

"See, we're safe here with Mr. Sutherland packin'." Noah giggles when we enter.

Dad confirms with a firm nod. "Gotta protect my baby and grandbaby."

I can't help the emotions flooding through me at how excited he is to be a grandfather. Even if I'm a single mom, knowing my dad will support me gives me the courage to do this alone.

"You told him?" Noah asks, smiling wide.

"Kinda had to when I threw up, and he was worried the turkey was bad."

Noah snorts. "I told the whole family at Thanksgiving lunch, too."

"Oh my God, you did? I bet they freaked out!"

"Yep, ugly cryin' and all."

I flick on the lights and am brought back to the other night when I walked in here for the first time.

"Shit, Mags. I'm so sorry this happened." Noah puts her arm around me. "But fear not, we're gonna get this place back into tip-top shape."

I blow out a deep breath as we walk farther in. "Dad called to get a security system put in, but they can't get here until Monday."

Noah lowers her gaze as if she's hiding something. "I should probably tell you..."

Before either of us can get another word in, there's a faint rapping on the open door.

I jump, quickly spinning around. My eyes land on Tripp and they narrow in confusion.

"What're you doin' here?" I ask softly. He looks good as usual, but the dark circles under his eyes match mine as if he's not been sleeping either.

"Hey, Sunny. Nice to see you, too." He smirks, stepping inside.

"You must be Mr. Sutherland?" Tripp stretches out his arm and my heart pounds, anticipating my dad's reaction.

"I am." Dad shakes his hand. "You're Tripp Hollis."

Of course my dad would recognize him.

"Yes, sir. The boyfriend."

What the fuck? I know he wasn't taking the breakup well, but I didn't think he'd still be in a delulu state of mind.

"Nice to meet you officially, sir. I'm here to help move Magnolia to my place."

"Excuse me?" I blurt, stepping between them. "What're you talkin' about?"

Tripp looks above my head, and when I glance over my shoulder toward Noah, they're having a secret conversation.

"When you didn't show up for lunch yesterday, I told Tripp about the break-in and he told me what happened between you two..." Noah pops a scolding brow at me for not telling her, but I'd planned on it today. "He thinks you'll be safer stayin' in his guest room."

"Absolutely not," I immediately argue. "The chances of them comin' back are slim. I don't think they even took anything. I'll have ADT and a doorbell camera. It'll be more secure than ever before."

"Are you really gonna *feel* safe here, though?" Noah challenges, and I scowl.

Whose side is she on?

"Sunny, just hear me out." Tripp gets closer. "I wanna protect you and can't do that if you're fifteen minutes away. This way, you don't have to worry. Even houses with big-ass dogs were broken into. It's not gonna stop someone if they have their mind set."

"Plus, most of your furniture got ruined. This way you don't have to worry about replacin' everything at once and can save up for a new place," Noah adds.

"So you think I should completely move into Tripp's guest room? And what about when I give birth? Just tuck the baby into the closet?"

Tripp snorts as if this is hilarious to him.

"I'm being serious. I've lived here for four years and am just supposed to let some creepy asshole push me out of it? It might not be much, but there'd at least be room for a crib."

"I will make room for you and the baby, Sunny. Hell, take my bedroom too and turn it into a nursery for all I care. As long as you're safe, that's all that matters to me."

I cross my arms because he's being ridiculous. "And where will you sleep?"

He shrugs. "The couch. On an air mattress. In my truck. Who cares. As long as you're safe, it doesn't matter."

His heated stare glues me in place. How can I refuse when what he's offering would protect me and give me the opportunity to save money? But if this is some ploy to get us back together, it's not going to work.

"If we're gonna do this, I have rules."

His face splits into a wide grin. "Whatever you want, Sunny."

"I'm not payin' rent," I say firmly.

He matches my stance. "Wouldn't accept it even if you tried."

"Don't expect me to cook for you."

"Considering I've never seen you cook a day in my life, I'll be the one cookin'."

"I'm not sleepin' in your bed."

"Didn't ask you to."

"This doesn't mean we're together."

This time he visibly disagrees. "We *are* together."

Shaking my head, I step back. "This is why it won't work. You don't respect my boundaries. I tell you it's over and you say *no* as if it were a multiple-choice question."

He closes the gap between us and tilts my chin. "Fine, let me rephrase. I am *yours*. I will always be yours. Whether or not you accept that, I'm not going anywhere. I'll be here to support you in any way you allow. If you want to return to being only friends, then okay, but in terms of a relationship, I'm taken." He tenderly grabs my hand and flattens my palm over his chest where his Billy and sunflower tattoos are inked. "I will always belong to you."

He's hell-bent on not making this easy for me. My brain and heart are fighting each other as it is.

"How are we supposed to live together when you want *more* than I can give you?" I ask softly, trying hard not to get emotional.

"I think you forget I spent the past seven years wantin' you while you dated Travis and my brother, and I survived, didn't I?"

"Okay, I didn't *date* your brother," I say, then turn to my father to explain because I know he's hearing all of this. "It was one date."

Dad stays silent, but the faint smirk on his lips tells me he's enjoying the show.

"Either way, I'll respect your wishes, Sunny. I'm not gonna force anything on you. We'll be roommates, and I'll help you with whatever you need. *Please*. Stay with me."

I blow out a defeated breath at this disaster in the making, but living here by myself would creep me out. Not that they need to know that part.

I turn toward Noah and scowl. "This is just temporary," I say to them both. "Once the criminal is caught, I'm findin' a new apartment. Should probably get one with two bedrooms anyway."

"And when that time comes, we'll help you move again. Won't we, Tripp?" Noah shoots him a look.

Tripp shrugs. "Sure."

"Great!" Noah beams. "Now that it's all settled, let's get this place cleaned up, pack your bags, and then move you into Tripp's guest room."

I force a smile. "Perfect."

I'll have to let the landlord know and will probably lose out on my deposit, but oh well. Not having to pay rent for a few months will be nice.

"I'll grab trash bags and start on the kitchen and living room. You and Tripp work on your bedroom and bathroom. If I notice anything missin', I'll let ya know," Noah says.

"I'll take out the broken furniture and put it in the dumpster," Dad offers.

"Okay, please take pictures first," I remind them.

"Will do!" Noah singsongs, and if she weren't my best friend, I'd disown her for blindsiding me.

When Tripp and Noah walk away, Dad leans down and whispers, "I like him."

I groan. "Of course you do."

"Vowin' to keep my daughter safe and expecting nothin' in return? He's got my vote."

Chapter Thirty-Three
Tripp

I spent the early morning cleaning the guest room and bathroom before I drove to Magnolia's apartment. She'll have plenty of room for her stuff since these duplexes were designed for two ranch hands, and each bedroom has its own master suite. The only thing we'll share is the kitchen and living room, but I'm hoping she won't mind considering she lived by herself. Growing up in the big house with four siblings, I'm used to sharing everything, so when I moved in here at the beginning of the year, it felt strange to have so much extra space.

It's only a matter of time before my brothers find out she's living here, so I plan to tell my parents this weekend before they hear it through the rumor mill. Especially the being pregnant with Travis's baby part.

By dinnertime, Magnolia's fully moved out of her apartment and into my place. Once she went through everything that wasn't salvageable, not much was left. She packed up her clothes, toiletries, and everything else she'd need for the foreseeable future.

I cleared a space in the kitchen for her espresso machine and supplies. My fridge is typically only half full, so she can add in whatever else she needs. The linen closet has two empty rows for towels, blankets, or storage.

There's still plenty of room for her and a baby if she decides to stay longer.

Which I hope she does.

Even though I knew she'd fight the idea, I wanted her to be as comfortable as possible without feeling like she was invading.

"Are you hungry?" I ask when she curls up into a ball on the couch with one of my fuzzy blankets.

"I dunno."

"Thirsty?"

"I dunno."

"Tired?"

"Yes," she mutters.

"I can make you a coffee...or attempt to?" I tilt my head at her machine and all the buttons. I'm sure I could find the instructions online.

"I'm not supposed to drink caffeine, which is why I'm draggin' so much ass."

My brows pop up. "None at all?"

"I think there's a recommended daily limit, but I'm a go big or go home kinda coffee girl, so it's just best if I stick to decaf."

That's going to be torture for her to work with coffee all day long.

"Okay, do you have any of that?"

"Not here."

I pull out my phone and click on the notes app, then add to my Magnolia notepad I created earlier when she mentioned needing a specific kind of detergent I didn't have.

Can't drink caffeine - get decaf.

"Alright, so no coffee. What about tea?"

"I only like lavender tea. Have any of that?"

Opening my cupboard, I look at the variety box with green, black, and white. *Fuck.*

"Nope."

Back to my notes app I go.

Lavender tea - her favorite.

"I'll take you grocery shoppin' tomorrow so you have everything you need."

"I gotta get back to work, so I'm going to do the farmer's market in the mornin'."

"That's fine. We can go afterward. Or if you aren't up for it, just text me a list, and I'll go."

"You really don't have to be this nice to me. I'm fully capable of feedin' myself."

I smile to myself. "You're so used to assholes, you can't even see when someone is just being a decent person. I've never been mean to you, so why would I start now?"

"Because you should hate me. Why you don't is makin' me question your mental state."

"Sorry to disappoint you, Sunny, but I could never hate you."

She stays quiet, and I don't push her to talk. I know she's had an emotional day between throwing out so much of her belongings and moving into a new place that doesn't quite feel like hers. I'm determined to make her feel at home as much as I can.

Instead of asking what she might be hungry for, I decide to cook something and pray she'll like it.

Digging through my cupboards, I find a box of bowtie pasta and a jar of Alfredo sauce. Mom would kill me for not making it from scratch, but I could never make it as good as hers anyway. But luckily, I have the ingredients to thicken it up and add in a healthy dose of fresh parmesan.

"You can eat chicken, right?" I ask before grabbing some from the fridge.

"Of course."

"Okay, just checkin'."

I'm not sure what all the pregnancy food rules are, but if I'm gonna take care of her, I need to know as much information as possible. So I make a new note.

Order pregnancy books.

Look up foods to avoid and a nutrition guideline.

Once the garlic toast is done, I add it to our plates with the chicken alfredo pasta and then bring them over to the coffee table. I make two glasses of ice water and then sit next to her on the couch.

"This smells so good." She sits up and gets a better look. "Wow, you made this?"

"Yeah. It's pretty easy and is my go-to when I don't have much else. Nothin' fancy."

She gives me a look as she stabs her fork into the food. "Your *nothin' fancy* is my idea of an over-the-top dinner date." Then she takes her first bite and moans. "Oh my God. This is delicious. If I wasn't already pregnant, I'd have its babies."

I chuckle, dipping my toast in the sauce. "Gotta up those standards, Sunny."

Though I do love that she appreciates my cooking, it beats eating by myself, too.

"Yeah, well, they've been in hell for so long, I'm not sure they exist."

There's sadness in her tone, but I don't pressure her to talk about it when she stays focused on the TV screen.

"What're you watchin'?"

"*Hart of Dixie.* It's my comfort show. I can change it to something else if you want."

I smile at her offer, but I rarely watch TV to care that much. "Nah. It's fine."

As we eat, I notice her mouthing the lines.

"How many times have you seen this?" I ask, genuinely curious.

"Hmm...the limit doesn't exist."

I chuckle at her blunt honesty. "So, a lot."

"Noah and I used to watch it religiously and fight over who Zoe should end up with." Then she chuckles. "We still do."

"Based on the twenty minutes I've seen so far, I can make an educated guess on your pick."

There's no way she'd be rooting for the beloved town lawyer. Wade's the guy from the wrong side of the tracks and sleeps with half the town.

"What's that mean?" she asks, almost offended that I can read her as well as I can.

"It means you have a type, sweetheart."

"That sounds offensive."

"Are you tellin' me Wade ain't yours?"

"See, this is where you're wrong." She shoves a forkful in her mouth.

"About what? Educate me, then."

"Me liking Wade better isn't because he's who I'd go for. It's because he's way better for Zoe than George is. She just doesn't know it because she's blinded by his shiny job and good hair."

I snort. "Is that the priority for choosin' a life partner?"

"I'm sure it doesn't hurt, but no. George is known as the nice guy. The good family man. His family is wealthy and well-known, so everyone adores him."

"Sounds like a decent catch," I say.

"Except he's a *cheater*. He finds Zoe on the side of the road and offers to drive her into town. Doesn't know much about her, just that she's pretty and obviously not from around there. Which would be fine and all except he conveniently forgets to mention his *fiancée* — his high school sweetheart — and low-key flirts with her. He leads her into thinking he's available and interested. Which means Zoe has to later find out he's engaged to the wicked witch of the South. A woman who's nothing but catty to her for no reason besides her being an outsider and a well-educated woman."

"When does he cheat?" I ask, feeling like I missed a chapter.

"*Emotional* cheating. Instead of being upfront with her and making it clear he's taken, he catches feelings for her. But Zoe's to blame, too. Even after she knows, it doesn't stop her from being flirty. But it should've been his responsibility to stop it from the start."

I nod, agreeing with her because if a woman approached me, I'd make it crystal clear I wasn't available or interested.

"Meanwhile, Wade never pretended to be anything he wasn't. What you see is what you get. No surprises. He's a manwhore, but you know that from the beginning. Hell, he lives on the Mayor's Plantation where she can see women coming and going because they're neighbors. It's almost all sexual attraction between them at first, but the more you see 'em together, the more you realize they're way more compatible."

I soak in every word she says, even if I'm trying to wrap my head around the storyline. I'm going to have to watch this from the beginning to properly understand the characters.

"That's quite the assessment for a TV show," I half-tease.

"Well...the men in this show aren't bad to look at. Wait till you see Mayor Hayes. Former linebacker in the NFL. Won two Super Bowls. Built like a tree I'd fall on my ass tryin' to climb."

Now that cracks me up. "You're tellin' me a two-time Super Bowl NFL player decided to retire and become the mayor of some small town in Alabama?"

"Yes, why?"

"I mean, sure. That's realistic."

She rolls her eyes. "Okay, Mr. Judgy. You don't watch these shows for the *plot*."

I furrow my brows. "Then what're you watchin' it for?"

Just then a shirtless Wade appears with sweat dripping down his six-pack abs, and she points to the screen with a grin.

"Ohh, so this is like porn for women disguised as a CW show."

She smirks, shrugging. "Now you're gettin' it."

323

We get through two more episodes before she passes out with her feet in my lap. I figure she wouldn't like me carrying her even though I'm tempted to so she doesn't wake up, but I softly brush my thumb across her cheek and whisper her name.

"Hmm?" she mutters with her eyes closed.

"Let's get you into bed. You'll be more comfortable in there," I tell her, moving so I can help her up.

"I'm fine right here." She snuggles deeper into the couch.

So damn stubborn.

"C'mon, or I'm throwin' you over my shoulder and puttin' you into bed myself."

She manages to glare at me with one eye open. "You wouldn't dare."

"Try me, *roomie*." Then I flex my arm and waggle my brows.

"Ugh, you're insufferable."

She takes my hand, and I pull her up until we're both standing.

"I'll be up at six, but I'll keep it down so I don't wake you," I tell her as we walk to the hallway.

"I'm gettin' up at six-thirty anyway, so no big deal if you do."

"Okay, well, good night." I kiss her forehead, then turn to go toward my room.

"Wait." She wraps her arms around my waist, pressing her cheek on my back, and my breath hitches at the intimate touch.

"Thank you for givin' me a safe place to stay. I know I fought you on it, and I probably will continue to, but I appreciate it nonetheless." Her soft voice is filled with remorse and it has me fighting the urge to spin around and claim her mouth.

Instead, I rest my palms against the back of her hands and hold her to me for a moment.

"You're welcome, Sunny." Then I pat her knuckles. "Sweet dreams."

"Night." She releases me, and it's not until I hear her door shut that my feet finally move.

As I lie in my bed, it feels wrong.

Wrong that she's across the hall instead of next to me.

But if I'm going to stay true to my words and be respectful of her boundaries and wishes, I'm not going to steal her from her bed and put her in mine.

Even as much as I want to.

Chapter Thirty-Four
Magnolia

10 WEEKS PREGNANT

I've never peed so much in my damn life. Just when I get comfortable in bed, I have to get up and go again. Since I'm avoiding caffeine and coffee overall, I've been sucking down water nonstop. It's not a major issue when I'm at home, but while I'm at work, it's the biggest inconvenience not having a nearby bathroom. With it being the Christmas holiday season, downtown is packed with shoppers who need their caffeine fix. I have to put up my "Be Back in 10" sign every thirty minutes to run to the bookstore across the street, and if I don't purchase a book soon, Mrs. Weis is going to ban me.

Hell, I'm about to bring a bucket to squat over because it's getting ridiculous at this point. Apparently, it's because my uterus is starting to push on my bladder, but it's only going to get worse as the baby grows, too.

TRIPP

> I'm leaving in 5. Need me to bring anything before I pick you up?

I'm closing early today since I have my first ultrasound

326

appointment to officially confirm my pregnancy and due date. Of course, as soon as I made the appointment, Tripp was adamant about going with me so I wasn't alone. Noah offered to join me, but she decided to put on a holiday festival at the ranch with a few weeks to spare, so I didn't want to take away any of her valuable time. Plus, it's not like Tripp wouldn't have tagged along anyway. If I didn't know any better, he's more excited about the baby than I am. Since we've become roommates, he tells me each week what fruit size the baby is.

At ten weeks, the baby is the size of a kumquat, which is one inch in diameter.

Yeah, I had to look that one up too because what the hell is a kumquat?

MAGNOLIA

No, I think I'm good. But I'm gonna stop at the store quickly for a bag of Goldfish crackers so you can pick me up from there.

TRIPP

I just bought four bags when I went shopping this morning so I'll bring one with me.

MAGNOLIA

You did? The Flavor Blast kind?

TRIPP

Yep. I saw your cheese fingerprints on the cupboards and then saw you were getting low so I grabbed more.

My cheeks heat at how he notices such small things but still takes the time to buy more for me. He knows they're my go-to snack because I can keep them down easily and although it's not the healthiest, it satisfies my cravings in the middle of the night when I need something cheesy and crunchy.

MAGNOLIA

Well, thank you. I'll wait at the coffee trailer, then.

This isn't the first time he's restocked my snacks for me either. After I moved in, we went to the grocery store, and I stocked up on my favorite Greek yogurts. Sadly for me, certain yogurt flavors made me sick, so I've been sticking to the one that agrees with me. When he noticed I was out of the banana cream, he went out of his way to get more, but the store was out of stock. So instead of skipping it, he drove fifty miles to another store and bought me three cases so I wouldn't run out.

Unfortunately, now banana cream makes me nauseous, probably because I ate it three times a day for three weeks. I felt horrible telling him, but he just shrugged and said no biggie, he'd eat some and share the rest with his brothers. They were more than happy to take them off our hands.

As I sit and wait on the curb, I admire the town's holiday decorations flooding Main Street. All the small businesses are covered in red, green, and white. I added some garland outside the coffee trailer, and once I launched my new holiday drinks, it finally felt like Christmas. It's been a weird month, but I'm excited to spend Christmas Eve with my parents tomorrow and go to the Hollises on Christmas Day.

"Hey, why aren't you inside the trailer where it's warm?" Tripp asks, jumping out of his truck after he parks.

"Because I already locked it up and you were on your way," I argue, taking his hand when he offers to help me up.

"You're gonna get sick out here," he scolds, wrapping his palms around my cold fingers and blowing warm air on them. "C'mon, let's go. Truck is toasty warm for ya."

The weather has cooled down to the fifties, but he's acting like we're in negative temps. I'm already bundled up as much as I can tolerate, but I don't fight him on it.

"Are you nervous?" he asks as he pulls back onto the street.

"A little, I guess. This'll make everything feel more *real*, but it'll be interesting to see how it looks on the screen, ya know?"

"It'll be cool to see. Like a little minnow swimmin' in your belly."

My mouth falls open and he laughs at my reaction. "Don't call my baby a fish!"

"I looked it up on YouTube for ten to twelve-week ultrasounds, and that's legit what it looks like!" He squishes his lips together and makes a fish face. "It can be their nickname: Baby Fishy."

I glare at him, and he smirks. "Not onboard?"

"Well, it's better than your Baby Kumquatty idea."

"Only until next week when it's the size of a peapod. Then we'll call it Petey. Get it?"

Tilting my head, I study him. "Did you memorize the baby size chart or somethin'?"

"I have a pregnancy app on my phone so I can keep track."

"*You* do? Why?"

"It's cool to watch, and I like reading the updates. At ten weeks, the baby has all of its organs. Oh, and it officially graduated from an embryo to a fetus this week." He leans over and fist-bumps my belly, which is no longer flat and instead looks like I'm bloated. "Congrats on the achievements, Fishy."

I stare at him in shock and awe that he's not only keeping track but reading about it.

"Oh, and it says you may start to get more constipated so maybe add more fiber into your diet."

"Okay, no more reading for you," I deadpan.

Talking about my bowel movements is where I draw the line. I'm still trying to wrap my brain around how a baby the size of a watermelon is going to launch out of my vagina without tearing me in half. I'll probably never have sex again.

"It's common in the first trimester!" He waves out a hand as if this is general knowledge to everyone. "It also mentioned mood swings, so..." He side-eyes me as if he's waiting for me to snap at him any minute. "You might be crankier or weepier than usual, which is totally normal for the first trimester. Resting, eating healthy, and avoiding stress are key to help balance your hormones."

"Are you seriously mansplaining hormonal changes to me?"

"Nope. Just sharin' the data. But there was an informative section about vaginal discharge too if you wanna —"

"Please shut up."

He clamps his mouth and stays quiet for the rest of the drive.

It's bad enough I have to go through these changes. I don't need the man I was sleeping with to know about them, too.

Although he's respected my wishes to return to friends, he continues doing sweet things for me and making it hard to resist falling back into old habits. Even though he's not crossed any lines, he's still acting like a caring boyfriend, and that messes with my head. I have to remind myself that this is for the best.

We arrive at the hospital, and after he helps me out of his truck, he takes my bag and holds it as we walk side by side. The receptionist smiles when she sees us approach, and I know it's only a matter of time before someone asks if he's the dad. I haven't quite figured out how to answer that question without it making things awkward.

No, he's my ex who I broke up with after I found out I was pregnant with another man's baby and although we aren't dating, we live together.

Totally normal.

"You can take a seat, and the tech will be out shortly to grab you and your boyfriend."

Welp, there it is.

"Thank you, ma'am." Tripp grins, then grabs my hand and intertwines our fingers. "C'mon, *love.*"

There's a faint smirk on his face, and I know he enjoyed that way too much.

I follow him to the waiting room and sit next to him in a separate chair.

"Ya know, it's only a matter of time before people find out I'm pregnant."

"Okay, and? Are you plannin' to deny it and say you're just puttin' on weight?"

I smack his thigh at his smart-ass comment. "And if you let

people think you're my boyfriend, they're gonna assume the baby's yours. So you might wanna correct 'em before rumors spread."

"And say what? That I'm your gay best friend here for moral support?"

I roll my eyes at his dramatics. "That we're *friends*. Or even roommates."

He leans in closer. "Hmm...doesn't feel appropriate for someone who's had their whole face in your pussy."

"Tripp!" I whisper-hiss, glancing around to make sure no one else heard him.

He shoots me a grin, then places his hand on my shaky leg. "Relax. Who cares what they think?"

I swallow hard, lowering my gaze. "Well, I figured you would. Not gonna help ya out in the whole *dating* department if chicks think you have a baby on the way."

"No? Because I've heard lots of women dig single dads." He waggles his brows, and I know he's messing with me.

"I swear to God, you're intolerable. You're gettin' worse than Landen."

His bemused expression drops. "Hey, no need to insult me now."

"Magnolia Sutherland?"

I pop out of my chair and turn toward the ultrasound tech. She greets me with a smile and Tripp follows me toward her.

"Hi," I say nervously.

"Hi! I'm Ginny, and I'll be doing your ultrasound today." She points down the hall. "The room's down here."

We walk behind her and my nerves start to get the best of me. Although I'm excited, I've been reading horror stories of pregnancies gone wrong and miscarriages.

"Is this y'all's first baby?" she asks as we enter the room.

"Uh...yeah. First one."

"Well, congratulations! Don't worry, I'll walk you through

everythin'." She's cheerful and sweet, which I appreciate, but inside, my stomach is doing somersaults.

"That wand is going where now?" I blink as she explains a transvaginal ultrasound.

She reiterates what she told me about not being far enough along for a regular ultrasound so they do a vaginal one to get a better look, but there's no way that mammoth is going to fit up there.

"It's scarier than it looks," she says.

"I told her the same thing when she had a similar reaction to me the first time," Tripp blurts.

Oh my God. I'm going to murder this man.

Before I can, Ginny bursts out laughing. "That's funny. Already comin' in with the dad jokes."

"Oh, he's not—"

"I have the next seven months to come up with more," Tripp cuts me off, and I shoot him a death glare.

"I'll let ya change into your gown and be back in a few to get started. Don't use the bathroom until after because a full bladder helps us see inside the uterus better."

"Wait, so you're gonna shove that between my legs while I have to pee?"

Speaking of, I'm already fighting gravity to keep it in there.

"Yeah, I'm sorry. I know it's uncomfortable, but as soon as I get the baby's measurements, if you really need to, you can go and let a little out before I grab some photos."

A little? Once I start, there's no stopping it.

"Okay, thank you."

"Be back in a few."

Once the door closes, I let out a breath.

"Sunny, are you okay?"

"I have to pee," I say urgently, rushing to the bathroom.

"No! You can't." He quickly blocks the door. "You have to hold it."

"I can't! It's gonna leak down my legs soon."

"Yes, you can. You're stronger than you realize. Just don't think about it."

"Easy for you to say." I cross my legs.

"Remember the time you and Noah snuck out to go to some field party?"

I nod but what a random thing to bring up.

"You guys drank for like three hours straight before Noah finally called and asked me for a ride. I was fuckin' pissed, but y'all knew I couldn't say no. By the time I came out, you were clenching your legs together because you had to go so badly."

"Yes, and you told me to go squat by a tree." I make a disgusted face because hell no was I about to expose my whole ass and vagina where bugs live.

"And since you're stubborn as shit, you wouldn't, and I warned you that you'd have to hold it until we got home."

"Which was over thirty minutes away."

"And you begged me to distract you so you wouldn't think about it."

"Oh yeah." I smile at the memory of him giving me his undivided attention for a solid half an hour. "You talked about *Twilight* with me the entire ride home and by the time we got back, I didn't even have to pee anymore."

He shakes his head as he chuckles. "Fuckin' vampires, but yes. So you already know you have the self-control to do this. I'll be right next to you to keep you distracted. Okay?"

I nod. "Okay."

He holds up the gown and opens it for me. "Pants and underwear off."

Twirling my finger, I motion for him not to look. Instead, he closes his eyes and stays put. Once I slide my arms into the gown, I spin around, holding it closed the best I can so he doesn't see my bare ass, and then he ties it for me.

I situate myself on the table, and when Ginny returns a few minutes later, she turns off the lights and explains more of the process and what she'll be looking for on the screen.

She lubes up the mammoth wand and slowly slides it between my legs. It's not as bad as I anticipated since she's not shoving the whole thing up there. Just a little discomfort.

"Alright, you see this here?" She points to an avocado-shaped bubble. "That's the amniotic sac and right inside there is the baby. You can see their two little legs and arms."

"And a big head," Tripp teases, gripping my hand with both of his.

"Yep. And it's movin' a lot. Very active. That's a good sign," she reassures me.

My heart's ready to beat out of my chest as I stare at the screen and take in everything she's telling me. I can't believe that's *inside* me.

"Told you it's a little minnow." Tripp chuckles, and I grin.

"See that little flutter in the center? That's the heart beating."

A quick, loud squishing noise fills the room, and my eyes gloss over because for the first time since taking those pregnancy tests, it feels more *real* than before. Being able to see and hear it makes a huge difference in understanding all the changes my body's going through.

It hits me that I'm going to be a *mom* in seven months. A wave of panic hits me alongside excitement. I thought I'd be much older when I'd have kids, but now that it's happening when I'm twenty-three, I can't say I'm mad about it. Despite how it happened and being scared for what the future holds, I already love this baby more than anything in the world.

"The heartbeat is 155 beats per minute, which is perfect," Ginny says. "I'm gonna measure from the top of the head to the feet and do a few more to see how far along you are and get your estimated due date."

I nod and Tripp squeezes my hand.

Ginny looks between us. "Dad, if you wanna record the screen, feel free. I'll print out photos at the end for y'all."

Tripp looks at me, either waiting for me to correct her

assumption or give him approval to take a video. I'm not sure. But I tell him to go ahead and start recording.

"The baby is measuring exactly ten weeks."

"Yeah, that's what I thought. I track my cycles and knew exactly when my last period was."

"Perfect. That means your EDD is mid-July," she says.

"My app says July fourteenth. My best friend is two weeks behind me, so our babies will hopefully be born in the same month," I tell her.

"Oh my gosh, how excitin'! Was that planned?" she teases.

"Um, no!" I laugh. "Neither of us was tryin'."

"Well, then it was meant to me. Built-in best friends for life."

I smile warmly at that thought. "I hope so."

Tripp continues recording while never taking his hand off mine.

"Alright, I got some great pics."

Once they're printed, she hands them to me, and I can't contain the smile on my face.

Baby's first ultrasound photo.

If I were any good at scrapbooking like Noah, I'd make one for all the pictures and milestones, but framing it for my bedroom will have to do for now.

"Good to go?" Tripp asks once I'm dressed and have used the bathroom.

"Yep. At least until I have to pee again in fifteen minutes."

He takes my hand, lacing our fingers, and leads me toward his truck. "We should celebrate."

"Celebrate?" I ask when he opens the passenger door for me.

"First ultrasound. First photos. First time seeing him or her. It's a big moment!" He beams, handing me the roll of pictures. "Since we're here, let's go shoppin' at a baby store."

"You wanna look at baby stuff?" I confirm, jumping inside the truck.

He licks his lips as if he's holding back. "I'd fuckin' love to, Sunny."

Then he winks and goes around to the driver's side.

"And we can grab some food while we're out."

"Okay. Let's do it."

I might not be able to eat a lot since everything either makes me sick or doesn't look appetizing, but I still enjoy hanging out with Tripp regardless of our situation. He's been nothing but supportive, and we have fun hanging out, so why not?

It can't hurt.

Well...it might hurt.

Chapter Thirty-Five
Tripp

After buying the cutest baby onesies with horse silhouettes and cowboy hats on them, being mistaken as the baby daddy by three employees in the store, and taking Magnolia to Texas Roadhouse where she devoured four rolls and a steak, we arrive back to town way past dark.

She's passed out by the time we get home, and this time, I don't want to wake her. After I bring in her shopping bags and takeout boxes of desserts we couldn't finish, I lift her into my arms and carry her inside.

The Christmas tree lights guide me through the hallway, and once I place her on the bed, I remove her jacket and shoes.

"Tripp?" she murmurs with her eyes still closed.

"You're okay, love. Just gettin' you into bed."

"I'm so sleepy."

"I know. Do you want under the covers or should I bring in an extra blanket?"

"Yeah."

I chuckle and decide to grab her one from the linen closet so I don't have to move her.

She snuggles into her pillow as I tuck her in and a cute little moan escapes her throat.

"Night, Sunny." I brush hair off her forehead, then lean down to kiss her there. "Sweet dreams."

She's silent as I tiptoe out of her bedroom and close the door.

With it being Christmas Eve tomorrow, she's not working and can sleep in if she needs to. She's had a busy month, and I know she could use the extra rest.

Once I get our food in the fridge, I take a few minutes to tidy up the rest of the house. Looking around at the decorations we put up a few weeks ago, a part of me is sad we'll have to take them down soon. The memory of that day is a good one, considering she had just moved in a week earlier and we were still adjusting to the awkwardness. Bringing out all my bins and getting the tree set up while watching one of her favorite holiday movies was a nice icebreaker to put us back in the friendly hangout zone.

Every time I'm near her, I'm tempted to pull her into my arms and kiss her senseless. I can't help wanting to touch her in some way, even if it's just holding her hand or rubbing her back. Forgetting how it feels to be with her isn't something I can do, and sometimes I can't hold back.

Two weeks ago, the sheriff announced Travis as a suspect in the robberies and break-ins, and it seems ever since then, she's more determined than before to keep me at a distance beyond friendship. She thinks my being associated with her will somehow put a bad light on my family because of his bad reputation. With her dating history being tied to him, she's really stretching the line between his criminal behavior and it somehow affecting me, but still, I'm trying to respect her decision.

No one outside of my family and her dad knows the baby is his, and if it were up to me, I'd keep it that way.

It wasn't much of a shock to learn Travis was into some sketchy shit, but him breaking into her apartment is where I'm confused since he didn't even take anything. The only thing that'd make sense is if he thought it'd rattle her up enough to run back to him for safety.

Well, good job, motherfucker. It brought her to *me* instead.

Stay With Me

Even if we aren't "dating" per se, she's here in my house and in my life.

That's all that matters.

But he's only a suspect, and now he's missing.

They released some of the footage they got from the break-ins where you can see the license plates of the car he runs back to afterward. Dumbass isn't even smart enough to know to cover his plates because there are cameras everywhere now.

I hope he stays gone and then she'll never have to tell him.

As I stare at the ultrasound photo, I feel a warmth of pride and hope. I want to be a part of the baby's life as much as Magnolia will allow and if she lets me, I'd be here for every step and milestone.

I snap a photo of it and then send it along with the video I took earlier to Noah, my brothers, and parents. Looking at it, I get an idea for the scrapbook I started weeks ago. Even if all I can ever be is "Uncle Tripp," I want to document everything.

WILDER

You sure that kid's not yours? It's got a big head just like you.

WAYLON

And it has a little peen like yours, too.

TRIPP

You dipshits, that's the leg. And how would you know?

LANDEN

Is it a boy or girl?

TRIPP

We don't know yet. Not until she's twenty weeks.

NOAH

Awwww what a cutie!

Brooke Montgomery

TRIPP

Five different people thought I was the dad today.

LANDEN

Yikes. How'd that go?

TRIPP

Well, we didn't correct them.

WILDER

I know I give you shit 99% of the time, but you need to be careful. You're gonna get attached to the idea of a baby that isn't yours, and she could walk away at any time.

LANDEN

Magnolia wouldn't do that.

WILDER

Maybe not, but Tripp's putting himself in a position to get hurt.

TRIPP

Are you actually worried about me? Is that love I hear?

WILDER

Fuck off. Don't get used to it.

A laugh bubbles out of me because this is a whole new side to Wilder I haven't seen in a long-ass time.

TRIPP

I appreciate the concern. But trust me, I know. I'm willing to risk it.

WAYLON

You still think she's gonna change her mind and wanna get back together, don't you?

Stay With Me

TRIPP

I'm hoping that, yeah. We were good together.

And I'm madly, deeply, stupidly in love with her.

NOAH

She's still processing all the changes she's going through on top of this Travis stuff, so it's possible she'll eventually realize she doesn't want to lose you and will admit she wants to be with you, too. But you can't push her about it. She has to decide on her own about this.

I'm well aware and would never give her an ultimatum in order to stay in my life.

TRIPP

Hmm, do you think the diamond ring I got her for Christmas is too much?

I'm only messing with them, but their consistent wave of messages cussing me out is amusing as hell.

TRIPP

Christ, y'all are gullible.

NOAH

Don't do that to me, asshole! I'm pregnant too in case you forgot. Don't be giving me a stroke.

WILDER

Wait, does this mean she's technically single?

TRIPP

It means if you don't stop gawking at her like I keep catching you doing, I'm going to find a Hawk to pluck out your eyeballs so you can never look at her again.

WILDER

I don't think that's possible.

341

WILDER

It's not, is it?

When no one responds, he continues.

WILDER

IS IT??

I bellow out a laugh because one quick Google search would tell him what an idiot he is.

Even though I make jokes with my siblings, I did get Magnolia something special for Christmas, and yeah, it's probably something that screams more than *just friends*, but I meant what I said. We'll never be just that.

I bought her a rose gold charm bracelet with charm sentimental pieces—a sunflower, cowboy hat, baby onesie, iced coffee, tiny axe, dinosaur, pickup truck, and then in the middle the letter M with her emerald birthstone.

She might hate it since it'll remind her of our short-lived relationship, but even if those memories are all they will ever be and nothing more, I want her to never forget what we once had.

Chapter Thirty-Six
Magnolia

20 WEEKS PREGNANT

"Whoa, what're you watchin'?"

I'm curled up on the couch with a blanket, a large bowl of extra butter popcorn, and a Sprite when Tripp walks in from work. His eyes are wide as coasters, and his tone is harsh like he's caught me watching porn.

"A movie. You wanna join me?"

"*My Girl*? Have you never seen this before?"

"No, I never heard of it until thirty minutes ago. But I saw that kid from *Home Alone* was in it, and the trailer looked good. It's one of those oldies from the '90s. It's cute so far."

He cautiously sits next to me, worry etched across his features. The movie features a little girl named Vada and her best friend, Thomas J, growing up in the '70s. Her dad owns a funeral parlor and his new makeup artist, Shelly, is talking to Vada in a bathroom about makeup and boys.

Like I said, it's cute.

I shove popcorn into my mouth and a few fall down to my chest and over the ski hill I call my baby bump. It's growing faster than I can keep up with buying new clothes, so I've been stealing

Tripp's T-shirts. He hasn't complained, so I assume he doesn't mind.

"I-I'm not sure you should be watchin' this, Sunny. It has a sad scene."

"What're you talkin' about? The trailer made it look sweet and happy."

Considering I cry at the drop of a hat, I understand his concern, but he must be confusing this one with a different movie. It's about an eleven-year-old girl going through some new life changes, to which I can relate on a different adult level, and witnessing her father dating for the first time in twenty years.

"Trust me...you're not gonna like it."

"Just because I'm emotional and pregnant doesn't mean I can't handle a somewhat sad movie. Plus, that Bingo scene was kinda funny. I don't think you know what you're talkin' about."

He scratches his head, presumably giving up on trying to convince me to turn it off. I've had a busy week at work, I'm tired and feel fat, so I treated myself to a movie night.

"How was work today?" I look over at him watching me.

"Kinda busy actually. Had five new check-ins at cabin call and they all requested Wilder as their horseback riding tour guide, so I have a sneakin' suspicion he's been posting thirst traps on social media again."

I burst out laughing at the idea of what a horseback *thirst trap* could entail, but now I must see this. "That's hilarious. Well, now ya can't say Wilder doesn't help bring in money."

"Yeah, well, I didn't tell you they were all women in their forties and fifties."

Now I'm laughing so hard my side hurts.

"I need to get to the retreat side more often and watch the twins at work."

"Don't even think about it," he warns, which has me fighting back a smile.

I go back to the movie, and the family is hosting a Fourth of July party. Vada clearly doesn't like how close Shelly is with her dad and is trying to sabotage them in every way possible. But then Shelly's ex-husband and his brother show up, threatening to take the camper she's currently living in, and Mr. Sultenfuss obviously doesn't like them.

"Holy shit, did he just sucker punch her ex in the gut?" My mouth falls open, and I inch closer to the edge of the sofa to watch the drama unfold.

Then Mr. Sultenfuss delivers the best line I've ever heard.

"Then you'll probably be visiting us here quite often." And when the brother asks, *"why,"* Mr. Sultenfuss says, *"Because if he ever tries to take Shelly's camper again, I'm going to bury him in my front yard."*

"Oh my God! Now tell me that isn't something a book boyfriend would say." I exaggerate by fanning myself. "Holy shit, that's pretty hot for an old guy."

Tripp gives me a look like I'm insane.

"What? He stood up for his lady!" I hold out my hand toward the TV.

He crosses his arms. "Oh, but when I hit Travis, I'm dodgin' assault charges."

I snort, patting his leg. "This is the '70s, babe. Different times."

He rolls his eyes, and we sit back comfortably on the couch as we continue to watch Vada, who's decided she's running away to Hollywood.

And then she gets her dreaded period and wants to outlaw sex.

I hear ya, girlfriend. Periods and sex *should* be banned.

"Oh my gosh, Vada's in love with her poetry teacher. That's adorable."

He coughs. "That's a felony."

I give him a side-eye for trying to ruin my vibe.

The way they say the Pledge of Allegiance after they share their first kiss has me cackling.

"I dunno what the hell you're talkin' about. This movie is adorable."

He clasps his mouth shut, glances over at me, and remains quiet.

"Aw, he went back to find her mood ring."

Tripp's body tenses beside me.

"Oh no, the bees are back."

He glances at me again.

"Why isn't he running away?"

Okay, that was weird...

The scene just ends with Thomas J surrounded by them, and now we're back at Vada's house.

"Wait...what happened?" I smack Tripp's arm, who's unsettlingly quiet.

Now the sheriff is at the house, and her dad's walking up to Vada's room.

Her dad looks like he's about to cry...and I don't like where this is going.

"What does he mean he was allergic? No...there's *no* way."

My chest squeezes as I fight back the tears when I realize Thomas J died from too many bee stings.

And then the dam breaks when Vada runs to the doctor and says she can't breathe. Poor thing is having a panic attack.

Is that how Tripp felt when Billy died?

When they show the stretcher going into the funeral parlor, I swear I'm hyperventilating.

"Why didn't you warn me?" I cry out when he wraps his arm around my shoulders. "A *child*? This should be a crime."

"I *tried*..." he whispers, pulling me into his chest.

"He was her only friend..." I sob through my words as he holds me close.

Watching Vada cry for him and scream out how he can't see without his glasses at his funeral has me no longer able to see the screen through all the tears. And when she runs off to her teacher, Mr. Bixler, and finds out he's engaged, I'm done.

Tapped out.

This little girl is feeling so much pain, and it's breaking me.

Tripp rubs his palm over my hair, trying to calm me, but there's no point. My heart is shattered.

When I wipe my cheeks, my vision clears enough for me to continue watching. I might as well finish this horrible movie and see it through.

But the ending crushes me almost just as much.

When Vada runs into the little boy's mom, she tells her that her mother, who died after childbirth, is in heaven watching over Thomas J.

Then she goes back to class for the last day and reads her poem that's clearly about Thomas J. It's equally sweet and heartbreaking.

And then the "My Girl" song plays as she rides off on her bike with her new friend, Judy.

"See, it gets a happy ending," Tripp says.

I sit up and give him a look of disbelief.

"Are you serious? She loses her best friend."

"That's part of life, Sunny. Now she's learning to cope and how to move on."

I pull away, rolling my eyes and refusing to accept this movie as anything but a tragedy.

It has me wondering how much he thinks about Billy when he watches these types of movies. I'm not sure I could ever watch a sad one if anything happened to Noah.

"I hate this movie. Zero out of ten. Do not recommend." I grab the remote and turn off the TV.

"So I'm guessin' you don't wanna watch *My Girl 2*?"

"There's a *second* one?" I shriek. "What happens in that? Her dad dies next? Gets a puppy and then they accidentally run him over?"

The corner of his lip curls up as if he's fighting back a smile. "No, she goes to visit her uncle to learn more about her mother and shares a kiss with her step-cousin at the end."

"*What*? You're lyin'."

He full-on laughs at my reaction. "I swear. She's only thirteen, and there's no relation."

"I still don't trust it." I fold my arms. "Now I need to watch somethin' else to cleanse my brain and remove my memory of the past two hours."

He stands, brushing dirt off his jeans, and then looks at me. "Find a new one to watch while I take a quick shower. Then I'll make us something for dinner. What're you in the mood for?"

"Hmm...I'll let ya know when you're done."

He smirks. "Okay."

Before walking away, he leans down to meet my eyes. "Are you alright? You're not gonna stay out here and cry while I'm gone, are you?"

"No." I sniffle.

He cups my jaw and brushes his thumb along my cheek. The way he looks at me has me in a chokehold and unable to move. Almost as if he's trying to see into my soul.

"I'll be back in fifteen." He dips down, kisses my forehead, and walks toward his bedroom.

You'd think after over three months of living together, we wouldn't continue to have this unspoken connection that is still there after one month of dating. Sometimes I daydream about what it'd be like to tell him I want to get back together and how nice it'd be to give into these feelings. The ones that hit me so strongly, there are times I forget I can't just go up to him and kiss him because I drew the line between us.

After ten minutes of searching, I finally land on a new movie to watch. *The Last Song* with Miley Cyrus and Liam Hemsworth. Surely a movie with her in it won't be sad. It looks like a teenage girl reconnecting with her dad after her parents split.

As long as no one else dies, I'll be fine.

The trailer has upbeat music and a Miley Cyrus song, which we love to see.

Plus, a little eye candy never hurt anyone either.

Bingo.

Stay With Me

I cue it up and wait for Tripp. Lately, our movie nights have been few and far between with him working late. Sometimes I wonder if he's purposely working more because being around me is getting too hard for him. I'm invading his home and space, and although he told me it was fine for me to be here, I might be overstaying my welcome.

But then I look down at my wrist and the charm bracelet he gifted me for Christmas that was definitely more than what you'd gift someone you didn't want living in your house. When I first opened it, I was in shock that he'd do something so sentimental and sweet. Though I should've figured because this is Tripp we're talking about here. He's nothing if not extra thoughtful. It really outdid the gifts I got him, but he didn't make me feel guilty about it. I wear it every day and can't wait to add the baby's first initial once I settle on a name. My next ultrasound is in a few days, and then I'll get to find out the gender.

I've considered looking for a new place since I've been able to save money by not paying rent, but I'd need enough for a security deposit and to actually furnish said apartment, plus all the baby stuff. Only my bed and dresser survived Travis's wrath when he trashed it.

As I scroll through my social media, my phone rings with an unfamiliar phone number. Curiosity gets the better of me, and I pick up.

"Hello?"

An operator asking if I'll accept a call from the Sugarland Creek jail is the last thing I expect.

My first thought is one of the Hollis boys got arrested, and when they couldn't get ahold of Tripp, they'd called me. But then a voice I never expected echoes in my ear.

Travis.

No fucking way.

"Maggie, are you there?"

"Depends. Whaddya want?"

"I needed to hear your voice and make sure you're okay. I've been worried sick about you."

"Worried before or after you broke into my place and trashed it?"

"Baby, no. I didn't do that. Someone's after me. You gotta believe me."

I scowl because of course he'd lie.

"Uh-huh, and who exactly is that?"

"His name is Emilio, and he's dangerous, baby. I owe him some money, and he went after you to send me a message."

"Stop with the *baby*. What the hell are you talkin' about? Why would he come after me?"

"Because he followed me around for a couple of months and realized you're someone important to me, which is why I'm tellin' you to be careful. Now that you're on his radar, you're a target."

So he's using me to get to Travis? Or was it to get him out of hiding?

And wait—

"When did you get arrested?"

Last I knew, he was still on the town's wanted list.

"Last night, but they just now allowed me to make a call."

"And you're responsible for the robberies?"

"I was tryin' to get the money to pay him back so he wouldn't come after you. I was protectin' you."

I scoff in disbelief.

"How much, Travis? How much do you owe him?"

This wouldn't be the first time Travis got himself into money trouble. He likes to place bets he has no business placing.

"It ain't that much."

I roll my eyes, growing frustrated. "That's not what I asked."

"A hundred."

"A hundred *dollars*?" I ask, confused.

"Grand, baby. I gave him half of it already from the money I stole, so he just needs the other half, and he'll leave us alone."

"*Us*? Why am I involved in this?"

"I just told you. He knows you're my girlfriend, so he's

threatenin' your life to pressure me to pay him the other fifty. So I thought if I could borrow it from you, he'd leave us alone."

"First, I'm not your girlfriend or your baby, so stop that. And second, you're more delusional than I thought if you think I have that kind of money. I lost the majority of my things in my apartment, and I'm a small business owner. I'm not drownin' in assets here."

"Can't you take a loan out on your coffee thing?"

"Hell no. Even if I could or had the means, I wouldn't give it to you."

"Maggie, this is serious. He's gonna come after you worse than messin' up your place. Next, it'll be your car or your trailer. Or hell, he could *take* you."

My heart beats so hard in my chest I can barely hear him over the pounding.

"Why would he suddenly come for me after months of nothin'?" I ask, trying to piece all of this together.

"Because I was missin', but now that I got arrested and he knows I'm not dead, he'll start harassin' me and you again until he's paid."

"Who is this guy?"

"A bookie and he doesn't play around."

"Is he the type to wear an all-black suit and drive a Denali?" Flashbacks of that random guy who stopped by months ago hit me.

"Yes, that's him. He sent me a photo of you workin', which is why I had to keep stealin' money. Once I paid him the first half, it held him off for a bit, but he's gettin' impatient for the rest."

"Well, if he comes back around, I'll just tell him I have nothin' to do with you."

He chuckles darkly. "It don't work like that. He already knows you're an asset to me and will use you to get what he wants from me."

I blow out a frustrated breath because this isn't making a lot of sense to me. "Well, I have nothin' to offer him."

"That's not the point. You offer him leverage on gettin' what he wants from *me*. If I hadn't gotten caught, I have no doubt he woulda done something to you to smoke me out of hidin'."

Well, that's not reassuring in the least.

"Speakin' of which, where're you stayin', by the way, since you're not at your apartment?"

"That's none of your business."

"Maggie, I just wanna know that you're somewhere safe."

"I am."

"If you see anything suspicious, run away and call 911."

Anger boils inside me as the reality of his words crashes into me. "Why do you have to pull me into your bullshit, Travis? Just tell him we're not together and that you don't care about me anymore. You're a pro at lying and manipulating people. I'm sure you can convince him."

"Yeah, see, it's kinda hard to do that when you're walkin' around with a baby bump. He's a smart guy to put two and two together."

My breath hitches, and my heart implodes. There's no way I heard him correctly.

"Were you gonna tell me?" he asks when I don't speak.

Sighing, I blow out a defeated breath. "Eventually."

"So it is mine." He's not asking.

My head falls against the couch, wishing I could go back to five minutes ago before I picked up the phone.

"Yeah. But it doesn't change anything. We're not gettin' back together, and I want nothin' to do with whatever BS you got yourself in. How'd you find out if you've been in hidin'?"

"Emilio emailed me photos of you walkin' around town lookin' a little plump. He wrote, *Turns out you have two assets I can take.*"

I snarl at his choice of words. "He's followin' me around?"

"I've been tellin' you…and now, he knows you're knocked up. So if you have the money, it'd keep him off our backs *and* the baby's."

My throat tightens as I fight back angry tears at the mention of my baby.

"I already told you I don't have that kind of money," I hiss between my teeth.

"He also had a picture of you with Tripp Hollis."

"So?"

"You two together?"

"Again, none of your business."

"Well, I know your little boyfriend has more than enough money to cover fifty grand."

"How would you know that?"

"Everyone knows the Hollises are loaded. Look at their ranch and all the property they own. It's the most top-rated equine retreat in the South. Everything they own is the best of the best."

"Okay, even if his parents are wealthy, doesn't mean he is."

"It's only a matter of time before Emilio connects the dots and comes after Tripp and his family. They'd be payin' for their safety and protecting their business without puttin' a dent in their wallets. So it'd make things a lot easier just to have 'em give it to me so I can pay him off right away and no one has to be in danger."

Fuck me. This is exactly why I broke up with Tripp in the first place.

"They have nothin' to do with you."

"If he's associated with *you*, he's a target," he confirms. "I wouldn't put it past Emilio to do whatever it takes to get the cash."

The phone beeps, and Travis sighs. "My time's running out. I'll call you in a few days, and I'll need your decision by then. I'm safer here, so I'm not even gonna try to get bail."

"Wait, *what*? You're leavin' all the responsibility of this on me and hidin' in there? You fuckin' coward."

"I don't have the money, Maggie!"

"Neither do—"

The line cuts out before I can finish, and I'm seething before I even set my phone down.

This cannot be happening.

Chapter Thirty-Seven
Tripp

Once I've showered and changed, I walk into the living room to ask Magnolia what movie she picked. When I approach her on the couch, she's hardly breathing and is pale as a ghost.

"Hey, you alright?"

She doesn't move or speak for several seconds.

"Sunny?" I sit on the edge of the coffee table and cage her in with my legs. "What's wrong?"

Finally, she blinks and looks at me. "Travis just called and said he's in jail."

My brows shoot to my hairline and my spine straightens. "What're you talkin' about?"

She goes on to explain what he said, talking about some guy named Emilio and how he needs fifty thousand dollars to pay him off. Describes how he knows she's pregnant and basically how we're all in danger if we don't find a way to get this guy his money.

"Travis wasn't arrested," I tell her once she finishes.

After he was named a suspect, I asked the deputies to let me know as soon as he was found since Magnolia's apartment was one of the targets. He's been in hiding for months, and I figured he was long gone or *hoped* he was dead.

She tilts her head, narrowing her eyes at me with confusion. "Whaddya mean? I got a call from the county jail. That's what the operator said. I heard a warning beep about five minutes in and the call ended thirty seconds later."

"I mean, he's still missing. They haven't arrested him."

"How can you be so sure? He said they brought him in last night."

I pull out my phone from my pocket and call the sheriff's office. The dispatcher immediately puts me through to Sheriff Wagner.

"What can I do for you, Tripp?"

I put him on speaker so Magnolia can hear.

"Did you arrest Travis Boone last night?"

"No, son. I told you when I had him in custody, I'd tell ya."

I give Magnolia a pointed look.

"Travis called Magnolia just a few minutes ago claimin' he was, and the operator said the call came from Sugarland Creek jail."

He chuckles, and my irritation level ramps up.

"Wendy, did you send a call to Magnolia Sutherland tonight?" he calls out to his dispatcher.

"No, sir."

"Sounds like he faked it. Probably had someone pretend to be the operator or downloaded one of those voice talkin' apps you kids use on your phones. Either way, he's still on our wanted list. If we had him, the news woulda spread all over town by now."

"That's what I figured. Thanks for confirming."

"What'd he want?" he asks.

I explain everything Magnolia told me and by the time I've finished, the sheriff's cussing up a storm.

"He's pretendin' to be in jail so she'll give him money to pay off his bookie?" he confirms.

"That's what I'm assuming. A few months back, there was a guy matchin' his description who showed up at her coffee trailer in a blacked-out Denali, and it was obvious he wasn't from the area. Travis is also claimin' it was this guy who broke into Magnolia's apartment and not him—to give him some kind of *warning* that he'd go after her if he didn't pay up. But he fessed up to the other robberies."

"Give me his details, and I'll add him to our watch list."

Magnolia shares it with him, and I have to physically stop myself from digging my nails into my palms at how angry I am at Travis and the possible danger he's put her in.

"Alright, got it. What's the number he called you from?"

Magnolia pulls up the contact and rattles it off.

"That's a Florida area code," Sheriff Wagner tells us.

"He's probably using a burner phone," I say.

"Most definitely, but it gives me a location to start with to send out his wanted profile. If he's hiding and has limited funds, he's probably stayin' with someone or at the very least, somewhere cheap. Someone might recognize him down there. I can also cross-reference similar crimes from that area when I speak to their department. I'd be surprised if he's still around here with everyone lookin' for him."

"That's somewhat of a relief to think he's not even in the state," Magnolia says and adds, "How do I get a restraining order against him so if he comes near me, I can get him arrested for that, too?"

"You'll have to come in and fill out some paperwork for a temp order, but it shouldn't be difficult to get it filed," he explains. "But if he's found, he'll get arrested either way, sweetheart."

"I know. I just want some legal order of protection if he thinks I'm gonna help him or that he'll be safe comin' to me."

"We'll stop in first thing tomorrow," I tell him.

No way I'm letting Magnolia out of my sight now.

"I'd still be on alert in case he does come around here or if this Emilio guy resurfaces. Don't let your guards down," he says.

"Don't worry, I'm keepin' an eye on her."

"Alright, kids. See ya in the mornin'."

We say goodbye, and then I wrap her in my arms because she's visibly shaking.

"Sunny, it's gonna be okay. You know I won't let that fucker put a finger on you."

"And what 'bout you? They could come after your family, too."

He chokes out a laugh. "I'd like to see 'em try."

"I'm so pissed I bought his bullshit so easily. What the fuck is wrong with me? After all these years, I should know he's a goddamn liar."

"You couldn't have known with how he made it seem real." I soothe a hand down her back as she angry cries.

"How am I gonna work without constantly lookin' over my shoulder? I can't *not* work. My taser and pepper spray aren't gonna be much help if the guy has a gun."

"I'm gonna come with you every day."

She pulls back, wiping her cheeks. "How're you gonna do that when you have a job?"

"You only work till three, right? I'll get Landen or Waylon to cover for me during the day, and then I'll make sure you're with someone at all times while I do cabin call and catch up in the evening. You can hang out with Landen or Noah."

"You can't stay with me at my trailer for seven hours and then go work for another however many. When will you sleep?"

"I work till nine or ten and then go to bed."

Her head falls back on the couch with a groan. "This is all my fault. If I hadn't made him think there was a chance of us gettin' back together, I wouldn't even be on Emilio's radar."

"That's if Emilio is actually involved in this. Travis could be using him as an excuse to get money out of you or me."

"I dunno...he creeped me out when he showed up. He said my name in a provocative way, and the whole encounter was very odd. I think Travis could be exaggerating about him going after you for the sake of scaring me into gettin' him that money. But there's just so much that doesn't add up..." She rubs her temples.

"For all we know, Emilio could be leadin' this whole scam and forced Travis to tell me this story or throw me under the bus with him. Fuck, I dunno. There's a million scenarios running through my brain, and I can't keep up."

I grab her chin and tilt it up until she meets my gaze. "Whatever the situation ends up being, if it comes down to it — protecting you and the baby or giving this guy fifty thousand — I'd pay up in a heartbeat."

She pulls back abruptly. "You can't. That's way too much."

"Not when it comes to your life, Sunny."

"What if it's just Travis's way of scamming you out of the money and he doesn't even owe this guy? Or he already paid him off and he wants the cash to run off for good?"

I shrug. "Still safer to just give him what he wants. I'd pay double if it meant he left for good."

The look on her face has me wishing I could freely kiss the sadness away.

She snarls. "I hate him so much. And I know I shouldn't wish ill will or death on someone, but if he is in Florida, I hope an alligator eats him."

I snort out a laugh. "Out of all the ways to die that's what you'd pick?"

"Why not? Sounds horrifying."

"True."

After a beat of silence, she sits up. "Do you think I need to be worried about my dad? He didn't mention him, but I wouldn't put it past him to threaten him next."

"Yeah, you should probably tell him just so he knows. The more people are aware, the better so they're not blindsided."

She nods.

After we go to the sheriff's office, I'll update my parents on what's going on and then grab my handgun from their safe while I'm at their house.

"Well, what're you hungry for?" I ask, hoping we can end the night on a better note.

"Don't laugh." She looks up at me through her eyelashes, a hint of pink on her cheeks.

"Okay?"

"I'm cravin' mac 'n' cheese and two hotdogs. Like the Kraft kind." She purses her lips, then adds, "Well, the *baby* is."

I smirk at how cute she looks flustered over boxed pasta. Considering I have plenty in the pantry, she has nothing to be embarrassed about.

"Your secret's safe with me." I wink. "Just don't tell Gramma Grace or she'll be in here teachin' you the family recipe."

"She could stand next to me, hand me the ingredients all measured out, and never take her eyes off me, and I'd still manage to mess it up. It's a miracle I can bake boxed muffins."

I laugh at her dramatics, and each time she says something so oddly specific like this, I fall even harder for her.

"Did you decide on a movie?" I ask once I'm in the kitchen.

"*The Last Song*. It looks like one of those cute young teenage romances."

I quickly revert back to the living room and swipe the remote. "Were you sheltered as a child? You cannot watch that."

"Why the hell not?" She furrows her brows, reaching up to steal it back. "I like Miley."

"It's based on a Nicholas Sparks novel. You know, the author of *The Notebook*, *A Walk to Remember*, *The Best of Me*." I arch a brow, hoping she'll understand what I'm implying.

No happy endings.

"Oh." Her expression drops. "Someone dies in this one?"

"Yeah." I turn toward the TV. "Here, I'll pick something."

"Disney Plus?" She groans when I scroll through the 'family-friendly' options.

"Here we go. A classic."

She snorts. "*The Parent Trap*?"

I shrug. "What's wrong with it? At least it has an HEA."

She inches closer to the edge of the couch. "In what world do two parents break up and think, yeah, let's just each take a child and split up twins, live on different continents, and never talk again or see our other kid. Or tell them they have a sibling." She crosses her legs and folds her arms as she leans back on the couch, shooting me a look of disapproval.

Just when I think she's done and I hit play, she continues.

"And for eleven freakin' years! The staff knew everything, which makes it worse. Then, you're tellin' me all it takes to get 'em back together is a boat dinner date? You *hated* your ex so much you left one of your children presumably for the rest of their life, and all it would've taken to put your family back together is one conversation!"

She's having a full-on meltdown at this point, and I'm not sure if I should laugh or be scared at how passionate she is about this.

"You're aware you're analyzin' a Disney movie when you read alien and monster smut?"

"You don't read those for the plot...or logic. Those are meant to be fun!"

I chuckle, clicking the remote again. "We're never gonna find a movie at this rate."

After going back and forth for ten minutes, we finally agree on something safe—one where she won't cry from devastation or send her off into a script rant. Then once our food is done, I stir the cut-up hotdogs into the pasta and serve it in a bowl, per her request, and we sit next to each other on the couch.

Every time we're this close, the urge to pull her in and kiss her is so strong, I have to constantly remind myself not to cross the line. In order to get back together, she's going to have to make the first move. The ball's in her court, and I stay a sitting duck until she realizes we belong together.

I'll wait for as long as I have to. Until she drops her guard and lets me back in.

It's not until the last ten minutes of *Erin Brockovich* that Magnolia loses her battle with trying not to cry. But this time it's tears of happiness.

"Oh my gosh..." She grabs my arm and leans against it as we

watch one of the final scenes. "Imagine your life being changed so drastically overnight and makin' a huge difference to hundreds of families' lives."

"I forgot how good this one was," I admit when Erin's boss drops off a two-million-dollar check on her desk. "Hadn't seen it in years."

"I love how independent and strong she is for her three kids. She made mistakes along the way, but she didn't let it hold her back. She demanded respect, and it paid off."

"And she had a full career after that," I say.

"Do you think she and George stayed together?" She gazes up at me with hope in her brown eyes.

I already know they didn't based on what I remember seeing years ago, but I'm not about to break her heart when she gives me that look.

"Definitely." I grin.

She smiles, then yawns. "I think I'm gonna try to go to sleep."

After the night we've had, I don't blame her. "Me too."

I grab our dishes and bring them to the sink. When I turn slightly to open the dishwasher, I bump into her stomach and quickly wrap an arm around her waist to hold her in place. "Shit, sorry."

"It's my fault. I didn't know you were gonna turn around." She licks her lips as she studies mine. "I was just gonna ask if you needed any help in here."

"No, don't worry about it. Gonna finish rinsin' these, then wipe down the counters, and I'll be done. Go ahead and get ready for bed. We have a busy day tomorrow," I remind her.

She nods and then gives me a side hug. "Okay, night. See ya in the mornin'."

Before she walks away, I press a kiss on her forehead and keep my hold on her for a split second longer than I should. "Sweet dreams, Sunny."

As I lie in bed, staring at the ceiling, my mind races with every negative thought involving Travis and how he's capable of hurting Magnolia. I don't know what he's up to or what the truth of the situation is, but I'd take a thousand knives to the chest before letting him get to her again.

After tossing and turning for an hour, a soft knock on my bedroom door grabs my attention.

"Come in," I say, pushing myself up against the headboard.

"Hey, are you awake?" Magnolia asks quietly.

"Yeah. Can't sleep."

"Me neither." She steps in and stares at the sunflower tattoo on my chest. "I'm too anxious."

Same. "You wanna lie with me for a bit?"

She plays with the hem on my T-shirt that she wears every night. It slides up her bare legs, revealing her white panties and little baby bump. I don't think she even realizes she's doing it, but I've noticed it's one of her nervous habits.

"Would that be too weird for you?" she asks.

I scoot over, pulling the blankets back. "Nope, get in here."

She smiles and crawls in next to me, lying on her side away from me. Once she's situated, I cover us up and snuggle in next to her.

"Do you wanna talk about it?" I ask. "Maybe it'll help you feel better."

"Not really."

"Okay. Lemme know if you change your mind." I stay on my back, but we're close enough to share each other's body heat.

Fifteen minutes of silence pass between us before her breath hitches and she gasps. "Oh my gosh, the baby kicked really hard. Gimme your hand."

Rolling toward her, I circle my arm around her waist, and she puts it on her stomach. "Hold on. She's super active at night."

"*She?*" I ask.

Her shoulder lifts. "It feels like a girl."

I smile at that. A moment later, a little nudge pushes against my palm.

"Did you—"

"Yep. Wow, that's incredible. A little boxer in your belly."

She giggles. "No kiddin'. I've felt little flutters all week, but this is the first big one."

Instead of releasing my hold on her, I lean up on my elbow and stay put.

And she doesn't take her hand off mine either.

"Do you remember that girl name you suggested a while ago before I even knew I was pregnant?" she asks after a few minutes of silence.

"*Belladonna?*" I tease.

She elbows my chest with a laugh. "Willow. If it's a girl, that's what I think I'm gonna name her."

"It's a beautiful name."

"And if it's a boy, Finn."

My mouth dips to her shoulder, and I instinctively press a kiss there. "After your dad. He'll be so honored."

"Yeah, I think so too."

"But now you know what that means? If you do have a girl, you'll have to try for a boy so you use that name."

"You think I'm poppin' out more than one of these? My vagina's already been violated by the wand mammoth, and once the baby comes out, it'll never be the same."

"I don't think that's true," I argue. "Want me to check?"

"Tripp!" She bursts out laughing, and I do too.

"From a friend to a friend, ya know? Just a little *friendly* favor."

"Oh, sure. In that instance, I could ask Landen."

I tighten my hold, inching closer to her ear. "Landen's already heard you screamin' my name through the ceiling and knows if he goes anywhere near your pussy, he's a dead man. You wanna be responsible for his murder?"

"That seems quite extreme for a *friendly* medical exam," she retorts.

"Then I wouldn't push for it, Sunny."

I imagine her rolling her eyes at me, but when she doesn't push me away, I stay snuggled up behind her with my hand on her belly and close my eyes.

Dreaming of the day I get to openly claim her as mine again.

Chapter Thirty-Eight
Magnolia

"Hello, welcome! How can I caffeinate you today?" I greet a new customer.

"Hi, um…I'm not sure. What do you suggest?"

I lean over the counter and point to my menu with all my beverage options and explain a few in detail.

"If you like sweets, I'd suggest the Maple Me Crazy Latte, but if you have a more bitter spicy palate, then I'd say the Basic Witch Spice."

He nods as he reads what's in each one. "Actually, I'll try the Hot Mess Express. Sounds good."

"Amazin' choice. That's my favorite." I wink. "Can I get you a muffin with your drink?"

"Sure, whatever you have."

He reaches for his wallet as I ring him up. When I glance to my left, Tripp's glaring at me with his arms crossed.

"That'll be seven-fifty," I tell him, leaning over the counter again.

He hands me a ten and tells me to keep it.

"Aw, you're too kind. Thank you." I smile at him, then get started on his latte.

Instead of Tripp sitting on the bucket like I've asked, he stands and makes his presence known to the guy.

"Haven't seen you 'round here. You a local?" he asks the guy.

I groan at the harshness of his tone.

"Just moved here. I work at my aunt's bookstore across the street."

"Mrs. Weis is your aunt? Oh my gosh, I *adore* her." I gush but am lying through my teeth. She's the one who writes in her notebook every time I stop in to use her bathroom. Not sure what she plans on doing with her little notes, but if she doesn't want me squatting on the sidewalk in front of her store, she'll deal with it.

"It's only temporary until I go to college, but yeah, not a bad job," he says.

I turn around and set his drink down, then bag up his muffin. "Guess that means we'll be seein' a lot of each other."

"Yeah, there aren't many coffee places here."

Which benefits me greatly.

"Have a magnificent day. See you soon…"

"Grant," he supplies.

I hold out my hand, and he takes it. "Magnolia. Welcome to Sugarland Creek"

Before we can pull apart, Tripp's hand comes between us. "And I'm the boyfriend."

I grind down on my teeth to stop myself from causing a scene.

"Nice to meet y'all." Grant nods, taking his items. "See ya later."

"Bye now." I wave before he walks across the street.

"Are you freakin' kidding me?" I turn toward Tripp and whisper-shout.

"Do you have to flirt with every single guy when I'm here?"

"I'm being *nice*, Tripp! It's how I get tips. I know you've never worked in customer service, but this is literally part of the job."

This is our third argument about it in three days.

"You're more than just being *nice*."

"No, I'm not. I've never given any of them my number nor

have they ever asked me out on a date. Even if they did, I wouldn't have agreed to one."

"So you leanin' over the counter with your tits out is for tips?"

I glance down and take a moment to appreciate how good the girls look in my T-shirt. Though I'm wearing a fleece jacket, I didn't zip it up because with two people in this small space, I get warm.

"Surprised you didn't read about it in one of your baby apps, but breasts can double in size during pregnancy. I can't help that. Blame the hormones."

His eyes roll as he crosses his arms over his chest.

"Are you tellin' me you don't flirt with the customers during cabin call? Just a little friendly 'Howdy, sweetheart. How y'all doin' today? Need me to carry those big, heavy bags for you with my massive muscles?'" I mimic in an exaggerated deep Southern accent.

He pops a brow. "You think I have massive muscles?"

"Oh my God!" I smack his chest, and before I can pull away, he grabs my wrist and yanks me closer.

"Sunny..." His warning tone sends shivers down my spine. "I don't flirt with other women. Hell, I haven't even looked at one since the moment you became mine. I know we're *just friends* and roommates, but I have no interest in anyone but you. And before you say it, there is no movin' on for me." He shrugs helplessly. "There never was."

Goddamn him. Doesn't he know I'm an emotional and hormonal mess these days? It's bad enough I had a full-on cry fest at my ultrasound appointment yesterday when we confirmed the baby was a girl.

And the day before that when we went to the sheriff's office, I had to give a full statement about my phone call with Travis, and it had me in tears again just thinking about all the shit I'm dragging Tripp through.

Then again when I told my dad.

So it's safe to say I'm tired of crying.

The morning sickness hasn't been as bad in my second trimester, so that's been a blessing, but the heartburn at night is killing me. She better come out with a full head of hair after this.

A throat clearing grabs our attention before I can respond to Tripp and find Landen staring at us with a shit-eating smirk.

"What's a guy gotta do for some service 'round here?" he taunts.

"Show me your abs and dick," I blurt, fully aware I'm adding fuel to the fire that's Tripp's patience level.

He pops a brow, amusement written all over his pretty boy face. "Is this a game of *I show you mine and you show me yours?*"

"I swear to God, you two." Tripp shakes his head, clearly done with us. "If I thought you were actually tryin' to get into her pants, there's no way I'd leave her with you."

Tilting my head toward him, I glare. "I'm not a puppy. I can be left alone and not chew on the furniture."

"Then *behave*, Sunny." He kisses my forehead before walking out of the trailer. "You too," he warns Landen, and the two of them share a moment before Tripp drives off in his truck.

Since they need him for cabin call at three, and I don't close until then, Landen stays with me for thirty minutes so I'm not alone. Then he'll drive us back to the ranch, and I'll either hang out with him or Noah at the training center until Tripp's done with work.

"How do you spend all day with him?" Landen asks once Tripp leaves. "He seems moody."

"That's because he's not a sit and do nothin' kinda guy. He needs activity and to be outside workin'. Like a wild animal."

Landen paces the small area as I wipe down counters, and I laugh to myself at him being exactly the same way.

"Mags."

I'm on my hands and knees looking for a box of straws when he says my name. "What?"

"Stay down there."

"And what? Give you head? Har har, very funny."

"I'm being dead serious. Do. Not. Get. Up."

The panic in his voice is making *me* panic.

Moments later, I hear a deep, recognizable voice when he responds to Landen's warm greeting.

"You're not Magnolia," he says. His tone is meant to be lighthearted, but I hear the seriousness in it.

"Nope, you caught me." Landen bemuses, and when I take a peek at him, I see his firm stance as he crosses his arms. "I'm just helpin' out while she's away. In New Jersey. Visitin' her Italian family. A big reunion."

The fuck?

That is weirdly specific.

"Ah. That's interesting. Sutherland is a Scottish surname."

"She's Italian on her mom's side." Landen's response is immediate.

"Explains her dark hair and complexion."

"Guess so. Can I getcha a drink or muffin?" Landen prompts.

"Just a black coffee."

"Comin' right up." When Landen turns around to grab a cup, I hear the recognizable sound of a gun cocking. I can't see the other side of the counter, but Landen's spine goes ramrod straight.

"Tell me where she really is," Emilio demands. "Now."

I cover my mouth with my palm, trying to hide my heavy breathing as my heart beats wildly.

"I already told you," Landen says, spinning back toward him. "She's not here."

"And I know you're lying. So you either tell me or I'm going to shoot up this whole little trailer and then light a match and leave you inside it."

Oh my fucking God.

I don't know how he's keeping his cool, but he swipes his tongue along his lower lip as he smirks. "No, you won't."

The fuck is he doing? Why is he arguing with a man who has a literal gun to his face?

My phone's in my back pocket, but I'm too scared to grab it. I don't want to make any sudden movement and alert Emilio I'm in here. But if I don't, he could kill Landen.

"Pretty confident for a guy who's facing a death sentence. Tell me where Magnolia is and you won't get hurt."

Landen scrubs a hand over his jawline, looking more amused than anything.

"This is the problem with you city-slickers who handle guns. Y'all gotta be real loud and flashy about 'em. You don't just whip it out and pull the trigger like a man."

Landen Michael! I swear to God. If he survives this, I'm going to kill him!

"Excuse—"

It happens so fast that I barely have time to register Landen's hand reaching behind his back and underneath his shirt. Seconds later, he reveals a handgun, aims it at Emilio, and then fires within three seconds.

My whole body jumps at the booming sound that echoes throughout the trailer.

"Holy shit!" I scream, unable to hold it in.

"See? That's how we shoot down here in the South. We don't just wave it around like a flag. If it's in our hand, it's to be used."

Landen's talking to him, so that must mean he's not dead. Then I hear a faint groan.

"Mags, call the sheriff. Tell him cleanup on aisle seven."

"W-what?" *That is not even a little bit funny.*

"He's not dead. Yet," he reassures me. "But he will bleed out if we don't get him an ambulance."

"Where'd you shoot him?" I stumble, getting to my feet, but Landen takes my hand to help me up the rest of the way.

Landen's devilish smirk doesn't ease my panic. "His groin."

Jesus.

Landen walks out of the trailer, kicks Emilio's gun out of reach, and then looks down at him. "So on a scale of one to ten, what would you rate our Southern hospitality so far?"

I finally manage to take my phone out with a shaky hand and

dial 911. When Wendy picks up, I tell her a quick recap, and then she informs me the EMTs are on their way.

"Tell the sheriff to come too, please?" I plead.

"He'll be there, sweetie. Just hang tight."

Once we hang up, I stand next to Landen.

"Where'd you get a gun?"

"Tripp. He always hands it off before leavin'."

"Wait..." I swallow hard. "He's been packin' this whole time?"

Tennessee is an open carry state, but that doesn't mean I want one near me all day while I'm working. Though I guess if he hadn't, Landen would've been killed.

"Yep. Did you assume your boyfriend wasn't unhinged when it came to you?"

Oh God. Tripp is going to go feral when he finds out this happened, and he wasn't here.

People start coming over from the other businesses and a small crowd forms. They're looking at Landen and me, waiting for an explanation, but I'm too shell-shocked to speak.

"Dude, you can't be groanin' like a little bitch or you'll lose all street cred for takin' a bullet in the first place."

Emilio snaps his eyes open. "Fuck. You." His words are barely audible as he lies half-hunched over. Then his gaze meets mine, and it's lethal.

"Magnolia, are you okay?" Grant walks over from the bookstore. He looks down at Emilio, who's nearly passed out from the blood loss or perhaps the pain. "Who's that?"

"His name is Emilio. He threatened Landen with a gun, but Landen shot him first."

Grant tilts his head as he studies Emilio's face. "He came into the bookstore yesterday and asked about you."

"He did?"

"Yeah, he wanted to know when you'd be parked out here again. I told him you come every Monday, Wednesday, and Thursday. I'm so sorry."

"It's not your fault. You couldn't have known."

Sirens break up the chatter of everyone whispering, and soon the EMTs rush over with a stretcher.

"This the guy?" Davis asks as if Emilio isn't the only one bleeding out on the ground, grunting and groaning in agony.

Landen nods. "Yep. Got him right in the dick. Gonna be messy. Sorry 'bout that."

Davis smirks. "I'll pass your sincerest apologies to the nurses."

Landen and Davis graduated high school together, so neither is taking this as seriously as they should be.

Davis and another EMT get Emilio hooked up to an oxygen mask, apply bandages on his wound, and then get him onto the stretcher.

"Wait…" I blurt.

I stand next to Emilio and his eyes are half open. "Where's Travis?"

His mouth opens, but nothing comes out.

"I have nothin' to do with him, so I suggest you don't return after this. If you think Landen's insane, wait until you meet his three brothers."

Landen chuckles next to me. "I'll let Tripp tie you to my breeding mount and let Rocky have at ya. He's a horny little stallion."

"Oh my God, Landen," I scold. The visual image that just entered my brain is going to haunt me in my nightmares.

"What? He is."

I roll my eyes at his inability to take anything seriously.

"We gotta go," Davis says.

"Good luck, Emilio. You're gonna need it." Landen smacks his leg, the one close to the wound.

The sheriff and his deputies pull up, and Landen immediately steps away from me and holds up his arms.

"Drop your weapon," Sheriff Wagner orders, holding his gun toward Landen.

Wait, what's happening? I freeze in place, watching his every move.

Landen pulls his out from his waistband and drops it to the ground.

"Anyone else?"

"Just me," Landen replies when everyone around us stays silent.

"Alright, I'm not gonna handcuff ya." The sheriff holsters his gun. "But I do need to take you down to my office. You too, Magnolia. We need to get statements."

The sheriff orders one of his deputies to collect the gun for evidence, and then another starts taping off the area around my trailer. Considering we're downtown, there should be plenty of surveillance cameras to prove Landen acted in self-defense.

My heart hasn't calmed down since this all started, and I feel the rapid beating throughout my body as the reality of what just happened catches up to me.

"I-I need to call my dad. And Tripp. Noah, too," I tell the sheriff.

"You can, sweetheart. But protocol dictates we take your statement first and then y'all will be released."

"C'mon, Mags." Landen wraps his arm around my shoulders. "It's kinda fun at the sheriff's office. They have a popcorn machine."

"You've been inside a few dozen times, haven't you?"

"Nah, only one or two." He winks.

"How're you so calm right now?"

He pulls me into his arms and presses his face into my hair as I work on catching my breath. "It's the adrenaline. Well, that or the fear of Tripp giving me a vasectomy if I let anything happen to you. And I'm rather fond of my balls."

"Is that why you took Emilio's?" I choke out a laugh.

"That was just a quick draw roulette. And a lucky shot."

Landen and I sit in the back of Sheriff Wagner's car, and I text Tripp first, then Noah. They must both be working because by the time we arrive at the sheriff's office, neither has responded. No doubt my dad's already heard about it on his scanner, but I send him a quick message anyway to reassure him I'm okay.

"Alright, kids. Start at the beginning." He sits behind his large wooden desk, and Landen goes first.

It helps that Sheriff Wagner already knows the history with Travis and his bookie, so we don't have to repeat everything.

I'm in the middle of explaining what I saw and heard when a loud thud echoes in the reception. Then a door slams.

"Ah, shit." Landen smirks as if he knows what's coming.

"Mr. Hollis," Wendy says.

"Where is she?"

"She's being interviewed. Please take a seat and I'll — "

"Where. Is. She." His booming voice sends a shiver down my spine.

"You can't go back there. This is an open investigation and — "

"I'm not askin'."

"Fuckin' Christ," Sheriff Wagner cusses, then presses the intercom on his phone. "Wendy, let him in. It's alright."

I push off my chair and wait for his impending arrival.

My whole body is still shaking. Hell, it hasn't stopped since I heard Emilio's chilling voice.

When the door flies open, Tripp's gaze immediately finds mine, and he charges for me. He pulls me into his arms so quickly that I nearly lose my balance.

"Sunny." A sigh of relief leaves his lips as one large hand presses against my back and the other cups the back of my head, fusing us together. My arms circle his waist, holding him as tightly as I can.

After a moment, he cups my cheeks and his eyes scan over my face. "You're okay?"

I nod with tears in my eyes. "Perfectly fine. Well, physically."

"I've never been more panicked in my fuckin' life. I was drivin' so fast, my tires were barely touchin' the pavement."

I knew he'd flip out, but this side of him has my emotions in overdrive. I want to kiss him so badly but in front of Landen and the sheriff isn't the time to make the first move after over three months of staying platonic.

"I'm fine too, by the way. Thanks for askin'," Landen calls out with a smart-ass tone.

Tripp cups his shoulder, meets his eyes, and an understanding passes between them. A look of appreciation and love.

"I dunno how to properly thank you for protecting her, but I'm eternally grateful."

Landen pats Tripp's hand with a nod. "You could make me the godfather of your kids?"

Tripp glowers at him, and I fight back a laugh.

Landen's lips twitch into a genuine smile. "You know I woulda taken a bullet for her. Woulda hurt like a bitch, but I woulda been a man about it and kept her safe through my last breath."

"Landen." My bottom lip trembles. "That's so sweet. But please, no more talk of gettin' shot on my behalf."

"There's still the situation with Travis," Sheriff Wagner interrupts us. "I've alerted the other departments in the state. We'll find him."

My gut threatens to bottom out at the mention of Travis. As much as I hate him for how he's treated me, I just want this to be over. I want him out of my life for good and to stay gone.

"Detective James on line two," Wendy says through the intercom. "He says it's urgent."

The sheriff picks up, and his face pales after ten seconds of listening to whatever the detective is saying. It's unnerving to see his expression change so quickly and then his gaze meets mine for a split second.

"Alright, I'll ask if she wants to identify him or I'll send a deputy to his mom's," Sheriff Wagner tells him, and my whole body goes cold.

He hangs up and brushes a hand over his bearded jaw. "They found a body in the back of Emilio's Denali. They sent him to the morgue, but they need someone to identify if it's Travis or not. We haven't informed his family, but I can send someone to tell her."

My knees buckle out from underneath me, and Tripp quickly directs me back to my chair. His hands squeeze my shoulders as he leans down to my ear.

"Breathe, Sunny."

How? I was just wishing he'd go away for good and now he could be dead.

"His mom shouldn't have to see him that way," I tell him. "I'll do it."

"I can drive y'all over there if you want," the sheriff offers.

"We'll take her," Tripp says.

My mind spins out of control as he takes my hand and leads me to his truck. Travis was a shitty person who did a lot of bad things, but that doesn't mean I wanted him to get murdered.

When we arrive, Landen takes the lead and speaks to the detective waiting for us.

"He's not been cleaned up yet, so prepare yourselves," he says.

"I change my mind. I don't think I can do this. Maybe you should check," I tell Tripp. He knows what he looks like just as much as I do, and if I have to see Travis's dead body, I might collapse.

"Sure, love. Stay back here." He kisses my temple.

I stand next to Landen and watch as Detective James leads him to a table on the opposite side of the room.

He pulls off the sheet and Tripp's spine straightens. Tripp gives the man a quick nod and then the corpse gets covered back up.

When Tripp returns, he drops his head. "I'm sorry, Sunny. It's him."

My eyes flood with tears, but I refuse to let them fall.

I will not cry for that man.

He's taken enough from me, and I refuse to give him my sympathy for the choices he's made.

Choking back my emotions, I swallow hard and clear my throat. "Can we leave now?"

"Yeah, baby. Let's go."

He takes my hand and we walk out into the cool air. It's too quiet out here. My chest tightens, and I forget how to breathe.

"Sunny?" Tripp cups my face, but my eyes are glazed over.

The anxiety attack takes over and with each second, breathing becomes harder. Spots invade my vision, and I fold over as I fight for control.

Tripp kneels beside me, squeezing my hand as I fight through the pain.

"He's dead," I say, needing to confirm the words aloud. "He's...*dead*."

He rubs a hand over my back. "Take a deep breath and focus on my voice."

"I—" I shake my head, flattening my palm over my chest. The tears threaten to pour out, but I stop them. "I-I..."

Finally, the air stuck in my ribcage releases and eases the tightness.

"There you go, Sunny. Slow, deep breaths. This'll pass."

After a few moments, I meet his eyes, which are filled with concern.

"I didn't want this." Shaking my head, I try to clear the thoughts taking over. "I just wanted him to leave me alone."

Tripp brushes my hair behind my ear, tilting my chin. "This isn't your fault, love. He made the decision to get involved with a bad man and paid the ultimate price for it. I know you two have history, but this has nothin' to do with the choices you made."

I nod as he wipes my cheeks with his thumbs.

Landen approaches my other side and meets my gaze. I've never seen him speechless, but his lips twitch like he's trying to find the right words to console me. So instead, I wrap my arms around him and hug him.

His body stiffens for a moment as if he hadn't expected it, but then he circles my waist the best he can with my bump and relaxes against me.

"Thank you," I cry into his chest. Without him, we could both be dead. "I know we joke around a lot, but what you did was really brave and it coulda gone completely different without your quick thinkin'."

The tears pour out of me.

For how close we were to death.

For Travis being so goddamn stupid and leaving our daughter without ever meeting her biological father.

For Landen being put into a situation where he had to shoot a man in order to protect us.

For Tripp being so possessive and keeping me safe even when I argued about it.

The turn of events would be so different if it weren't for these two men who care so much about me. It's hard to process after feeling so disposable in my relationship with Travis.

"You're welcome, Mags. I'd do it again in a heartbeat if I had to."

I pull back and find him grinning at me.

"Plus, imagine the badass street cred I'm about to have." He waggles his brow, and I choke out a laugh.

"Ellie's gonna be trippin' over her boots to get a piece of you," I tease.

"Pretty doubtful after the knife I found in my tire from her."

I can't even pretend to feel sorry for him. Ellie's gonna give him a run for his money.

"Let's go home, Sunny." Tripp pulls me to his side, kissing my forehead. "Noah's freakin' out and wants an update."

I nod because *home* never sounded more perfect.

Chapter Thirty-Nine
Tripp

It's taken a month for things to feel normal again. Even though the two men threatening Magnolia are out of the picture, it's been hard letting her go back to work alone and unprotected. She tried to reassure me Grant was just across the street if she needed anything, but it had the opposite effect. Instead, I went into his bookstore and made it very clear to him what would happen if he touched her or said anything inappropriate.

Poor kid was ready to piss his pants by the time I left.

After Emilio made it through surgery, he was arrested and charged with assault and homicide. His gun was analyzed and tested against the bullet they found in Travis's skull to determine he was the shooter.

I'd never seen a dead body before, but I felt nothing when I saw his. I hate the pain it brought Magnolia, but the asshole got what he deserved, and I'll never feel sorry for him.

That night, I tucked Magnolia into her bed, and when I got up to leave, she asked me to stay with her. So I did and every night since then, we're either snuggling in her bed or she comes into mine.

But I promised myself I wouldn't kiss or touch her intimately until she gave me the green light, so I continue the forehead kisses and tender hugs until she's ready for more.

Landen's even more insufferable now that he's been labeled the town hero.

As we eat and talk during Sunday night supper, he goes on and on about the interview they just printed about him in the state newspaper. Then he continues to say how he's collecting so many chicks' numbers from the bar, he can hardly keep up.

Except the one girl he wants to impress still acts like he doesn't exist.

Magnolia keeps giving him ideas, but he shoots and misses each time. I think it's hilarious that he's getting a taste of his own medicine since he acts like every girl should be tripping over their feet to be with him.

After dessert, I stay for scrapbooking night so I can keep working on the one I'm making for Magnolia. She's at her parents' tonight, so it's the only time I have where she won't see it before I'm done.

"She's gonna love that, Tripp," Noah says, sneaking a look. "I love that you take polaroids of her belly progress each week."

I tape the most recent one to the page and write "24 Weeks" underneath it.

Magnolia has no idea what I'm doing with these, but when the time is right, I'll gift them to her. Underneath each photo, I list out any new cravings, milestones, or symptoms she's experiencing. Every week is different, so it'll be nice for her to look back on it someday.

There's a page with all the baby's ultrasounds from ten weeks and twenty weeks. She's scheduled to have one more at thirty weeks, and then I'll add that in.

"I hope so," I say, admiring how beautiful she looks. She's glowing in this shot, with one hand on her bump and her head thrown back as she laughs. I made a joke about her giving birth to an alien baby because she's so active at night that it feels like there are six limbs kicking her stomach. She laughed until her side hurt, but it made for one hell of a perfect photo.

Gramma Grace sits across from me, but she's not scrapbooking tonight. Instead, she's been crocheting baby blankets for Noah and Magnolia. Once they're finished, she plans to add the baby names to them. Then she'll gift them during their joint baby shower in a few weeks.

I already know the party is going to be over the top with decorations and food, but they're going to love it. We've been talking about it over supper, and everyone's pitching in to make sure Magnolia has everything she needs for Willow. She hasn't mentioned moving out now that there's no threat to her living alone, but I'm hoping she'll stay anyway.

After an hour of scrapbooking, we start packing up for the night. I'm exhausted and ready to cuddle with Magnolia.

"Night, Ma. Thanks for dinner." I kiss her cheek.

"So when're you showin' her that?" She nods toward my chest.

"When it's appropriate to." I shrug because I've been hiding it from Magnolia. I don't want it to sway her decision about us, so when the time is right, I'll reveal my new tattoo. I purposely wear a shirt around her, even in bed, so she doesn't see it.

Mom gives me a look that says she disagrees with my decision. She thinks I should be the one to make the first move, especially after everything that happened, but the last thing Magnolia needs is a guy who can't respect her boundaries. Men have crossed them so many times in the past, and I don't want to be grouped with them.

"You love her," she says pointedly.

"More than anything," I agree. "Enough to wait."

"I just want you both to be happy. Y'all are meant to be together. I can feel it." She places a hand over her heart, and I nod because I feel it, too.

Magnolia needs time to process things on her own terms, and I'm not about to push her to be in a relationship while she's struggling with the guilt of what happened. Especially after watching her go through an anxiety attack, I knew she wasn't ready.

Even though she was a victim in the whole thing, she feels remorse for his family. Travis's mom loves Magnolia, and they had a decent relationship throughout the years they dated.

So the day after his funeral, I took Magnolia to get some flowers and drove to his mom's house since we didn't attend. Ms. Boone cried when she saw the ultrasound photos and learned she's going to be a grandma. Apparently, she and Travis had a rocky relationship, and he only came around when he needed money or a place to crash. Jade loved her son the best she could but knew it was only a matter of time before his poor decisions caught up to him. She's obviously upset about his death, understandably so, but now she can find solace in knowing there'll be a piece of him left behind.

And if I'm being honest, I'm happy she gets to have that, too.

Magnolia was worried about how people would react to her being pregnant with his baby after he broke into their businesses and homes. For months, they assumed I was the father, and since we never corrected them, they were shocked to learn I wasn't. But everyone's been respectful and kind, even showing up at her work and bringing her gifts for the baby.

Once I say goodbye to the rest of the family, I head home. I'm relieved when I see Magnolia's SUV parked in the driveway because I missed her all night. Being around her settles the anxiety being away from her creates.

When I walk in, something feels different. The lights are off, minus one lamp on the side table. Assuming she left it on for me and already went to bed, I tiptoe down the hall to check on her.

I open the door as quietly as I can, but it's pitch-black and silent. She usually has a white noise machine on with lights that reflect on the ceiling.

"Sunny?" I take out my phone and turn on the flashlight.

The room is empty.

Her bed, nightstand, dresser. All the clothes that littered the floor.

Gone.

What the fuck?

Did she move out?

Her car is here, so where the hell is she?

When I go toward my room, I hear the shower running, which is odd since she has her own bathroom.

Everything in my room is the same except her dresser is now next to mine and her full-length mirror she had in a corner is now in here.

The bathroom door is ajar, so I push it open all the way and find Magnolia humming a tune in my shower.

"Sunny."

The curtain whips open just enough to see her face and her eyes widen in surprise. "You're home earlier than expected."

"It's nine-thirty," I tell her. I'm actually home later than usual on Sunday nights.

"Is it? Shit, I lost track of time and worked up a sweat, so I wanted to rinse off before you got back. I'll just be a minute longer."

She closes the curtain and continues showering.

I step closer until I'm leaning against the vanity that's now covered in her stuff and watch her silhouette move through the curtain.

"What's going on? Are you movin' out?"

"Um…not exactly. It was supposed to be a surprise."

"What was?"

She stays silent, but I can't take not knowing. Without thinking, I whip the curtain open. Once I see her wet body, I realize what a mistake this was.

I haven't seen her naked in months, and fuck me, she's still as stunning as before. Her round belly is adorable. The temptation to take her into my arms and kiss every inch of her is so strong I almost do it.

"Shit, you scared me." She jumps slightly, draping her arms over her chest as if I haven't already seen and licked her perfect tits.

"Tell me what's going on."

Her shoulders relax, and she blows out a breath. "Fine, but if you insist on knowing right this second, at least get in here and close the curtain. It's cold."

My brows pop up because I hadn't expected that response.

"With my clothes on?" I ask, unsure if she meant for me to strip down to nothing or just come in as is.

"Do you normally shower with them on?" she teases.

"No?"

I remove my shoes and clothes until I'm completely naked, but when I step in, she turns away from me and faces the water.

"Okay, well…" She fidgets with her hands. "Just know I had something way more romantic planned." She releases a deep breath as if she's nervous to say the words out loud. "But I don't want us in separate bedrooms anymore."

My heart races at how unsteady her voice comes out.

Is she saying what I think she's saying?

"Turn around," I demand. "I don't wanna have this conversation with the back of your head."

When she does, her brown eyes find mine, and I grin at how many times I've gotten lost in them.

"That's better." I cup her jaw, rubbing my thumb along her bottom lip. "Where's your bed?"

"Noah said I could put it in one of your storage barns, so my dad helped me move it out. I figured we'd need room for the nursery furniture."

My cheeks already hurt from how hard I'm smiling.

"Please tell me this isn't where you say you're stealin' my room, and I get the couch."

She giggles, leaning into my touch. "No, this is me tryin' to propose girlfriend-boyfriend matrimony to you."

I smirk at the same words she said to me at Noah's wedding when I confirmed she was mine and I was hers. Circling her waist with my other hand, I inch as close as I can without pushing into her belly. "I thought that was my job."

"You were takin' your sweet time, and I got impatient."

"I was waitin' for you to tell me you were ready."

"I'm ready," she says confidently. "I want us to be together."

Thank fuck.

"Okay, let me do this properly then." I grab her hand and get down on one knee. "You're mine, Sunny. And I'm yours. Got it?"

She nods, and although the water stream hits her back, it's her face that's wet. "Yes. So much *yes.*"

I press my lips to her ring finger, which I plan to claim once and for all someday, and then stand so I can kiss her properly.

But then her eyes widen as she stares at my chest, and I freeze in place.

"What's that?" She presses her finger to the Willow tree inked above Billy's name on my left pec and leans in for a closer look.

I look down at where she's touching. "The two most important people in my life are always close to my heart, so it was only fitting to add our baby there, too."

"Tripp..." More tears fall down her cheeks. "You consider her *ours*?"

Grabbing her hand, I flatten it over my racing heart. "Willow's a part of you, which means she'll always be a part of me, too. I witnessed her first ultrasound. The first time you felt her kick. And I hope to experience many more firsts with you and her."

"You're unreal," she chokes out, then shifts her body to the side so the water hits us both. "When did you get this?"

"After we found out it was a girl and you decided on her name. Sorry to tell you, there's no changin' your mind now."

She giggles through the sobs as she covers her mouth with one hand. "I don't deserve you, Tripp. Are you sure you want this? It's a lifelong commitment and responsibility."

"I think you underestimate my loyalty to you." I press my lips to the tip of her nose. "You're the love of my life, Magnolia." Then I kiss the corner of her mouth next. "It's always been you, and it will *always* only be you." And then my lips brush the other side.

"I'm so in love with you," she breathes out when my mouth hovers just above hers. "Kiss me. *Please.*"

Lifting a brow, I smirk. "Since you beg so nicely…"

I give her exactly what she needs, swiping my tongue along her bottom lip before fusing our mouths together. Heat and urgency feed our need to desperately taste each other.

She melts against my touch as I grip her hips and keep her pinned to the wall.

"I've missed this so much," she murmurs when I wrap a hand behind her neck. "I wish there were a way to rewrite history so you were the one to get me pregnant. Then we wouldn't have lost all this time together."

I tilt her chin and stare into her sorrow-filled eyes. "We didn't lose anything, baby. I don't consider anything with you a waste."

She nods, though I see the regret across her face.

"If it's any consolation, now we can play into your little breeding kink without reservations and practice for next time." I wink.

Her face splits into the widest smile I've ever seen, and she laughs. "You mean *your* kink."

"Well…" I glide my hands up the sides of her body. "Whaddya want me to do to you?"

"You already know." She hears the implication in my voice and goes along with it. "Knock me up, cowboy."

"My fuckin' pleasure, Sunny."

Chapter Forty
Magnolia

Tripp's body blankets mine as he thrusts into me, careful not to squish my belly as I wrap my legs around his waist. His tongue plunges into my mouth, moaning and whispering sweet nothings as we reconnect after months of staying platonic.

We're still wet, but neither of us cares. As soon as he carried me out of the shower, and I begged him to fill me up with his cum, he couldn't wait any longer.

But neither could I.

His hands on my body, tender kisses, and groaning in my ear have me falling apart. Sex while pregnant is a whole different experience but in a good way. Everything feels more sensitive, and my hormones have been out of control, but I can't stop touching every inch of his body.

"Fuck, Sunny. You feel so good," he breathes out.

"Take me from behind," I plead. "You can go even deeper."

"I don't wanna hurt you."

"Trust me, you won't."

He sits back on his heels, helps me flip over, and then repositions his cock against my pussy while I arch my back. When he teases his tip up and down my wet slit, I'm close to losing it again.

"Tripp, *please*."

"Please what, Sunny?" He slaps a hand across my ass cheek. "Beg for it."

"Please spill your cum deep inside me. I need it," I pant out between each word.

"Jesus Christ." He slips into me, slow at first, but then squeezes my hips and goes deep and hard.

"Yes, right there. Oh my God, I'm so close."

Tripp gives me everything I ask him for and then slides his hand between my thighs and rubs my clit until I explode around him.

"Such a good girl, Sunny. Fuck, you're so tight. I'm—" His fingers pinch into my hips as his words fall off and he tenses, groaning through his release.

I'm still catching my breath when I feel him pull out and lower between my legs, spreading my cheeks apart.

"What're you…"

"I want my cum sittin' inside you all night, love."

His tongue laps up my pussy, and he shoves his tongue inside, pushing his release back inside me. The sensation sends my nerves into overdrive, and when he buries his whole face in my ass, I cry out at how good it feels.

"You taste so good, baby. Especially mixed with my cum. You wanna try it?"

I nod and am nearly out of breath by the time he helps me roll to my back. When he brings his mouth to mine, I soak in every touch and kiss.

He cups my cheek and gazes at me with so much tenderness it makes me tear up. "I love you so much, Sunny."

I rest a hand on my belly. "We love you, too."

"A little to the left," I direct as Tripp and Landen move the crib for the thirteenth time. I can't decide which wall I want it against, so they've been showing me every possible angle.

"What about on this wall but like angled into the corner? You'll have direct access from your bedroom without having to go through the whole room and trippin' on shit in the middle of the night," Noah says, standing next to me.

"Oh, good point. Okay, let's try that."

Landen groans as he and Tripp move it once again.

"Isn't this the first option we showed you?" Landen complains.

"Maybe, but now that Noah mentioned it, I like the idea of it being closer to the door. Knowin' me, I'd trip over a toy and break my nose."

Tripp smirks as Landen curses under his breath.

A moment later, I beam at how perfect it looks. "Yes! Now we can bring in the changing table, rocking chair, and dresser."

"How did I get roped into this again?" Landen asks, walking toward the door.

"You wanted to be the godfather," I tease, and that puts a smile on his face.

"Okay, fair enough." He fist-bumps my belly before heading to the living room. That's where they spend the first half of the day putting the furniture together.

Tripp leans down and kisses my temple before going to help Landen.

At thirty-eight weeks pregnant, I can't even see my feet, so I'm no help in carrying anything. Not that Tripp would let me anyway. He waits on me like I'm on my deathbed, but I don't mind. He loves doing things for me, and I love making him happy.

"I can't believe you only have a couple of weeks left," Noah says, taking a seat at the breakfast bar. "I feel ready to pop now."

"Physically, I'm ready to get her out and be able to take a deep breath without feelin' like I'm gonna crack a rib, but mentally, I'm still scared shitless."

"Why?"

I take the chair next to hers and lift up my swollen feet.

"I'm worried I won't be good at it, ya know, being a mother. I don't have a great relationship with my own, so how am I supposed to know how to be one?"

Noah gives me a sympathetic look and reaches for my hand. "You'll learn as you go. Just like all of us first-time moms do, but no matter what, you're not doing it alone. Tripp's read all the baby books, has like twelve apps downloaded on his phone, and even took a Zoom class to learn about proper feedin' and diaper changin'. You're in good hands."

I laugh because it sounds insane when she says it aloud.

"Plus, you have me, my parents, and Landen. It sounds like Ms. Boone wants to be involved as much as possible, too. You have a large support system, and you can lean on anyone of us, okay?"

I wrap my arms around her and try not to cry.

"And I'm nervous about becoming a mom, too. Fisher never thought he'd have more kids after Lyla died and is scared he'll drop the baby now. Ya know, PTSD and all. But together, we're gonna figure it out and be a team. Just like you and Tripp."

"I really am lucky to have him. There's no way I'd be here if it weren't for him. Actually, I have a surprise for him…"

I reach across the counter to the pile of papers and pull out a painting I had made for him from one of the local artists who has a shop near my coffee trailer. It's of a sleeping baby wearing a white onesie with text on it that says, *Will you be my daddy?* Underneath, it reads, Willow Jade Hollis.

I'd originally planned on giving her my last name, but I want her to have the last name of the man who's never left my side. Who got her tattooed on his damn chest. Who loves her unconditionally and she's not even here yet. I know we'll get married someday, and I'll take his last name, too, but for now, I want him to know how much he's loved and appreciated.

"Oh my gosh, Mags! He's gonna love this! What a sweet thing

to do for him. He better cry at this or else." She giggles, and I do, too.

Noah and I have both been overly emotional during our third trimester while Tripp always holds himself together. I know part of that is because he's learned to be guarded over the years after Billy died, but I love that he never makes me feel bad for it. Sometimes they're happy tears, and sometimes they're sad ones, but either way, he just brushes them away and kisses my forehead.

"I just need to put it inside the frame and then decide how to give it to him."

"You should put it somewhere in the nursery and see how long it takes for him to notice," she muses.

I laugh. "I was thinkin' something a little more romantic." Considering the last time I tried to do something sweet, he ruined it by coming home too soon.

"Sunny, come take a look," Tripp calls from the nursery.

I manage to slide off the stool without pulling a muscle, and Noah waddles behind me as we walk down the hall. The rest of the furniture is in place, and I beam at how great it looks. It still needs a lot of decorating, and I have to organize all the clothes and supplies I got from the baby shower, but I love it already.

"Whaddya think?" he asks.

I wrap my arm around his waist and lean my head against his chest. "It's perfect."

He reaches for my belly and rubs his palm over it. "Pretty soon she'll be here."

Tilting my head up, I reach for his face and pull him down for a kiss. "It could be sooner if you have sex with me and put me into labor."

"Christ. Could you two wait until we leave at least?" Landen grumbles, covering his eyes as if we're about to get naked right now.

"Why're you actin' so shy? I thought you liked to *watch*..." I taunt.

His arm drops immediately, and he glares at Tripp, who holds up his hand in mock surrender. "I didn't say a word."

"I snooped through his phone and read your text messages," I admit shamelessly.

Landen's brows draw together as he crosses his arms.

"What? I got bored, and Tripp doesn't care." I shrug.

"Great. Now I can't send those dick pics to you anymore."

"Oh no, what a tragedy," Tripp deadpans. "But honestly, you can stop that in general. I don't need to see it in eight different angles with various lighting."

"I sent *two*, fuck you very much."

"Wait a goddamn minute…" Noah finally chimes in, blinking between her brothers. "You share dick pics?"

Landen and Tripp both shrug.

"*Why?*" Noah asks.

"I had a manscape question, okay? Not all of us like to be completely bare, but I wasn't sure how short to go."

Noah gags, and I laugh at how pale her face is.

"Personally, I liked the third photo you sent. Neatly trimmed without taking away from the main attraction. Plus, the girl won't get a pube rash from it being too scratchy, especially if she's bare," I tell Landen.

"See? Should've been askin' Magnolia in the first place," Tripp says.

"Well, pardon me for not wantin' you to murder me for sendin' her pics of my junk. Wasn't aware that was an option."

Tripp's smile drops, and he narrows his eyes at him. "It's not. *Ever.*"

Landen rolls his eyes, and Noah looks like she's questioning a few life decisions.

"So wait. Rewind. Who's Landen watchin'?" Noah asks.

Landen shakes his head at me, and I chuckle.

"He's into voyeurism. You know, watchin' people engage in *activities*."

Noah's nose wrinkles. "Isn't that just porn?"

I giggle. "In real life, babe. Or a cam website."

Noah's mouth falls open as she stares at Landen.

"Did you really have to call me out like that in front of my sister?" Landen sighs. "It's bad enough you knew."

"Where do you...watch?" Noah arches a brow, and her mouth twitches like she's trying to hold back laughter.

"I'm not havin' this conversation with you." He shakes his head, walking toward the door to leave.

"Why the hell not? You can talk to Tripp but not me?" Noah asks, offended.

"Exactly." His voice echoes in the hallway.

"Well, that was fun." Noah folds her arms. "Except, you two share way too much with each other," she tells Tripp.

"Oh, and you and Magnolia don't?"

"We're not related!" she defends. "Askin' her to help me shave my lady bits ain't weird when it's your best friend."

Tripp blinks, then looks at me. "What?"

I shrug. "She helped me, so I had to help her."

"Yeah, you're welcome," Noah smarts off to Tripp.

He shakes his head. "You two have no boundaries with each other. It's a little weird."

"Says the guy who just admitted to sharin' dick pics with his brother," I say.

"That was against my will," he defends. "I never sent one to him."

We walk into the living room, and I hug Noah before she leaves. We both have doctor appointments tomorrow, so we're going together, but I'm sure we'll talk before then.

"Tell Fisher I said hello and to do his part in helpin' you go into labor," I call out as she walks to her car.

"Same goes for you, Tripp!"

"You hear that?" I tease as I meet him on the couch and lie down.

He pulls my feet into his lap and begins rubbing them. "Mm-hmm. But now I'm worried I'm not manscaped right."

My head falls back on the pillow as I bellow out a laugh. "Want me to send a pic to Landen for you?"

He glowers as I reach for my phone and imitate taking his photo. "Cute."

"Oh, I have something for you. Stay here."

I walk to our bedroom where I hid the frame and then go to the kitchen to put the painting inside it.

"Okay, I wanted this to be a little more special, but I can't wait any longer." I sit next to him and put the frame face down on his lap. "I thought this would be cute to hang up in the nursery."

My heart races as he flips it over. He stays silent as he continues staring at it and the longer he goes without speaking, the more anxious I get.

Finally, his throat moves as if he's swallowed a huge lump. When he looks up and meets my eyes, I see them.

Tears.

"I can't even express how much this means to me, Sunny." He shakes his head as he wipes his face.

I take his hand and press my lips against it. "You deserve to be her daddy and for her to have your last name."

He cups my face and crashes his mouth against mine. I moan as he weaves his fingers through my hair, tilts my head back, and deepens the kiss.

"I love you both so much," he murmurs. "I have something for you, too. But it has to wait until she's born."

Sticking out my lip, I pout. "That ain't fair. You can't tell me that and then not show me."

He smiles and kisses the tip of my nose. "It'll be worth the wait. I promise."

I grab the frame and set it on the coffee table, then straddle his legs the best I can with a watermelon-sized stomach between us. Wrapping my arms around him, I kiss him.

"Then you better help me get her out so I can get my present sooner."

Stay With Me

He chuckles against my lips as he squeezes my hips. "I waited seven years for you, so I think you can wait two more weeks."

I spread my thighs a little wider and grind down on his thickening bulge. "I don't think *you* can, though…"

With a deep, throaty groan, he cups my ass and rocks me over his erection. "Take your clothes off. Grab my hat. And then ride my cock."

My pussy throbs at his words.

He doesn't have to tell me twice.

Epilogue
Tripp

"You look so much like your mama."

As I hold her in my arms, I'm in awe of this perfect little angel. Barely eight pounds and was only born less than twenty-four hours ago, but I already know I'd move heaven and hell for her.

It all happened so fast. By the time I got Magnolia to the hospital, she was eight centimeters dilated, and it was too late for an epidural. Of course she thinks she had an easy labor because of all the sex we've been having the past two weeks.

I told her it's because Willow couldn't wait to meet her daddy.

Every night in bed since Magnolia and I officially got back together, I'd talk to her belly so she'd recognize my voice. Her cute little baby kicks always made me smile in return.

They felt like our first father-daughter bonding moments.

Either way, I'm beyond proud of how well Magnolia handled everything. She nearly broke my hand squeezing it so hard and screamed in my ear for a solid thirty minutes, but she never gave up. She put every ounce of strength she had into pushing through the pain.

I was also pleased with myself at how well I was taking

397

everything in and not letting my emotions take over since I wanted to be strong for Magnolia.

But then they asked if I wanted to cut the umbilical cord and that's when I lost it. Magnolia cried as soon as she saw Willow and then there was no chance of me keeping it together anymore.

After they cleaned Willow up and got her wrapped in a blanket, Magnolia got to hold her for the first time. Watching the love of my life become a mother is a moment I'll never forget.

When Fisher and Noah showed up a few hours later to visit, her water ended up breaking, and they took her into her own delivery room. Four hours later, Poppy Underwood was born.

Now our girls share the same birthday.

My family, Magnolia's dad, and Ms. Boone all came before visiting hours ended.

Jade cried when she heard Willow's middle name was after her.

Mr. Sutherland teared up as he held her. He and Magnolia shared a sweet father-daughter moment together.

Landen walked in wearing a black T-shirt with "The Godfather" written on it and then made me take his photo with the baby for his new dating profile picture.

Waylon was too scared to hold her.

Two seconds after I put her in Wilder's arms, she spat up breast milk all over him.

Needless to say, it was the best day of my life.

After my parents visited us, they were able to go next door and meet their other granddaughter.

Two in one day.

The luckiest grandparents in the world.

"Alright, Willow. You wanna help me surprise your mama? We gotta take your picture."

After Magnolia fell asleep, I put her in the onesie I secretly packed. The framed painting she surprised me with that's now hanging in Willow's nursery is what inspired this idea to go along with the scrapbook. This photo is the final touch, and then I can give it to her.

Carefully, I set Willow down in the little bassinet and pray she stays asleep while I get the shot. Luckily, I do without waking her up. *Dad win.*

When Noah came up to visit, she brought me my secret bag with everything I'd need, including my polaroid camera, the scrapbook, and double-sided tape.

"Perfect," I tell her when the image clears. "You look so cute."

I can't help gushing at how adorable she is. Magnolia really said copy/paste.

Once I wrap Willow back up into her blanket, I grab the scrapbook and tape her photo on the final page.

Underneath the photo, I write all of her newborn stats: date and time of birth, weight, and height.

But I have a feeling it's going to be what's written on her onesie that'll either have her squealing or crying.

Probably both.

Willow wakes up to eat thirty minutes later, and Magnolia breastfeeds like a pro. Well, a pro for as well as she knows how to. From what she's told me, it hurts like a bitch and feels like Willow has teeth.

She switches Willow to her other side, and we chat until she's done, then I offer to burp her.

"Remember that gift I mentioned a couple of weeks ago?" I ask Magnolia, and she nods. "I brought it with me."

"You did?" Her eyes light up. "Do I get to see it now?"

"Yep."

I put Willow in her bassinet, still wrapped up, and then grab it from my bag.

"I made you something." I set it in her lap, then sit next to her on the bed.

"Oh my gosh. A scrapbook?"

"Of your pregnancy," I confirm. "I found this beautiful picture from the ranch and the pink sunset reminded me of you."

"It did?"

"Every time I'd come across that photo during family scrapbook night, it made me smile. There was just somethin' about it, the contrast between the greens and pinks, the beauty in that one image just made me happy anytime I saw it. So finally, I took it for myself and decided that's what I wanted on the cover until we had a family photo to replace it. But yeah, it gives me the same feeling as when I look at you."

"Tripp Chattanooga Hollis," she weeps, reaching up to touch my cheek. "I've cried enough today. But that's seriously so sweet. I love it."

Then her fingers play with the little decorative wheat pieces surrounding the photo, and she smiles when she sees the flower.

"A little *sunflower*." Her eyes gloss over and she sticks out her lower lip. "You thought of every little detail, didn't you?"

"Noah might've helped me a little, but I'm takin' credit for ninety-eight percent of it."

As soon as she opens to the first page, her eyes widen and she covers her mouth. "Look at my little belly," she coos.

"Only ten weeks."

She touches the image and then reads what I wrote underneath.

"Tripp, this is so freakin' sweet."

She flips to the next page and reads it again.

"Eleven weeks."

Flips again.

"Twelve weeks." Then she looks at me. "Did you do every single week?"

"Of course. Up until her birth, actually."

"You're jokin'."

She continues to flip through each page, laughing and crying when she reads the notes and reminisces about the size of her bump.

"Oh, my chocolate ice cream and pretzel phase." She giggles

when she remembers some of her cravings. "Can't ever go wrong with a sweet and salty combo."

"Unless it's two in the morning and we're out of ice cream..."

"Whoops." She smirks. "But you were so nice to get me some."

When she gets to the thirty-eight-week photo, it's of her in the nursery for the first time. We've busted ass the past two weeks to get it ready. Laundry, organizing the closet and dresser, putting out all the diapers, and decorating it exactly how she wanted—in light pink, yellow, and white. She wanted it bright and homey.

My heart rate ramps up a notch when she goes to the next one. *Thirty-nine weeks.*

The week of Braxton hicks and lower back pain.

"I can't believe that was only seven days ago." She shakes her head.

The next page has two photos.

On the left side, her bump at forty weeks before she went into labor, and on the right is the photo of Willow in her special onesie.

She flips the page, and her smile widens as her eyes dance across the pages. Until it lands on Willow and she reads what her onesie says.

Her gaze snaps to mine, and her mouth falls open. "When did you take this photo?"

"Earlier when you were sleepin'."

She looks back down at it and blinks. "Will you marry my daddy?" She reads it aloud. "Is that really what it says?"

My face splits in half at how stunned she is.

I pull out her ring from my pocket and hold it out for her to see. "Willow really wants her mommy and daddy to be married. She told me."

She chokes out a sob. "Is that so? Our one-day-old baby said that?"

"Oh, she told me weeks ago. You were asleep, but we were up late chattin', and it's what she demanded, so I said okay, I'll go buy a ring. Then we made a plan on how I'd ask, and here we are."

She squeezes her eyes as she holds back tears.

"That's pretty impressive of her."

"She's a smart baby," I tease and then take her hand.

"Okay, I'm going to propose for real now." I place a kiss on her knuckles and give her a wink. "Sunny, I hope you know by now how much I love you. But in case you ever forget, I will spend a lifetime reminding you because you changed my life. You brought light into it and gave it meaning again. You took my demons and made them your own. You make me laugh like no one else ever could. You are truly my best friend. You gave me the greatest gift anyone could ever give me—your love in return. You made me a dad. You gave me our own little family. And I don't want to spend another day without you as my future wife. So, please...say you'll marry me."

By the time I finish, she's a sobbing mess. I reach up and wipe her tears, then cup her face.

"Yes." She nods frantically as she repeats the word over and over. "I'd marry you right now if I could."

I chuckle as our mouths crash together in a desperate, hot kiss.

"I love you so much," she whispers against my lips. "But how dare you propose when I'm in a hospital gown? I look like a grandma wearing a moo-moo."

Pulling back, I rake my eyes over her body. "Well, then you're a hot grandma because you're gorgeous."

Her face drops and she's anything but amused. "You're lucky I love you so damn much."

I slide the ring onto her finger, kiss it, and then kiss her lips again. "Trust me, I know."

Bonus Epilogue
Magnolia

You'd think with Tripp's truck filled to the brim with bags and baby gear that we were going on a cross-country three-month vacation.

Nope, just an overnight trip to the rodeo.

With a ten-month-old.

It's Willow's first time at the Franklin Rodeo, and we're meeting Noah and her family to watch Ellie compete. The Hollises go every year for the full duration of the event, but I'm not that brave to spend three nights in a camper with an infant.

Being here brings back so many memories. Not only have I gone every summer with Noah's family, but it's where she met Fisher. Well, technically, it's where I found Fisher and pointed him out to her. I'm the only reason they actually met, and I will take credit for their love until the day I die.

Noah and Ellie have been training extra hard these past few months. Ellie's at the top of her game and has crushed every event she's had for the past year.

"Da!" Willow points toward Tripp as I carry her on my hip. "Da!"

"Yeah, he's comin', sweetie."

Go fucking figure I'd carry her for nine months, and that'd be her first word.

But I can't even be mad because Tripp's an incredible father. For the first six months after she was born, he got up with me for every feeding and diaper change. Luckily, now she sleeps through the night, but he still continues to cook all of our meals. Hell, he does the laundry most weeks because I forget. He never complains even after working a ten-hour shift.

The day Willow was born and the day I married the man of my dreams were the two best ones of my life.

As soon as he's within reach, she holds up her arms and squeals for him to pick her up.

"Hey, sweetheart." He kisses her cheek.

I let him take her out of my arms, but I make a pouty face about it.

"Don't worry, I'll lift you up later tonight." He winks.

I snort at his cheesy line but can't help the smile that sneaks onto my face. *Damn him.*

Even after everything we've been through—being first-time parents, juggling a newborn and work schedules, finding secret moments to steal—he still makes me laugh.

We're staying in one of the Hollises' trailers, so we only have to bring the stroller and baby bag to the arena. By the time we arrive and find Noah, the barrel racing event has already started.

Noah and I stand in the front by the railing, ready to scream for Ellie as we always do. I turn around and laugh at the image of Tripp holding Willow and Fisher holding Poppy. It's like a hot dad's club.

"Did you ever imagine this would be our lives? Three years ago, I was pushing you to go talk to a man twice your age, and I was chasing after Tripp like a lovesick puppy."

"I'm startin' to wonder if Tripp's a victim of stalker syndrome? Ya know, kinda like Stockholm syndrome? He couldn't get away from you, so he had no choice but to fall in love with you," Noah teases.

"Call it whatever you want, but it worked." I shrug with a smirk.

Landen walks over and stands behind us. "Is her division next?"

"Yep, she'll be the second runner," Noah says. "Get ready to scream your guts out."

"Your brother will be rearranging my guts later, so I can't do that."

"Gross." Noah laughs.

"You're tellin' me. I live above them." Landen groans, standing behind me like a bodyguard.

I pat his arm. "Oh, you poor baby."

The emcee announces Ellie's name with her horse Ranger and the crowd goes wild. When she flies into the arena, we cheer as loudly as we can.

"Yes, Ellie!" Noah stands on the railing, screaming louder. "Go, go, go!"

Ellie goes smoothly around the first barrel and quickly races to the next.

She gets around the second, but then I notice something off about her posture as she rushes toward the third.

Just as Ranger whips around the final barrel, Ellie falls off and smacks her head on it. There's a loud, audible gasp in the crowd, and Landen clutches my shoulder. She tumbles to the ground, rolls a couple of times, and then ends up face-down in the dirt.

"Oh my God!" Noah sprints toward the exit to get down there, and Landen quickly follows.

"Holy shit." I gasp, feeling helpless as people start to make their way over to her.

Tripp comes to my side with Willow and puts an arm around me. "Jesus. I hope she's okay."

"I've never seen that happen before." I stand shell-shocked. "I thought something was off after that second barrel."

"I wonder what happened," he says as we watch a medical team arrive.

It takes a good ten minutes before they get her on a stretcher and move her out of the arena. Tripp puts Willow in the stroller, and we exit with Fisher and Poppy to go find Noah and Landen.

"Is she okay?" I ask when we see them outside near the ambulance.

Noah shakes her head, and I see the concern written across her face. "I dunno. She wasn't responsive. They think it's possible she had a seizure."

"Does she have a medical condition?" I ask.

"Not that I'm aware of or it'd be too risky for her to be ridin'."

"Poor thing."

"Landen and I are gonna meet them at the hospital," she tells Fisher, then looks at me. "I'll text you when I hear anything."

I give her a hug and an extra squeeze for luck. "Please do. I'm gonna worry about her."

Noah gives Fisher and Poppy a kiss, and then she and Landen leave.

Instead of going back to the arena, we decide to let the kids play back at the trailers until they return.

Except they don't until close to midnight.

The girls are long passed out, but I hear them walk in and immediately sit up.

"Hey," I whisper. "Where's Landen?"

"He's still there. She woke up finally, but you're not gonna believe this."

I furrow my brows. "What?"

"Between the seizure and how hard she hit her head, she's lost part of her memory."

My hands cover the gasp that slips out of my mouth. "Oh my God!"

Noah chuckles, and I'm thrown off guard by how this could be funny. "She doesn't remember Landen."

Just when I think I couldn't be any more shocked, I'm proven wrong. "Wait, what?"

Noah looks like she's struggling to keep it together but laughs again. "I know it ain't funny, but she doesn't remember not liking him. After she woke up, she recognized me, but when she looked at Landen, she got all flustered like she had a major crush."

"Shut the fuck up!" I whisper-shout. My mouth falls open in disbelief.

"Dead-ass serious. Landen was so shocked, he didn't know what to do. Ellie asked if he'd stay, so he did."

"This is wild, Noah! What if she remembers she hates him in like a week? Landen will be even more crushed after gettin' his hopes up."

"I asked the doctor what to do, and he said *nothing*. If we tell her too much, it'll just confuse her, so it's just best to wait it out and let her memory return naturally."

I blink hard, trying to wrap my brain around all of this.

"I can't believe Landen agreed to stay knowin' she'd normally want nothin' to do with him."

"He didn't wanna hurt her feelings or her to be left there alone," Noah explains. "Her parents hadn't arrived there by the time I left."

"I just don't want Landen to get hurt," I say.

"Me neither, but it's his decision."

We chat for a few more minutes before she calls it a night and goes to her trailer. I slide back into bed next to Tripp, and he wraps his arm around me when I snuggle into him.

"If I lose my memory and forget that I'm in love with you, would you fight for me?"

His eyes are closed, but his lips curve up in amusement. "Sunny, I'd do everything in my power to make you fall back in love with me, even if it took the rest of my goddamn life. I'm not lettin' you go in this lifetime or any other."

I rest my head on his chest and smile. "And that's why I married you."

He leans down to press a kiss on my hair. "Thought you married me for my cookin' skills."

"Well, of course. And for your oral game."

"I knew it," he deadpans.

My hand slides down his bare torso and explores beneath his boxer shorts. He gets hard in less than five seconds, and I smile to myself at my ability to get him aroused so quickly.

"Say cowboy…"

"Hmm?"

"Whaddya think about tryin' for baby number two?"

His eyes whip open. "Don't play with me, Sunny."

I bite down on my lower lip and stroke his shaft. "So you don't wanna knock me up?"

He growls as he captures my wrist, rolls me underneath him, and then pins me to the bed. "Be very careful what you ask me, love. If you say those three words to me again, I will fill you with my cum and then hold your legs up in the air over and over until you're pregnant. And that's not the *kink* talkin'."

Good God, I could get pregnant from his dirty talk alone.

But just in case that doesn't work…

"Knock. Me. Up. Cowboy." I drawl out each word as he presses into me, his cock hard and throbbing against my stomach.

His dark gaze is filled with hunger, and when he lowers his mouth an inch above mine, he whispers, "Beg for it, Sunny. Beg for my cum."

I can't help the smile that fills my face, knowing I'm getting exactly what I want and he's all too eager to give it to me.

"Fill me up with your cum. *Please.*"

Read Tripp & Magnolia's bonus scene on my website:
brookewritesromance.com/bonus-scenes

Curious about Landen and Ellie?
Find their story next in *Fall With Me*

Fall With Me

A dislike to lovers stand-alone from small-town romance author Brooke Montgomery about a barrel racer who loses her memory and the rowdy cowboy she once hated but no longer remembers...

About the Author

Brooke has been writing romance since 2013 under the *USA Today* Bestselling author pen names: Brooke Cumberland and Kennedy Fox, and now, **Brooke Montgomery**. She loves writing small town romance with big families and happily ever afters! She lives in the frozen tundra of Packer Nation with her husband, wild teenager, and four dogs. When she's not writing, you can find her reading, watching ASMR and reading vlogs on YouTube, or binge-watching a TV show she's most likely behind on. Brooke's addicted to iced coffee, leggings, and naps. She found her passion for telling stories during winter break one year in grad school — and she hasn't stopped since.

Find her on her website at
www.brookewritesromance.com
and follow her on social media:

facebook.com/brookemontgomeryauthor

instagram.com/brookewritesromance

amazon.com/author/brookemontgomery

tiktok.com/@brookewritesromance

goodreads.com/brookemontgomery

bookbub.com/authors/brooke-montgomery

x.com/B_Montgomery15

threads.net/@brookewritesromance

Also by Brooke Montgomery

Sugarland Creek series

As Brooke Cumberland:

Pushing the Limits

The Intern Trilogy

Shouldn't Want You

Someone Like You

As Kennedy Fox:

Checkmate duet series

Roommate duet series

Lawton Ridge duet series

Only One series

Make Me series

Bishop Brothers series

Circle B Ranch series

Love in isolation series

Made in the USA
Monee, IL
12 March 2024

54897169R00249